THE
CLAIRES
AN ASCENDERS NOVEL

THE CLAIRES

AN ASCENDERS NOVEL

C. L. GABER

THE CLAIRES
BY C.L. Gaber

© C.L. Gaber

Copyright © 2019 by C.L. Gaber All rights reserved This book, or parts thereof, may not be reproduced in any form without permission from the publisher, exceptions are made for brief excerpts used in published reviews.

Published by
Big Picture Media
An imprint of Big Picture News Inc.

www.ascenderssaga.com

This is a work of fiction. Names, characters, corporations, institutions, organizations, events, or locales in this novel are either the product of the author's imagination or, if real, used fictitiously. The resemblance of any character to actual persons (living or dead) is entirely coincidental.

For more information contact
C.L. Gaber at CLGaber@Yahoo.com
Edited by Mary Altbaum
Cover Design by Adrijus G from Rocking Book Covers
Special Back Photography by Tiffany S. Bell
Interior designed and formatted by

emtippettsbookdesigns.com

Books by C. L. Gaber

Jex Malone

Ascenders Series:
Ascenders (Book One)
Ascenders: Skypunch (Book Two)
Ascenders: Omorrow (Book Three)
Ascenders: 11:11 (Book Four)
Ascenders: X-Catcher (Book Five)
The Claires

CLAIRES' TIMELINE

BORN IN 1911   DIED 1928
BORN 1928   DIED 1945
BORN 1945   DIED 1962
BORN 1962   DIED 1979
BORN 1979   DIED 1996
BORN 1996   DIED 2013
EXISTENCE INTERMISSION   FREAK ISLAND
DIED 2017   INSTITUTE OF
     TROUBLED TEENS
BORN 2017   CHICAGO

THEY ARE SEVENTEEN YEARS OF AGE.
QUADRUPLETS.
THEY ARE NOT IDENTICAL.
BUT EACH IS NAMED CLAIRE.

Claire V (Violet) is Clairvoyant.
Claire S (Sophia) is Clairsentient.
Claire A (Alice) is Clairaudient.
Claire C (Clover) is Claircognizant.

They were born with overwhelming gifts, including:

Clairvoyance. She was born with clear future vision. A seer who has psychic tendencies, she can witness the future and it's shown to her as snapshots or "flickers" behind her eyes. She sees real-life "coming attractions" played out to her like a movie. In her wildest dreams, she can also sense impending darkness. This is a weighty aptitude. How much should she share with the others? And with outsiders?

Clairsentience. She was born clear feeling. Not only can she sense the mood of others, she co-opts their most private feelings. When someone cries, she cries. Someone's euphoric; she's giddy happy. She dwells in the exact soulful state of others. She also feels love strongly, despite her low self-esteem and lack of her own emotional identity. This is a good-bad capability, as it keeps her inner sensitivities cranked up to ten.

Clairaudience. She was born with clear hearing. Granted the ability to hear voices of the dearly (and not-so-dearly) departed, she can "speak" to her deceased bio-mother who "calls" from the grave. Thanks to a ringing or buzzing in her ears, the spirit world summons her attention prior to announcing an otherworldly message. This is an unthinkable (if not unbearable) ability, as it's impossible for her *not* to hear what she doesn't want to hear from dead, evil forces.

Claircognizance. She was born with clear knowing. One of the most misunderstood of the siblings—and the most powerful --- she is the Yoda. She just *knows* things and can manifest thoughts and ideas. Rarely wrong, she can easily tell future prophecies—and also manipulate all the tomorrows in dramatic ways—thanks to her creative, renegade mind combined with the heart of an enforcer. She's the ultimate definition of knowing too much for your own good.

SISTERS
IN LIFE
AND DEATH

THE CLAIRES

*For all those with something extra...
revel in your splendor*

1.

THE FOUR CLAIRES, as they would come to be known, should never have been known at all. Nonidentical quadruples, they were often singularly described by a word that rhymes with *witch*. Clearly, there were hexing strands in their DNA, but what made them noteworthy—verging on extraordinary—was the fact that each was born with a distinct and separate *clair* force or power. This caused underground governments, not to mention world powers, to act with great haste. Human rules *always* dictate that what can't be understood must be destroyed.

Before they were born, the girls were given an expiration date.

The Allotment of Life certificate confirmed that all Claire children will be put to a most wretched and painful death (just to be sure) on their seventeenth birthday.

After the cake.

But before the presents. Which made sound and wise sense.

One should not carry needless "things" into the afterlife.

Baggage was baggage—alive or dead.

2.
LONDON
1890

THE TIME LIMIT on this proclamation was most curious and read as follows: Granted by the Patriarch of Paranormal, sequestered in the nethermost bowels of London's underground tunnels, this covenant will hold until The Extinction of All Living Things.

THE CLAIRES

But there was fine print, too, which was where the story always lurks. It declared: This agreement extends to each and every Claire lifetime in the unfortunate case(s) that they die and are refreshed and refurbished for another seventeen rather pointless and painful years.

Reincarnation wasn't just a theory with them, it was a promise as sure as their dreamy smiles, bloodless, porcelain skin, and iced-ocean-blue eyes marred by the shadows of secrets that were buried in the centuries.

3.

THEIR ALMOST-NEVER-SPOKEN-ABOUT LINEAGE could be traced to an unsavory grandmother, the cobalt-blue-eyed Penny Louise Pitcher. A woman of formidable witching, she spent "the tender years" from ages twelve to seventeen at a place known as The Clink. In 1890, it was the most notorious medieval prison in London and a hellhole where dirt-poor inmates who were lacking friends, family or funds were given cells that overlooked the rutted cobblestone streets. The detainees would do their daily bidding by begging those who passed by for scraps of food and by dangling rusted tin cups from the bars as they pleaded for fresh water.

"Please sir, I beg of ye," Penny cajoled as she turned the brilliance of day into the gloom of night when a passerby left the cup dry.

"You're a witch! You would rather eat us!" children would taunt. They slowly and deliberately chewed their biscuits and sipped their tea inches from a pale face pressed to iron.

"By chance, I am empowered. Not by choice," Penny said in a raspy voice laced with illness and regret. And then she made it rain cold pellets on those juicy little brats while she explained in her stern, British tone, "I don't wish to dwell in darkness. Darkness, however, wishes to dwell in me."

Penny, with her long black hair, thin face, and extremely pointed nose, was what they called a "loaded" one. She was dressed in rags and laden with heavy irons, which made walking, standing up, or lying down most excruciating, though not as absolutely horrendous as burning at the stake, disembowelment, or beheading—which were the other unmistakable menu options of the day.

But let's leave politics and fine dining out of it for a moment.

Penny was there for reasons that had absolutely everything to do with her murky reputation and even cloudier DNA. Was she a child witch? Or the devil's daughter? Or something else not even the Patriarch could pinpoint. Penny could predict the future, read thoughts and, most disturbingly, communicate with spirits and souls long since passed.

Yes, she was also born with a few "parlor tricks," like manipulating weather and bestowing an occasional tail, but those were only the incidentals.

Her burning had been on the dockets for years, but every soul in charge of her was . . . one-thousand percent chicken-shit when it came to drawing the first flame.

As Penny waited to barbecue, she found the perfect pastime in tormenting the prison guards with promises of their own heinous futures, threatening immediate lunacy conjured from her spells. To that end, she would swirl damp tea leaves in an almost-empty porcelain cup. Occasionally, they gave her the brew, plus the fancy china in order to hear their own fates. One squinty-eyed glance from Penny combined with the pursing of chapped lips and these men knew it wasn't good news and cowered in drafty prison corners.

Turns out, there weren't enough guards or unoccupied edges

THE CLAIRES

in the Old World. But there was another reason she didn't get the torch. That would have been a sin of the highest order given the fact that two—*mother and child*—would have perished. Therefore, Penny was given a one-way ticket, no return passage on the *Mauretania*, a ship that boasted the first steam-turbine engines on a passenger liner and was built for speed. She was on her way with great haste to the New World because she carried a gift waiting to draw first breath.

Incidentally, there were whispers. Weren't there always? But the father-to-be in this case wasn't an abusive prison guard checking a box to hell by making a nightly call. Her visitors included seekers of futures, including the prime minister and another dark-haired, lanky fellow named Jack who never had a formal last name. He would historically and infamously add this surname: the Ripper. And, yes, Penny knew full well that he was Queen Victoria's "troubled," yet devastatingly handsome grandson.

Alas, she had a thing for bad boys.

Moving along . . . .

Young Lula Fair Pitcher, her daughter, was born in a mild hurricane on that wildly rocking boat to America. She was a precious child with beautiful black hair and eyes that were golden-yellow and seemed to collect the glints from the sun and keep them. Of course, there were conditions concerning their dual relocation because there always were (and still are) in matters of life and enchantment.

Lula, who would grow to be a lively, smart, and spiritually gifted one, would be allowed to live her childhood in one of the newly established boroughs of New York, where she would meld into a sea of immigrants and new arrivals, Catholics and Jews, Italians and Poles and peoples from Ireland, Britain, and Germany looking to better their lives and grow their families.

Lula's American dream came with an exhausting list of rules.

She would be allowed to live with her mother, only if Penny immediately married, as nothing was to appear improper. To that end, Penny chose to sink her claws (literally) into a meek, skinny Italian shoemaker who came to the New World alone at the elder age of 22—and had no shot of resisting the love potion she dipped her hands into before bewitching him into matrimony. Sadly, he perished during the first hard winter because a woman needed only so many shoes.

There was one last law sent from England for Lula's "future." Drawing breath would be allowed, if and only if, Penny agreed to put her beloved child to death on the day the girl turned seventeen.

Since the beginning of time, no child in this universe was allowed to possess three distinct *clair* powers in one mortal body and Lula was born a quadruple threat—clairvoyant, clairaudient, clairsentient and claircognizant.

She could predict the future, sense human feelings and emotional states and possessed the telepathy to hear voices of both the living and dead. Most horrific for those born without such "extras" was the last trait because it signified that she was all-knowing, and no mortal needed to be *all*-anything.

She was quite simply and forever, a Claire.

NEW YORK
1907 (OR 17 YEARS LATER)

C. L. GABER

1.

THE ORDER, AS they called themselves in the New World, assembled on a frosted fall night by a whispered oral invitation given at dawn. Slanderers, nags, or gossips who dared speak in audible tones about such a gathering would be given the cruelest punishment of all called the Scold's Helm. It was your basic heavy iron cage that covered the gossip's head, combined with a spiked tongue of silver metal that was thrust into the mouth. Ironic that this was when the term "tongues wagging" was coined.

But enough trivia.

The formal name in America for this underground group was the New World Order, which meant that they governed all magic, mystery, and mayhem of an otherworldly variety on the shores of the colonies.

Few knew that one-third of the colonists possessed something "extra," which is why England and other countries expelled them in the first place.

Young Lula was about to turn seventeen, and hushed words naturally revolved around her imminent demise. This pleased Henry Handen, the leader of the Order, who had a perpetually running nose, hooded brown eyes and was six feet three, bone thin and all business, which is why he hounded the maternal source to discuss the arrangements.

Little did any of them know that this was the last thing Penny would ever arrange for herself or any others. In mere days, she would be found face down in a pickle barrel, drowned. Her last days of life were feisty ones and she used her wolf hounds to run Henry off the small front yard that was located in what someday

THE CLAIRES

would be called the Flatlands section of Brooklyn. On this day, however, it was nothing more than a row of cheap, makeshift, two-story red bricked farm houses plopped into free dirt.

"Madam, if you please, may I speak with you a moment," Henry fumed from behind a white-picket fence that she had painted black.

"Keep yer bone box shut!" Penny shouted from an upstairs window. "Ye may not speak—nor I."

Modern translation: Zip it.

He could only stare at the securely bricked house she shared with her daughter on Barberry Lane and shout back, "Trot!" Colonially speaking, it could have been worse. He was simply referring to her as a decrepit woman.

Henry was sick and tired of women in general. Five times now he had demanded details concerning this cursed daughter's scheduled death and had provided a laundry list of reasonable options to accomplish the task on the day Lula turned seventeen. Why, there were so many choices, including, but not limited to the following: bloodletting, gallows, hanging, or the good, old-fashioned Ordeal by Water.

As for the latter, the guilty would have their left hand or thumb tied to her right foot and her right hand tied to her left foot. At this point, the human was put in the deepest water of the closest lake. If said human sank, they were considered innocent while floating indicated secret admittance into the devil's service.

Either way, it was an ordeal that had only one outcome and it didn't involve breathing.

2.

IN THE MIDNIGHT hour that September night in Old New York, under the smallest glimmer of moon in a lonely sky, The Order convened under a hollow oak tree in the untamed woods, far from the prying eyes of the local witch hunters looking to earn their monthly stipend. The Order was far more important than some self-governed vigilante task force and remained consumed with far bigger paranormal threats. Their task was making sure that the new country of America wasn't overrun by insanely gifted mystical types who willy-nilly could plot to take over the colonies for their own fantastical reasons.

"I wish you a good evening, Madam," Henry lied to the woman in his presence now, who added up to only one, because it was the job of men, men thought, to rule the world, new or otherwise.

"Sir, I am your most obedient servant. I am heartily glad to see you," Penny lied back because she never trusted a man. Sadly, here she stood in the woods conversing with one of that breed.

"Miss Pitcher," Henry cut right to the chase, "there will be no further stalling. Lula Fair Pitcher's death date was determined and must be accomplished before her seventeenth birthday on 24 December. So, it was written, so it must be done."

Penny was a clever mind reader, so she already knew what he was going to say before the words formed. She cut to the proverbial chase knowing why her daughter's demise was required. "I do greatly admire your wisdom, sir," she interrupted. "But, one must heed a new life plan that I, as her mother, have formed. Here is my offering: My daughter will never flirt with a boy. Never marry. Never have a child. She will do absolutely no larking. Ever."

The latter was a lascivious thing that needed no explanation.

Penny came armed with what they wanted to hear, knowing

THE CLAIRES

if she promised her child would never have a child then, and only then, there might be life preservation. There could be a life lived.

"We cannot risk her joining with a man who might have any of the last four *clair* traits such as clairtangency, or clear touching, clairalience, or clear psychic smelling, clairgustance, or clear tasting, or clairempathy, which is plain old being a sap for any cause or person needing a lift. A child born from that union of potency would be . . . we don't know what it could be," said Declan B. Jones, a miserable type with big bones, wide farmer's hands and a mass of reddish hair. He considered himself the second in command. Jones with all his know-it-all bluster was a teacher of his own brand of new-fangled religion, which is why he was clear with his explanations of such moral treachery.

He was the one who secretly summoned the second woman to show up at tonight's gathering. It would be none other than soon-to-be-dead Lula herself. He incurred her teenage wrath when he woke her from her early evening sleep that night by tossing small pebbles against the glass of her bedroom window and informing her that her mother was in distress. The bonny, headstrong Lula with her blue-black hair and ivory skin cast a defiant attitude on him, preferring to run into the woods instead of ride on horseback.

Once she saw that Penny was alive and well, Lula decided to mess with prevailing wisdoms. Her face said, "Suck it." Her will said, "Make me." She defined teenage attitude by at first refusing to dance around the fire the Order had built to temporarily cleanse any wicked sections of her soul. Intense heat, it was believed, melted ill intentions.

"I don't dance," Lula said in a bored voice. "I don't go out at night. And I don't participate in pagan rituals either."

She wasn't finished.

"So, if you want to kill me, do it now," she said in a most defiant voice. "I'd rather be dead than bored."

In the end, her mother Penny provided one more stalling tactic in the form of a sealed letter that she produced from the ankle-length, A-line, black woolen skirt that was washed monthly. With great flourish, she waved the almost translucent parchment paper in a stray moonbeam, so the others could see the return address: The Patriarch of Paranormal, Beneath London. No street number was needed. None was given.

"The Order shall bless a fruitlessness potion sent from foreign shores," Penny read aloud, insisting the handwriting came from the Patriarch himself. "The potion is guaranteed to render the young lady sterile in the womanly arts. Lula Fair Pitcher has thus been granted a continuation of life if, and only if, she never bears a child."

Members of The Order couldn't hide their disappointment. There was nothing they loved more than a good town cleansing, but the sirs and madams were forced to accept the pronouncement and even blessed the small satchel Penny brought forth containing the elixir of herbs and roots sent from the Old World per the Patriarch's sterility recipe. The group respected authority, wantonly (by the removal of hats) sanctified the hottest blue fire from the dry dust below and then danced around it to serve as a blessing.

So, it was written.
So, it was danced.
So, it was decided.

3.

ON THE WALK home, Penny's practical side, along with her utter distrust of the English, created a worry spot in her heart. "What if the potion was actually a poison?" she fretted, wondering if she was actually about to kill her only child. It would be just like the ruthless Patriarch to take matters into his own hands and wield his power from across the great pond.

Had the little brown goat not stumbled away from its mother none of this would have happened the way that it did. But that foolish little, smelly beast came upon them at the exact right time and fate took an extremely hard twist.

The hungry goat ate the satchel in one satisfied bite, cotton and all. Tragically, he dropped in only two minutes and suffered the twitching, moaning, extremely painful death that had been scheduled for a certain local *clair* hellion.

Penny buried him, worried that some unsuspecting colonist—maybe even one or two that she *could* stand—would have a hankering that week for a hearty goat stew. Put simply, they didn't have enough people in the New World for needless and heinous demises.

A few days later, in a little red brick house by the Hudson River, the gifted Lula Fair Pitcher, discovered her mother floating upside down in the wooden pickle barrel that sat on their front porch. She buried the only one who had ever loved her in the blood field out back, a place for all things that had passed and blessed by the Cayuga Indian tribes that used to occupy these lands before they were "escorted" away.

4.

NEW YORK
1911

LULA OBSERVED THE traditional period of Old World mourning where she did not leave her home for exactly four years of moaning and memories. When she finally emerged in spring of 1911 to go to market, she was three times her usual size, which was unusual in a place where food wasn't plentiful. Nine months later, with no known father on record now or ever, she gave birth, with the help of a midwife girlfriend, to four beautiful, non-identical daughters.

Quadruplets.

En masse, she bestowed upon them the name the Claires, giving each a middle initial that would later signify their most sacred trait. There was no need for the Patriarch to worry. There was not one child who possessed all the sacred gifts this time. The Claire traits had splintered amongst the next generation producing four genetically powerful specimens. Redheaded and clairvoyant Claire V could see the future.

Blonde clairsentient Claire S felt the emotional state of others.

Dark-haired and clairaudient Claire A heard the voices from here and beyond.

And finally, the pixie of the group, curly, golden-haired Claire C was claircognizant, and the most dangerous or potent. The beautiful imp could see right through anyone as if she was looking through tissue paper. She was the one who knew much too much.

But didn't that describe every damn Claire who ever lived?

A VOYANT'S STORY: V

Los Angeles, California
March, 25 2013

1.

FOURTH PERIOD.

English class.

Kill me now.

I was giving Johnny *the look* that could only be described as resting witch face. I knew it would leave him feeling unsettled and a bit perturbed, but that was no shocker since I was born knowing, though they never put that on your birth certificate. Imagine it: Seven pounds, three ounces, red hair, blue eyes AND clairvoyant . . . . as in she has her unknown father's eyes and her mother's spiritual juju.

Good luck with that one, kid . . . now, go out there and act normal. Don't spill the tea, i.e., talk up the family tree or future events or even how you live under an ancient curse, one that dictates your seventeenth birthday will also serve as your death day. For those who enjoy mathematics, it was our 16th year and we had nine months or approximately 270 days and counting.

And I, the one they called V, was stuck in high school. Perhaps that was the cruelest fate twist of all.

My classmate Johnny couldn't even guess any of the above, which is why he leaned over and whispered, "V. . . yeah you . . . What's up? You look stressed." I can't answer him honestly as in: *Wassup? Well, the economy is about to take a dip . . . and the world is in turmoil . . . and they caught two kids at some local school with guns last week . . . and Iron Man is . . . no plot spoilers here. And I have to figure out a way to break an ancient curse in a few hundred days or I'll be a corpse before you can say Christmas vacation. And Fred Turner in the back row had beans last night. You didn't need to*

THE CLAIRES

be voyant to know the last one. You just needed a nose.

I can't say any of it, so I fall back on the standard, sixteen-year-old response.

"Nothing," I whisper back, trying to find one date-able trait in his entire being and coming up all zeroes.

Besides the mind-boggling task of trying to survive through senior year, I had one other focus this lifetime, our sixth trip around the sun. I was going to lose my virginity, no slut shaming, please.

Imagine that you've gone through five entire lifetimes, living up until age 17 with hormones raging only to die a virgin. Well, not this lifetime, because it wasn't happening to me again. There was going to be some motion in the ocean if you know what I mean and that had nothing to do with the fact that I lived in California by the Pacific. Some of our more literary students at Santa Monica High called it bumpin' uglies or spelunking, but whatever the label or how gross you wanted to be about it, I was doing plain ol' doing It.

It would be my own personal victory, which was always my goal. Winning was one of my favorite personality traits, and it made sense because I was the oldest and most competitive of the sisters. I wasn't necessarily competitive with my siblings, but with the world at large. It's why I was on every academic team at SMHS including the Math Gurus (not a fertile ground for virginity loss) and the Academic All-Stars (even worse). I didn't always understand the answers, but as a voyant I'd find them before they could tumble off the lips of any of the other giant brains from one of the other schools. Just last week, we did Academic All-Stars against those pampered Hollywood High School low IQs.

Question: Chateau Gaillard overlooks the Seine, but it was built by this Leonine ruler who lost it to the French in 1204.

No one answered. I knew they wouldn't.

And just before the buzzer rang, I smiled, blew imaginary dust off my fingernails and said, "Richard the Lionheart ....obviously."
#smokedthem.

2.

OKAY, BACK TO the virgin thing. My sisters do slut shame, and it's because they're all virgins, too. My sister S, the petite clairsentient with long, honey locks, absorbs the feelings of others. She claims to feel too much to get into a real relationship where actual hips dip.

Then there's A, the dark-haired clairaudient who can talk/see actual ghosts. She brings these hot Viking, pirate and dead movie star hunks to our room just about every night and takes them to her bed. It's not real sex, but she has a *very* active imagination. "Regular high school boys just don't measure up to having JFK stop by on a cold Friday night," she mused one night.

"JFK is married," I told the history buff.

"Didn't stop him when he was alive," she retorted. "And did you see pictures of him when he was alive?"

And then there is my all-knowing sister C who is the hellion of our little group, meaning that just about every guy and girl at school is scared to death of her. Yes, she can be vigilante-tough with her short, pixie, blonde curls and defiant stance, but I know somewhere she had a heart and other working body parts that want to do the nasty before she hits the grave again.

She claims not to care, but one cannot deny hormones, especially when one has less than a year to live and is almost seventeen years doomed.

THE CLAIRES

3.

LONG AGO, MAYBE 100 or so years but who was counting, I had decided that this was the lifetime that I actually fell in love and lost my virginity – hopefully in that order, but not necessarily because my time and choices of partners was limited.

I know, I know, too much for English class? Then again, literature was about great loves and lovers, right? Was it too much to ask that I find a boyfriend in this lifetime and he had broad shoulders, sinewy muscles and a mane of long, light hair to let my fingers roam in? A tat or two? Facial stubble? Yet, it felt as if the universe had some sort of delete button when it came to my lips on ones belonging to that someone special because there was no one special at Santa Monica High – even when you cruised the senior class. Well, maybe there was one.

My last crush, well, we'll get to it. It ain't pretty.

As usual, the non-contenders will not go away. "Maybe the bag of bones forgot about today's quiz," says Johnny, who is six feet four, gangly in body and has these little wired rimmed glasses. He was nice, smart and observant, but definitely not under the covers material.

He was talking about our English teacher, the distinguished Miss Evelyn Ehm, age sixty-two, an OG, polyester-wearing, long, baggy sweater aficionado known for being forgetful and for trying to suppress her lunchtime activities. It's not that she was dealing drugs: I *knew* she was a food-lifting thief who drank well over the limit of warm liquids for someone in her mid-sixth decade of this life.

A weak bladder. Her Kryptonite. Our gain.

My hand shot up.

"Yes, V," said the above-mentioned bone unit, who was

standing in the front of the room droning on about Tom Joad and *The Grapes of Wrath*, two subject matters that left most of the room, including the cheap seats in back, two breaths short of an educationally induced coma. (I had actually lived during the Great Depression, and could teach this class and most of my history courses).

Let it be said: I was nothing if not helpful. "We only have twenty minutes left, Ms, E," I began. "If you don't give us the quiz you mentioned yesterday, we'll have to wait until Monday, which in teenage and dog years equals a century of having to contain all of our knowledge of the Joad family."

What happened next was strange for an average American classroom, even one in the outskirts of Los Angeles in Santa Monica, Cali-for-ni-yay. The others in my age bracket didn't groan or throw things at me. Heads nodded; hidden phones were shut off. These kids knew the deal. We had done it several times before . . . and would again in the name of GPAs and $$$.

"How could anyone ever forget poor Tom Joad? But your fear over such matters is understood with all the social media these days. Heartbreaking, yet beautiful foreshadowing, dear," Mrs. E. said, walking around the room to pass out the quiz.

If only she knew.

My entire life is one gigantic foreshadowing. As I said before we got to my lack of a sex life, they called me Claire V, or V for short. All packs have their alphas and I was the alpha female at home, and certainly a mover and shaker at SMH.

No one, except my sisters, knew I was gifted with clairvoyance, which means that I possess the power of inner vision or clear seeing. If you want to get all fancy about it, it's *clair* in French, which means clear, and *voyance*, which means to have vision or the ability to perceive things or events in the future.

The CliffsNotes: I can see your tomorrows.

THE CLAIRES

As for my own, our lives as Claires were covered in a rather black cloud. Until we lifted a curse handed down over a hundred years ago by some really unreasonable adult who called himself the Patriarch of Paranormal, we would dwell in darkness.

When you're born knowing that you only have seventeen years to live, it instills a certain screaming desperation in your soul that I never show anyone. It's better to just get on with it and cry in private.

Of course, all of the Claires subscribed to the theory: If you've done something one way your entire lifetimes and it's not working out, then do something different.

Truth be told, we did a few bad, bad things in the past. And as our death day became closer, we had this natural inclination to embrace the darker parts of our souls. So, this lifetime the sisters swore that we would become do-gooders to prove that we should be allowed to live. *Not that this was in any rule book. But it couldn't hurt.* Altruism and a keen need to survive meant that at night, we walked the beaches and neighborhoods of Los Angeles looking to right any perceived wrongs by pooling our collective gifts. By the way, it was far more interesting than just binge-watching TV, and provided the kind of drama that we relished.

Was it working? Who knew? As I just said, in each life and as we neared our 17th birthday, the pull towards hideous and abominable behavior along with recklessly dreadful thinking verging on the appalling revved way up as if someone was pushing a lever inside of all of us and we were entering a red zone. I could feel myself headed in that direction, which frightened me to the core.

It meant that time – the most precious gift of all -- was winding down until that day when the world simply faded to blank.

We had one last hope: A trip to our ancestral home in New

York City was supposed to shed light on this curse that kept killing us. You know, the whole origin story thing, but I don't want to jump too far ahead.

Knowledge was power and perhaps knowing what we were dealing with would help us break it once and for all. How did we know this? Well, our dear old original Ma, a clever clair and part-time witch named Lula Fair Pitcher, was still in direct contact with all four of her beloved daughters proving that helicopter parenting was invented far before even helicopters were on the drawing board.

"You were damned and couldn't do anything about it…until perhaps now," Ma (as we called her) reminded us. "How will you know if you don't go home to New York and try to end this darkness? The answers are waiting there."

Nine months wasn't much to reverse an ancient dooming, lose my virginity and make sure my entire English class aced the final.

Good thing I'm always jonesing for a challenge.

4.

HOURS AGO, IN second-period algebra, I saw the flash in my third eye. Then, like always, the picture came floating on by the inside of my closed eyelids. I "saw" that Mrs. E downed one of those ocean-sized Starbucks at lunch. She not only sipped the last sip, but then made that horrible snorting sound with the straw to draw any renegade drops.

Even worse, the owner of the aged bladder, the hydration queen, followed that liquid fest up with a clandestine trip to the fridge in the teacher's lounge where she recklessly chug-a-lugged some gym teacher's two-liter Coke *right out of the bottle.*

Pause for disgust.

THE CLAIRES

I saw it all for good reason.

"You're clear seeing V," the Patriarch of Paranormal in London once told me before he sent one of the more infamous serial killers to murder us, but that's a story for a snowy night around the fire. The Zodiac killer. What a gas.

Here's how the clairvoyant part works: I focus on a person or place until a burst of brilliant white light explodes behind my eyes, eventually clearing to reveal a scene like a black and white documentary playing out in my mind. All I have to do from this point is close my eyes and watch the show. Or I can stare out into the distance while the immediate and occasionally long-range future of someone else's life plays out on a long, continuous loop.

Did I mention that my faculties work on everyone else, except me and my sisters? Their mad skills don't work on me either. Damn it, but there is no time to lament.

Shall we take what does work out for a spin?

2:20 p.m.

FLASH!! Mrs. E. presses her knobby knees together.

FLASH! She curses herself for running out of her Depends. TMI, I know.

FLASH! She attempts to . . .WHAT . . . hold it . . . is she nuts? Yes, there's a drought in California, but this school doesn't have flood insurance.

FLASH!! No, she's going to make a run for the border, which is actually the frontier between the English and history departments where there is a girl's room . . . where right now Ashley Hamilton is doing the nasty with OH MY GOD, that gym teacher who will make the evening news by this weekend when he's fired for not observing boundaries.

FLASH! Our teacher stands and does the perp walk from behind the desk, moving uncommonly slow as to not stir up her innards. FLASH! She knows what we're thinking. She looks like an old lady version of a duck, fast waddling like Donald's ancestors.

"Children, I'll be right back." The voice is clear in my head before the actual words are spoken.

2:21 p.m. Ten seconds.

"Children, I'll be right back."

"You're on the honor system." She will say . . . now.

"You're on your own personal honor system," she says.

Vague threat coming. About the future.

"Your futures depend upon it," Mrs. E says.

FLASH! Her future can be described in one word: Drenched.

FLASH! New wool gabardine pants are neatly folded in the trunk of her sky-blue Chevy Malibu.

5.

A SWING OF my naturally wavy reddened hair. I stand and move to the front of the classroom like I'm the heir apparent to today's lecture on *The Grapes of Wrath* and other tart literary fruits. I do a half curtsy and the crowd responds by silently clapping their hands without their palms touching. They know the routine, welcome it, and beg for it.

I would have dressed up for the winging if I would have known three boys would wolf-whistle loudly. I pull down my skirt a bit. Why was I so curvy now? It's why I wore a long black number—a black shirt covered by a long black sweater and tiny skirt. The shit-kicking rounded black construction worker boots weren't for show. They were for later.

This was a time to do some business. No one in the room had studied for the quiz. Anyone, even without supernatural strengths, could tell you that.

THE CLAIRES

"If only Steinbeck had an Instagram, we would be Rhode Scholars," says Kenny Davis, who had last cracked a book in seventh grade.

At Santa Monica High, most of the student body was simply too bored or distracted, and this included the cheerleaders, jocks, nerds, bullies, future actresses and actors, models, moguls and various other generic dramatists operating from a script known as our mostly unremarkable teenage existences.

FLASH! I see the number 11. That's when I knew our teacher would be gone a blissful and exact eleven minutes. I close my eyes and then with one hundred percent precision accuracy pop them open again to write down (correctly, as always) all twenty multiple choice questions concerning the minutia of *Wrath*.

I began a slow loop across the room starting with the above-mentioned Johnny whose glasses slip when he looks down. He's painfully shy, but manages to gaze up in that puppy dog way and mouth, "You're a goddess." When he passed over the cash, he allowed his fingers to linger one beat longer than necessary. When I pulled back, he resumed his regularly scheduled program of gazing at the floor tile.

Then there's Rylan Williams. He sat directly behind me in one of those uncomfortable plastic desks. Rylan's father JAX (who went by only one name legally required to be in caps because why not) was one of the biggest action stars in Hollywood. JAX was also a vicious, bald by choice, womanizing narcissist who stopped by the school once a year for a photo op to accompany a story about why fatherhood is "the most important thing to him next to going to church on Sunday and saving homeless kittens." *I saw him kicking kittens once ... not to mention costars.*

I didn't feel sorry for Rylan who was one of the most gorgeous jack-holes in school. He had that slightly long, messy black hair that required long stretches in front of a mirror and constantly was pushing it out of a perfectly chiseled face that benefitted from weekly dermatology visits with Dr. Lancer. Some girls fell for his deep blue eyes that were reportedly "soulful," but I tried to resist. Urges based on looks led to purges of emotions when the guy turned out to be a total waste. All you needed was five minutes with his personality and such resistance was not futile.

Right now, he was kicking Johnny's desk and when the beanpole with the thick black glasses and mass of black hair whipped around, it was Rylan who said, "Hey, douchebag, go back to your regularly scheduled mediocrement."

Rylan wasn't smart enough to come up with that on his own. Instead, he spoke in former movie lines that his Dad said once upon a script ago on screen, which was his mediocrement. Rich Daddy or not, I could see his future in three words: Rehab/Walmart/Divorce.

Rylan pulled two crisp bills out of his wallet and pressed them into my palm and at the same time called poor Steve Dunbar, minding his own business in another row, "A stupid, worthless ferger." Ferger, of course, was invented by some cop drama starring JAX and meant "fat, hairy and made out of trash."

"Sorry, you couldn't study last night," I chirp as a quick subject changer. "Tough to read when you're at a premiere eating face with that girl from that Netflix thing. She's 15. Disgusting."

"Did I make TMZ? You could make TMZ with me," Rylan whispers. He is hopeful. His name in bold is his goal.

You won't make TMZ. Not until next month, Mr. DUI. I don't say it out loud. And I don't report on the rest of his life including the drugs, the arrest, leaving rehab, the living on the street... really ....the street? Sad. But, true. I'm never wrong. And then there is the *Dateline* special. *Kids of the Rich and Famous: An Ultra Cautionary Tale.*

Speaking of cautionary, he has already asked me to the school's

THE CLAIRES

winter dance on December 23 at the famed Hollywood hot spot, The Chateau Marmont hotel. Dream come true time, right? Knowing the pickings might be slim, I gave him a distinct maybe because I was scheduled to die the next day on my 17th birthday on Christmas Eve. Yeah, the Universe had some sense of humor. But I had the dance. And if all else failed, at least I could…well, you know. And he was technically more beautiful than me, so the scenery would be a good going away present.

He's actually number 10 on what I secretly called V's V List, which I hide on my phone and examine in detail before falling asleep each night.

The list must be hidden. If my rental parents from this lifetime (because they're hosts and breeders to us Claires) ever find it then I will be at one of those homes for wayward girls, the kind last seen in a Winona Ryder movie from the 2000s. For God's sake, my current father was a police detective. The idea of him finding the list…well, they might hear the yelling back in some time loop in the early 1900s, where our lifetimes began.

Right now, with my list safe and sound, I make the rounds, stopping at each desk where a perfect twenty-dollar bill fresh out of the cafeteria ATM is swiftly slapped into my palm along with heaps of gratitude, some even genuine. I heard it all before: "You're saving my life"; "My grades have been killer"; "You're scary smart"; "I don't know how you get these answers"; "Did you hack the school's main computer?"

Yes, they thought I was just a standard cyber thief who hacked into the school's mainframe on a regular basis, and thus had all the answers, all of the time.

There is always one naysayer.

Sarah Conway, daughter of no one, glares up at me, refusing to dip into her backpack. "I did the impossible," she snipes. "I actually read the book. You know, that thing with pages, V."

I want to crush her. I will get an A plus to her A minus today. I will be the first seat at every Academic All-Star event, which will have her weeping on the way home. I will "see" every argument from every student in the debate club and pulverize her.

Of course, I am nothing if not incredibly polite to her face. My current mother didn't raise Dr. Phil material.

"Scara, you might want to get out your inhaler," I say.

She begins to wheeze. Which I knew would happen.

"Welcome."

Saving lives. It's not just a job; it's also a burden.

"Can I kiss you, V?" Declan Rogers inquires after putting the cash in my palm.

"No, Mr. Mono," I say. *Shame because he's number three on my list, but since I'm scheduled to die soon, the last thing I need is some contagion rendering me bedridden for the next few months. Who needs home confinement with a mother who is at home doing her painting thing just a few rooms away? And making your soup. And putting her hands repeatedly on your forehead. And hovering. No, I couldn't risk it.*

"I do not have mono," he stammers. "How dare you air my private medical information with the entire class. There are Hippa laws and my father is an attorney who works for Universal."

"A disbarred one who handles merchandising," I chirp. "And yes, you do have mono. Check the results of your blood test." *He also had this rash, but well, never mind.*

Back to real world issues.

The last stop is the lecture stand in the front of the room. I cut to the chase.

"The answers are A, C, D, E, B, B, C, D . . . and . . ." I rattle off. "Row one, make sure you miss at least one question from the first set. Mix it up. Row two, miss two questions from set two. Row three, you're geniuses today. You get 100 percent."

THE CLAIRES

We had been through this routine many times.

In many classes.

In the end, it was a profitable day in class with over $640 raised for my future endeavors, including the small, one-bedroom apartment us Claire girls kept at the iconic Hollywood Tower Apartments, a secret from our most recent and unreasonably suffocating parents—the above-mentioned overly involved, stay-at-home-artist mother and tough cop father. Rounding out the family tree this go around is our older brother by one year, Cass.

C…A….S….S.

He was the hero type, if you know what I mean, in the most basic sense of what those words mean. I mean, square jawed, muscular type with broad shoulders, long, sinewy legs and miles of sandy blonde, sun-kissed, California wavy hair pushed casually off his devastatingly handsome mug. There was one Marine tat of an eagle on his upper right arm that got him grounded for a good two weeks. At his most magnificent, he forgot to shave and had facial stubble that made him look wild and reckless. Damn it, but he just always looked like he stepped off the cover of some vintage romance novel….the kind where the image made your knees melt and breath catch.

I know, I know. It's not the usual way to describe your *brother*.

But was he? Is he? My brother, I mean. Our odd way of being born to various families now meant that we had absolutely no DNA link.

Technically speaking, he is more than a possible sibling. He is a possible everything.

He is also number one on the V List.

6.

Saved by the bell.

"Have a good weekend and say a prayer for Tom Joad, y'all passed," I mock a drawl as Mrs. E sailed back into the room with fresh pants, a flat stomach, and a quizzical smile playing upon her lips.

"How hopeful. What are the odds that they all passed, dear?" she asks me.

"Hundo P," I reply, which translates to one-hundred percent.

What I couldn't tell her: I was just your average entrepreneur with a third eye committed to the excellence of a new generation—one boring ass quiz at a time.

A SENTIENT'S STORY: S

Los Angeles, California
2013

1.

THE NOISE ROSE from the scratched wood floors, bounced off the oatmeal-colored cinderblock walls, and reverberated like an entire marching band gone AWOL inside my head. It was unbearable—like a herd of wild rhinos stomping over every inch of grey matter. Like those beasts were auditioning for *So You Think You Can Dance*.

The racket of pandemonium was why I always sat in the farthest reaches of that hideous room, the worst in any high school. It was why my head was currently pressed to the coolness of that long, faux-wood table that contained the fingerprints of youth long since passed. It provided a surface for so many cold tater tots, greasy slabs of meatloaf, and raw human emotions that were served up daily.

A mental institution? No. It was our high school cafeteria.

Lunchtime at Santa Monica High and time to break bread (although no one ate carbs anymore) with your friends, crushes, enemies, formers (as in loves), and the rest of the peeps that fell somewhere between "adored them" and "wanted them run over by a city bus."

For me, the one they called S, the hour-long feeling fest went on (and on) five days a week, over culinary delights served on orange plastic trays as if the shocking color might stun us into some sort of decency. If only it was just the food that caused the pain. Today's offering was your typical gray slab of tofu pretending to be meat surrounded by steamed kale that had given up its will to exist and all of the above was decorated with slices of brown-

THE CLAIRES

green avocado. Welcome to California. I couldn't eat, and not just because of the dismal menu.

Things went just a little bit deeper here for yours truly, which was typical for someone like myself who was born with clairsentience, or clear feeling. In case you get the question on *Jeopardy* someday, and I feel that you might, I have the ability to experience the emotional energy of others in an intuitive way and then absorb it into my own system.

But, first things first.

Claire S, nice to meet you. Genetically, I inherited yellow daffodil hair and sapphire eyes from a mystery source. I did manage to snag my original parental unit Lula's long, lean frame, hatred of green beans, and the ability to feel the present, past, or future emotional states *of others*. It's an awful, awful gift, thank you for that, mother dear.

This is what you will never read on my permanent record in this realm: As previously discussed, I can sense other people's feelings while experiencing another's deepest emotions as if they are my own. If you want to get fancy about it, it's called psychic sensing. I can feel things about people and places, all the while draining myself of every ounce of my own personal energy while I tune in to the other being.

Clairsentients feel things—every little freaking second—so strongly and profoundly that we're just-ran-the-marathon mentally exhausted after wandering into a large group of people with all their emotions popping.

Imagine taking on everyone else's bad day, sad day, or day of joyous euphoria. It's enough to make you long for your pillow and a week-long nap. For instance, right now, I'm crying actual tears *and nothing remarkable happened to me this morning* beyond fighting with my brother over the last of the breakfast cereal.

Each day, I eat lunch alone or with my sisters if they can

manage to ditch their classes and find me. Most days, one of them finds me in mid-panic attack from what I'm absorbing. My hands sweat; my heart races. It's not easy to make a cold compress out of soggy cafeteria napkins, but I do it.

My panic today concerns that sophomore, Carrie Armstrong, over there who had a knock-down this morning with her stepfather, Steven. I'm deeply tuned into her, which means I'm forced to feel her feelings as if I own them. Thus, it becomes our shared pain, our sadness, and our disappointment. And then it happens. A terrible stab of terror makes goose bumps rise on my arms. She/me have this strange fear that something even worse will happen later when she goes home. That's just a hunch, but what is dead-on is the feeling of abject dread. What did her stepfather say to her in the driveway? If I think about it hard enough, it comes to me on playback and makes me cry. "You're a throw-away child," he told her. "You're not even my real daughter."

Body shaking tears flood over me in overlapping waves of emotions until I turn slightly to my left, gaze at another table and surf the next human mini-drama. *The boy over there, he can't afford college. His mom taunts him: "You were never supposed to amount to anything much, so what does it matter?"* I look two tables over. *There's the other girl who tells her parents she was sexually abused by her uncle. Her Dad's response: "You're talking nonsense. Making shit up."* The back table. *The girl with the pink hair who just buried her mother. Oh, poor baby.* Grief begins to overwhelm me.

I can also sense the overall energy in the room, which today can be summed up as: Quiet desperation, served with brief period of joy and undercooked tater tots.

If you add the fact that this will be my last spring when it comes to drawing breath followed by my last summer and last fall -- not that I'm dwelling on it -- but, if you ask me, there's not enough Kleenex in the world.

THE CLAIRES

2.

"S, DON'T, HONEY. Don't lose it. We have our big trip to New York coming up," says my sister V, who quietly slides in next to me and holds my hand firmly, like only she can. She doesn't have to sit this closely given no one ever eats lunch with me. There's an entire bench of room at the other back table. "Take a deep yoga breath. Keep your shit together if you want to live – if you know what I mean -- – and you do," she says in that V-the-Conquer voice. I almost half believe her because every family has one person who is the muscle. V is always flexing for the greater good.

She reminds me that we have two chances at extending this lifetime:

One: We were already racking up lots of good deeds as a sort of penance and possible bargaining chip, although good deeds didn't get you as far as they used to, we were told by our first Ma (Lula) who tapped into universal sources to ask the question.

Two: Speaking of Ma, she was a bit of an old-fashioned nudge. She had begged us for decades, during former lifetimes, to travel to our ancestral home where we first grew up with her. Lifetime #1. She was talking about our red bricked turn-of-the-century New York house that sat on woodsy land in the hot real estate market of Brooklyn. Like many historically protected homes and buildings, it was mostly untouched as was the forest land that surrounded it, which also fell into the protection of preservation groups.

Ma, as we called her, was still harping that our grandmother Penny had buried something of interest either in the house or around the property and what she hid pertained to a curse that caused us to always die at age 17 and then experience a rebirth in another part of the world to a different family. Poor Granny was tossed head down in a pickle barrel and drown before she shared what-or-where with Ma. In past years, we thought she was either nuts to ask us to go there and/or it was impossible for us as children and young teenagers to travel to New York. It was always something that prevented the journey, from adult interference to a complete lack of finances that kept us away from where it all began.

This time was different. We had four tickets booked for this spring break and a lie of epic proportions already in motion to buy four beautiful, un-parentally supervised days out of town.

Just thinking about breaking a curse should have me melting down emotionally, but the truth is I feel the thrill of wanderlust combined with solving an ancient mystery. If only I could get through this day, we'd only have a few more until the above-mentioned spring break and four cramped seats on Delta Flight 587 from LAX to JFK.

V reminds me, "You can't freak out again or the school will call home and suggest meds. They always suggest meds. It's the easy way out in many cases. You don't need anything but your sisters and a clear head and open heart for the trip."

"Plus, comfortable shoes," I interrupt.

"Well, yeah," she says.

I breathe even deeper and this time I see stars. "That's it, honey," V says, getting out her phone and pressing the screen into my face. V's on the Calm AP (better than meds!) and right now I'm staring into a roaring fireplace. "No good?" she poses and clicks over to waves lapping on a beach. "Now, you're making me want to go to the bathroom," I say with a tiny smile. "All that swooshing water."

V smiles and flicks over to a picture of Chad Johnson that she took…I don't even know when. Chad is a sweet 16-year-old math nerd who looks like that actor Timothee Chalomet, but with his own wave of glossy black hair, big brown eyes and a shy, curious smile. A few weeks ago, he stared down at his shoes and asked me to the winter dance. For once, my heart did a tiny flip. I could

THE CLAIRES

also feel his nerves dancing, which made the whole thing a bit exciting. I said yes; we stared at his shoes. And then I gave him half a sandwich to seal the deal.

"Enough with Chad," I tell V. Then I make a mock mad face. "He better not be on your V list. I didn't even eat lunch today, but if he is I might toss my cookies."

"I don't poach from my sisters," she insists, "even the ones I've single handedly brought back to life today in the cafeteria."

V likes to boast, and we don't mind because mostly we ignore her bravado. Yes, she's super confident and the most competitive person on earth, but she is the oldest by at least a full minute. But this virginity thing…please? I think V deep down is a hopeless romantic who has just never had a romance. Just when she gets to her prime age of hormonal nirvana, life is yanked from her, which is tragic to say the least. I want to cry just thinking about it, but hold back the waterworks.

Now that I'm calm, she pulls up what we call our Exist List. She's big on the lists to keep order in each lifetime.

Our Exist List is a random inventory or catalogue of things we will do *when (you have to manifest things if you want them to happen, hence the when and not if)* we live past age 17:

Mine includes getting through one lunch period without losing my mind, doing a perfect backflip as a world-famous gymnast, finding my significant other, adopting countless dogs and cats and maybe a few babies.

Other sisterly agenda items are mostly spoken of late at night when the lights are off.

Our sister A wants to get her Ph.D. in history and have five children and a little cabin in the woods with 1000 channels on her TV and a moat, while badass C wants to save all the mistreated dogs and children in the universe and join the Avengers, if they really existed – and she believes in her heart that they do. If not, she'd like to invent them in real life. V talked about living until she was a hunched over little old lady with a cane and a Poodle named Prissy. She would collect the years like trinkets, cure cancer and marry three times to enjoy a variety pack of men.

These were all lofty goals, sure, but when the lights go out at age 17, you might as well dream big. Most of us had a long list of agenda items, if and when, we were granted the time to make them into realities.

Or not.

"Nine months and counting, honey," V reminds me. *It's all the time we have left and the last year of our lives is always the worst because you're forced to count. That's just human nature.* Is that actual moisture in her eyes? "Not that we're going to freak out. We have time now – and this time we're going to beat the clock. We're going to outrace impending doom. We'll look for the signs and work to break the curse."

Want to hear the weirdest thing of all from a Universe that had an odd sense of humor? Strangely, the sign that we were about to draw last breath was the sighting of a goat. A few months ago, in science class, our teacher brought in a farm animal for study and my heart, along with V's, stopped cold.

"Not a goat, not a goat, not a goat," we began to chant under our breath.

"Hey fellow PETA members, I'm hoping it's not my lost cat," said the above- mentioned Chad.

Turns out the thing making all the noise in the school garden was actually a sheep.

"We will win," V re-affirms with all the confidence of someone whose life has been given an end date. Her words say one thing, but her voice is hollow with fear.

THE CLAIRES

3.

OUT OF THE corner of my own moist eye, I spot the baby of our bunch, C, who bursts through the cafeteria door in a manner where the actual steel of the door hits old concrete and creates a tiny cloud of particle dust. She is 100 percent lethal bravado backed up by a badass streak that is 100 years in the making. Right now, C is doing her snarky walk, eating up tile with every step, as she saunters up to the salad bar. As usual, the line is long, but she cuts right in front.

Rule embracer Sarah from V's English class says, "Excuse me, the front of the line is waayyy back there. Have you been struck blind?"

C gazes over her bronze, round, John Lennon sunglasses and purses her lips. Then she slaps Sarah across her right cheek. "Have you been struck stupid?" C says with a slight smirk.

"Ow...you can't....ow...I'm calling my ....," Sarah stammers, rubbing her cheek. "That's bullying. I've been bullied! You are a bully!"

"Hearsay," C says, grabbing a plate and remarking, "Plus, I don't see any witnesses." Heads fall in unison. The next 20 people in line become immediately absorbed in their phones.

C, who is claircognizant or all-knowing -- the most powerful of the Claires -- is the supermodel of our group with a killer body, dangerous curves, naturally curly blonde hair that flows perfectly just past her perfectly sculpted chin and innocent-looking, saucer blue eyes that make mere mortals melt. She looks like a fairy minus wings from some country you've never heard of, but has a dot on somebody's map.

Unfortunately, C's kingdom is Santa Monica High where she downplays every single thing about her princess appearance.

Besides the little round glasses, she plops a black beanie on her head and wears a black sweater about five sizes too big over skinny jeans. She's in her own personal witness protection program from high school.

Her personality isn't designed to win her any awards either. She has always been extremely physical and once sunk her baby teeth into a boy on the playground for looking at her for too long during recess. "That girl is a bat," he reported while bleeding.

"A bat out of hell," she retorted, licking her lips.

At the time, C was only five and tested negatively for rabies.

Right now, the student TV show is playing overhead, which is enough for C to drop her salad bowl on the ground. As arugula flies everywhere, Rylan, our anchor, is announcing the "court" for this winter's big dance. "And rounding out the list of possible winter dance queens is C Danko," he says and then looks right in the camera and makes the "call me" sign as he says her name.

"Son of a bitch!" C says. And loudly.

And she's not done.

"Are these assholes kidding?"

She had a worse reaction last year when the cheerleading coach delicately asked her if she wanted to be on the varsity squad. It involved a series of ripped up pom-poms and a backflip where she stuck the landing on some cheer queen's face. It was the day the school found out that polyester shirts actually did absorb blood.

C's current emotional state is mortified with a touch of white hot anger. "Can you freaking believe it?" she fumes, sliding down next to us. That dancer's body means her moves are like rushing water. "The theater teacher cast me as the lead in 'Oklahoma' and I didn't even try out. Someone named Miss Nadia wants me on her dance team. What's wrong with these people? I'm only passing time here. I don't do high school."

THE CLAIRES

"The nerve," I say, stealing two cherry tomatoes from her greens.

"Four words," she says. "Get off my ass, muther….."

"That's five words," I say.

"Do you want me to hurt you?" C retorts, but it's an empty threat. She would never hurt her sisters, and was in fact, one of our fiercest protectors from vermin known as society at large. You saw a lot of society when you roamed around LA at night.

On the other plus side, C had been helping Dad with some of his more difficult police cases and this had gone on since she was eight. A hard ass in life, she had a keen sense of street justice and that included protecting those who were younger, smaller or truly vulnerable. She wasn't a superhero by any means, but if she had a cape, it would shelter the downtrodden of the land.

Rylan was not one of the needy. He was hovering in front of us now, fresh from the superstardom of the noon student news. Ignored, he took it upon himself to actually kneel at C's feet like we were in the middle of some Victorian melodrama.

"Oh, for God's sake," C sighs when Rylan gazes up and starts to beg her to be in the dance court. Then he asks her out. "You already asked my sister to the winter dance," she says with disgust.

"You can have him," V chimes in.

"Please," he begs C. "Dinner and a movie? Friday night. You. Me? My hot tub?"

Her answer this time is a hard shove that causes him to fall backwards and hit his head on the cold tile floor. "I have yearbook pictures later today," Rylan gasps. "That was uncalled for … even if you were going to say no."

Dean Walter Simpkis isn't content to watch teenage love in all its glory play out before his eyes.

"First the slap – and now you've almost paralyzed that boy," Dean Simpkis says.

"Oh, please," C begins to defend herself. I think. "If I really wanted to paralyze him, I would have shoved him into one of the folding tables and then smashed him into the wall. Far more effective in terms of crippling."

"On your feet, young lady," he says.

C stands and then slowly reaches over to my sandwich from home which is uneaten and of the tuna fish variety. She takes the slowest bite ever, and chews it 26 times because I count and know this is accurate. I feel Simpkis' fury. He wants to shake her violently, but he can only go so far because he knows our father would kick his academic ass.

V chimes in. "Dad is already on his way. You know how he feels about school injustice. Plus, he's on a big case. Needs your help, C. You won't be at school for much longer because he's about to sign you out." (V's winning also extended to beating any and all faculty members at their own game. A victory for any Claire girl was her trophy, too.)

"Toodles, girls," C says, blowing us kisses. She secures the John Lennon's in place and asks V, "How much longer?"

"Exactly seven minutes until Dad is in the parking lot," V responds. "See you in the funny papers, Mr. S."

4.

MY SISTER A pops in for a quick chat, waving a bathroom pass. "Did I see C with Simpkis?" she says. "I hope he has health insurance. She'll eat him alive and we'll need a new dean."

V and I laugh ourselves silly while A, the one who speaks with spirits and has fallen in love or deep infatuation with quite a few, informs us, "I'm supposedly on a hall pass to the john. I can stretch it because I informed Mr. Danvers it was women's issues and that

THE CLAIRES

time of the month. Then I said a word that made him almost barf ... flow."

We nod. That works every time in every lifetime.

"How are you, sweetie?" she asks me.

"I'm overly responsive today," I whisper. "Exhausted, a little anxious. Overwhelmed. Look at Matt Whitcome over there. Tried to . . . last night. In a closet with rope. But what else is new?"

V looks at me and nods. "But he didn't . . . and he won't," she assures me. "His mom did the right thing and called the counselor. And anyways, he can't do...that. He's number nine on my list."

"You're disgusting," A tells her with a smile. "And delusional. I'd put him at six or seven at least, if I had a list, which I do not."

"It's my list," V says, eating the rest of my tuna sandwich. "The two of you might consider a little jungle boogie before we trip out of this lifetime. Just saying because I'd like you to die with a s-smile this...." When she stops talking in the middle of her favorite subject, I give her a curious look.

The fearful look on her face has my heart pounding.

What? I mouth. A host of possibilities enter my mind, like bomb threat or school shooter, but I can feel that her mind is outside these high school walls.

"Missing kid in Santa Monica," she says. "That's why Dad is picking up C. He's four. Sad situation. It's about to hit the news. In exactly three minutes." We wait until the text comes over her phone and then my phone as an amber alert.

I tap into the world outside the doors of this school and feel the pain of a young mother searching for something just outside of her reach. She's not alone.

So many seekers in this world; so little answers.

My attention is temporarily diverted back to the cafeteria. I see her in another corner, the girl with the long, silky reddish hair and big hazel eyes. She lives next door to us and is being raised by a single, way overly protective father named Gene who is another cop and our father's partner. Her name is Annie and she has no mother (her own died years ago). She hangs out at our house a lot and borrows our current mother, if you can call it that, which I do. Mom is always hugging her and taking her on little shopping trips.

She sees me and lifts her hand to wave. I return the motion although V snaps, "Don't wave. We hate her. Remember?"

Annie and I are secret friends because my sisters don't like her that much, especially V. I do not feel the same way – not by a longshot – which is why I find moments to talk to Annie outside on our driveways or in the bathroom at school or even in the few classes we share together that luckily don't include my sisters.

For some reason, V and I both gaze at Annie at the same time, but we look at her differently. We always do. I find pity for our motherless next-door neighbor while V gazes at her savagely. And then V and I stare at each other for a silent minute like I don't really know what's going on, which is a lie, but sometimes lies are just easier.

Annie has a "thing" with our brother, Cass. They call it friends.

This "friendship" is why V doesn't call Annie just Annie, but refers to her as "deadshit Annie." It's like V is trying to combine the worst fate of all – death -- with the word shit. She's a walking dictionary of these nasty combinations and some are so bad that I hesitate to even think them.

"I saw what deadshit Annie did," she begins.

She saw it; I felt it. She still sees it – and she could kill her for it. *The thin line between love and clair hate.*

I'm sure they're not. Just friends, that is. I'm talking about Annie and Cass. Naturally, neither will cop to it because it's just easier to be neighbor best buddies. That part was established at the tender age of five when they used to make mud pies together in the backyard. The mutually agreed upon denied love between

THE CLAIRES

them as high school seniors makes it that much more intense for all involved. Rejecting the obvious just makes the obvious that much stronger.

And then there's V. She feels the same thing for Cass.

All I do when I feel the love vibes at home from V to Cass is think, "He's not really our brother in terms of DNA or blood or bone or muscle or even eye color type. He's not really out brother at all. He's not really our relative in that way. So, really, what's the big deal if V wants to go to bed with him?" I think she's also in love him. In her own way.

Cass. A story for another time.

Our "brother" remains a murky entity to all of us Claires, and we don't like murk. All of the sisters feel quite wary of him in a way that brings out the worst in us. For starters, we never get emotionally involved with our host families, which just makes it easier to move on. Secondly, he has morphed into this technically gorgeous specimen of manhood, a fact that *three of us* can easily ignore for some reason. Since he's not a blood relation, I can tap into his feelings and know that he is desperate to deny who he is.

We hate people who dismiss a great gift.

Rocking our world is that Cass is our only so-called relative ever who came to the party with "a little something-something." He frightens us because we're used to dealing with average Joe mortals, but this six foot four mountain living in the bedroom next door with his wavy surfer blond hair down his back and those blazing blue eyes also has strong psychic gifts that he has only begun to explore. I think he's dangerous and avoid him at all costs.

He returns the favor. The only thing we actually have in common with Cass is an address.

His "friend," Annie is eating alone again because they don't share the same lunch period. *Why not tap into her? It's easy to do...*

and... She's scared down to her bone marrow because... because ... she's hiding some sort of massive secret that will upset... no, devastate, her father, big, bad Gene who really has a heart of gold. Not that he isn't tough because he is a decorated police detective, our father's partner and one bad muther at the same time.

I feel her worry enter the panic zone.

And then my heart races like it will burst. There is something I haven't shared with my sisters or anyone else on this planet. When it comes to Annie, I don't just feel sorry for her family situation, but I have other feelings for her, which means that Annie-Cass-V aren't really a love triangle. If you add me to the mix, we're a love quad.

5.

I NEED TO recharge on this Friday afternoon, the last day before, thank God, spring break sets us free and fortunately/unfortunately we embark on our supposed week up in Northern California cleaning plastics off various beaches. But we're not really going to the land of Big Sur and Pebble Beach.

We've saved enough money for the first time ever to sneak away to New York City on our own for an entire, beautiful, peaceful parentless four days. The rip is that we're actually going on the advice of our DNA Ma who all, but signed our permission slip for the trip back in the 1800s.

I shudder to think of all of the emotions that will bombard me in the biggest city of all. Quiet time is the only solution before we leave tomorrow, which is why I excuse myself today, and on most days, from the bulk of afternoons at school.

It's salvation.

There is nothing like going home early to put my throbbing head under a pillow in the name of simply being hormonal, which doesn't cover the half of it.

AN AUDIENT'S STORY: A

Los Angeles, California
2013

1.

Sixth period.

Miss Makayla Butler's AP history class. We sit in these hard, wooden chairs in "pods" of four, just in case Ms. B calls for the horror known as a group project. Big bro Cass is not only in this class, but in my pod. Really? I mean, what are the Vegas odds on that one happening?

Right now, Ms. B is showing some sort of power point on a screen about something historical. I only have nine months to live, but if I spent every single day in this class, in this pod, it might seem like nine million months. And counting.

Obviously, Cass feels the same way. He's pretending to take notes, but I see him looking down at his phone and occasionally typing something to Annie when he thinks Ms. B isn't looking.

I can't exactly hate Cass, although I try, because of the sisterly peer pressure that goes this way: C doesn't trust him, S feels too much sisterly love, so she clamps it down and V feels another kind of love for him, which weirds us all out as in "get a room, but not one in our house because sister-brother love is just so Lifetime TV."

I have an added burden, which is that Cass and I share certain "plusses." He sees dead people; I see dead people. His room in the middle of the night is a revolving "who's who" of the afterlife; mine is mostly confined to an in-your-business super dead Ma from the 1800s who keeps popping up, plus a long list of hot guys from history who I invite to the old bedroom for some late-night fantasy interaction. Some girls can simply dream, but I can visualize and actually talk to men from the past, lonely types who like to make war and love.

THE CLAIRES

Last night, there was that amazingly gorgeous WWII fighter pilot named Charles with his dreamy blue eyes, short dark hair and a form that said "come fly with me, come fly away." If it wasn't for our alarm clock ringing at six thirty a.m. then I might have joined the historical mile high club.

"I'll need your homework now," Ms B interrupts anything resembling joy.

"Cass," I whisper across the table and he gives me his almost adorable, completely snarky half grin. "Didja do…" I begin.

"The homework?" he whispers, slipping me a piece of paper that has multiple choice questions circled in a bold pencil. "You owe me," he says. "Keep V and C away from me. And clean the bathroom."

"Done," I nod and smile. "You do those essay questions this weekend and I'll see what I can do about you getting a whole ten minutes in the communal bathroom sometime soon – clean and solo bathroom time."

"Don't be too good to me," Cass says, grinning wide. "I won't know how to handle it."

"Don't worry, I won't," I reply.

"Miss Danko would you like to share what aspect of history you're discussing with the rest of the class?" Ms. B interrupts.

"Well, I was mulling over the plight of the fighter pilot during World War II," I begin.

"We haven't even studied World War I," Ms. B interrupts.

"She loves history so much that she reads ahead," Cass chimes in. "I see her do it. She stays up all night reading the textbook."

A teacher save.

Slick move of the highest order.

He made it almost impossible to hate him.

2.

TEN MIND-NUMBING MINUTES go by where I allow my mind to wander to more pleasant and enjoyable topics like Sven, my Viking warrior ghost lover. He is six-foot- five with wild reddish hair combed by the brisk sea winds, a sturdy jaw dotted with sexy stubble and a body made out of carefully molded steel in the form of muscles upon muscles. No, he didn't go to Planet Fitness, but his exquisite form was from tangling and tussling with Anglo-Saxons, Norwegians, Icelanders and the Danish. My man of the Mediterranean was a ghost who made frequent visits to my room late at night because ...well, mentally I called to him as in, "Hey, Sven, are you out there?"

Being clairaudient, I could call all sorts of interesting potential boyfriends back for some late-night chit chat and kisses that I actually felt down to my toes. True that they didn't have mortal lips, but I had an active enough of an imagination to fill in the blanks similar to mere mortals reading a really hot romance novel and feeling all the tingles.

Viking men and fighter boys, plus all other vintage males, had ruined your standard high school boys for me. Consider: Who wanted some tall, skinny math geek crushing on you when you could have Sven promising eternal love and your own castle with bridges and moats? Yeah, the boys in my class at SMHS could be on the football team, but my soldiers were on the front lines saving the world and looking so handsome in their flak jackets.

Normal boys: Regular girls could have them.

True, I was slutty when it came to my ghost boyfriends and rotated them at will. One night, it was Rollo, the first ruler of Normandy and Viking with a bod like Aquaman and a heart of gold and the next it was Bjorn Ironside, my brave *other* Viking

THE CLAIRES

man (so many Vikings, so little time) who once pretended to be dead and had his men ask the town priests to bury him on sacred ground. When his coffin was carried into the church, my man Bjorn jumped out, fought his way to reach the city gates and opened them in order for his men to invade. By the way, he gave the best ghost massages. As a spirit, he would sit on the edge of my bed and run those strong fingers over my back.

Midnight in my bedroom. You could say I was just a girl who couldn't get enough history.

One of my biggest crushes was on Eric Bloodax who didn't just have that rad name, but raided the Baltic and European coasts. As with all men, you had to weigh the good with the bad. Sure, he also murdered his brothers, but no one was perfect and families were always complicated.

I was about to call for Eric right now….if only Ms. B wasn't so loud and shrilly. She was making it tough to concentrate on Mr. Bloodax with all his blood bruises that needed tender loving tending and those full lips with just a hint of wind burn from the open seas and then his ….

"But how do we knooooow," Ms. B stands right in front of me now and drones, "what Harriet Tubman said on that historical day back in …?" At this point, I put my dating life on hold because I could use some choice class participation points before the quarter ends.

Harriet . . . Harriet? I say the name silently in my mind. *Come on Harriet. Don't fail me now. And please don't play hard to get.* As a ghost, she's Beyonce time. She's standoffish, which is the norm with these historical icons. Many of them are divas who go AWOL when you need them the most such as on the AP history exam day. Still . . . it can't hurt to knock. Maybe she's having a slow day in the great beyond or feeling altruistic or just bored out of her gourd.

You can never predict, with pinpoint accuracy, the daily vibe of the spiritual world, but as a clairaudient, reaching out to them is my thing.

Just when I'm facing certain doomsday failure for class participation, I hear the small, tinny taps in my left ear – *ping, ping, ping* -- and then feel the small shockwaves race up and down my spine. Slowly, her words come into my mind as if someone was whispering them into my frontal lobe. I remove my big silver hoop on that side, so her voice doesn't vibrate to the point of being overwhelming. But it still does . . . even *I* get a chill when the ghost is this revered.

"What I said was: I grew up like a neglected weed—ignorant of liberty, having no experience of it," Harriet whispers. I nod to no one, which makes me look like I've lost my marbles or I'm going into a shoulders-up seizure. The good news is everyone is so apathetic in high school that no one even notices.

"A, you owe me," Harriett says. "Go do something good for humanity today. I'm watching."

"Touch your heart and hope to—" HT adds, but then stops. "I'm sorry. That was insensitive. I know you only have less than a year to live. Please don't report me Upstairs."

I flash the peace sign under my desk. The rest is lost because I dismiss her with a mental footnote, *Be gone now, you ghost.*

"Earth to A? Am I disturbing you?" demands Ms. B, who is now hovering over me. She has done the teacher sneak attack where they invade your personal space and then wait for full wattage embarrassment to set in. I hold tight for the threats—and Miss B doesn't disappoint. "As you know, A, half of your grade depends upon class participation and I get the distinct feeling that you didn't read the material last night."

In a bland voice, I repeat. "I grew up as a neglected weed . . ."

Ms B.O., a favorite nickname for her, stands there like she is in the thick weeds of disappointment now. She's stupefied. But now I'm having a good time. A *very* good time. "Um, yes, that is exactly what she said. Very good, dear. Very . . ."

The bell saves us all.

3.

IT IS ENTIRELY time-consuming being clairaudient, which means clear hearing, and also means listening to distant sounds and voices when no one else does because they can't. By the way, this chit-chat does not mean you're crazy or losing your own freaking mind, although historically speaking too many clairaudients have logged times in the mental institutions of the world. When you talk to yourself and insist it's ghosties communicating, there is a good chance that a padded room will be reserved at the looney bin.

Quite simply, I hear way beyond normal range, which originates in my fifth chakra, if you want to get technical about it.

Let's take it out for a spin. Yes, I can hear gunshots from miles away or the moan of a person who is in pain—or *was* being harmed. But all of this is only my opening act.

The big show is I can hear spirit voices. They come on quickly, marked by a change of pressure or a pop in my ears, as if I was rocketing upward in a plane. Then comes the ringing, buzzing, or knocking. Spirits are nothing if not polite, announcing their presence and then dissipating when asked to leave. That's in the rule book.

Request that they leave and the "visitor" from beyond must – and you should never have to ask twice. Most of the time, they will appear when I specifically ask them questions like the lovely Ms.

Tubman, but not always. Good luck asking Albert Einstein or my beloved Mac Miller a rhetorical question. Some of them have their own version of call waiting as in *forever hanging onto an answerless line.*

The one I loved the most, our beloved OG, Ma, always answered. You could say quite simply that I was born a Mama's girl. I hadn't seen my dear Ma since she/we died in 1928 – our first death – but she remains in constant touch no matter what lifetime we're on or what family calls us their own. We called them host units.

It was lovely that I could summon her anytime, like now, while taking a quick pee in the empty girl's room. I'm in one of the stalls talking very low.

"Ma, you there?" I whisper.

"My beautiful child," she replies from way out of town.

"Rough day, Ma," I mouth. "Teachers are like raptors here. They gang up in threes, which is why I have two papers due Friday and a test. I might flunk out of school, which I know doesn't really matter since we never graduate."

It's such a bitch to die at 17 and never, ever wear that cap and gown. Since 1928, I've longed to toss my tassels.

"My darling Claire A," Ma responds from …where I'm not sure, but it's beyond these walls. "As long as you're learning skills for future lifetimes, then you've graduated in the school of life."

Motivational to the backbeat of six toilets flushing at various times.

"Bye, Ma. Check in with you later, gator," I tell her.

When I emerge, two sophomores are standing by the mirror, glossing and looking at me like I lost my mind.

"School…play," I mutter. "Running lines. Dedicated to my craft. Living in the moment, theatrically speaking."

They buy it. Nod furiously. Underclassman hope so desperately to bond that I could have convinced them that I was reciting the Gettysburg Address in there.

Another trait of clairaudients: We like to talk to ourselves—and quite honestly can't help it—especially when contemplating or experiencing a stressful event.

Tonight, we would go prowling which almost always proves to be a stress- inducing-palooza. We do almost every single night. We—as in me and my sisters—vowed that this life in sunny California would be . . . different. We would act as servants of a better humanity in order to earn extra years of life. Not that anyone told us that this would work, but a life of charity couldn't hurt. And what better way to do it than at midnight when California got interesting.

I could already feel it was going to be a night of tales we would tell far into future lives.

4.

It should be mentioned that we live on a relentlessly sunny residential street a few miles from the white foam of the ocean, which doesn't mean that we're living a lifestyle of the rich and/or the famous. It's a cookie-cutter neighborhood where the tasteful ranch houses are the same adobe-colored Spanish style, all identical in size: medium-small. It was a neighborhood made up of elevated blue-collar families. Not cops, but detectives like my dad. Not plumbers, but the dudes who owned the company. The houses were purchased decades ago, when Santa Monica wasn't an "attractive" address. It was just cheaper and the families never left.

This lifetime with the Danko family was definitely middle-class all the way, which was fine because we didn't like getting too attached to a place or a time. Rich attaches you because you never want it to end. But, end it must. And time does fly when you're only given 6,205 days for each go-around or 17 years. Yes, I did the math.

The minute I round the corner of Camrose Court in our white VW, a present from this life's Daddy-O, I can hear the radio or TV playing ... in each and every home on the block. Props to our next-door neighbor's landscaper for listening to O.A.R., though right now some pesky newsperson is cutting in with a special report.

"A, do you think you can find him? Is that missing boy alive?" Cass shouts from the living room, the freaking minute we walk through the door. *I mean, the exact second we appear and he's primed to jump.* He also has his own car, a vintage Jeep that Dad worked on until he could get it up to speed. It's black, fast, and Cass drives like a lunatic, which is why he always beats everyone home except S, who takes a lot of half days to emotionally refuel.

I can see Cass's watching TV with laser-beam focus, head in his hands, on the small brown leather couch in the den. He's XL everywhere so I see more of him than couch. I stand behind him and listen to the police code on the scanner my father leaves on by mistake. I can read between the lines as does Cass, who is older by a year, but this has nothing to do with elevation of supernatural abilities. Our mutual curiosity is revved up to a ten thanks to growing up as the kids of a cop, which puts us both on the same heightened "crisis" level. Each day on that scanner is a different melodrama with real life consequences – tragic and fascinating, if you're into these kinds of things.

Today, it's a 207, possible 273A, which is a shame. The first is kidnapping and the second is possible child neglect. It happened earlier today and V told me that Dad was on the case. A four-year-old boy has gone missing near Venice Beach. His distraught

THE CLAIRES

mother and her boyfriend told the police that they brought the kid to the beach and he "just vanished into thin air" while collecting shells. The Coast Guard had combed the surrounding water and had found nothing, which was concerning. Sharks were also spotted in the area the previous weekend.

I knocked again into the spirit world and hear a lot of kids running and playing, but not this specific voice. And no one was swallowed into the ocean in this town today by prehistoric creatures. Even underwater, I would have heard the screaming.

"Is he alive?" Cass repeats.

He's not asking in the normal way...as in give me your best hunch. One day when I was extremely bored, I started talking about ghosts and Cass started talking about spirits and we told each other -- in not so many words -- what happens to us via the spirit world. I didn't judge him; he didn't laugh at me. We've never spoken about it again, but there is a quiet understanding that these gifts are there. Cass explained it away saying "our" mother (really his mother) had these abilities, too, so it must have been handed down through the bloodline.

"Uh huh," I said. "Yep, you got it all figured out."

Like I really couldn't say, "By the way, your mother was only our birth host and we don't share any DNA with her, your father or you. Have a nice day."

At moments like these I needed to focus, and I did before telling him, "I don't know what will happen to the kid. I don't think he crossed over yet . . . and for that we can be grateful. I can ask...." I almost followed that with the words "the spirit world" and wanted to add, "But you can do that, too." I didn't say a word of it. Why jump into topics that felt so damn uncomfortable?

"I don't see the kid in the afterlife," I say.

"Me neither," Cass seconds.

"If you go out and look later, I'll cover for all of you," Cass promises. "Or maybe I can go with you." He looks at my face. "Or maybe not."

It's an offer backed up by the fact that we both knew it would never happen because the other sisters wouldn't allow it.

"I'll keep you informed," I say.

"Right back at you," he replies.

Actual discussion might not be necessary. We crossed wires a few times in the past, so to speak, when it came to the great beyond. For instance, while in elementary school, Cass and I found ourselves on the receiving lines of some very motivated and greedy ghosts with messages galore, so they ping ponged between us. Both of us ignored the fact that we were on a party line. It was like running into your teacher in the Target dressing room. You did the too fast head nod and then pretended it never happened.

It was moments like this one, when I felt my brother's big heart, that it was hard to completely dismiss him in a forever type of way. In a few months, we'd be nothing more than his dead sisters and would never see him again. But forget all the boo-hooing over that fact although I wondered if he would miss us. Would be begin sentences with words like: "When my sisters were alive..."

As Claires, we had survived the centuries not attaching to any other stray siblings, and it made us nervous to let even one in . . . . even a little bit. Cass was the first one ever who could power up in ways we understood. It provided moments that made me feel a little bit too close to him, which went against our self-protection mechanism. Hatred was always a far more manageable emotion than love followed by impending loss.

But there were times when I opened a window . . . just a crack.

An audient's plight in life is the expectation of providing profound advice and I didn't disappoint him.

"I do believe that if there is a thin line between life and death then our presence tonight will make the line waver definitively one way or the other because every interaction, every moment, produces a Butterfly Effect of reactions," I reply. "Remember, I said 'our' as in the girls and I."

    He stands, takes a large step back, and I get it. He's backing off. He even heaves a compliment.

    "My sista," Cass says, raising a hand to give me a high five that I ignore.

    "Better than Oprah," he says, slapping the air.

5.

AFTER MY CLOSE encounter of a Caspian Danko kind, I walk through the circular Spanish arches into our warm and sunny kitchen with the terra cotta colored, tiled floor. We have beamed ceilings and bright red-and-beige rugs. After a little ice-cream out of the container, I nav the small rooms of this house and make my way up the wooden back staircase to our room. Yes, the four of us girls share.

    Dad broke down a wall and all four of us co-exist in what was once two rooms and now is called the Claire Compound. Mom is lenient with everything including the decorating advice and allows us to be the very definition of the word eclectic. She chooses to believe we're going through a phase, which is why we live in a style that can only be described as early 1800s not-so-shabby chic.

    "This Victorian-Early Americana phase has lasted about ten years," Mom tells guests.

    I should caution here that Mom is our word for our Mom in this current lifetime. It might sound too cold to call Mrs. Danko our host, but frankly that's exactly what she was for us. She was pregnant with us and birthed us because we were placed in her womb by forces beyond anyone's control. In many ways, these mothers or Mom now were like surrogates while our first Ma, Lula Fair Pitcher, was our real Ma or maternal figure with whom we share actual blood. We treated the hosts as nannies of sorts. There to comfort and care, but we never latched on. They weren't our Ma.

The air hangs heavy in our warm, dark room where the only light flickers wildly from real oil lamps subjected to a modern invention known as ever-blasting arctic air-conditioning. Mom was at that age: hot flashes, moody, forgetful. Our lamps, each identical and made of brass, sit on small, sculpted walnut nightstands placed next to four pristinely made single beds.

Each bed was framed by a turn-of-the-century white wrought-iron headboard and covered with an elaborately embroidered quilt in pinks, greens and purples. There were four beautiful antique ivory-covered porcelain bowls next to each bed with a matching water pitcher inside of it and a white cloth nearby.

The beds were lined up in a neat row on dark, hardwood floors with a faded-looking wool rug in muted colors next to each. I see S in her bed with two large feather pillows pulled over her head and the glow of her phone providing light. It was a wonder the girl didn't suffocate herself.

My nose twisted at what was beside her—a small, off-white bowl with a handle and yellow liquid settled inside. If they knew at school that we lived this way, then we would certainly make the yearbook under the category: Most Mentally Deranged. So what if we *sometimes* did "our business" in old-fashioned chamber pots, invented in the days before toilets. We didn't do it all the time. Only when we were feeling "nostalgic."

It was like listening to '80s music. We yearned for the good old days.

S, the foulest of all of us, hadn't carried her personal swill to the actual bathroom today to dump it into the real porcelain throne. This was a cause of contention. "Hey, Downton Abbey," I called

THE CLAIRES

out. "There are no maids at this palace. Can you hike the mellow yellow down the hall and flush it?"

"All you had to do was ask," sniffed the emotional mess. *Oh great, she was watching some Netflix melodrama and now was picking up the emotions of all the characters, plus the actors. S was such a sap, but it worked for her. She could deal with the fleeting feelings of others; her own emos were just too hard for her to grasp.*

Standing in front of our large walnut wardrobe where we kept our clothes, I took a quick glance inside and pulled out a thin sweater. My hoop earrings were on our antique dresser that was void of any electronics. We couldn't deal with TVs, computers or too many electronics. Yes, we had cell phones, but only for emergencies like lying to our parents about why we were out at two in the morning. Tech made our minds swim. And we got a little too vicious when tossed into the deep end of so-called progress.

It was all because of her.

On one wall was a painting of a woman in a dark cloak with her face partly shaded, framed in heavy, somber walnut. Her eyes seemed to trap me in some kind of a snare that made it nearly impossible to look away. We told these parents it was a school art project, and it was. We worked together to paint her likeness – or what we could remember -- during each lifetime.

"Hi, Ma," I said to the image. "Nothing much has happened since our bathroom convo, but you'll be happy to know that your daughter has been missing you all day today and longing for that shortbread you used to make us with fresh cream. Can't get much fresher than going into the field, milking Bessie and then making cream. You were the original Pioneer Woman, but without a book deal and TV show."

I missed her, but I did have my "phone line" to her, which was comforting during good and bad times. I could hear her—clearly—but never saw her like I did other ghosts. She was just a voice from beyond, but I was grateful that she felt comfortable speaking to me anywhere at any time. Like any motherly unit, she also liked to maximize the drama by popping in at the worst possible moments: SAT tests, driver's exam . . . and, oh yes, moments before our impending demise.

Excuse me. Demises.

6.

"Hang on, Ma," I say because another entity has entered the room, and this one is made of actual flesh and bone.

V walks in and stops cold when she hears me talking to myself. She uses sign language to inform me, "For shit's sake, don't tell her I'm here. I don't need the third de—"

"I'll tell her," I say into the air. Then I mouth to V, "She knows you're here, genius, and she's pissed that you didn't charge them more in your class." Our Ma might be dead, but she still didn't believe in leaving money on the table . . . be it just a penny or a pound. She had that entrepreneur mentality born out of life circumstances such as starvation combined with the occasional plague or famine.

Sometimes, I would imagine her settling into the old wooden rocker in a long flowing white gown, staring into her tea glass, with that thin-lipped smile of any parent with concerns regarding their extra-long-distance children. We were the high-risk type of kids. You know, the ones who have a penchant when it comes to engaging in matters involving spiritual suicide. That's just a fancy way to describe our post-midnight monster hunting.

It's hard to ignore Ma and her worries. She frequently announces her presence with the great subtlety of a bomb. I hear what sounds like the foghorn of an ocean liner, but what else can

THE CLAIRES

you expect? The deceased from your actual family tree can be so unreasonably demanding.

When they want you, they want you *now*.

"Yes, Ma," I said aloud as the gaslight lamp in the corner flickers while it sounds like she's banging on the front of a gong to get my attention. "School was fine . . . No, we didn't maim anyone . . . That was last lifetime . . . We're trying to be law abiding citizens this time around . . . We're helpful little earth dwellers . . . Yep, V and S are home. No one has seen C all day. I'm sure she's fine . . . I don't know where she goes . . . No, there are no boys involved . . . I don't know if any boys we know have *clair* traits. I'll test their auras . . . Sorry for having a smart mouth . . . But no, we're not doing any rutting or having wild sex or running naked at school, if that's what you mean . . . Sure, I'll wash out my fresh mouth with a bar of soap, but we don't use soap. We use cleanser. What is cleanser? Never mind . . . Yeah, we know. We know. When we get to New York City, go to the address you gave us . . . Tell no one. Okay, for the seven millionth time, we will find it even if we don't know what it is. . . . Right, I know you're trying to help us, but you don't know what Granny Penny left either. Freakin' old-world superstitions. I know she felt if you knew then they would kill you, too…... Yes, it will give us what we need to survive well into the future . . . No, that does not constitute a return of my 'ever loving attitude.' By the way, we call that female empowerment now."

"Turn off the channel. Enough!" S says, her head still buried in fluff.

"I'll show her empowerment," V pipes in as she catches my eye roll.

"Love you, Ma," I said. "I wish you could live to experience air conditioning, showers and the song stylings of Drake."

"Did you say Rake? Does this family make you do yard chores? Son of a b…."

It was just like any other mother/teenage-daughter relationship. Times four.

Except...

Over the years in the great beyond, she had sadly developed quite the potty mouth.

Right now, my sister is exasperated as only a Ma from the 1800s who did the nasty with "Jack"—can make her. "I'm so sorry. I know this is certainly no way to treat your hundred-year-old-plus mother who is wrinkling by the moment from her inter-realm concerns," I say. "Um, sorry Ma, I love you. I respect you. I honor you. I hear a door that's about to slam. No, it's not a boy trying to get into my pantaloons. Try thong. Bye."

"C's home," V whispers to me. "Maybe Ma can haunt her world."

7.
A QUICK HISTORIAL INTERLUDE
NEW YORK, APRIL 1, 1917 – NINE P.M.

"You can call me Uncle Woody," said the serious looking man who arrived in the cloak of night in a horse drawn carriage. He would be the last president to arrive this grandly because automobiles had just been invented, but he refused to fully embrace change. Why use some new-fangled motor when a trusted beast named Fred on four legs would do?

And now, despite the long ride, he looked a bit formidable standing on our front porch with his oblong face, pursed lips and enough crevices that his skin looked like a road map of worry. He was tall, thin man and swept whatever little brown hair that was

THE CLAIRES

left into a low, comb-over capped with a snow-white fedora. The small specs across tired eyes made him appear kindly while the three-piece black suit with a crisp white shirt and black tie made him look like an undertaker.

"No, sir, I cannot call ye Uncle anything. Ma said that would be deplorable," I replied in my six-year-old scratchy little voice.

It took so much courage to open the door (although Ma said to do it with great haste) and say those words despite that I felt a tiny sweat break on my brow. That in itself was odd. It was early April in New York City and the wintry ice that still formed on the grass sparkled at our house a little brighter than at most of the other dull colonial lodging establishments along Barberry Lane, Old New York.

My sweat was born out of nerves because standing on our stoop wasn't just a former governor of New Jersey, but also the 28th President of the United States.

Here stood a history maker of the highest caliber, but we were used to his ilk. There was a serious man with serious problems showing up almost every single evening now.

Men came knocking at our door in a way that said it was all quite clandestine. When you want to go inside an establishment, it was common to robustly pound three times on those thick wooden doors. Those who made calls at one, two or three in the morning were there on hushed missions. They made their presence known with a low three taps.

I think some half-hoped that the door stayed shut.

Ma told us to treat each night caller with the utmost respect and such care began with our cleanly scrubbed faces, hair that was swept way up into tight little knots a certain Princess Leia would co-opt one day and the wearing of those elegant white, party dresses with the blue sash. We never dressed that fancy except on Sundays when we stood in the woods outside the church to say our weekly prayers. We weren't allowed inside. Sinners were made to stay approximately ten feet away so their evil wasn't catching.

"Sir, I cannot call you Uncle Woody," I reminded the leader of the free world who now stood in our dimly lit parlor. "My mother told me that I should call adults Mr. or Miss or Madame. But when the president of the United States comes to our house, I must address him as Mr. President, sir."

"What a charming little girl with so much insight," said President Woodrow Wilson. My sisters appeared from nowhere and we curtsied like we were meeting a king. In turn, he handed us four hand-sewn country girl dollies and then snapped his fingers.

Instantly, two men with bowed heads brought the most beautiful stuffed teddy bears in through the front door and placed them gingerly on the front room couch. They always brought offerings…candy, puppies, stuffed teddies and apple or blueberry pies that would make your mouth water before the first bite. No matter the gift, the men thought correctly that the way to the gifted one's heart was through her children.

"Presents and treats for the most beautiful girls in the county," said the President whose staff seemed to evaporate like smoke.

"I'm hoping to find your mother in a sharing mood tonight because these are grave times," he said grandly, knowing that this little meeting had been prearranged by secret messenger who had arrived yesterday to announce that the president would be visiting again. Never mind if it was a president or a pauper, Ma was always in good form and shared from the deepest vestiges of her heart when helping to decide the fate of one family or the world. She was a forward thinker and believed in freedom, joy and finding one's bliss in each lifetime.

Before I took my leave, I had the moxie to motion to him to bend down. Ma said this man during his presidency advocated for farmers and small businesses. But he had tried to remain neutral

THE CLAIRES

when World War I began in Europe in 1914.

V had the courage then to step up. "Sir, I see the future," she said. "Boys will die. By the thousands." I nodded and told him, "I hear dead boys crying to be sure. Boys wishing for their mothers before the fog rolls in."

"But you must fight," V said. "You must save the world from the despots in Germany or we are all doomed."

"The dead boys will understand," I said and that nice president took a hanky from his pocket and dabbed his eyes. "Just like the ones who died in the Civil War knew it was for the greater good. You were a boy during that war. You watched Confederate president Jefferson Davis marched in chains through Augusta, Georgia. You know how many men sacrificed their mortal lives. It's comforting to know their souls go on," I reminded him.

"How do you know so very much, my little pretty?" he asked me.

"They talk to me. The dead have messages from the beyond. A few are here right now," I said, knowing that he would need proof. "Mister, your mother Janet is here. She used to nurse wounded Confederate soldiers in your father's church down south. He's here, too. Joseph Wilson, right? He was a Presbyterian minister who reminds you that this time you should be on the right side of history."

Many times, I didn't fully understand the messages I was delivering or comprehend it at all, but I tried hard to provide a solid account.

"What an odd little girl," said the President of the United States who was on the brink of World War I. I smiled up at him and said, "Our mother has hot tea for you in the parlor, Sir."

As children, we knew when to charm and when to take our leave, which didn't mean we would tuck ourselves into our four small beds with the white wrought-iron headboards. We'd hide in the hallways and listen silently. Our mother fully approved, insisting, "This is your education."

Ma served her best corn biscuits with fresh strawberry marmalade and hot Earl Gray to our commander-in-chief. She was on her second cup when she told President Woodrow Wilson that he must enter World War I.

"We cannot remain an isolationist country. We must fight for democracy and join the others," she told him. Then she paused to stare up at the ceiling. "You will fight Germany more than once."

"When will the war with Germany be over?" the President demanded.

"Nineteen hundred and forty-five," she said in a wobbling voice.

"This country can't fight a war for three decades!" the president boomed. "It will be the end of us. Now, you're speaking utter nonsense!"

"No, no," Ma said. "There will be two wars. It will bring a new beginning."

"But will we win?" he demanded. When she smiled and nodded, he handed her a small box filled with gold bars from a secret treasury stash. It was V who kissed that nice president's hand on his way out and said words to him that he couldn't understand at the time, but would haunt the world forever.

"Hitler," she whispered. "Tell the others. Remember that name."

"What is a Hitler? Is that a plane? Or a machine?" he asked. "A type of gun?"

"No," she replied with the innocence of someone who was only six years into a short life. "It's a monster."

"Rubbish," said the president. "There are no such things."

"Hitler is as real as women voting for president, which in January of next year you will advocate and then the states will

THE CLAIRES

ratify the 19th Amendment in August, 1920," V told him. "Thank you, in advance."

V wasn't done. I motioned for the president to lean down. "Our first lady and your sadly dead wife Ellen Louise says hello from the great beyond. She's three years gone and her soul is troubled. She isn't happy that you're sparking to the widow Edith Galt…or with that woman Mary Peck."

"Young lady, I bid you good night," he stammered.

Incidentally, the day after our visit, on April 6, that nice Uncle Woody went to a joint session of Congress to request a declaration of war against Germany. Ma told him it was the only way to make the world safe for democracy and it sure helped. She also predicted for him that a ceasefire and Armistice would be declared on November 11, 1918.

By the way, that nice president would die of a stroke on February 3, 1924. Ma left that part out because he had enough on his head and there wasn't a fedora big enough to grapple with your death day.

Just ask us.

One last thing: His new wife Edith would later remember that his last word was an odd one. "He said something like hit her or Hitter," she wrote. "It made absolutely no sense."

A COGNIZANT'S STORY: C

Los Angeles, California
2013

1.

The principal's office is filled with the spirits of students who had long since passed through the portal to hell a.k.a. Mr. Edward Wright's inner sanctum of torture. You can't visibly see any of the vintage alumni, but I feel their emotional baggage – the tears, the pain and their balls to the walls rebellion – the very things that brought them to the bad girl's chair in front of a rather imposing steel gray deck.

I could only celebrate any personal uprisings that had ever taken place in a room defined by yellowed file folders and the stench of decades of burned coffee and squashed spirits.

Mr. Wright glares at me, so I did the only thing reasonable under such circumstances. Reaching into my purse, I smile as I grab for the small box. I put the cigarette between my lips to light it. Flame touches the tip and I take a deep inhale.

"Young lady, do not test me. This is a non-smoking, environmentally conscious school experience," Mr. Wright says, frowning deeper when I take another puff and then agree, "Yes, it's an experience, all right."

He waits until I stub the rest of it on the side of his personal World's Best Dad ceramic mug some kiss ass kid made for him.

"First, I must ask you what you want out of this school year," Wright begins.

He's going for the existential questions.

"I just want to live," I reply, slinking back into the chair.

"What is that supposed to mean? Do you feel suicidal?" he must inquire.

"Suicidal, you wish," I say. "I just want to make it to 18, which

THE CLAIRES

doesn't mean I'm thinking dark things – if you don't count the fact that I don't have a long-life expectancy. No one in our family does. Not that it's any of your business."

"Are you ill?" he asks. "And smoking doesn't help."

"I am sick of this line of questioning," I reply. "And you better make it fast because my father is on his way, plus I'm getting curvature of the spine as I sit here."

"Is there a reason, C, that you refused your holiday dance court nomination?" Wright swerves, thinking that he will catch me off my feet.

A rookie!

"What am I being nominated for….fashion, beauty or wearing a crappy Party City crown on my head. Those are major life accomplishments, true," I say. "I'll just leave them to someone else to remember when they're 50 and find the crown in some attic surrounded by rat turds."

Wright just looks at me harder and shakes his head. "Young lady, you could have a wonderful high school experience if you were just a bit more open minded and embraced the possibilities."

I knew the possibilities lecture was coming. Was there any possibility he would stop now? That would be a definite no.

"The dance court is your business. But the school cafeteria is mine. I won't have you slapping students. There will be severe consequences if this ever happens again because we don't allow bullying in this school."

"We're solid," I blurt, staring at him although I know what's happening just outside the window. I never take my eyes off our principal when I announce, "My Dad's here, so if you want to suspend or pummel me, please do it. I could use a vacation from this place."

"We're not done," Wright warns.

"Yes," I say in a clipped tone as I light up another cigarette and blow this smoke his way. "We are."

2.

MAYHEM. MURDER. MISSING persons.

The town is spiritually burning. It hit the noon news, but I knew the moment it happened.

A child has gone missing. In Santa Monica. He is three or four with dark hair that curls every which way, and large brown, almond-shaped eyes. He's wearing blue shorts that have been put on inside out because he did it himself, and a yellow duckie shirt with spaghetti sauce stains from last year. They're not his stains. It's a Goodwill outfit. "What else, honey?" begs our current father, Detective Joe Danko, who has already signed me out of school via phone and is waiting in his black, non-descript SUV in the high school parking lot.

It's funny how we have this system. When he needs me for a case, he never calls me. He just shows up at school and I know to go outside.

No one else can know that he did this . . . does this . . . on a regular basis, except our assistant principal, Mr. Antonio Moretti, who is a big, teddy bear sympathetic party when it comes to my father putting the scumbags of the earth away.

Dad is the most non-woo-woo human to draw breath, but he's still a believer in leaving no stone unturned. When I was a little girl, his sharp detective instincts couldn't deny that I had that special sauce. Over the years, he watched closely as I grew into my abilities while I relished being the most gifted of the sisters. I'm sorry, but

THE CLAIRES

that's just me. No, *excuse me world, I'm shy and don't want to talk about myself because it's not fair that everyone wasn't born with this power, folks. Screw the rest of the world.* I'd scream the joy of being me from the highest tree or tallest mountain. The fact that I am me – good and bad, plus again and again, throughout every lifetime -- is the definition of a miracle.

Dad knew I was the most advanced of the sisters. He wasn't sure what I had or why it was there, but instinctively his cop sixth sense told him that I was his secret crime fighting weapon – and why not? Together, we ran our own personal and private justice system. He tested me as a little girl by asking to find his missing car keys and later missing people. Now, I'm his ace, Claire C, the one who is all knowing.

Today, I was on a major case – *yee to the haw! You wanna test me suckers, let's go!*

A quick word about my altruism: I do most of my good deeds for entirely selfish reasons including the fact that it's in my DNA to want to be the enforcer. By that I mean if I smell wrong doing, I'm racing in, tires squealing, and trying to turn it around while also giving the bad guys the worst day of their entire existence. If a case involves small or frail things like children or animals then I go full-throttle medieval.

Some teenage girls look for love (no thank you, no time), and more power to them. I look for injustice.

"Dad, he's still here," I say.

A large head nods.

"As in alive?" he says. His voice is hopeful. He actually lets out a breath. Just one.

"As in . . . in town," I reply in a slow voice because I don't always want to know . . . what I know. And I can never forget what I'm shown. It's like having front row seats to a car crash with multiple fatalities. You can't unwatch it.

3.

A CLAIRCOGNIZANT, LIKE me, simply knows things about *everything* including the past, present, and future. My sister V, as a non-souped-up, regular clairvoyant, only has visions of the future, which is nice if you're into those things, but not the whole enchilada. A claircognizant sees a far broader picture, even if we don't know why we're seeing what we see in that moment. After all, cognizance means knowledge or awareness while *clair* means clear (although one of my other sisters already explained that.) I was born with the much-coveted power of clear thinking—or as close to the Patriarch's worst nightmare as possible, thank you Ma and grandmother Penny. I'm top of the line. The A-lister.

Top of the kill list, too.

When we die as Claires, I go first followed by my sisters in reverse order of how we were born. Or so I'm told. You can't exactly keep a photo album of what happens at the big event. We die minus all worldly possessions and the next thing you know we're swimming again in utero thanks to a brand-new host Mom.

Fun fact to dazzle the relatives: All mortals are born with a touch of claircognizance, although few light the fuse or even notice the ember. They call it intuition and expect daytime TV talk-show hosts to explain it to them. It's buried, and we don't trust it or live by it. What a shame. Unused intuition is like having a hot, red Ferrari parked in your garage, but you never turn the key or press the FOB. What just sits there, rots, until it's filled with dust and sticky muck and thus unusable.

There are times that red Ferrari must take itself out for a spin, if you get my analogy. It's why you suddenly veer from your usual routine and take a new route . . . only to find out that your usual way was the location of a ten-car pile-up. Sometimes intuition actually saves your non-woo-woo ass.

THE CLAIRES

As the most powerful Claire, my sisters (among all others) are always coming to me for the ultimate answer because... let's face it. I'm always right. I'm quick to interrupt them as they explain things because my mind works at supersonic speeds. I'm not alone in my visions. Many full-blood claircognizants walk amongst us, calling themselves writers or musicians. Some of the best songwriters of our time—claircognizants, all. Madonna. Bruce. Bono. Gaga. Fellow members of dat pack.

Above all, I know facts about future events with one hundred percent accuracy. It's an innate sense. A mighty ability—and responsibility.

The downside? Like all of my sissy's, it only works on other people and never on any of my blood relatives or myself. Damn. Damn. Damn.

Did I mention I'm better than V? Call it clair rivalry. A plain, old, regular clairvoyant sees future things after she goes through her flick-and-see process, which is so rudimentary. I just *know* things – past, present and future. There's no pregame. I'm aware with complete sureness in my gut, except for myself and my sisters.

Detective Joe, a.k.a. Dad, uses me and only me, for his police work. He asks me about the more heart-wrenching and vile case questions, knowing I will come up with an answer even if I have no previous knowledge of the subject matter. It has been that way since I could speak. Missing wives. Lost kids. Hiding perps. Lost cats. Lost loves. I've solved a lot of his cases over a midnight bowl of cereal at the kitchen table.

Detective Joe, tough ass with a heart of gold, looms large in his police cruiser in the SMHS parking mecca.

"Where is that missing boy, honey?" he asks through an open vehicle window. No hello. No bullshit questions about school. We get right to it. No matter how awful I might have acted in previous lives, I've always had a soft spot for those who are defenseless and the ones who try to protect them. *Just don't tell anyone because over several lifetimes, I've found an aloof, rather badass reputation is the way to go. But I digress.*

Time was ticking. As it always did in cases of child kidnapping ... or worse.

I will my mind to go blank because white space is how information is transferred from a higher power.

"Near the water," I say. "He wasn't kidnapped. He was put there. By the beach. By someone ..... no, two people, who know him."

"That's good," Dad says like we've wrapped. "Do you want to go back to fucking class, honey?"

"Would you like to go home and mow the fucking lawn?" I toss back.

We only talk to each other this way when no one is around. Our priss mother is the artsy, woo-woo type and would have been mortified.

He's used to it, so he backs off. Once I'm in, I'm all in. We lock eyes in a way that only two similar beings who search for things in this world can. If I was sent to know, he was sent to help. Most of the time, it's a potent combination that contributes to the good side of the line. Since I was devoting this lifetime to good deeds, I felt a bit giddy as we briefed each other on "our" case.

Did I love my father in these moments? No.

I will never allow myself to wallow in any father's *love* because I don't consider this Dad or any others my real anything, except sometimes Det. Joe's a real pain in the daughterly ass, if you know what I mean. But he is the closest I've ever come to opening my heart to one of that breed even if my heart only opens a sliver due to a self-protective mode instilled by my true age and the fact that I don't even know my natural father.

When I accidentally hug him in the front seat of the cruiser,

THE CLAIRES

it's a meaningless, reflex human emotion run amok for no good reason whatsoever.

"Stop smoking, honey," he says because immediately after that skin-to-skin I light up.

Really.

Busted while on a case.

It's belittling and charming of him to act this way even if he's just my meal ticket and the reason why I don't sleep in the woods.

4.

WE REACH THE beach by Santa Monica Pier and the ocean is as turbulent as my state of mind. Foaming waves of white crash onto cool spring sand, and are instantly rejected and sent back to a mighty power that is the quivering sea. I could stand at the water's edge forever as the most mesmerized voyeur, but I don't. They won't let me, and by they, I'm talking about the mortals who are amongst the living.

Santa Monica beach at 10:00 a.m. on a workday is mostly filled with those on vacation, with a good sprinkling of the homeless wandering amongst jobless middle-aged men who like to stare at the water for answers. They also enjoy propositioning young women.

I race ahead of Dad, the pint-sized, five foot nothing, super skinny runt of the Claire litter with short, blonde natural curls that barely touch the bottom of my dimpled chin. Think Princess Di hair, but with loopy, curls that always look as if my head was just removed from an open car window.

"If you were a Transformer, you'd be my Optimus Fine," shouts the oily haired man-bitch sitting directly in the sand in black polyester slacks, white athletic socks with the swoosh, and a shirt that looks like a black and white checker board. He's late 50s coming onto a sixteen-year-old, which is just plain gross to infinity. Then he notices that my father, who is six foot two, sports the shoulders of a NFL linebacker, and wears a perfectly pressed black suit on the beach. Detectives don't wear the standard police garb, but they still carry that harsh, grim face, which in this case features a long nose, stubborn jaw bones, and eyes that flash the official "back off, Jack" signal.

"A movie buff . . . just what county lock-up needs since she's clearly under-aged," Dad says under his breath. The harsh lines of his lips force the man to cast his gaze toward the horizon as in, "Checked into it, but now checking right back out."

"Mr. Perv looks like the human version of Sid from *Ice Age*," I reply as his story floods my frontal lobe. I don't feel for him, but I do know what happened. *Screenwriter. Wife walked. Took all the money. And two kids. Back to Michigan to live a so-called normal life. Took all the hope with her, too. That was eighteen years ago. He sits here every single day thinking about walking into that ocean and never walking back. The eternal swim. I can smell his regret laced with the desperation of only the loneliest souls.* I'm half-assed sorry about the Sid thing, but not really.

I look to the water again to cleanse that vision. These types of waves are known as a swash, a violent layer of natural liquid that washes up on the beach as incoming surges break. There's the uprush or the onshore flow and then the backwash or the onshore flow. It dawns on me in the moment: There's not enough backwash in the world to cleanse the human race.

We press on, walking the beach in silence. Dad knows the drill because I need to absorb the surroundings on a cellular level.

"Refresh my memory," Dad says, because he knows *that I know* every detail of this case that's breaking his heart, but they all do a little damage. All of them chip away a little piece. What's left

THE CLAIRES

embeds in his being. Today, he has very few details and I feel his internal panic. He wants to push me, but holds himself in check. He will delicately pick the meat off the bones.

I dial in. It's not long before I can barely breathe.

"Mom's name is Tiffany. Really? Yep, Tiffany. Figures. Trailer park. She's twenty-five. Knocked up four years ago. Not the first time," I rattle off. Dad nods. He knows all of the above because it was Tiff herself, the mom, who called it in. *The mom with the spotty job history of convenience stores; the DUI; the bottles of oxy in the medicine cabinet. Now, she has a kid who has gone missing. Most of the time, she lets him wander off like some sort of unwanted puppy. She always seems shocked to find him again.*

There were projectile tears when she was telling Dad about how she, a single parent, was building sand castles with her son, *name starts with a B,* on the beach then she turned her back for just a split-second to take a phone call. When she turned back, the boy was gone.

"Would he have run into the water?" Dad asked her. Once. Twice. Three times.

"I don't know," she sobbed. "He can't swim."

It's so convenient that this kid, the one her new boyfriend can't stand because the boy cries all night long, can't swim and she took him to the water's edge of the Pacific Ocean. She turned around for a minute. And now he's gone, baby, gone.

"Ben. They call him Benny," I state as I stare out at the fog-covered horizon. "He's four years old and two months. Big eyes. Dark. Brown bowl-cut, curly hair. A nervous little guy who cries at night because the boyfriend makes him watch scary movies with Chucky and Freddy." Then I see the rest of it. "Benny hates baths. He would have never run into the water. He's scared to death of it. Idiot boyfriend showed him *Jaws.*"

Dad makes a noise that sounds like relief, but the sound is

muted when I swallow hard. When I square my shoulders, Dad knows.

"Kid hates haircuts. Hates carrots. He loves his mom; wishes he had a real dad. Big welts on his arm. Red ones. Mom has a new boyfriend. He's forty. Unemployed. Hates noise," I rattle off. "Hates kids."

"His name is Chester. The boyfriend. I see him. He has a wide face, like the baby doc dropped him on it and smashed it flat. I see him screaming at Benny to shut up. 'Get in the bed or I'll feed you to the boogey man.' I see Chester making a two-in-the-morning trip from their apartment to his SUV to load a black nylon gym bag into his truck." *Why the hell is he loading in the middle of the night when all he covets is sleep? And why is that thing so awkward and heavy?*

I stop and look at Dad more closely. There isn't an iota of doubt in my mind, which is why my face crumbles as the grief becomes overwhelming. Tears spill down my cheeks as they always do in the case of this world versus the plight of children with no champions. I don't show the world this side of me; Dad is another story. "Benny is always crying. He cried for hours last night," I hear darling Tiffany informing Dad. *As if crying is the real crime here.*

I feel the malice of ill intent. *They planned this for a week. They waited until the gym bag went on sale at Target. Chester likes a good deal.*

Dad's eyes well with tears, which he keeps on the QT, too. It bonds us in a way I don't accept *because he is just some cop and host for this lifetime.* I turn my back to him and look at the water. At the same time, I feel a warm rush flood my upper chest like lukewarm tea was spilled inside the first tender layers of skin. It has always served as my confirmation, but at the moment it feels as if I'm only eighty percent glow and ten percent glacial. *I'm not all the way there. And if I know one thing from my many lives it's this: Almost never counts.*

"Maybe the kid ran away. Things could have gone the other way," Dad says in that hopeful voice.

"Yeah," I reply. "But they didn't."

5.

I GO HOME, race upstairs, and find my sisters in varying degrees of distress. *Really?* The almost-gone bag of Oreo's is a clue. Frankly, I can't deal with it today. The thing with the kid has leveled me.

V is counting her cash and knows we will need more for our trip, plus it also pays for an apartment we secretly keep at the infamous Hollywood Tower Apartments, built in 1929 and still haunted by the ghost of Humphrey Bogart. We go out *a lot* at night, which is convenient and smart since this is when Dad mostly works. And we can go racing in and out of the house, which is only under the prying eyes of our big brother Cass or Mom, if and when she has all her marbles in the right place. But, that's another story.

V was the one to have the brilliant idea. "We should get our own place…for privacy and group meetings," she said, in an expressionless voice *like four then twelve-year-olds secretly renting an apartment was a total no-brainer. I mean, who needs a room when you can have a sixth-floor walk-up with a galley kitchen?*

One day, V took about $4000 in cash she had collected at school and dressed up like she was twenty-five, or her idea of that age, which was a little hooker-ish, if you ask me. No one questioned her when she rented us a she-shed, as we like to call our apartment, or Claire's Central. We don't have much furniture there except a black metal desk and a flaming red leather couch. The place serves as our "office" for evening activities. Someday, we muse, the city should pay the rent given all the good deeds we've done during this lifetime. (Incidentally, we've had the apartment for four years now. And have continued to write that monthly check from our "earnings" at school. A win-win for all.)

Our time at the parental pad is always a bit crowded as we share what once was the master bedroom, but this house is small. On days like today, I know I will never be alone. To wit, A is flopped on one of our beds at home with her headphones on to drown out the spirit world and another visit from our real parent. She is exhausted after chatting with our Ma, but hopeful they will talk again later. *Cut the cord!*

"Do you want to know what Ma said today?" she asks me.

"La-la-la," I sing, "Bother someone who cares about a message from the great beyond."

"You're a shitty daughter," A grumbles.

"And proud of it," I reply, looking upward to make sure the roof doesn't fall in on me, but Ma doesn't do cliché physical things. None of us do. It's all a mental game of wits and knowing, which causes far deeper pain. The fact that I stub my big toe on the big dresser has nothing to do with anything, at least that's what I convince myself.

I'm sitting lotus-style on my bed now reading the tea leaves like my grandmother did all those years ago. *That little field trip to the beach. It was what they called a story in progress. A real life first draft.*

"What do you see?" V asks. "I'm a bit murky about the missing boy for some reason."

"Death and despair," I retort. "The despair is, as always, served first." Pause. "You asked."

And then the portal to our world bursts open. I wish I could classify this as a supernatural jaw-dropper, but it's just our dork

THE CLAIRES

brother Cass who has never met a closed door that he could respect. He never knocks either—not that it matters, because we can all feel his presence before one of his little "break-ins." This is just one of the ten million reasons the femmes in this family and the lone young male get along like oil and water.

Then there was that thing that V tried to start with him thanks to her no-virginity world tour. What exactly happened is something none of us speaks of since I'd like to keep my lunch down.

"Anyone home?" Cass says in a way that makes me want to kill him. Oftentimes, I've wondered why I have such an intense dislike of him, but it was easier to figure out who shot JFK than to put a fine point on Danko sibling rivalry.

Oddly enough, we've never had a brother in any of our previous lifetimes. Preliminary findings: His species is big, messy and there are pee stains on the toilet seat. He uses our products to combat his natural "woodsy" smell and he always eats the last piece of chicken or all the leftover pieces of anything else. Idiot puts the cardboard take home boxes from restaurants back in the fridge empty after eating our stuff…as a joke. Nothing like being starving, getting excited about that half of burrito that was your dinner and opening a box that just has a twig of parsley left in it. I want to kill him.

Even worse is that fact that Cass isn't just some schmuck brother, but he can communicate with dead things, which wigs me out. I also sense more to him, untapped natural gifts of the super freak variety, and that makes me fear for our collective safety in a way I never have in any previous existence. One thought keeps running through my mind when I think of my "brother": *Maybe he won't damage us in this life, but in another . . .*

Pushing it over the edge is the fact the he balks at anything he deems otherworldly. Denies it even exists. Like he has to stay one step ahead of what's really in his DNA in order to lead a normal, i.e. boring life with a home and 2.2 kids and a SUV in the driveway.

You don't deny what is rare.

It is the biggest insult of all.

Today, like all days, no one answers him, so he just stands there in our door jamb like he's a statue of normalcy.

Cass just shakes his head and those annoying long, honeyed strands fall into his face. All of the girls at school melt in his presence, which makes most of us sisters vaguely ill verging on hurling up a lung. He spends all his time with the stick-figure waif next door named Annie who is so sweet and helpful, I'd love to run the lawnmower over her. Several times. And then I'd get out the weed whacker and stage a do-over on her face.

Alas.

Annie lives with an overbearing father, Det. Gene Coleman, our father's cop partner. She's so fragile and sweet in those little printed dresses and leggings and ballet shoes. Yes, I do like to protect the weak, but there is something about her that doesn't jive. She's steel, wrapped up in the façade of a Disney heroine.

Why in the world does she need the long, red, tangled hair and big hazel eyes? Of course, it completes a picture. It defines a type. She is a little would-be princess stuck in suburbia with her overly protective Daddy and "best friend" Cass a finger flick away in case she runs smack into danger. Like if a bug landed on her. Or someone frowned her way. Both would ride in for a quick, but effective rescue. The Princess would be saved, which is not the plot twist I look for in my stories.

V hates Annie for obvious reasons, and dreams of striking blood. Personally, I don't think we go in for the topple. Since we truly want to live past seventeen, we hold back with her, although it's almost too tempting not to just mildly maim her a bit. You know, maybe sneak out in the middle of the night, infiltrate her

THE CLAIRES

room, and cut her hair down to one-inch stubble. A harmless prank!

Not that we're not going to necessarily do it… at least not tonight.

V reads my mind. "One more story about helping stray animals, though, and I might have to bite her," she says. "Or drown her. Or push her…"

Oh, V. She's jelly belly jealous, which makes me queasy and worried despite the fact that I usually try to ignore matters of lust and longing. *Crap! Maybe if we lived in Arkansas, but really V? Your faux brother?*

This was why I avoided love entanglements at all cost. All that emotional hootie-hoo was just too much to manage. White hot rage was much easier to embrace and it did a teenage soul good.

Oh, one more thing.

Cassy, gassy, mostly assy, is consumed with walking around pretending that he doesn't like Annie "in that way." They're "just friends." Or so he says. My two cents: Annie's technically beautiful, but even if a moron like him "liked" her, I didn't see a future for it.

I knew it was his destiny to fall down that slippery slope toward love with another woman and she would also be just a hair beyond his reach. Jury was out, however, when it came to the win. But, I could see that one would physically resemble Annie with reddish-brown hair, big eyes, and a sweet side that was also just thinly covered iron. The future love of his life would possess the spirit of a hellion and an over-questioning nature. But she still has cracks. She could be broken . . . and she might never fully love him because there was another.

What a sap. Always looking for broken little birds. And then falling for them.

"Did you find that missing kid? he asks. (Why weren't we born with wands to zap people in oblivion?). He's that blunt with us, but loving with Mom, Dad and even our Labradoodle Alfa as in Alfa Doodle.

V frowns at him, flips him the bird and slams the door in his face.

"Well played," I tell her.

"I'm over it. He has slipped to number five," she insists, bringing up that damn list of hers again. But then in another voice that's much sweeter asks the universe in general, "Is it too much to ask for a date to the winter dance and to lose my virginity before my next vile and painful death?"

"Dear Abby," I begin. "All I want to do is pop my cherry before I'm put in the ground in a wooden box – and nail a suitable date to the winter prom. Signed, Desperate and Dateless."

"Enough," S moans.

"What's today's haul?" I ask, pulling a subject changer although I already know that she earned $470, wait, no, $480 at school today.

"Good deeds?" S inquires, finally throwing her pillow to the floor.

"I helped with the missing kid—and I'm still trying to find him," I say in an exasperated voice. I'm furious with myself for not finding the answers, but I shrug it off.

"Saving lives and taking names—our mantra," I say, which earns a three-way laugh.

Old school style in a Mead notebook, we actually keep a list now of all the mortal lives we have saved. To track them. You know, to see if it was worth it. "Last life we saved absolutely no one and died promptly at seventeen," I reminded the room. "Our experiment with penance is still a question mark. If we lived to be seventeen and one day, it would be worth it." Time was time. You had no choice, but to grab for it. To that end, we would save a few needy humans from forces beyond their control.

I really wanted to survive to see twenty, thirty, forty, ninety...

THE CLAIRES

But, I wouldn't dwell on it now. I'd drown out all the voices by playing the Rolling Stones cranked to full volume.

A head with a mass of long, blond hair pokes its way back through the door jamb. He's back. Like a fungus.

"That's a fascinating plan. All of you doing good deeds to . . . what? Did you say something about a curse? Or maybe I'm the one that's cursed. Either way, can you all turn it down a few notches. Thin walls," Cass begs. "I have a physics test tomorrow."

"Oh, you'll be flunking," V taunts, slinking past him closely enough until "accidentally" their fronts touch. He recoils and takes a large step backwards.

I clear my throat and look at A who is also giving me a sideswipe look that says, *WTF are we going to do about this!*

It's easier to place our thoughts elsewhere and to that end, I dial into myself and "see" that Cass would infuriatingly collect another A-plus in psychics, making our half-sib even more dangerous because knowledge was the most potent weapon of all. He was just a little too smart, which is why we keep such close tabs on him.

After all, he was the one who would eventually help the others kill all of us.

6.

It's the last word I want to hear.

"Dinner," V informs all.

"Lunch," Mom yells up to us about a half second later. It's a real punch to the gut because she was beyond the beginning stages of Alzheimer's and the decline has been at a rapid rate.

Eleanor Danko, mother of this lifetime, was ill. I knew it

although the rest of the parties in the house tried to pretend that it was just "that time of life" or simply a "bad day." Facts were facts, and I could diagnose anyone from that guy across the room coming down with a common cold to the woman at the bus stop who will find out that she has cancer. Eleanor or Mom, in this case, was in the middle stages of Alzheimer's, quickly sliding toward the latter and most devastating parts of the disease.

We were extremely fond of this caring, warm maternal unit who did her best to love and protect us, although we refused to allow ourselves to completely melt into her generosity of spirit. Remember, we could never fully love *them* as in the host families. The damn shame of it was that I liked this one the best of all because this Mom had a soft way about her. Her hugs were like falling into a cloud although I kept a pocket of air as distance. Mourning one mother was enough. This current specimen of maternal joy was a painter who spoke in a whispery, lyrical voice and had skin as smooth and pliant as a newborn baby's cheek.

It ripped at me that she had been forgetting things all the time now, and mixing up other particulars. Mom had an appointment with a specialist at the Mayo Clinic in Phoenix for a cognitive health exam next week. It was there that doctors would tell her with grave certainty what we already knew.

What we all knew.

CASS

Los Angeles, California
2013

1.

CHUGALUGGING STRAIGHT OUT of the milk carton makes mom do the cringe dance. I do it on purpose because it's the exact reaction I want from her.

The lips purse. She looks stricken. She had been behaving so oddly lately that anything normal such as her reacting to disgusting behavior makes me feel like raising a fist in the air. Small victories. *This wasn't happening to my family.* I chug; she makes a completely revolted face and rattles off a laundry list of germ concerns. That always comes after the dance of *Cass I love you, but you're filled with bio hazards.* Resoundingly normal. Thank you, God.

We have a small kitchen covered with brightly colored Mexican tiles, white cabinets, and black countertops. It's the kind of place where there is always a threat to remodel, but it never really happens because of last minute family needs or lack of funds.

There is a big table in a cramped dining area where you can sit all of us—especially now that Aunt Sondra took the baby back to live with her, so we were minus the high chair. She was over her marital crisis and probably didn't trust our increasingly not-so-normal mom anymore with her eighteen-month-old, late-in-life surprise baby.

"Honey, do you know where I put the roast?" Mom asks me. *Boom!* The joy of the milk incident leaves the building.

How many places could a roast be lurking . . . fridge, oven, her bedroom? I smile, although my heart is being ripped open. I see exactly where it is—and by "see," I don't mean in a psychic sense, but a normal "oh it's over there." Our closet-sized laundry room is right off the kitchen and I spy the roast in there. The wind slips from my chest. She put the spices on top of the plastic wrap. *Oh, Mom.* Then she purposely placed the thing on top of the hot dryer that has nothing inside it, but she still turned it on. I smell chicken cooking in the oven. Obviously, she forgot about the roast until now, but still made the chicken.

The whole thing was a colossal tragedy.

I couldn't deny it any longer. Mom has early-onset Alzheimer's disease that is progressing, though Dad won't admit it. It began about a year ago, with difficulty planning and solving problems, and progressed to her struggling with completing familiar tasks like making her famous lemon cake, which basically required only lemon, sugar, and flour, plus the baking soda and powder. She forgot the lemons. Then she remembered, and put three lemons in another pan and turned on the oven. Her keys were missing; then she couldn't find the car, which she parked in the neighbor's driveway. She forgot that she painted with actual brushes and not her bare hands. That was a messy one.

She wasn't always so sure now what time it was or what day, but this didn't happen every day, which gave us hope. And then there was the struggle when it came to making even the most basic decisions. Did she want butter on her bread? She couldn't figure it out. One day was good; the next unsettling at best, although Dad pretended it was just some "change of life thing."

The truly terrifying part was that it was about to be diagnosed in Phoenix at the Mayo Clinic by a top specialist thanks to Dad's primo health coverage. Of course, he put this off as long as possible for a solid reason.

The next few days would make it real.

I never want to embarrass her, so I casually rip open the oven door and take out the chicken before it burns. Then I quickly wash off the roast and put it back in the fridge. She smiles that sunshine

I've known my entire life. It's like liquid heat flowing from where she is to where I am.

As long as she remembers my name. For as long as she can.

"Love you, Momma Mia." I can't say it enough because the girls never do. They were born with ice in their veins, though everyone chalked it up to them being closer to Dad. I don't buy it. C looks like she has our DNA, except in the height department, but the rest of them could easily have been adopted. Not that there was anything wrong with adoption, but there were pictures of my mother pregnant with all of them. On bed rest for the last few months because the girls grew so big and so quickly. There were the usual beaming hospital photos of my parents with their quads, even though multiple births didn't run in either family.

The chances of having quadruplets was only one in 800,000. Quads were much rarer than twins or even triplets. In fact, there were only about 3500 sets existing worldwide. The fact that my parents were one of those families always struck me as . . . . odd.

I couldn't exactly put a handle on my sisters because—stupid as it sounds—they never felt like family. I thought of them as visitors.

And there were other variables. I remember when I was four and they were three. V bit me so hard on my right arm that I needed stitches.

Then at ages ten and nine, respectively, she did it again because I told her about my recurring dream. It was the one where a guy named Jack was their real father.

"Jack who?" she smarted. "The Ripper?"

"Makes sense," I retorted. That's when I felt her dental enamel almost embed in my arm bone. This was followed by all the denials. *No, Mommy, I didn't do it. Cass bit his own arm.*

I frown just thinking about it now, and Mom still tries to make it all better.

"Love you, my sweet boy," Mom says. And then I wait for it.

THE CLAIRES

Pray for it. One, two, three seconds. "Caspian Danko, prince of the sea," she adds. From the time I was born, she always used my full name when I was hurting, and she still knew my name and when I was in pain. *It's all I need. Just the name.*

"Can Annie come by for dinner tonight?" I ask her.

"Sure, honey," she says.

I can breathe again.

Until I look into her confused hazel eyes.

"Annie, is she a new friend from school?" she asks. "A girlfriend? You should date a nice girl, honey."

"You've known her since she was a baby," I remind her. "Annie. My friend from next door. Gene's daughter. Sometimes you call her your fifth daughter." This was the exasperating part. "You already love her, Mom."

"Oh, right," she covers up nicely, but the fog has rolled in for the day. When it will roll out, only God knows. She must feel it and is instantly shamed, which is why I drink out of the bottle of milk again. There is no confusion ever when it comes to a son putting his lips to the family's source of liquid moo.

"Caspian James," Mom says. "Don't be gross. And I'd love to meet your new friend. I hope this Charlotte is a nice girl. She better be good enough for my baby boy."

My middle name is Scott. Her name is Annie. But that's okay.

All things considered, it's still a good day.

2.

DAD IS A master in the art of denial. He believes in meat, potatoes, clean garages, and real diseases like cancer and the flu. He can understand a heart attack or a stroke because they're thunderclaps of fate. His wife's memory loss is something he won't buy into because he can usually find excuses. The morning she asked him why he was in *her* house, he finally agreed to more advanced tests, but still with a skeptical mindset. He's waiting for a pill or a miracle—real things that fix broken things. He plans to administer the pills and keep the order of his life intact. Nothing less will do.

I've been slotted to study computer programming and have a nice, safe, if not mind numbingly boring, computer desk job. No thanks, Dad. You glue your ass to a chair.

Mom often returns to a hundred percent lucid when I talk about becoming a marine first and a computer expert as a distant fallback. I would be a man of adventure who saved lives, not a guy who pushed around numbers until his head exploded.

"There is no reason to go to Afghanistan and get your legs blown off," she tells me. So, I go to the other source, who is even less supportive. "Dad, I'm going to join the military like you did when you were eighteen," I insist. "I don't necessarily need college. I need the world—and to get a world away from here."

"Last time I checked, genius, there was a war going on in the Middle East and a president who doesn't know his ass from a . . ." Dad begins his ramble. I allow my mind to wander as I always do during these lectures. *Here we go again. He'd lock us in cages and stop time if he had those powers, but he doesn't. It still doesn't stop him from trying to box us in. Dad's superpower is discouragement. He's the Discourager.* "It's not the right time for you to go play devil dog and test if you have the balls of your old man," he concludes.

Dad has to bring balls into it—as if this will stop the argument cold because he has the biggest balls of all. My whole life, it has been his balls vs. my balls and his always win. He's a detective who stops killers, rapists and other evil scourges of this earth and he's sure that the one with the smaller balls (his son) cannot man-up to his level. Thus, he will stop me from doing dangerous things until my pair down below has a growth spurt.

THE CLAIRES

Far more dangerous are the genes I was given from Mom's side that somehow skipped her generation, like blue eyes often do. Only this wasn't about some physical marker.

My grandmother, Mom's mom, Evangeline, was a lot of things in her life, including a nurse, a mother . . . and someone who would supposedly "talk to herself in the middle of the night." Some thought she was out of her mind or maybe borrowed a few pills from the hospital and popped them with her evening Tab cola.

Except she wasn't some nut, and the only pills she popped were an occasional Excedrin. Talking to herself, she insisted, wasn't what she was actually doing because there were "others" in the room with her. Or so she tried to tell anyone with an open mind, which was no one in her direct family.

"Others?" they would mock her.

Others only she could see.

I see them, too.

But more about that in a moment.

I'm seventeen, and joining the marines, for many reasons. One has to do with the uncomfortable vibe in our house ever since my oldest sister... I can't talk about it. I can't even think about it. *What the hell was she thinking? Maybe she was drunk. Drunk would be good in this case. Drunk explains things. Not that I'm advocating it, but drunk (i.e. reckless behavior) would be a reason. High would be another. The idea that she was sober and really meant to come into my room and....I can't even wrap my mind around it. She's my sister.*

The only thing I feel for her now is pure disgust and a wary sense of unease. I can barely even look at her, let alone talk to her or even be in the same room with her. The way she looks at me sometimes... or how she walks too close in the hallways...is wrong. One day, by accident last week, she whipped open the shared bathroom door while I was in the shower naked because generally that's how one does the whole hose yourself off thing.

"Oh, you're in here," she said, slowly, while still standing there. She didn't miss much because I always leave the curtain half open for some reason.

"Yes, I'm in here and you're not anymore," I yelled, ripping that plastic shield closed. Why was she still lingering? Was I losing my mind? Like I said, I'm joining the Marines as my one-way ticket out of dysfunction land.

This meant a clandestine afterschool trip to a recruiter's office a few days ago. It's on Route One, sandwiched between the Aldi's supermarket and some second-hand bookstore that's always going out of business. "C'mon in, son," said the friendly soldier who sat under the largest American flag I had ever seen. "Tell me why you want to serve your country?"

I told him about the most satisfying moment in my entire life, which was the day Annie nearly drowned in her backyard pool. We were seven, and her father was out busting perps and, by then, her mother had flown the coop. The babysitter was sleeping when Annie heard the splash.

From my upstairs bedroom window next door, I saw Annie trying to pull her beloved poodle, Tag, out of the pool, but she lost her balance and fell in with a giant splat. My legs couldn't pump hard enough. I pulled Annie out first and then the dog. Dad taught me how to give mouth to mouth, so I did it first for the person and then the canine. "I needed to rush in for the rescue like people need air," I told him, staring down at my shoes. "I felt like I held their lives in my hands and I could do something to make it better."

The recruiter reached down to take the paperwork out of a file, reminding me that to join the marines, I'd need my parents' consent or I'd have to wait until I'm eighteen. There is no third choice.

"All marines must go through the thirteen-week boot camp," he told me. "Then there will be additional combat training and

THE CLAIRES

specialty schools to attend." My ears almost twitched; I wanted it so bad.

"Sir, tell me what we can do," I begged.

The glass door to the office slammed at that moment. Dad was always one step ahead. One of his cop friends working a car accident in the same parking lot tipped him off after seeing my Jeep pull up. He watched as I walked into the recruiter's office and made a quick phone call.

Before I could sign any paperwork declaring my future, my past showed up. Dad, all two hundred and fifty pounds, walked heavy on his heels and stared down the solider who backed so far off, it was like he moved out of the country. Then, our ever-protective Dad went to work nixing my wildest dreams with one severe look.

"Cass, get your ass in the damn car," Dad said.

Balls. His won, again.

"There are other recruiting offices in LA. And I can choose basic training in South Carolina—far away from you," I man up to tell him as we faced off outside on the sidewalk covered in old gum and abandoned shopping carts. We stared each other down with the intensity of two wild animals who stalk each other first and go for the kill shot later.

Over. It's not.

Dad rams one of those carts from the Aldi's into the brick wall and I swear the building will crumble. But then he becomes something even scarier: quiet calm.

"You can get your smart-ass attitude in my car," he said in an annoyingly relaxed tone. "I'll have someone pick up your car and drive it home. I'm not done with you, yet." Even keel is his M.O. now. He has that cop thing where he doesn't have to yell. But he's yelling. In your head.

Dad: 1. Cass: 0. He likes it that way.

3.

Her name is Annie, and she soothes edges.

She lives next door and I've known her since the beginning. I was always a big, lumbering kid who felt like the Hulk; she was bony thin with long reddish-brown hair halfway down her back, a sprinkling of small freckles, button nose, and heavy lids hiding sparkling hazel eyes. She was the most beautiful thing I had ever seen, and my world was a better place when she was happy, which wasn't always.

Annie's mother, Samantha, flew the coop when Annie was just five. I remember the night when the woman with those same hazel eyes stood in the sway between the front lawns screaming that she didn't want to be a cop's wife anymore—and certainly not the wife of someone who constantly asked her, "Where did you go? Who did you talk to? What did you do? Who do you know? Did you talk to any men?" Trusting, her husband was not.

That night, Gene hovered in the door, half in his old life and half in his new one as a single father—although he didn't know it at the time.

Big, not-so-bad, warm-hearted, control-freak Gene, bald and 300 pounds of muscle, has always been my father's partner, but he was in a different kind of trouble that night than what they usually encountered on the streets of Santa Monica.

"Stay in the house," Dad warned all of us as he hung back in the garage. Just in case someone needed help, he would immerse himself in a woodworking project and listen hard. Word on our street was that Samantha was "fooling around with her boss," although I didn't know what that meant in those days. The only part I "got" was the fool part, which seemed to describe Gene, who was begging her to stay.

THE CLAIRES

"You're forgiven for what you did," he kept ranting. "You're a wife and a mother. You're sorry and I forgive you."

V slipped through distracted parental eyes to wander outside, despite the fact it was just shy of midnight. Before my father could stop her, she looked up at Samantha, smiled sweetly and said, "You will go off to die—and die you will."

Hello.

That certainly caught everyone's attention.

"You're a horrid little girl," Samantha railed on her. To which, V promptly called her a *die hure,* which later we found out meant whore in German. How she knew how to curse in German is still confounding.

"V!" Mom scolded, racing outside to pick her up. Then she turned to Samantha and shouted words I had never heard before followed by the instructions to "never again talk to my children." A stream of apologies followed to a distraught Gene while they turned their backs on a desperate-to-get-out-of-there-Samantha. "I'm so sorry. Why would V say something so horrible?" Mom kept saying.

She stopped short of swatting V on the behind when she hissed like a snake at poor, nearly hysterical Annie.

Mom always covered for the girls no matter what the peculiarities, including how they walked at six months, spoke in an odd language by age two, *communicating only with each other,* in words that only they understood, and boasted about hanging with what S called "ghosties in the middle of the night."

"Where are these ghosties? Under your bed, honey?" Dad would ask.

"No, silly," S said, rolling her eyes. "They're levitating over it,"

As in any fool could....Well, no one could see a thing, but them.

"Lights out," Dad snapped. He didn't want to entertain how a two-year-old knew the word, "levitating."

The night her mother fled, Annie was outside, clinging to her long legs and short skirt, although Samantha was quick to shuck her off despite having a hard time pivoting on sky-high gold heels. She peeled off her daughter's fingers like she was removing alien tentacles that kept reattaching. Annie began to scream.

"Make another choice; live a different story," C taunted while doing a little dance on the lawn with S who had wandered outside to join her. Naturally, S was hysterically crying, which was normal for her.

"I hear the sound . . . of tears," A began. She was there. From nowhere.

Five hours later, they found Samantha's body on the I-15 outside of Vegas, twisted and mangled in a five-car pileup thanks to a trucker who took a five-star snooze while driving. I got a black suit, the sad kind for a little boy, who only needed that kind of clothing for either a wedding or a funeral.

As for Gene, well, he never remarried, but instead decided to devote himself to ridding the town of scumbags and making sure that none of them even glanced at his one reason for living: his only daughter.

Mom had her hands full with me, my four sisters, and the semi-orphan girl next door that got all the mothering she needed. I never got along with my sisters who would hit and trick me, so even as a little boy, I stuck to Annie like glue. Best friends. Two peas. One pod. Confidants. Never more. Until a couple months ago.

It was a middle-of-the-night, needy, stupid, but beautiful mi—. Wait, I would not call it a mistake. That would be a lie.

It was something else.

A marvel.

THE CLAIRES

4.

Three birdlike taps on the back door stopped the mind trip down memory lane.

"Well, look at you," Annie says, side-stepping me as she walks into our kitchen. She's an eclectic dresser to say the least. Today, she's wearing a little yellow sundress, black leggings, a Mickey Mouse watch and those cat-eyed sunglasses that make her look like Audrey Hepburn's stunning Irish younger sister. I couldn't stop memorizing her.

She always says the same thing. And, so do I.

"Well, look at you, sugar," I respond. "Now that you're here, I guess we're out of the woods." I think we heard it once in a movie – or maybe we just made it up. At this point, nobody knows. All I do know is that her ruby red lips, so soft and kissable, curve into a small smile while her spirit brightens the room like a twinkling light that jettisons across the night sky.

Just being around her makes me feel like we are indeed on terra firma, riding shotgun under a blaze of stars.

Today, I could also see some trouble was brewing. I knew this girl. Every bit of her heart. Every ounce of her soul. Plus, I could trace every worry line and pinpoint its origin story.

I rub my index finger across the little fret line on her forehead. It feels deep.

"Anything up?" I ask. No need to be pushy about it.

"Oh, it's all downhill from here," she says with a frown.

"What does that mean?" I ask in a lighthearted voice. I'm not much of an actor, but somehow, I dredge up only vaguely concerned.

"Is that your mom's Italian chicken that I smell?" she hedges.

Annie likes to dance, and I usually let her lead. If she wants to drop it, we'll drop it. For now.

We end up next to each other in our cramped dining room where the crowd has gathered and the decibel level is at around seven or eight out of ten. Over the "pass the corn," I've already leaned over to whisper to her, "We could ditch this fam fest and go to In-N-Out. Three food groups that matter: burgers, fries, shakes."

"If you promise onion rings, I'll meet you in the Jeep," Annie whispers back, before handing my sister S the platter of freshly baked rolls. Mom forgot the baking powder, so they're more like little flat pancakes. No one says a thing beyond Dad shouting, "These are sure tasty, honey."

"Over here, it's a two Tums event these days," I whisper to Annie, while hack sawing into chicken that's more than a little rubbery. I expect to hear the cluck.

"But it's better than when I'm just with my Dad," Annie says, mentioning Gene, who is often here for dinner, but not tonight. "When I'm home, it's all kale, grilled chicken and vitamins galore. He hid two Brussels sprouts in my cereal the other day."

After "the tragedy"—as everyone on the block officially labeled it—Gene morphed into the ultimate helicopter parent who didn't allow Annie to date, drive, eat fast food (or so he thought, which is where I came in), or develop an interest in anything beyond going to UCLA one town over while living at home. The plan was she could become a teacher at a school he would guard one day. We joked that she was lucky to be able to breathe on her own.

He was a cop and jailer; she was a prisoner of his good intentions, which still meant that she was doing time, one day at a time.

Gene wasn't mean about it, but firm. He explained that his "overly protective Dad routine" was just a reasonable, if not prudent, reaction to having to act as both parents. The idea that his daughter was becoming a woman was the worst of it. He still saw her as age four, in a little straw hat, with a hand that needed holding to cross the street after he put gobs of sunscreen on her pure white skin. It figured that the last guy who asked Annie out was actually "detained" after school in Gene's cop car, scared down to his bone marrow, and interrogated for over an hour. In the end, the idea of possible water boarding made him withdraw the idea of a simple date of dinner and a Tarantino movie.

"What's next Gene, the stun gun?" I joked with him while we washed cars in the driveway. "Maybe you could try it. A few volts to wake the idiot up."

Hey, I wasn't so thrilled with the idea of her dating high school dudes.

"I like how you think, Cass," he said. "Low voltage could serve as a warning without destroying any vital tissue. Smart boy."

"Warn away," I taunted him. "The guys at school are pigs."

Gene trusts me because of my son-of-a-cop DNA, although he doesn't know the weirdness that flies in this house because our own father keeps that on the QT. It's not like he's announcing to his detective partner, "By the way, my wife comes from a long-line of women who talk to the dead, amongst other talents, while my four daughters are . . . well, we're not sure what they are, but we live under the 'don't ask, don't tell' plan when it comes to any supernatural surprises. Go to the john in the middle of the night at your own risk. The ghost of Aunt Helen might be waiting."

It was only common for outsiders to wonder about V, A, C and S.

For instance, Annie constantly wondered why V always looked at her like she wanted her dead. "It's like she's jealous of the time I spend with you," she observed a few days ago. "I mean, she's your sister. It's just plain weird, if you ask me."

"V is just plain weird," I reminded her.

But it was true. Each time Annie entered the room, V went nuclear in her own quietly devastating way. Earlier tonight, as we sat down, she managed to give Annie a humiliating full body once-over and then say under her breath, "Someday your boobs will come in…sooner than one might expect."

"What's this . . . thing . . . . with your sisters?" Gene asked me one day while we cleaning out his garage.

"I call them the spawn from hell. Not to their face . . . at least not all of the time," I told him. He nodded because it sounded normal and I was good at making up stuff that made us appear to be the all-American family.

"I could never get along with my sisters, either, kid. They're back in the Midwest somewhere torturing new relatives," Gene tells me, the son he never had. He passes the ladder, so I can take a good look at his Army metals that he keeps in the rafters. "A few years from now and you'll go your separate ways or become best friends. There really is no middle ground."

I don't add my response: *If we all survive our suburbia sentence.* Sometimes, I wondered if we would.

MY SISTERS' NIGHTLY bullshit is like nails on a chalkboard for me. Take V, who announces what we're having for dinner down to the last lima bean before her butt is in a chair because she just "knows." A insists that a low radio playing is "killing her" because her hearing is that sensitive. S is always crying because "of future tension, so it's best to cry it out now." C is the best one of all. She's the doomsday forecaster with her nightly report of our future dystopian society. "Doomed, we all are," she says, stuffing her face with various varieties of lettuce. "If global warming doesn't wipe us out, then certainly it will be something bigger, like the first

THE CLAIRES

invasion of our nation from a foreign nation."

"What?" Dad demands. "Stop watching Netflix."

"*I know* you won't pass the chicken, rude one," V says to me tonight. My attention returns to the dinner from hell. My sister licks honey off her fingers for just a little too long. *Here we go again.* V's sultry act is the worst. Even Dad is grossed out. "Get a napkin, V! Now!" he barks. On purpose, she talks a little too loudly because calling people out on what they won't be doing is one of her favorite parlor games. The only thing I pass her is a disgusted glance.

I can only hope she doesn't start a round of her *I know* game. Some of her greatest hits: "*I know* you'll never graduate college; *I know* you'll never truly have the girl you really want; *I know* that you'll die young." Those are her life predictions for me.

"Want to read my palm, sis?" I ask her, instantly regretting it. "Pull a few pins out of the voodoo doll you probably keep in your backpack?"

"That's for amateurs," she taunts.

"She knows—and I confirm," C chimes in.

They work as a tag team of fatalistic forecasters of the unknown while S and A daintily chew their meat like young coyotes who haven't been fed for weeks. V and C are the badasses of the quartet; the other two are wing women. Put it together and it's fucking weird. It's why none has ever been invited to another child's birthday party since they were in preschool, let alone a sleepover. "It's like my girls have a shadow over them, socially speaking," Mom once opined.

C sends the most threatening of vibes because I hate to say it, but it must be said, I wasn't sure *what* she was, although it was anything but normal. I know she helps Dad out with his toughest cases, which also leaves me uneasy. Why her? What does she possess…or is she possessed by what?

Just before Annie arrived, I saw Sister Dearest whispering with Dad and knew it was about that missing kid. After Dad made a U-turn back to the den, I threw my two cents into the mix. "Make sure you tell him everything," I said, knowing that they liked to "investigate" on their own. Holding back info was a Claire sister trait.

"Bastard," she said to me. "You're a true waste of human tissue."

"Do you really think she would withhold information about a child?" V seconded.

Since V was involved, I left the room, head down, like a guy with no life raft who was bobbing in the middle of the ocean. It was a dead man's survival mode.

Both of them glare at me from across the dinner table. We're baiting each other, waiting for the other to say something first. Annie glances between the five of us. She has seen this play out countless times and there are always bruises.

"Is everyone excited about spring break?" Dad interrupts, because he keeps it on track between North and South Korea, aka, his children/mutants. It's called maintaining an uneasy sort of peace. Mom going into the kitchen for more rolls provides a minor distraction, but the drill sergeant is back to business in a quick second.

"Your mother and I will go to her appointment in Phoenix and Cass will stay home to study for his ACT's," Dad rattles on. He's giving the spring break "orders." "Girls, I'm so proud of you for going on that Green Peace trip to clean up the ocean. Let me know if you need any money for those four days, but I guess you won't need much if you're camping out." *What a crock of shit. Sometimes I wonder who has the fogged brain in this family. Who would even believe for a minute that those four were doing charity work over spring break? They were probably going to Cabo.*

"*I know* we won't need much because we're going to be cleaning

THE CLAIRES

the beaches all day and the lodging in those tents is free. We've been told that there is spotty cell service in the woods," V says. "I'm sorry that we won't be able to call home much."

Annie smiles up at me in that way non-blood-related beings do when family tension mounts. "Sounds interesting," she suggests.

"We're going to save the world, one sea otter at a time," C says giving her a predatory smile that troubles me. They never smile at Annie, which makes me wonder.

"Hopefully, Cass spends the entire week studying for those college boards," C taunts. "I know he will have to take them about 22 times to get a score above basic moron."

"He can do it," Dad boasts. "Instead of going off to faraway places, our Cass will use his well-developed brain to get a good job as a computer expert."

"Cass is an expert at nothing," C interjects, sipping her iced tea with a dainty pinky finger off the glass.

"*I know* something else about Cass," V interrupts as she rips into a drum stick like she's killing the chicken all over again. She chews slowly and finally leans back in that superior way she does when she really *does* know something monumental.

Eyeballs rotate until the entire table looks her way, which is the way she wants it. She's a spiritual show boater, but tonight's performance is put on hold.

"Gene's here," she says, although no one hears a thing.

A beat. Then two. The screen door slams.

"Italian chicken!" Big Gene says, walking in without any notice, like he always does, because this is his second home and second family. Our dinner table is his dinner table. S taps into his pain. "He's not a moocher; he's lonely," she says under her breath, but most of us hear. He kisses his daughter on the top of her head, which he has done since she was small, but now makes her visibly recoil.

"Hi, Daddy," Annie says in a monotone. "We weren't expecting you."

"Yes, I was," V chirps.

"Honey, can you go get your old man a plate?" he says to his bio-kid, looking around the room at all the tense faces. Annie rises because she's also the designated maid, cook, and housekeeper in the casa next door. A location change doesn't mean she's off the clock.

"Did I miss anything?" Gene asks, shoving a pancake roll into his pie hole.

5.

GENE'S NEED TO know the trivial details of our family powwow pale in comparison to his quest to fill his rumbling, wife-less, fast-food receptacle of a stomach. He's an XXL guy like Dad at about six feet four, but instead of being dark, he has reddish hair, ruddy skin and a big, wide smile that makes him appear approachable if you like to walk up to grizzlies. He's the son of Irish and Italian immigrants, with a round face, light eyes, and an auburn mustache that he uses as a resting spot for his right or left hand, depending upon which he uses as a comb. Add a commanding personality and one of those big senses of humor that can be contagious if you're in the mood. Not exactly aware of his own strength, he uses one of his baseball-glove-sized mitts of a hand to give me a slight and completely painful shoulder shove as a hello and I fall forward, stopping inches from my food.

"Cassy, gotta get up earlier than you do to tangle with me and your old man," he boasts, pointing to the butter. Annie actually blushes because it's their little routine. She butters rolls for him, which at this age is just plain weird and in return, he overly watches

THE CLAIRES

to make sure she eats all her veggies. They've done this routine since she was five and could hold a knife, and it never gets old. For one of them. The one who can't allow the other to grow the f-up.

Annie and Gene are frequent guests at Casa Danko where the table and food magically seem to stretch like an endlessly supple rubber band. In fact, everyone has their place at the table and a role to play. Mom is the main waitress, and despite the family style mode of serving will pop up like a Jack-in-the-Box to serve her patrons. It takes only a second for her to load a plate full of bird, potatoes, and veggies for him. Sadly, she hands Gene a spoon instead of a fork, but he quickly smooths it over.

"Smells so good, hun, that I might eat it with my hands," he teases. Gene is the always-positive food critic combined with the life of the party.

"Ladies," Gene nods to my sisters. Ever since that thing with his dead ex-wife, they clearly unnerve him, so he treats them like a pack of dogs that he isn't so sure won't rip his arm off. But he has to acknowledge them, which is the polite thing to do.

"Why?" they say in unison like they're singing it.

One thing about my sisters is they have the oddest reactions to those who converse with them. I don't know if they do it to throw people off at first, but their strangeness, especially in unison, makes Gene stare at me.

I call their opening remarks the initial hazing.

"Why? Why not?" Gene poses, smiling because he doesn't sweat it, but he still doesn't get it. He thinks my sisters are just plain nuts and his work as a cop has him dealing with a lot of psycho brain matter. It entertains him. "Why is the sky blue? The earth round? Why isn't Beyoncé married to me?" he says, pointing to another roll. Annie slathers it up.

"Now these are the questions of our time!" he informs the table.

"Why does the Universe mess with kids?" Dad adds, as he swaps a knowing look with his partner. Dad puts on a good game face, but we all know that he's consumed with his current case and both men will work on it until the wee hours of the morning. As life-long cops, they're both good at compartmentalizing, but I can see that this missing boy is weighing heavily on both of them.

Maybe it reminds them of the time long, long ago when I was four and Mom "lost" me at Marshall Field's department store in Chicago when we were visiting relatives. For a heart-stop thirty minutes, as she tells it, I was MIA until everyone figured out that the gourmet food section was the perfect spot for a hungry five-year-old intent on opening and then diving into $50 boxes of gourmet chocolate chip cookies. Maybe the answer was as simple for this missing kid although it had been hours since he had vanished.

I just pray I don't see him at night from the other side.

I know a lot about that fine line between here and there. Since I was a kid, I've received the kind of middle-of-the-night visitors who don't exactly hide in your closet or under your bed. Spirits of dead people are extremely pushy and quite often plop down on your bed or hover just above your face like translucent trapeze artists trying to capture your middle-of-the-night attention.

Ever since I can remember, I could always see them—*clearly*. Plus, I could talk to them either in real words or in my mind, and even commiserate with their plans to reach out to a beloved relative. I've never been open for business on that front. I couldn't possibly grant these requests as I was no spiritual messenger boy. I had to go to school and try to launch my own life as a Navy Seal, although a few times I made exceptions. Those ghosts came with so many tales, so many opportunities lost, so many loves left behind, and so many shattered pieces, that it broke my own heart, if not my resolution, to dismiss them.

Of course, Mom was the only one who would talk about it with me from time to time because she saw them, too – and had since she was a little girl growing up in Sedona, Arizona. It followed that she never told Dad who couldn't handle what he called her "flights of fancy" or "a visit to Woo Woo U." Dad and Gene had a way with me of keeping it "manly" and always bringing any conversation back to grades, college, or sports—their Bermuda triangle of interests that no teenager wants to discuss with a parental type.

"How about the Kings?" Gene booms. "I think we're headed to the Stanley Cup."

My sisters hate talking about sports. This much I also know. They're good for an almost immediate subject changer if the topic turns to anything with a cheering section and a jock.

"*I know* something interesting for *all*," V announces in a vile, ruthless voice. She turns her entire body toward me, which should make me turn way. But for some reason I do not move. Well, maybe it's not for just some reason. Frankly, I'm sick of her crap.

"I know something about Annie," she taunts. Her tone is enough to capture Gene's head swivel while Annie looks like she's drowning again. One thing about my girl. She bounces back with great speed. Annie has also been V's victim for years and even more so now that V has staked some weird claim on me. Annie knows to cut her off at the pass.

"You're right, V," Annie says in a sheepish voice. "I was going to tell you, Dad, after dinner. I got in a little fender bender with the car yesterday."

"Are you okay? Are you hurt? Was the car damaged? Was it a hit and run?" Gene drops his fork. The interrogation begins without even a formal reading of her rights because she has none.

"Darling girl, this has nothing to do with some silly car."

V again and Annie does a double take.

"And I got a D on my history paper, but Ms. B says I can do a re-write," Annie interjects as she goes into full teenage confessional mode.

V stands, as if this news is so enormous that it cannot be released in a sitting position. I can see Annie's eyes fill with freaked out tears as her unknowns are splattered in front of her. *I know everything about Annie. For the life of me, I can't imagine it's worse than the car or the paper – two items that are old news.*

But this is worse than she could imagine. That "we" could contemplate.

"I *know* our little Annie here is knocked up." Pause for V to suck down a victory breath.

"By our dear brother," she blurts.

"Who is about to become a father!" V gushes with self-satisfied sham merriment that's one-hundred percent mercenary. She's not smiling and looks at me viciously when she forces herself to say "Mazel tov, kids! You're having a baby!"

It can't be, but V is shaking as she speaks. Why is it that she appears to be devastated?

I know something, too.

Life. As we know it.

Is over.

6.

EIGHT WEEKENDS AGO, we found a line that was daring us to cross. It revealed itself at Tommy Malone's party on an unseasonably warm night at Venice beach. We trusted that it was safe to eat the bean dip that we later figured was laced with pot, and a lot of it. I mean, most of us know to question brownies, but this was chip dip. I had asked if the food was clean because I didn't do that. Tommy lied. Welcome to your so-called social life in 2013 when you have to BYOE (bring your own everything) or take a chance.

Life is full of those roulette moments and we got a good-bad spin.

After, we couldn't go home because we were a little bit high (neither of us went for seconds, but took liberal firsts) our fathers are cops and would want answers that led to names, angry accusations, fists, and bail. What followed was a plan to squander a little bit of time until our pops were snoring in front of their respective wide-screens. My own Dad was good for a *Godfather* marathon that night and rarely got past the Ellis Island part before he was sawing wood; Gene liked to retire early with Cameron Diaz, or as close as he could get to her, which was his DVR.

Annie and I, our second chapter, began with an impromptu, semi clothed midnight swim on a starry beach – my best friend doing a little strip down hidden by the shadows of night. It wasn't long before she was swinging that tumbling red hair forward, covering bits and parts, before daring me, "Cass, live a little." My clothes evaporated although I put them too close to the water. A flirty swim had me chasing her, holding her and then … why were her arms now wrapped around my neck. Water was followed by a small, roaring fire—drying my pants and sweater, and her flimsy new hopeful-green spring dress on sticks—and then wrapping our underwear-clad bodies in a blanket I found in the back of my Jeep. I convinced her that we were cold, but it was Indian summer warm.

This was trailed by one of those midnight talks you can only have with someone who knows you down to your bone marrow.

Annie's face looked like she wanted to blink those pretty eyes and transport herself to places unknown.

"My Dad doesn't really want me to go to college. He's irrational when it comes to the idea of his daughter having a real future," she said. "He just won't let me go. And he wraps it in all these fears about how dangerous it is out there. All this cop shit. I can't take it anymore. The thing is he won't allow another person he loves to walk out that front door."

"Everyone leaves," I said, not knowing how true those words would echo.

"Cass, I don't know if I'm destined to become anything. Maybe I'm just some girl who makes C's and is on no teams and never does anything much. Maybe my future is sitting alone on this beach on weekends, and the rest of the time I'm taking classes at the local community college where I'll be like the rest of the zombies masquerading as human. I'll march off to school, work a part-time job, and die a little each day just sitting in my cell, my child's room."

I stayed quiet, but my legs opened and then my arms. She climbed in, I closed any gaps and we melted together while she continued to pour out her heart.

"I have to do something drastic to get out of here," she said, her eyes welling up. "It's live like this -- his idea of life – or create something beautiful on my own."

I felt her entire body shake and when she started weeping, I broke and held her even tighter. When she wiggled around to face me, I dried her face with my fingers, like always, but this time I allowed my skin on her skin to linger.

That's when I knew.

When did this happen? When did I cross the line? Or fall down that slippery slope where loneliness leads to companionship and then friendship becomes love?

Her damp, rosy cheeks were the site of many dried Annie outpourings, including the wretched days after her mom left or when Brandon Smith broke her heart by kissing Shelby Jones at school. Not that Annie could have ever dated Brandon. Her Dad would have KO'd it.

On the beach, backlit by moonbeams, I watched her cheeks

flame red. "Sorry, babe," she said to me. "Now, let's do you."

That's when I told her about the marines.

"Cass, it does sound dangerous," she said, rubbing her cold little hands on my knees in concern. You can do that when you're spooning in a sitting state. I half expected her to tell me that I could get my legs blown off or worse when she added, "I feel a real panic creeping into my own being knowing you might not be around. In fact, I might not be able to breathe anymore. I can barely breathe now."

"How do I do me . . . without you?" she asked and shivered. This time I pulled the blanket up around us and tipped her back until she was practically lying on top of me as I stared up at the stars. I closed my fingers around hers. Tight. Super tight. "Sugar," I told her, "life is dangerous, but the only alternative is not to really live it. And maybe for the next few years, we live it solo. Then we don't."

"Don't what?" she wanted to know.

"Solo it," I boldly offered. "Maybe then we . . ."

I couldn't say the words, so I flipped the subject.

"You're destined for the magnificent, sugar," I told her.

She loved those words and wanted to dwell on them. So, she curled up into me with her legs tangled through mine. "Well, maybe I should become a marine, too," she teased, which felt normal. "I mean, I don't know about this military stuff," she added. "Even bigger is I don't know if I want to be me without you."

I smiled up at her. At the same time, she pivoted her head and gazed at me.

"Well, look at you," she said.

"Well, look at you," I whispered.

This time she punctuated it with something she had never done in the past.

Sweetly, she pressed her lips to mine and then didn't take

them away. I willed myself not to react—*kissing is dangerous to our emotional health*—but she pressed harder, lingering. I felt her tongue on my bottom lip. And then a rope broke and I kissed her back with every bit of uncertainty and promise in my tender and hopeful heart.

When I walked in the door that evening, it didn't make sense.

The kitchen looked like a tornado had swept through it. On the table was a tub of ice cream, a half an eaten pizza and a tray of cookies that looked like someone smashed them with their fist. In the midst of it all, sitting in a lone chair backlit by the lone light, my sister V was alternatively shoving her face with food, crying and then slamming cabinet doors. I think she broke one off the hinges, which woke Dad up.

"Wassamatter," he called as the Godfather shot another one.

"Nothing…everything," V cried.

"Saw their naked asses on the beach a few weeks ago," V continues now, snapping me out of my rewind. *My rage towards her was bad enough before, but now I felt close to homicidal in this moment.* "Which, frankly, was far too much Cass than we ever wanted to see," she announces.

Uproarious laughter. My sisters are in the kill zone and they love it.

"V!" Mom scolds, but it's far too late. I stare at Annie because she hasn't said a word. *Not one fucking word.*

"You're six weeks along, aren't you dear. I can hear the heartbeat," A says. "Ba-boom, ba-boom, ba-boom. It's beautiful, life's little percussion section." V gives her a stare that could drain blood. "Well, it is," S insists and this time I feel V kick her savagely under the table until she screams out in pain.

"Seven weeks knocked up, genius," C corrects because she loves to ride shotgun when it comes to V's viciousness. "All healthy; all good. Due in early December. Happy holidays to the grandfathers to be! We'll all be one big happy family now."

What happens next is like a pin being pulled out of a grenade. At first, there is that sound of heavy silence hanging in air so thick that it's almost unbreathable. It's followed by the actual detonation. Gene pivots his body in my general direction and bellows, "What the fuck— were you thinking? Obviously, you weren't thinking, Cass, you stupid son of a bitch!"

"I see . . . . breakage," V says in a victorious voice.

Dad explodes because no one calls his boy a stupid son of a bitch. Launching upright, I watch his plate of food crashing to the ground, glass and torn pieces chicken co-mingling in a million little pieces.

Like a color commentator at the big fight, it's S who opines next. "Gene feels like he'd like to punch his way out of the pain of his wife leaving and now his daughter betraying him. It's either violence or biting the end of his gun, and tonight it will be violence."

Gene goes one better as he flies across the actual table to maim me with his bare hands, but instead finds Annie is a closer target. He grabs his only child by her bony shoulders and then violently shoves her away like she's a different person than she was one minute ago when she was buttering rolls. She actually bounces off the cream-colored wall.

"Annie, just so you know…you're absentee, dead mother doesn't really give a shit, but thinks you should hit the road – as soon as humanly possible," C taunts.

Launch-pad Gene, fueled on rage, hauls back with his fist squeezed. He's about to punch my lights out when Dad rips him around by the collar, plants himself squarely in his partner's face, and warns him that blood is thicker than anything. *It's not that he's upset that Gene is about to demolish my head. He wants to do it . . . . . . himself.*

"Mine!" Dad bellows, grabbing me by both ears until I'm basically howling in pain. I have never hit my father, ever, but his grip is so excruciating that I'm forced to head butt him back to common sense. Our frontal lobes crash into each other and I know I have a concussion. Points for my old man. His grip is so firm that he only lets one ear go.

Mom screams and grabs for his arm, but misses as I watch the bottle of wine they opened crash to its side and then pour over the thin, white linen tablecloth. It looks like long trickles of blood and might as well be since Annie has none of that substance in her ashen face.

She doesn't say a word, not a yes or no about this supposed baby, but her eyes flash the "gotta run" sign, which is my answer. We would flee, not fight. She is in motion like an athlete going the distance for survival. Annie almost slips in the puddles of wine and food and bolts with what may or may not be our baby.

If I was a guessing man, I'd say she's running for *their* lives.

That's when her father yells, "I'm going to kill you both."

"Don't be so dramatic, Gene. You know you're not going to shoot anyone," V taunts. But it turns out, he has to prove that he has the biggest cajones in the room now, even bigger than Dad's enormous stones.

He pulls the gun from his pants and Dad responds instantly by extracting his own. They're packing; cops always are. Escalation is certain when Gene points his gun at my heart, which freaks Mom's addled brain out. After dashing out of the room like a racehorse, she's suddenly back. One shaking hand is holding that spare little Glock Dad keeps in a lock box. How she remembered that code I'll never know. I do know one thing: she's a crack shot. Dad likes to take her to the shooting range as their evening cardio after a big dinner, once upon a time ago calling her his little Linda Hamilton from *Terminator*. Oddly, they've always found it romantic and would put the target practice sheets on the fridge like a child's art project and then retire to their room where the door would be locked.

"No one gets hurt in my home," Mom states. She's as calm as a still pond.

All I care about is Annie, who is now hysterically crying, as she rushes across our front lawn like an escapee. She's coursing over the grass and cuts into her own house. It takes only a few minutes for her to emerge with what looks like a few essentials that are now spilling out of a plastic grocery bag. I see her fling it into the little white Toyota her father gave her for her birthday. S, who has followed her, is *helping*. WTF! Annie gives her a small hug as a thank you and I watch my sister's face shatter like she's losing *her* best friend. When I reach out for the driver's side door to jump in, Annie's faster. She hits a button and locks it. And then she rolls up all the windows.

"We need to . . ." I begin, but it's too late. I run down the street after her, following red taillights that blur in my tears.

When I turn around, I see them. Three sisters. The fourth doesn't stand with them, but is hysterically crying.

The rest of my sibs are on the front porch, now flashing hundred-watt victory smiles. Even worse is that all of them are laughing. In spite of the self-control I pride myself with having, I want to rip the flesh off their faces, but all four choose to run like wild animals at full-tilt-boogie including the distraught S. They're on the street with whip speed, jump into their VW wagon, and then peel away. V punches it at the top of the street.

Our front door blasts open like it will fly off the hinges –

and that catches my glance. Out of the corner of my left eye, I see Gene and my dad acting like two middle-aged morons. They are grappling with each other like two past-their-prime wrestlers determined to never tap out.

I'm standing on the front lawn watching these two old fools sweat while wondering, *What if she's wrong? What if there is no baby? What if this was enough for her to make her exit? What if I never see her again. What if . . .*

A shot rings out.

She meant to scare them. Really, she did.

When I begin to yowl, Mom drops the gun.

THERE WILL NEVER be a police report because they cover it up. They're cops, after all. If they say it didn't happen, then it didn't. Mom begins to scream and shake followed by Gene standing down, so Dad can give me a quick once over and then take her inside. One sleeping pill later and he's sure she won't remember much, if anything, in the morning.

Forget the ambulance for me. It's my lucky night. The bullet only grazed me and then embedded in our large pine tree out front. Dad treats me with the medical training he learned thirty years ago at the police academy. It involves a brutal, deep cleaning of the wound followed by liberal amounts of make-me-see-white-stars hydrogen peroxide and topped with a big white bandage.

"We can't go to a hospital, son," he tells me.

"Yeah, I know," I moan with my eyes closed. "Just finish it up, so my arm doesn't fall off. I need to go find Annie."

Gene was already gone, probably looking, putting out a full

THE CLAIRES

APB for his missing, potentially pregnant daughter. Dad sits next to my bed offering me cold water to drink because I'm his kid and that means everything. "Your blood pressure is off the charts. Calm yourself down before you go out, Cassy," he instructs. "Thank God, you're okay. And it will all be okay. I promise. I'll make it okay."

One thing about Dad. He ruled in a crisis because that was his domain. He not only dressed my wound, but grabbed the gun, calmed Mom down, put her to bed and dug the bullet out of the tree so there would be no evidence. He told off two lookie-loo neighbors reminding them that "it was none of their damn business." Then he went to get me a cold drink.

The icy liquid tastes so good going down my dry throat, and I begin to gulp it. The room doesn't cooperate as it begins to spin.

Damn it.

"You're not looking for nobody, kid," Dad says, waiting for the pill he melted into my drink to kick in. "Night, buddy. Sleep tight. Pleasant dreams. I love you."

A VOYANT'S STORY: V

1.

The Chuck Box sandwich shop is a little hole-in-the-wall place that smelled like the heaven of freshly baked bread combined with the tart scent of dill pickles. It was conveniently located near lovely Santa Monica Beach and could be quite the tourist trap, but not tonight. The beach was barren, thanks to LA weathercasters losing their minds over an impending spring thunderstorm.

We sit in one of those too-cute white and red polka dot booths eating veggie subs like the world will soon run out of fresh produce. I'm on my second, which even catches the attention of the sub shop owner who raises an eyebrow. I eye the knife in his hand and he doesn't say a word. So, what if I'm an emotional eater of epic proportions?

"Aw heck, baby girl, I just lost 100 bucks," C says, wiping tzatziki sauce off her chin. "I didn't think you'd have the guts to out Cass and Annie for doing the beach mambo – and in front of an audience. Damn, I've known about it for a week too, but I kept my big mouth shut! I salute you, V. Why can't my gifts include clear insight when it comes to my own sisters?"

"Girls, wasn't that a bit harsh?" A pivots. "Even Ma jumped into my ear on the car ride here and she said what we did to Cass was moderately entertaining, but certainly beyond the pale. Ma was also wondering if our 'meanness gene' was kicking in early this lifetime?"

"Ma, Ma, Ma, Ma," I say in a sing-song voice. "You're 16. Grow the hell up. Be an adult for your last months on this earth and stop tuning into Mommy every five minutes." For a minute, I stop and wonder if this lifetime will end earlier because the level of

THE CLAIRES

vindictiveness – i.e. the Cass and Annie debacle – was a bit off the charts. We usually don't get this maniacal until just before dying when the bad blood carrying the most aggressive of our feelings floods our systems.

I choose to Gandhi it.

"I understand if you find my boldness offensive," I tell my sisters. Then I look specifically at A who actually speaks to Cass more than the rest of us. "I find your sisterly, sugar-coated caring when it comes to a certain brotherly person pretty offensive, too. Remember where your loyalties are, A. It's not like you're carrying this so-called brother into the next lifetime. In a few months, you'll never see this fool again."

"You don't have to be hurtful about it," A sniffs.

C even interjects, "I'm not so sure never is the right word here. I have a feeling we will see Cass again."

S tries to drive a wedge because she's absorbing so many conflicting feelings that she's going a bit schitzo. Whenever this happens to her, she opts to go for just the news, which she delivers in an unemotional way.

"If any of you bitches care for an update, here it is," she says in her best TV newscaster voice.

"Breaking news, girls: Annie left the block like a shot out of hell. Cass was in total despair, plus Gene was ready to kill someone," S spat out. "And, dear sisters, that doesn't equal our do-gooder plan to break whatever spiritual scourge we seem to be under. Shame on all of us for tonight. Perhaps this was a giant setback."

"I'm sixteen. I'm hormonal. *Laisse-moi tranquille*," C states with enough of a lift in her voice that tells me she enjoyed doing what we would later call "a bad, bad thing."

"In English, please," I demand.

"Get off my ass – and pass the soy sauce," she says. "There you go. Translated."

"He's so self-righteous. Cass, the prodigal son. Just makes me want to scream," I fume, but it's hard to lie to this crowd. The more I bash him and list his faults, the more they look at me dubiously as in *I know what you did last summer. Just thinking about it makes me blush.*

That night .....

He went to bed early and I stewed in my room for hours. Around midnight, I was reaching into a bag I kept way back in the closet to avoid my sister's prying eyes. The material that made up the barely-there nighty was almost translucent and it slipped through my fingers like air.

C dabbles in a bit of mind reading. "I saw the nightgown in the bag all the way in the back of the closet months before and thought, 'Oh no! This is some screwed up, we-really-don't-live-in-Arkansas-stuff. I mean, I've heard of kissin' cousins, but this....'"

"Shut up," I warn her.

"Can we do a subject changer," S bravely interrupts. "I'd like to keep my first and second dinner down."

"If he wasn't such a sap, he would realize that he's more powerful than . . . well, than he deserves to be. He doesn't even appreciate what he's been given," I fume. "Won't accept it. Won't entertain it. He's embarrassed by it. That's what makes me want to educate him. Or maybe I want to mess with him—although he has enough tragedy in his coming attractions," I say, quickly changing the subject.

"You don't want to educate him. You want to do the nasty with him," S begins.

"Hello, Arkansas," C jumps in.

I pick up my fork and point it in her face.

"Say one more word and you'll be joining our real Ma for tea and sympathy tonight," I warn her.

C's eyes flash. "Be careful who you threaten, sister dear," she

THE CLAIRES

says in a cool voice, John Lennon glasses down below her eyes for a second. "There is one of us who is ultimately more powerful – and I could eat you alive. Lucky for you, I'm a vegan."

Three sets of eyes look at me with pity, which is more than I can stand. "You're my sisters by blood. You know he's not my real brother. So, I don't see the big deal. The heart wants what the heart wants," I say with tears in my eyes. I know something that I won't share with them. I want more than just a physical experience with Cass. But I lie to the others. "I just want the experience," I say. "He's my type. Plus, he's easy prey. A virgin until that beach event. FYI, if anyone is interested."

They look at me with wide eyes.

"Cass was…." S almost whispers.

"A viiiiiirrrrrrgin," I repeat. "It seems to run in this lifetime. He doesn't hardly get any action, but when he does…look out. He's, uh, quite spectacular."

The three of them look stricken as if is TMI x infinity.

Then I deflect. "I guess I just thought, he's a virgin. I'm a virgin….And if not him then who?"

No one can answer because if you discounted the gays at SMHS, crossed off the total freaks and then sifted through what remained, there were maybe two or three decent male specimens at our entire school. One is a slave to a cheerleader; one is HIV positive; one got real nasty in a Chris Brown way with a girl years ago.

I didn't tap into Hunter Clark's vibe until it was almost too late.

Our one date last year was supposed to be dinner and a movie, but he switched it to dinner and a ride up into the hills. I can never see my future, but I tapped into his and clearly. This included the locking of the car door and the pulling down of his pants with the idea to rip down the front of my dress.

This is where it pays to be clairvoyant. In that one quick second before he hit the automatic lock on his Chevy Tahoe, I was able to wrap my hand around the door handle, pray, and then oh-so-silently open my car door just an inch. As Hunter was going for his zipper/car lock move that I knew he had tried in the past, I, the current daughter of a cop, went animalistic. A quick rising to a yoga pose that defied gravity followed by a knee to you-know-where had him folding forward and choking while I jumped out of the car and then ran at speeds that defied any P.E. class challenge.

I never told my father about it, but did something far worse. I told my sister A who put out a system wide call to several, extremely agitated feminist spirits. Let's just say that in this #metoo era, they weren't exactly pleased with a date rape scenario.

The haunting of his bedroom that followed for the entire next calendar year produced enough hair loss in poor Hunter, a high school basketball jock, that under his yearbook picture last year he was voted: Most Likely to Open His Own Personal Hair Club for Men.

C tries to talk around my crush on Cass. She's good at mediating tough situations. "What if we found someone else who was your type," she begins. "Tall, blond, big...not too stupid." Then she shook her pretty head. "You're right. It's impossible. We only have seventeen years, not seventeen million," she reminds the table.

Just another night talking scenarios and sex with your sisters.

2.

"In case any of you fools need a real-world update, our present Mom shot at the tree and nicked Cass. Dad drugged him. He'll stay home for tonight and then go look for Annie," C says.

"I see . . . disaster," I add, holding tight the nagging worry I felt when she said that my mother shot him. When my sisters

THE CLAIRES

stare hard my way, I fill in a few blanks. "Oh, the virgin-no-more princess next door is fine," I swallow hard and let C tell them the rest.

C nods. "Hiding out at some rich girlfriend's house in Beverly Hills. With our future niece. Yes, it's a girl. Just what this family needs—another gifted human girl. And this one is off the charts – a wild child whose hands will hold more swords than flowers. I can't see much beyond her birth – and she will arrive just before Christmas. Born in another state. We will meet her exactly once before we go.

"The rest is quite filmy," I sum up.

"Wouldn't the Patriarch of Paranormal shit a brick?" S poses. "Soon, we'll be just a few girls short of creating something like that island in Wonder Women. I call dibs on the first golden lasso."

We all laughed loudly.

"Well," C poses, refocusing us, "since this evening is shot to hell in so many ways, we might as well get back on the do-gooder track. First agenda item is to help fix Dad's other problems, so he can focus on throttling our so-called brother."

"The missing boy from earlier today," A says with her eyes filling. "I can't hear him. Not a peep. Do you think that means—"

"I can't feel him," S continues in a worried voice.

"Don't go there," I say, slowly. I wonder why I care. "I think he's alive, but I can't quite reach his frequency either. I do see a corporate logo, whatever that means. And blue nylon fabric. And darkness. Total black out."

"I know we need to be on the beach in exactly forty-six minutes," says C.

She drops that like a bomb.

This means we need to waste time because we certainly can't go home again. The problem was you can't occupy a booth in the sub shop for more than thirty minutes without everyone in line getting twitchy. To make those minutes pass and to amuse ourselves, we find ourselves dodging the light rain that's falling as we wander next door.

An ancient, faded gold couch with rub marks where previous rear ends have parked it is the only available seating.

Turns out, it will be dinner . . . and another show.

3.

THE PLACE NEXT door is called Santa Monica *Friendly* Psychics. If you pay, you can occupy one of their comfy couch seats, sip lukewarm tea from two days ago from a dirty kettle and have your future unveiled by a friendly, portly guy in a stained navy velour sweat suit named Bruce Bartholomew. He has supposedly been doing "readings" since he was six and took over the place from his parents in the '80s. They didn't predict futures, but sold beachy T-shirts and flimsy towels here.

According to the brochure, Bruce, a man brimming with otherworldly intellectual abilities, could talk to the dead, determine your future, and even create a love potion for an extra $15.99, minus taxes and tip. Ah, the rub. Love always costs you the most.

Bruce was not just a spiritual man. He was also a businessman.

We're the only ones in here because of the weather. No one in Los Angeles can drive or even tries to leave their house during even a light misting, let alone the drencher predicted tonight, which is why we feel like the last survivors of a zombie apocalypse—something Bruce can't conjure up, we don't think. But maybe he can for an extra $15.99.

Bruce *is* loud enough to wake the dead. He yells out from the back room in his thick Brooklyn accent, "Can ya's wait a minute while I clean up this mess?"

THE CLAIRES

Clean up from what? A blood-letting? *FLASH!* I see it in my third eye. Oh, he means clean up as in crumbs. He's on his third sub of the day. Scratch that ... the night.

"If he was really clairvoyant, he would have already pulled out a breath mint because he saw us coming," I say under my breath.

True grit gifted types resent all of these rent-a-fake con artists who set up psychic reading shops in strip malls and announce to the world that they're brilliant. You know the kind. They're there to tell you the generic: *Your (fill in the blank) dead relative loves you. He/She is near you. The future looks so bright you gotta wear shades.* I can barely keep it together when I spot a rip-off because it gives all the real special types a bad name. For instance, Bruce charges twenty-five dollars for a regular fifteen-minute reading, which seems outrageous, but the guy has to eat.

Bruce yells again from the back. "If ya's want to do selfies on the way out with me that will be an extra five bucks—a piece. And I got a camera out there, so I see all four of you. That's twenty-five buckaroos for each one of you and an extra five beans for the prints. No camera phones allowed."

C shrugs. "Wanna test him. Mess with him?" she offers. She has made a sport out of this kind of thing -- destroying the minds of many fakers over our lifetimes.

"If you want lotto numbers—" Bruce shouts.

"We know, we know, we know," A says. "What does it cost to breathe in here?"

"The air is free," Bruce spits back. "Me and Tony Soprano. We're generous guys."

Finally, he calls us into the reading room, which is decorated in basic New Age un-splendor with yin-and-yang posters on the wall, red velvet chairs, a small table, a deck of tarot cards, and an old, big-backed television set with an episode of *Law & Order*: *SVU* playing on mute. *Really?* Magic and Mariska? Then there's Bruce, who is about fifty, looks sixty, and assures us that he's the real deal, born and bred in Queens, but touched by "the heavens up above."

"I also come from a family of gypsies. From Romania," he says in a monotone voice while he sits on a folding chair on one side of the table. There is only one uncomfortable wooden chair on the other side, so I sit while my sisters stand behind me. "A cab ran me over when I was five. When I woke up in the hospital, I knew I was existing in more than one world."

"How did you know?" S asks. "Was it the drugs?"

Bruce gives her a silencing look that says he can make this room spin so she better watch her tart mouth.

"Ya's know, I started seeing dead people first in my bedroom and then on the streets. Yessiree, I followed one ghost into Queens Boulevard on a busy traffic day. It happens. Bottom line, poor Brucie. Concussion. Traction. When I woke up, wham-bam-slam, I began to see the future *and* I could talk to ghosts. The universe just upped the ante."

We stare at him blankly, but he doesn't care if we believe him or not. Since the "wow factor" is somehow missing on our faces, he goes right back to business.

"What sign were yer born under?" he asks me.

"A warning sign," I retort.

He clears his throat.

"Do you want to hear only the positive information about yerselves?" he asks me.

Rainbows and butterflies and cute guys marrying us in the future.

So not us.

"I only want to hear the negative stuff," I say and wait for Bruce to choke, which he predictably does two seconds later and on his own saliva. A little spittle runs down his chins.

"You ... what?" he sputters, actually putting down his

THE CLAIRES

sandwich. "No one wants to hear only the bad news." He pauses, leaning forward to say something I imagine will be insignificant, "That will be twenty-five bucks in cash ... now. *Before* we begin. With only the bad stuff – as requested."

S gets out her notepad and three ten spots.

With that he begins the routine including putting cards down on his crushed red velvet tablecloth. He does this all day long, which is why the cards are old and bent. A cough. On the cards. It seems so unsanitary ... and suddenly so real. "I'm not sure if you're a good person. If any of you are good," he says, pushing back in his chair to put some distance into the equation. "But maybe it's not your fault." He touches his forehead three times. *Tap, tap, tap.*

"You're older than you seem," he blurts out. "Much older. You've ....no, that's a big load of ...."

"You," he says, pointing at me, "are trying to get sexed up before you...."

"Die in December," I fill in the blank. "Yeah, we know all of the above."

"You are....," Bruce pushes himself back to the wall. "You're living under a curse from what I guess is the 1800s."

Then his face turns red like a tomato. We're pretty shocked, too, because suddenly this flimflam man seems to be the real thing.

"Well, polish my nuts and serve me a milkshake!" he cries, slapping his hand down on the faux wood. "I'm used to cheaters, lonely hearts and those who are brokedy-broke. But a real curse handed down from underground types in London. Holy Revenge of the Sith!"

"Keep it down," I implore.

He stops. Then looks at me. Hard. The cheap white shutters on the wall shake, but not because of anything *unexplainable* inside this room. Outside, black clouds have billowed in from the west and the scent of rain is thick and heavy. I hear a low crackle of thunder in the distance.

This is where it gets scary.

"You're right to try to atone in this lifetime. A little bit of penance is always good for the soul, but a "fix it" is not promised. It *is* worth a shot. Ya's never know. It's also why you need to get going," Bruce says. "That little boy, Ben . . . Benny. The one who is missing? After you find him, go into the water. *Into. The. Water.* Do you understand me, girls? They'll be there. They're hunting tonight. It's why I never go to the beach in the rain. They love inclement weather and inclement people. I'm afraid I'll get sucked down into their world. There's not enough dudes under da sea."

It doesn't really make sense, but C's head is bobbing up and down in slow motion. It's like they're on the same party line.

"And one more thing," Bruce says, standing up and pushing our money away as if he doesn't want any part of us to remain in this room after the next minute goes by. "It's not in the house. The thing you're looking for. It's outside somewhere. Your grandmother was a very clever woman."

"Ain'ts ya going to New York soon?" he says. "Look outdoors for what you want."

"Thanks, gypsy blood. We have to go to the beach now," I say as we stand, but we leave the cash.

The gifted must eat, too.

4.

IN THE HALO of an amber street light, the rain-soaked beach takes on a luminous glow. A hail of liquid bullets sends almost every ordinary person home for the night, leaving just a few bums pushing silver shopping carts on the sidewalk that runs the lip of

THE CLAIRES

where the road continues until the grit of the sand begins.

The wind continues to pound the windows of the VW as C pulls into the front driveway of a swanky hotel named Shutters where the rich and famous can buy a getaway with an ocean view. No, we weren't checking in, C informs the helpful, model-like doorman with the ski-slope cheekbones. He offers to valet the car, grab our bags and then perhaps carry us into the warm, lodge-like lobby. I wish.

We don't ask C why she pulled up here. We never do. Cognizants are a hot-headed bunch who don't like to be second-guessed. "I know this is the spot," C says followed by three affirmative nods. She knows; we follow. We've observed this law of sisterhood since birth.

C tosses the handsome one her keys, which means we have to step out into the vile weather, where the rain is coming down sideways. First things first: We yank some warm sweat jackets out of the backseat and put them on. The fleece hood part is low over our faces, which feels like a shield on a night when the sky has been split in two.

C has what's known as spiritual GPS, which means her spirit guides have an uncanny sense of finding. Blindly, we follow her to the end of the sidewalk and then off the concrete and into the vastness of miles of soaked sand.

"I honor my clear vision," chants C, spitting rainwater from her mouth.

She keeps saying it—again and again and again—on our swift descent down through the glossed ground to the water's edge where our four shadows are nonexistent in the turbulent, onyx waves.

The ocean is staging its own heavy metal concert tonight, focusing heavily on what sounds like a pounding, never-ending drum solo. The crashing waves look deadly, which doesn't stop

S, who goes a little too far out as she wades knee deep into the churning foam. A's the one who always pulls her back in—physically and emotionally.

C is crouched low now in the compressed sand, which worries me. Another wall of liquid turbulence collapses by our feet, and I know she could easily be swept away. She knows it, too, which is why she stands sturdy with her feet wide apart. She's mere centimeters away from the exact instant that separates life and death.

Those moment of time and chance were everywhere in the mortal world.

"I manifest thoughts and ideas into reality," she shouts. "What shows up in my mind materializes in the world." She opens her arms wide and says, "I am open to receiving the answers now. I am a vessel of the truth. My hands are helper's tools. Where . . . Is . . . The . . . Boy?"

When she stands and starts walking up the beach toward one of California's most famous landmarks, I blink the water out of my eyes once and then twice until I see the monument clearly. You can't miss it because it's that iconic. C leads us to stand underneath the slats of the bridge that marks the famed Santa Monica Pier.

Above us, the never-ending happy carnival music is absent and the whirl of the hazy red-and-blue lights from the Ferris wheel is on pause because the great machine has been put on hold. The storm has driven away all of the tourists and the pier is closed.

A interrupts me. She hears the sirens wail in the not-so-far distance. It's a police cruiser or two, a mile or two out, and I wonder if they're still looking for the boy.

C has an uncanny way of shutting off the world. Which she does now.

All she needs to do is *hear*.

"I'm hearing a little boy . . . crying like a harmed bird," C says

THE CLAIRES

in an even voice. Her words force me to look up. I pray it's not a boy crying above us because his parents just ruined his evening by telling him the rides are closed.

"He's not above . . . He's below," C says.

There is nothing under that pier, but slick-smooth sand. The grains aren't as wet here; they're glazed, but packed looser because the wood slats above protect from the elements. It's a shelter of sorts for other reasons. The ocean's waves can't quite reach us yet, but the tide is quickly eating its way up the beach.

"S, stay cool, baby," I tell our sensitive sister as I stare at C who has an internal movement meter that picks up any human or animal form.

"Movement," C says. Only none of the four of us is actually moving. We're barely breathing. "Twenty meters to the right . . . ten, nine, seven."

She looks down at her Sketchers that are suddenly all wet. Like a sprinting horse, C unglues herself from the caked sand, elevates a long leg and rushes ten paces to the extreme left, eventually dropping to her knees. From there, she starts a ravenous digging with her bare hands.

"He's in this world. Not the next," she states, repeating it over and over again as we all drop and begin to excavate. My nails dig into the ground and soon I'm removing fists filled with grit and sediment.

"This boy is destined to save his sister from drowning . . . This boy is destined to become a teacher . . . This boy is destined to create more acts of kindness than failures of hatred . . . This boy is destined to live," I say, looking deeply into his future.

C puts up a hand for us to stop. She stands and takes another three steps to the left. Crouching again, she takes her hand and runs it over what looks like water-lacquered silt. "Shit . . . ouch," she says as something stabs her. Looking closer, I can see what looks like a branch sticking out. But it's not.

C shines her cell phone light onto the orange tip of a plastic drinking straw.

And next to it, sticking up through the sand, are the blue-beige tips of five small fingers.

4.

FLASH! I SEE the little blue lips on the other end of that straw. He's buried down deep, and we dig with savage abandon until we feel smooth, cold, human skin. The straw was for oxygen; the goggles he wears was another way his parents were tempering the act of a child murder. They were playing Russian roulette with the whole process, pretending that fate would take the wheel.

Carefully, we dig now, feeling a tiny shoulder, an arm, and then the saturated end of a soaked shirt. It isn't long before C and I gingerly begin to hoist him, inching him into our arms. It's as if the ground has given birth to a little boy. Quickly, we shed our jackets, wrapping first with our warm bodies and then with our wet clothing. We don't want to scare him, but somehow, instinctually, he knows he is safe now. Little Benny has a sopping, sandy mop of plastered-down dark hair that makes his too-pale skin look like fresh white paint. His breath is thready; his lips the color of a summer blueberry.

"He's still alive. *Alive!*" I assure my sisters, moving C away with a slight shove to lay him down in A's lap. I lean down to give the nonresponsive boy mouth-to-mouth. By now, C is on the phone to Dad and the sirens in the distance wail louder as they get closer. Our poor sister S feels the boy's pain so deeply that she sits slightly away, quivering limbs over her knees, compulsively rocking.

THE CLAIRES

Dad roars up, minus Gene, but with an ambulance a scant second behind.

"I'm so sorry, Dad. I'm so sorry, kid," C repeats over and over again. "I couldn't see it clearly until the rain came and washed some of the blur away from this city.

"The parents. They did it. But they didn't always have him here, buried alive. They had him . . ."

She stops for a moment and sees it clearly now. I see it, too. *Monsters masquerading as humans.*

"He was in a gym bag. They drugged him and then put him in a bag in the trunk of their car. He stayed in that hot trunk for most of the day. It's a miracle he survived it. They kept him there until it got dark. In that damn bag. Parked by the hotel valet in their underground garage."

C is crying now, which is so unlike her. "Please tell me that he's going to be okay?" she begs.

The boy is on oxygen now and under a warming blanket thanks to the vigilant paramedics. They take him on a stretcher while Dad and I look at C.

Her sad smile is one party victory; all parts pain when it comes to the state of the universe.

At the same time, the EMT shouts what amounts to a miracle. "We have a heartbeat and he's asking for his teddy. We got him just in time. If the tide would have come in any harder, he would have drowned. Nice work, whoever found him. The kid had less than ten minutes left."

We wait for Dad to praise us, hug us, remind us that we have a place in this crazy world even if we're limited editions on limited time – although he doesn't know that last part. All he does is look at us *like he barely even knows us.* His disgust is palpable.

"You hurt your bother, you hurt me," he bites out. "And you better hope like hell that Annie makes it home safely tonight."

His threat lingers in the air; his voice is rough and dismissive. It's like he doesn't know us. Maybe he wished that he didn't. The only worse sound is a clap of killer thunder off in the distance.

"You're on borrowed time if anything else happens," he says. "There will be hell to pay if anyone gets hurt beyond the fact that your brother was shot. V, look at me. Your brother was shot by your mother who was so upset that she got a gun."

"Is he still alive?" I snap, knowing the answer.

The words land hard.

"I hope your conscious doesn't just hurt. I hope it bleeds," says Det. Danko.

He rises, walks to his police cruiser, slams the door, and peels away without saying another word. I'm dumbstruck. *So, that's how you'll play it. Not an offer of a ride. No, "congrats girls." No, "you saved a life tonight." Just stand in the rain and rot. If the weather doesn't do you in.... maybe I will.* Suddenly, I feel a type of blind fury. I shudder to think of the wrath of C, the one with the worst temper of any Claire. Not that you would know it by vocal tone, but just by deed.

I can see the slay factor in her eyes.

"Let's finish this bitch," C says, calmly. I know she's detaching from Dad and this earthly family. We tend to isolate during our sixteenth year—and moments like this just make it easier to sever the ties.

"The mother and her boyfriend did this," C continues in a tone that's deep and guttural. "They're out here on this beach. Right now. Looking. In order to put on a show of how much they love little Benny. They love him to death, if you know what I mean."

Her smile is bloodless.

My words are to blame.

"It won't be long for either of them. I know —" I begin.

"What do you know, hunny bunny?" C interrupts. She pulls a

small silver hunter's knife out of her pant pocket.

"Everything," I say, removing the stun gun strapped to my ankle that I stole from the old man. "What's that saying . . . an eye for an eye? A death for a death."

"You know it, too," I remind her.

5.

WE'VE BEEN ALIVE since 1911. We know the way the world works when it comes to this mother and her abused son, which now has our complete focus. It's easier to direct our rage towards *them*. There were enough of *them* out there.

I know that they—as in the mother and her boyfriend—will never do a day in jail for burying their boy alive. Real life isn't a movie where the bad guys pay with their own sorry hides. Mostly, they get a good lawyer paid by the state and get off because prisons are too crowded.

Here's how it goes down: *Abused girlfriend, dope addict, lost her mind, needs another chance, judge feels her pain and gives her the kid back. . . . Screw the kid. He has no rights. Not even the right to stay alive . . . No one notices when she forgives the boyfriend. She loooveees him. He's a really special guy.*

So what if he does a year for child endangerment, as if burying a child alive is simply 'endangering' him and not trying to kill him. And after a slick lawyer does his tricks, the boyfriend is back living with the mom and boy. By golly, they're going to make it work! It's so beautiful they say, but it's really not. 'Cause, the boy is a year older now and has nightly dreams of his sandy grave on that stormy night. He screams out in his sleep almost every night because he feels he can't breathe, which the boyfriend doesn't appreciate to the point he tosses the kid across the room and watches his little head bounce off a wall. So what? His own father knocked some sense into him, too.

Mom and boyfriend know the drill by now. By the time the kid is conscious again, he's stuffed into a new and slightly bigger Nike bag and they drive him into nature again. They're sick of the beach. What a crap show. But boy, those big mountains with thin crevices to hide a small body will do the trick. They bury him again, the boyfriend assuring the mom that someone will find him maybe and it's no worse than just abandoning a dog that no longer pleases you.

Before he left, I told our father (figure) a big whooper of a lie about the couple in question. "The parents—they're down the beach by the hotel."

God help me, but I point in the wrong direction and C knows it, which causes her to look down, so he can't read her face. He doesn't even try. Regular mortals were so easily pointed in the wrong direction and moved toward it with no questions asked in most cases.

"You're such a lovely and competent bullshit artist," C whispered into my left ear after Dad raced away.

She's not calm anymore. Vengeance is her drug, and she's riding that high with a slick smile that proves we're not do-gooders in the traditional sense of the word. We're more like good-bad doers. It's much more authentic for us to bank on revenge and retaliation in the hopes that something fair will come out of it.

This creed we take with us from lifetime to lifetime is blood for blood; bone for bone. One must be poured; the other crushed.

6.

WE GO TO the water, but not to cleanse our immortal souls. It was time to plead our case to the ocean, which is always breathing, always listening, always in motion for reasons beyond man's

THE CLAIRES

explanations. The ocean links us to other worlds, thus it is always churning and rolling toward something new. It gives, it takes, and so it goes on and on and on. This never changes.

The ocean cleanses in the most powerful way, which is why we stand together, arms linked as the mighty rain pours down over the city. I reach out and let the water flow through the grooves of my hand—and wait.

The water is icy cold and stinging—and as real as those bodies that live within it. Let me make one thing clear. These are not the dead bodies. I'm talking about the ones that are alive and claim the deepest reaches of the water as their homes.

A is the one who lifts her hands straight to the sky to do something that we save for only special occasions. She's not just clairaudient, but also gifted in the art of summoning, as are the rest of the Claires. We don't know why, but it's as if we have some internal beacon that calls for creatures or otherworldly beings when we're in trouble. Sister A is the best at it and summons as only someone with clear hearing and portals to other worlds can. The hard sloshing in her ears tells us that they're coming on quickly, but not from above.

Some dwell below.

There is a reason human beings can only travel so low in the open ocean. It's called trespassing.

7.

WITH A CRASH of the ages, a smooth and enormous round wave rolls in and I see the faint glints inside of it. The tiny twinklers look no bigger than glowing particle dust, but if you looked closely enough, and you didn't dare not, you began to see the specks bursting into blue, underwater flames. A blink. A gleam. And suddenly the next wave joins with the first until it appears as if it holds small flares illuminating the water from within.

We wait breathlessly.

We watch hopefully.

A glorious surge kisses the patient shore, and I can barely breathe as parts begin to materialize into fully formed mortal-like bodies that roll into the material realm like gymnasts doing forward somersaults. One more loop of liquid glory and they bob in the churned surf, lower parts hidden by the water while their top parts form iridescent chests, arms, necks, and human heads sporting long, flowing locks that gleam fire red.

What appears is half-human, half-fish, always female in form, and wonderfully ageless. Their kind ranged from very old women with the speed of the wind to grown females our age who seem to be in some sort of apprentice training. They look to their elders as the decision-makers, playfully poking each other in anticipation until an answer is rendered.

The first time I saw them, I thought I was losing my mind. "Shape-shifting water spirits?" I questioned. Then one of them touched me, transferring the cool smoothness of her water-logged caress, and I lost myself in the wonder of over-sized black eyes that never stopped crying salted tears. She explained why. "We appear to cleanse," she said. "And there are not enough tears in the universe to explain why."

This time, I welcome our visitors like any good Angelino does when out-of-towers arrive in the City of supposed Angels.

I don't fear them because S has given them a high mark of approval. "They mean no harm to us. They give only love to us because we're cleansing the planet."

"Same mission," I whisper.

They're standing now, gliding out of the surf, almost living silhouettes, although made out of . . . what? I don't know, but they

THE CLAIRES

sparkle and glisten thanks to translucent flesh with body systems flashing bright as greenish liquid flows through a complex vascular system.

S tells them it's better not to be this visible, so they move back into the water until all I can barely see is three heads bobbing in the darkness.

They listen as S tells the story of the boy who almost drew last breath, the drinking straw and the abusers. She tells it with so much emotion that I feel their rage churning as the words tumble into the night air.

They do not talk, but bow their heads in thought. To decide.

And now, they will wait, but not for long. C has located one of our guests of dishonor.

Benny's mother is a defiant woman, twenty-five, with butt-length bleach blonde hair, a crop top and jeans that are molded to her thanks to the rain. She has mascara running down her cheeks, but not from crying. She's cold, wet and extremely pissed off. *FLASH!* The boyfriend is the only thing that matters to her. Anything to make him stay because so many have not. And she feels a touch of victory. By now, she reasons, her son is in a better place. A watery grave. But she's not sure—and she needs closure for some reason. *FLASH!* The reason is the boyfriend is on probation for domestic abuse. He's no use to her behind bars. She wants to see a body.

She believed C who, just moments ago, discovered her on the pier above and informed her in her most breathless and innocent way, "We located your son in the ocean and saved him. I think you should come with me. He's calling for you. He won't stop crying. We don't know what to do with him now."

Even in the downpour, the mother puffs on a cigarette and spouts slews of curse words, but she follows until she's at the ocean's edge and staring at the four of us.

In her rage, she doesn't see them. She sees us. The ones stopping her from a dream life with the boyfriend who calls himself Ferryman. He actually drives one of those little tourist boats by day.

"I don't see no kid," she says in a tremulous voice because she can't be sure. "You're just trying to get some money out of me."

I cut to the chase.

"You placed him in a Nike bag. Buried him in the earth. Planned for him to drown." I state quietly.

"It's none of your damn business," the mom screams into the night. Then she calls out his name – again and again. Not her son's name. "Ferryman!" she cries.

"But it is . . . our damn business," I say, moving closer to her. "We come out at night to right the wrongs. And what you did was so very, very, very wrong."

Her back is to the water, which she ignores to focus on the glint of C's knife in the moonlight. My sister is agile and hones in on her, taking small steps while waving her weapon in the air. The mom is forced to back up, once and then twice, while puffing hard on her cig.

The female nymphs, a shade or two darker than the waves now, don't need to ponder any longer—*they've sensed more than enough*—and begin a forward swim. C slashes at the mom, who takes that one last step backwards. On the next wave, the translucents sway and then twirl forward as only those partially made of liquid can do. It's a gorgeous, fluid ballet that plays out without any music.

She must sense it. The mom turns around. A glint from the sea catches her eye.

"What the hell . . . is that?" she screams. "Wh-what are . . . those? Things? Are those eyes? Is …it…alive!"

"By the way, there's no lifeguard on duty," C says.

THE CLAIRES

We watch as they barely touch her, yet wrap around the mom as she's pulled backward into water that churns with the ferocity of a sudden riptide. We gaze at her living remains (for now) as her body bobs up once, twice, three times until the final glow of that cigarette is extinguished. A blink later and the rest of her is sucked away.

There is no rehab when dealing with forces of nature. No reasoning. No extenuating circumstances. Certainly, no parole. It's just, you did that and we do this. Cause and effect.

When it's over, I see that the last nymph is standing at the water's edge. Slowly, I walk up to her, all the while putting my right hand up and splitting my fingers into the peace sign. I know she won't harm me because we're on the same side. She feels it, too. I bow my head in respect and she sprays a fine mist of water into my face before taking a long, slow roll back into the dark surf.

For several long minutes, no one says anything. It's still now. Even the rain has retreated.

Finally, my sister A smiles and tells me, "I think she has a crush on you, but be careful. I feel she's not just a nymph, but a nymphomaniac."

We laugh hard. It's funny . . . and it's not.

"Job's not over," C says.

"I'm not sleepy," I reply.

8.

WE MAKE OUR way back to the actual pier where the city is blanketed in a black night sky ignited by stars. No one is on those post-storm wooden slats, which is why I look at C with a question mark in my eyes, but she just grabs my hand and keeps walking the boards. When we get to the farthest part, about a hundred feet out over the ocean, where the tourists stand to take their snaps, I see him.

Clearly.

The boyfriend, young Benny's captor, is about six feet two, truck-driver beefy, and looking out *into* the water as if he hopes to see something familiar like a body he recognizes floating by.

I whisper into C's ear, "He's worried about it now. Saw the cops racing over here, but he's not sure if the boy is alive. When he saw the flashing lights, he ran. But now he's back feeling uncertain. Did he get rid of his problem? Or does "it" still lurk? Was the boy just that one or two percent lucky or did he surrender to the inevitable?"

The man can't rest until he has his answer. He needs some kind of proof.

"How the hell is the sea supposed to tell him?" I snap under my breath.

"He's a kid-hating psychopath. Who knows what he considers proof," I retort.

A continues to whisper. "He needs closure. Like the ending of a movie. He wants the tide to come in and the kid to wash up on shore, so it can be considered an accidental drowning. He also wants to stand on this lofty perch and watch the grand conclusion of his big plan, so he can feel like something was accomplished here tonight. That he did something that couldn't be done to him."

Note: One thing you should never do in front of a kid-hating psychopath is speak out loud.

"Who-who's out there?" he yells into the shadows.

He's not a particularly smart man, which makes him even more dangerous. It doesn't help that he apparently has the hearing of a mongrel dog. He heard every single word A just said—and clearly—which means that now we've discovered the only thing he hates more than little kids.

Women.

A COGNIZANT'S STORY: C

1.

My sister A must be the loudest voyant ever to exist. Even when she thinks she's whispering . . . she's *yelling.*

The deranged Ferryman hears her clearly because he's standing at the top of the pier looking intently and listening hard in order to stay one step ahead of the police. I knew he would be there, but somehow my hunting knife doesn't seem like enough. It's like bringing a can of Raid to blow away Godzilla.

The worst of it is when S starts to cry. "He wants to kill us. He thinks he *can* kill us. What's four more?" she says. "He's murdered five people in three different states. It's just a numbers game to him now."

The interruption of garish carnival music, flipped on to full volume because the rain has now stopped, affords him enough time to advance his plan like only trapped animals do. He moves full-throttle, his large feet pounding those pier boards like he wants to demolish the wood.

When he twists around and coldcocks V in the stomach, I launch forward, but he evades, smashing his forearm into my hand, which causes me to drop the knife. The Claires play a mean mind game, but we're not physical fighters by any means. When S tries to jump on the back of this shitty-smelling gargantuan, he roars back like he's planning to ram her into the rail to break her spine in two. He doesn't count on her jumping off him just in time to fall to the planks below and roll sideways to safety.

"Who the hell are you bitches?" he bellows.

Fifty feet below us, the water is still swirling from the evening's storm and I know a repeat appearance from the nymphs is like begging for that second miracle.

HE'S A SIMPLE man—kill or be killed, trap or be trapped—and I can read him easily. He likes steak, WWE, and women who provide for their kids because then they will also provide for him. He knows enough from watching true crime shows to have disappeared when the cops stormed the pier earlier, but returned now to wait until daylight to dig up the little body, if it was still buried, and make a deeper hole.

Plan B was to finish the job followed by a big country breakfast. Biscuits and gravy. Shit on a shingle.

To celebrate.

He's stupid, but instinctual, which is why the man gazes at us knowing that we're here for a reason. He can't figure out the whys—doesn't much want to either -- so he will just eliminate the possibilities.

I dodge left, but he has survival mode on lock. The killer launches forward until he grips my flesh and spins me around, lifting me by my arm pits and now dangling me over the railing. It's a more than a fifty-foot fall with crashing waves underneath, maybe not enough to kill me, or maybe just enough for some maximum shattering.

"Don't, Ferryman," V warns him and he stops because of the obvious. How do we know his name? I go slack in the wind, my body waving like a sheet of paper. She has raced up now, and launches into his leg, but he easily kicks her away.

When I strike out with both legs and miss, he pulls me closer to savor the win. This rancid-smelling creep hisses, "Ferryman takes them all out into the ocean. Only some return."

He smiles while allowing his fingers to go lax, enjoying the moment as he releases me into the freezing cold drink, one meaty digit at a time.

2.

ARMS OVERHEAD, I shoot through the darkness, an excruciatingly fast descent to my ocean grave. Hands and feet flailing, I brace for impact as I fly back first through nothing but calm night air. Holding my breath, I squeeze my eyes shut until my entire face howls in pain.

But there is no water.

There is no death.

There are only a thump and then flesh as powerful arms catch me before even a drop of ocean mist slides across my bare skin.

He bandies those firm forearms around me, all but cradling me in his arms like a baby. *His baby.* I open my eyes in micro-millimeters. *No, it isn't possible because he defies the laws of science and physics.* I look down and see two black boots hovering in the sky inches above the swirling torrent. In that moment, he twirls a long finger and a fine mist sprays my face. The wet slap reassures me that *no, C, no for the tenth time, this is not a damn hallucination.*

I don't know what he is or what he possesses. All I know is what he is *not.*

He is not of this earth.

We've run into each other several times, in several time periods, always at night, and mostly during the dreadful.

My protector is over six feet five, over two hundred pounds of muscle, and of some sort of mixed race. I once saw him shirtless and he was made of light-black skin covered in light green tats and deep scars. Oh, but the best part was those almost-violet eyes, the color of plums, so unusual that he mostly covers them in the black vintage glasses of a scholar making him look like the geeked-out version of Superman.

No cape, however. He's in his early twenties and wears a long black trench coat tonight and dark, tight jeans with silver chains on his belt. He's not even damp because damp would make sense and, like I said, *his body hovers a few inches above the sea*, although he's not attached to a board or boat. He's just floating, or standing on air. *On his own volition.* I ignore that for a moment to do another scan. Yes, he's still that sturdy with a precise buzz cut revealing an almost bald head that makes him look animalistic and dangerous.

"Claire C, already a bloody legend," he says as those arms grip me tighter.

He still has the formality to him that is as British as his accent.

I'm the stammering American. "My sisters . . . this man . . . and there is the boy. We saved him. But my Claires. He's . . . he's going to kill . . . .," I rush in a breathy voice.

He's looking at me. Really looking. As if I'm the most fascinating creature on the planet. He's reading my mind. Like he did once long ago. It's easier that way. It's why I show him exactly what happened tonight after he locks in with a stare that makes my cheeks flame the brightest of bright red. He is imagining me naked telling him the story. I know it; he does, too.

"Bloody hell," he responds, followed by, "Yes, you did need a save. We all do from time to time. I'm glad you summoned me."

"I did . . . not."

"You did." He winks.

But the time for talking is over.

My erratic heart pounds against his coat while he jettisons both of us up until we're standing on the railing of the pier. Below us, my sisters occupy spaces on the deck where they have been manhandled and thrown. Ferryman stands over the lax body of V.

"I-I'll rush his knees," I begin.

"I got this, Miss Clover" says my fighter, who smiles now. "Enjoy the spectacle."

The rest is beyond reason, well-past bloody, and not a shred merciful.

Yeah, I think he kind of likes me, too, damn it because I don't need this. Love, lust or whatever you want to call it is not in my realm of existence. Not now. Not ever. And why did he have to call me Clover, my full name? Shit. It sounded sexy the way he said it.

Focus!

The man, the child killer, has four cracked ribs thanks to a fist to the gut which blasted him into the corner of the railing, which is partially in the ocean now. My protector could rip his limbs or break his neck, but he smiles at the four of us and decides to embrace...creativity. He begins to blow hard into the distance, which causes the water to roar up. We're spared, but the boyfriend begins to gurgle as the iced liquid is directed from the ocean blue directly down his throat.

I can hear him gasping for air and gurgling loudly as the water becomes too much and fills his lungs. His legs collapse. He's ... drowning. Finally, he slumps over, clutching his throat in pure survival mode as thick wads of seaweed fill his mouth, sealing his fate.

The boyfriend will never torment another boy. He falls forward onto his face onto the weathered slats. I count it down. One ... two ... three ... ten.

The storm. It's over.

THE CLAIRES

3.

He is kind enough to take out the trash.

In the pale moonlight, I see what looks like an unattached arm and just one leg floating in the momentarily calm sea. It's better described as chum, really, for the night feeders, rushing out to the horizon with their late-night snacks. It's an ancient truth: whatever is done in this realm washes out to the sea. Humans aren't always buried. Sometimes they just roll away.

By the time I lock eyes with the helpful one, he's got a satisfied look on his face and a calling card.

"Street justice," he explains, "is my trade."

He bows slightly to the other girls. Then he speaks again. In our entire history, he has said less than a hundred words to me, but each one is provoking. Maybe, I have a little book. Perhaps, I've written them down. Not that I dwell on this kind of thing.

"How wonderful that God created the mountains, ocean, and stars. Then he gave us you, sweet Clover, because he knew the world needed one of those, too."

"Victoria, Sophia and Alice, enjoy your night," he caps it off with nods to the rest.

Running toward the end of the pier, he barely touches my arm before turning his back and racing forward until he jumps over the railing.

There is a moment of silence punctuated by gentle laps and no crash.

"You saw that?" A whispers. "Cause there was that big handsome man in a long coat."

"We've seen him before. He wore the same coat," V says. "Maybe trench coats are so plentiful where he comes from and he could lend me one."

I give her the look.

"Remember two lifetimes ago when he showed up to help us. He said in that British accent and I quote, 'Excuse me ladies, but it's easier if I'm starkers. Don't mean to offend.' Then he took his clothes off," A recalls. "Bod of steel."

"Ah, the memories. I feel them. Down to my toes. I feel him...." S chimes in. "Down. To. My. Toes. All ten of them."

"I heard you the first time," I reply. "We should go. Before the night needs any additional street justice."

"Yes, sweet Clover," S torments me.

4.

THE MAN WHO caught me...

His name is Emin and he works between the hours of midnight until four. You could call it the night shift. In the spirit world, the day is just beginning.

There have been many lovely evenings in times past where he has just shown up to offer his assistance. Am I summoning something that majestic? I had/have no clue.

I looked up his first name once—the only name I had for him because he kissed my hand two lifetimes ago and told me—and found that, historically speaking, there was an Emin Pasha of Germany who was one of the greatest adventurers of the Ottoman Empire. I don't know if there is any relation or reincarnation, but I dare to dream.

I say his name once, twice, into the air.

It's a basic thank you for the assist – nothing more.

He is gone, but the wind lifts the ends of my hair until the tips brush over my parted lips.

THE CLAIRES

5.

Evening Wrap Up Filed: The news will report in the morning that the couple who tried to kill that precious little boy took off to parts unknown. There were supposed sightings of them in Phoenix and Vegas, but that was just fan fiction from weirdoes who dwell on the comings and goings of these kind of low lives. There is an active ongoing search on for them, but they haven't been located – and might I add, they never will be.

The bodies will never be found, but that sweet boy will find the most loving, grateful adoptive family.

As for his mother and her main squeeze …

Sometimes karma leaves no forwarding address.

As for us …

The Claires. We go on—somewhere between psychotic and iconic.

CASS

The Next Night

1.

She has two good friends and they live in the Valley and Beverly Hills, which in this light, misty fog means two words: road trip. Between swearing at other drivers—"You stupid SOB, learn how to drive"—I am given too much time to think. And thinking is dangerous, especially in my condition.

Post bullet wound, Dad kept me drugged pretty much the entire next day, but then my fog lifted. And after a good meal or two, I found clarity and my Jeep keys. I also found a white-hot anger in my gut that was threatening to detonate once and for all.

I despise them. And by them, I mean my sisters, but that has always been the case.

It began with simple play sessions when I was five and they were four. One minute we were playing, the next I was pretend sleeping and C put a pillow over my face until I was choking and gasping for air because I was *dying*.

"Honey, don't tease your brother," Dad would say with a laugh. And then he turned on me like a rabid dog, "You gonna let some girls beat you up? Toughen up, kid. She's the girl." Another breath: "Don't ever put hands on your sisters or any other girls." There was no winning. I would never purposely hurt any female, but this was different. These were alpha bitches from another planet.

There have been times when I've wished—with every molecule of my being—that they would simply vanish. When I was younger, this involved UFO kidnapping. And when that Meryl Streep movie came into our DVD collection, a more realistic, if not natural way of them "leaving" came to mind. "A dingo ate my sisters," I'd say and they would glare in a way that made me wonder if they would

THE CLAIRES

spontaneously turn into four rabid rats that would eat me.

"We don't live in Australia, asswipe," V would say. "There are no dingoes in Santa Monica, California although maybe we should import a few. Imagine our backyard gladiator games with real live beasts and the smelly beast that lives here, meaning you, Cass."

Freshman year of high school, I was nervous about a new school and making grades. That morning before Dad drove me, I put on my best boots and found myself sinking into something foul, cold, and rancid smelling. They had cleaned all the surrounding yards and filled my footwear halfway up with dog shit from various breeds. The note attached to my shoe read: "Have a shitty day, Ass."

I guess every sibling has entertained the idea of being sibling-less, as in: What if I were the only one? What if they just found another family? What if it was some sick joke and they never really belonged with us in the first place? I've felt this way since I was five and then again at age 16 after some heinous night when I asked the million-dollar question: Did quads or even twins run in the Danko family. The answer was no.

As we aged, we tested the limits of sibling rivalry. It was an unseasonably hot summer day when at ages ten and nine, they ganged up, all four, to push me to the bottom of our pool. And then they waited . . . one minute, tick, tick, tick. All four of them pushing down on my arms, my head, and C holding my feet, thus forming a force field between me and a deep breath. They were uncommonly strong and had eight arms and eight legs to my two of each appendage. My mother must have had a sixth sense about my thrashing and dove in. Immediately, they released me.

"Mommy, we were just playing a game—Duck, Duck, Cass," V said, shrugging it off like a harmless *misunderstanding*. I preferred to think of it as attempted murder.

As I choked, gasped, and sputtered on the deck, it was V who smiled, insisting, "I could see your future and sadly for us, dear big brother . . . you are still alive."

"Better luck to us next time," C capped it off.

They were like those night creatures you read about it books. The dark was their favorite time to prowl. Later that same almost DOA night, I was almost asleep when something caught my eye. The moon hit the mirrored glass of my closet door. A blink or two later and my eyes went wide when I saw that the door was slowly moving from closed to open. I was so used to spirits of the dead visiting me in the middle of the night, I didn't scream. I did sit straight up like an arrow and waited. The seconds that followed were painful ones as adrenalin-fueled anxiety raced through my blood. And then the closet door slid the rest of the way open with a hard crash that almost made the whole panel skip the tracks.

It wasn't that spirits were hiding in there. My four bitch sisters were sitting on the floor laughing their evil little asses off.

C skipped over to my bed and jumped into it. "We weren't kidding, Cass," C said. "You better tell Daddy that what happened in the pool was your idea of a game. Don't screw with us. There are so many ways for us to kill you. Beheading in the middle of the night comes to mind. Our dear A knows a few Vikings."

They weren't normal girls. They were vultures.

"Consider this your warning," V piped in. "If you want to live your short life in peace -- and a short life I promise you it will be, then don't F with us."

"Now, you're doing future predictions. You have a crystal ball in your head," I said.

"We'll witness your death, too, which will be a shining day," she carped. "It will happen in a big city and . . . well, that's enough foreshadowing for now. I don't want to be a plot spoiler."

Sister A grabbed my hand because she was one of the nicer ones. When I struggled, she squeezed harder until she lifted my palm to the thin shaft of light pouring in my bedroom window from the street lamp outside. "Yes, so sad. A very short lifetime as sister said," she confirmed. "But, not so tragically, because there is so much more if you just keep an open …"

"You're a monkey dancing on a razor blade, A," V snapped at her sister, which shut her up mid-sentence. This was unusual because they never fought in front of others in order to keep the pack tight.

"In other words, shut up, bitch?" A says to herself.

"Shut up, bitch," C confirms

Nothing would please me more than to rid the world of them. But bad people rarely got what was coming to them. They just spread the pain in waves until the good people were throbbing as they fought for their lives.

2.

I find Annie at her friend Becca Monroe's house in the plush 90210 zip, Beverly Hills. We know each other from school, or used to before Bec's father hit it big in the movie business, producing something about mutant reptiles and cashed in for non-ending sequels. They moved to Beverly.

A knock on the door and fashionista Bec, in some sort of flowing pink kimono, doesn't say a word. She just opens the door wide because she was expecting me and I duck under her fabric flowing arm. "Yeah, honey, she's here," Bec says. "Good luck."

And there she is . . . standing in the hallway like nothing has changed although everything is different now. Annie looks no worse for wear in a black gauzy dress with a worn jean jacket over it, leggings and shit kicking boots. It's like she's wearing half her wardrobe, so she doesn't have to pack it. She asks if we can be alone and it's easy because this white stone mansion has about a million rooms.

"I'll be in the great room," Bec says.

To me, they're all seemingly great rooms.

Annie and I are awkward at first, eyes on toes, but some of it feels familiar like a warm blanket.

"Well, look at you," she says in a low, tinny voice.

"Well, look at you, sugar," I say as I stare at tile so expensive it could probably pay for my college education. I hate that she does this nervous thing with her hands. *It's me, Annie. Why the stress attack?* I have so much to say, but we can't find two or three words to start it. So, we sit outside on a quaint front porch swing with enough overhang to keep us dry while we silently watch the drops of yet another spring downpour fall from the sky. It's nice; it's awful. It's everything.

Annie has no answers on her lips, but they're in her warm, now wary, eyes. I just sit and stop her from rocking by placing my feet firmly on the ground. One of us has to bring this back to ground level. The lack of sway catches her attention because it's always easier to fidget than focus.

She cuts to it.

"I don't know. I really don't know, Cass. I think so . . . but maybe not," she says about the idea of a baby. *Our baby.* "I missed my period, but it's only two weeks late. I'm too afraid to check. I'm paralyzed even thinking about knowing because it changes everything, so it's easier not to know. Do you know what I mean?"

Fat tears begin to a slow slide down her cheeks.

Here is what I don't tell her: My sisters might take a shot in the dark about certain things, but not about something this big. There must be some shred of truth. But, for some reason, it doesn't worry me. I don't think of it as a disaster. It's just new, so it feels odd. When

THE CLAIRES

I let it settle, it makes me ... happy. I know that's not the right answer at our ages, but it's my answer.

I try to convince her that the first step is knowing, but she'd rather exist in the question. At least for now.

Little lines on tests will make it too real for her. Since her mother left, Annie prefers to exist in the world of romance books and fantasy movies. She'd much rather visit Middle Earth than real Earth, especially if the topic concerns the reality show of her own daily existence.

Just touching her hand, I know that even the idea of a baby is beyond her mental pay grade. Annie is someone who has never-ending debates about mushroom v. onions on a pizza or Netflix v. Hulu and not babies v. freedom.

Maybe the timing wasn't great. Maybe we didn't have our own home. Or any money. Or much of a future at this point. We were young, but people had babies when they were as undeveloped as us.

We'd be two joy-seeking, future-morphing fools with a little madman or madwoman by our side.

I beam at her because it's us, and there is a lot of right here, too. I love her on a deep level, and that's the reality I've been avoiding. My heart versus getting it squashed.

There is no time like now. I hand my heart over and hope she is ready for the catch.

"I love you, Ann. I've always loved you," I tell her. "I have nothing else to offer you, but me. Just like tonight I'll always be right here with you. Just like always. And always it will be."

I search her eyes, and it doesn't take long before I hear what I need.

"I love you, too, Cass. For good. For keeps. For life," she says and puts her hand on top of mine. I put my other hand on top. She echoes it and does the same thing. Then, I lean down and press a light kiss on her lips to seal it.

Someday, we would remember this moment and it would seem almost cinematic with the rain and sliver of moonlight. We'd replace the words "in trouble" with "in rebellion." And we'd be glad for the whole damn thing.

Her eyes flash undeniably happy for a minute, but they don't drown in mine. I have no choice, but to follow her gaze as she scans the horizon like a dog looking for a weak spot in a fence to slip through, so she can run.

"I'm going to go far from here," she says. "I didn't want to tell you. I wanted to get gone first—and then let you know. I can't do this life here anymore."

"We can't do these lives anymore," I insist as I listen for some aspect of this plan that actually includes me in it. If she won't put me in, I'll do it myself. "That's why we will go. I thought about it on the way over here. I have about $1000 in my account. I took it out yesterday from the bank and it's in the glove compartment of the truck. It's not much, but it will take care of . . ."

She shakes her head wildly. "I don't want to be taken care of—not anymore, not at all," she blurts out, standing up. In that one abrupt action, our hands unseal and fall.

Her words aren't registering. I keep grabbing for plans, but I can see that my words are floating away into nothingness. "What if I go with you to get you settled. Just for a little bit," I offer, knowing I might be able to turn a little into a lot. "What if we move to Seattle or Oregon or even Alaska. We'll dance under the Northern Lights and—"

Annie turns to place her hands on the sides of my face.

"You have the best heart I've ever seen. You're the best friend I'll ever know," she says. The friend part stings. Then burns. Then aches.

"Don't I get some say in it?"

She pulls the box out of the deep pocket. It's one of those home pregnancy kits, which means my future depends on a sliver of plastic. She motions for me to stay here while she goes to the bathroom. I begin to follow her, which is the worst possible thing because she can't breathe.

"Sorry."

"I know. You can't help it. I'm the only one who can."

She moves back into the house for what seems like forever while I wait outside on the grass wanting to scream. I look at my watch every second until ten actual minutes have passed. I pace, chewing holes in that earth until finally a figure emerges from the front door. She's back, waving something in the air. It's the pregnancy testing stick.

"All good," she says, handing it to me. Before I can look down, she grabs a bag that's stashed in the dark behind one of the front evergreens. I feel the sink of disappointment. "I'm going," she says. "Please don't follow me."

Words won't form as the knife twists in my chest and gut. "Wait, Annie," I say. But it's too late. I see a car pull up in the driveway. She called an Uber from inside the house, and suddenly my future is barreling at me.

I trail after her, but she's walking fast now. I'm talking to her back as I begin to list all the reasons she needs to stay. It doesn't matter if there is no baby. We can still be together. We can still be us.

By now, she has her essentials in one hand and a wildly elated look of freedom on her face.

"Annie, we need . . ." I begin. "Can we sit again?"

"Tell my father that you looked for me. That I might be in Malibu with some friend from school. Buy me a few days to figure it out—and get far. I'll be in touch."

My words are cut off as she stops, turns, and impulsively kisses my forehead. "I guess we tested fate," she whispers into my ear. "I'll never regret it. In fact, I just did it again."

The words are just tumbling.

"You did…what?" I ask her.

My equilibrium off-kilter, I watch her walk into the distance. And then I stand there for several minutes while my life without Annie officially begins. One, second, two, three. Time is like ocean waves. Unstoppable, it moves us on as it always does, even when your heart has been removed from your chest and beaten into the dirt.

Bec is outside by now, and she's offering kind and useless words about it all working out one day and how lasting love is always tested. Her experience with lasting love: zilch.

Her pink dress dances in the wind.

"So, it was true," she says. "Sorry, Cass."

She's staring at my hand, which is dead at my side.

I'm not often this confused. "What?"

A quick glimpse down at the plastic stick in my right hand and I can't breathe. There is a pink plus sign. In case you're a total moron, it also tells you in words.

Pregnant.

By not looking down, I missed it. But that was life. Moments swinging one way or the other based on what we did see…and what we didn't.

3.

For the next three days, I drive the lonely man's highway, living in the car, stopping at gas stations to refuel and pee and then checking out spots that seem reasonable. If she ever mentioned it and it was

THE CLAIRES

around here, it's worth a stop. And then I'm off, merging with the rest of the seekers, on the way to the next probable location. I was aging rapidly behind that wheel. My emotions were like erosion.

The last night with $40 in my pocket, I buy doughnuts and stay in a cheap motel near San Diego. The TV doesn't work, and the black screen gives me entirely too much time to think. I banish all thoughts of Annie, which opens my mind to murderous thoughts concerning my sisters.

I will never forget what they did to me . . . everything they did that was either evil or lurid. The last part belonged exclusively to V.

I push that night away whenever it comes to mind, which isn't often because I won't allow it. It's just that on a still night in a strange place -- where no one knows you and doesn't really care if you evaporate into nothing -- the strangest thoughts float between your lobes.

I was sleeping for hours, naked under my bed sheet, because Dad kept the air conditioning at a broiling 85 degrees. Somewhere, surfing the middle of a dream, I heard something that brought me almost all the way back. It sounded like a door moaning on its hinges. Or maybe it was a window that wasn't exactly down. A hiss of air. A snap. Something was in my room . . . and it was real.

Or perhaps it was Them. Of course. It must have been the arrival of some pain in the ass spirit visitor ruining my chances to throw that game winning basket for the Lakers.

I opened one eye, just a bit, and in the haze of being barely conscious, I saw her.

Sexy. She wore a sheer nightgown that left absolutely nothing to the imagination although her face was blurred by shadows that she seemed to bring with her. Long fingers painted a faint pink slid the tender strap off a bony shoulder and then the other until the paper-thin dress pooled at her feet like a satin cloud.

"Close your eyes," she whispered.

It was easy to comply because it was exactly what I wanted. Then, she came closer, ran the tips of her fingers over my chest, and murmured. "It will be just like that night on the beach."

I felt chills as she trailed a finger up my neck and up until she traced the outline of my bottom lip. Slowly, like she was made of air, she moved my sheet and slid in next to me. Then she leaned over and silky, honey scented hair fell on my face; her warm lips pressed to mine.

"Mmmmmm," I moaned in my sleepy fog. I felt her. Visions didn't feel like this and I couldn't believe that Annie was doing this… and I loved it.

She licked the side of my ear and then whispered into it, "Do you think about it?"

"Always, sugar," I whispered. "Ever since that night."

She moaned.

My body began to respond, but then something odd happened. Ice began to form in my stomach, spreading upward to my chest and then it clutched in my throat. A cold feeling of dread began to permeate my entire being, which was why I forced my eyes to open. Wide.

My sister V was straddling my naked body. She slid down, touching below and then saying words that made no sense: "One hundred years a virgin, but no more. Do you hear me, Patriarch? Do you hear me? If I get pregnant, you cannot kill me."

Revulsion raced from my stomach to my throat.

"What the fuck?" I yelled, sitting straight up.

V ran a hand through my hair, placing my hand on her breast.

"Haven't you thought about it? Dreamt about it? I can't stop thinking about it."

"Are you out of your mind! You're my sister," I roared, shoving both hands to her waist. "Get the fuck out, you God damn freak!"

I lifted her off me and dropped her on the hardwood floor, hoping *she'd fall through the creaking floor boards to the center of the earth. After, I vaulted out of bed and then showered with the water turned to almost boiling.*

Every trace. I would remove every hint.

Just thinking about it now makes me want to full-throttle run away from myself. Grabbing my keys, I'm back in the car speeding wildly through the darkness of the Big Bear mountain range. Annie once said that she wanted to live in a cabin in the woods. I wondered how many cabins I'd have to check.

Staring into a blank canvas of night, I keep seeing V's face, but I blink her away.

You can't outrace a memory, but with the windows open blasting cold and your foot goading the limit on the gas, you can sure as hell try.

4.

OUR HOUSE IN Santa Monica at dawn is tomb quiet when I return alone three days later. Dad has put one of those sticky notes on the fridge with some scrawling writing on it about how he left three twenty dollar bills on the counter and how my sisters are gone for the next five days doing their spring break ocean project in Monterey. My parents are MIA, too, because Mom is having tests at the Mayo Clinic in Phoenix.

Dad could surprise me in the most unlikely ways. He wrote:

HEYA Cass: Just take a deep breath. We'll find Annie. Stay away from Gene. Keep your chin untucked. I love you, son.

I believe that no matter what, he actually does.

A SENTIENT'S STORY: S

1.

I'M GOING TO tell you exactly what happened on the plane: I almost lost my mind.

One hour of sleep (we didn't roll back into the house until 3:00 a.m. from a nightly prowl) combined with frantic packing and an unwanted visit from our Ma didn't help with my PTFD – Post Traumatic Family Disorder. I felt what could only be described as her intense pain. A wouldn't stop talking, frantically providing messages that Ma was sending as she went on and on and *on, about real estate*. V and C put their heads under thick feather pillows, earbuds firmly in, to try to drown her out, but unlucky me. Did I ever mention that I suffer from insomnia?

"She's demanding to know, 'Are you listening to me? I mean *her*,'" A told us.

"Yeah, Ma, with two sleeping ears, I'm hanging on every word," V grumbled. "Tell her that I'm turning Nirvana up to 10 to drown all y'all out."

"Ma says, 'Don't sass me,'" A related. "She said and I quote from the great beyond, 'You must listen and learn about our New York ancestral home.'"

"She says, 'Remember what I told you about our original property, circa 1911, in very old NYC, because this place contains *it*,'" said my sister.

We needed to find it – if it still existed because the last time Ma was there was at the turn of the century.

"Ask her, 'What is it, Ma?'" I said in my snot-laced voice. At this point, we go around and around via A.

Ma doesn't know exactly what it is—this thing to be found—

because her mother, Penny, had tucked it away so safely (good move), but never told anyone what it was or where it was (really, Granny?) "She says, 'Your grandmother knew that she had defied the Patriarch and the Order in the New World. She knew her days were numbered,'" A informed us. "At the same time, she had been begging the Patriarch for the real reasons her daughter was slated to die at age seventeen."

"He wrote her a letter saying that he had placed a curse upon Ma and any of her 'hopefully non-existing' future children, meaning us – a multi-layered curse," A informed us. "Gran knew the particulars of the curse, but didn't want Ma to know ….as if not knowing would enrich the years she had on the planet. Since she had defied the Patriarch and lived beyond age 17, he added layers to his curse to make sure it would never happen again."

"Gran said that any future generations would have to look for the origins of this curse -- if they were hopeful about living long lives," A said, adding, "Ma knows the answers are in or around our ancestral home in New York. She said we must go there. To live!'"

I had to live, sure, but first I had to pee, which she didn't appreciate. Quietly, A knocked on the door to inform me, "Ma said to tell all of us to be very careful and trust no one there, whatever that means. And she said to brush your teeth. Good night.'"

I cannot connect with the dead, but I feel our mother's dread as it drifts through the decades.

2.

CUT TO AN emotionally torpid time at LAX airport. Fun fact: There are 167 seats on our 737 and each one holds a body with their own emotional melodrama playing out in real time. For me, the one who dials into others' emotions, it's one huge sniffle bag of life's greatest hits. The guy in 3D is getting divorced from a real playa. Yep, she has a much younger boyfriend, poor dude. The woman in 7A just got engaged, but she doesn't really love him. Sad that 15 E just got canned at work. 3B is flying to NYC to talk about a gender reassignment. Then there's us—row 16.

A small mechanical problem leaves an hour on board at the gate to remember the emotional cesspool of the morning. Just standing in the security line, I felt a man in front of me dripping nervousness (medical tests), the woman with her heart heavy (missing her kids), and that young man shipping out (fear and adrenalin). The life stories kept hitting me like hundreds of tiny slaps. Even the sweetly round TSA agent with the big bandage on her arm who felt me up had her own woes: bankruptcy, foreclosure, relationship turns . . . *yeah, she took the kids and was hiding out at her friend Jean's house in Encino because he really shouldn't have hit her.*

"No one should hit you," I say while she gives me a double-take.

"How do you . . ."

"He will do it again, so go home and clean out the house now. Take all your things. Pack the kid's stuff," I told her while she shook her head convulsively. Like she was in a daze. You're not supposed to touch a TSA agent, but I put a finger on her bandage to snap her out of it. I began to nod, too, and she got it.

Truth always cut through bullshit, and it amazed me how women always knew when someone was telling them what I call "the actuallys." I called V over and she filled in the rest.

"Actually, you have a few hours until he gets there. He's at a bar now getting good and drunk before he tries to pound down your friend Jean's front door," V said. "Go now. Say you're sick. But go."

With those words, and a shout to her supervisor, she was gone. No questions asked – and no doubts either that we were telling her the truth. Sometimes you just know.

Our first good deed of the day, and damn it felt good down to my toes. I felt invisible life points being put into my equally invisible account.

When I shivered, V took it the wrong way.

"Keep it steady, honey," V begged me while rubbing my arms.

She always knew. It's odd what nags at you . . . and what you let slide.

It was spring break. Mid-April to be exact.

Eight more months to live this life.

And I wasn't ready to flip the off switch.

3.
AN AUDIENT'S STORY: A

THE NIGHT BEFORE the trip, we did couch and contemplation at the apartment we keep secret from our parents for obvious reasons, starting with the fact that they were parents.

It was my job to sit quietly in my favorite yoga pose in the spiritual corner where we placed fat, white, flickering candles on the deep mahogany floor of our mostly undecorated living room. There was no time or space to contact a Viking lover or a martial arts master looking for nightly lodging. Isn't that how the romance books would write it? Lost Irish warrior with cutting cheekbones named Liam who just needed....

"A, really?" V says. "I can feel you panting. Keep your mind on business."

As I said or was about to say after dismissing some lean Roman conquering type, less was more when trying to contact the spirit world to pick their dead minds. I wouldn't call it stalking. It was more like binge researching on the true dark Web.

C. L. GABER

The location was certainly conducive to some ghostly interactions. The Hollywood Tower Apartments—our unofficial, but actually official home away from home—had been a Hollywood icon since they opened the place in 1929. Even the architecture seemed Goth with a V-shaped building, ten stories high, that made the place look like a cream- colored French Normandy castle located on a small hill.

On a clear night, you could see most of the main drag when it came to Hollywood Boulevard including the cars filled with actors, actresses, writers, and dreamers all. So many rich, broke, living on fumes, and infamous names had called the place home, at least for a little while, including Humphrey Bogart, whose spirit I ran into once at the mailbox. Guy could never find his key. Vintage beauty Carmen Miranda, who got married in the building's lobby, reenacted the ceremony almost daily at dusk. I didn't mind that or the fact that our little pad was also the inspiration for the Tower of Terror ride at Disneyland.

On second thought: maybe that wasn't a good omen.

For sixteen hundred dollars a month, we could rent our own freedom in the form of a studio apartment, which was enough room for an overstuffed couch, plus a spiritual area in the corner where I had the above-mentioned purple yoga mat, several brightly colored pillows from T.J. Maxx, and hundreds of large candles, some real and others with batteries and fake, fluttering wicks.

We couldn't afford to burn the place down and were sensitive about flames since fire was one of the demons of our collective pasts. We remembered it all—the flames licking fresh skin as our first home burned around us until all that was left was four charred beds with dead bodies in them. The smoke did a silent job of taking care of that lifetime. One final, dramatic curtain call. It was a birthday present from the dear Patriarch.

But that was then.

THE CLAIRES

The big, churning spirit world could sense I was as open as a broad summer sky tonight, which is why I heard loud ringing in my ears and an almost constant buzzing, like they were pushing some invisible doorbell again and again and again. Spirits were like children in that they had no "wait" mechanism. When they came at me in needy droves, like now, it would change the pressure in my head and cause my ears to pop.

Tonight, the popping was like a machine gun going off. Their whisperings collected and turned into some kind of loud gibberish like thousands of conversations taking place all at the same time. So many needed attention and all came knocking with their urgent messages for loved ones. In many ways, it was like I had a remote in my head. I could easily mute the ones I didn't want to hear and "tune into" the one that intrigued me. It wasn't their choice; it was mine. The power of it made me feel everything from euphoric to guilty beyond.

I began to talk to myself. *Breathe in. Breathe out. Clear my mind . . . A small tinkling bell . . . No, it's not a bell, but the very distant sound of metal on metal. Bang! Bang! Bang! When I listen more closely, it sounds like a hollow metal object like a cup hitting . . . steel bars.*

Grandma. Granny. The OG. She got mad if I called her by her rightful name, Penny, because I guess it was sewn into that dirty grey prison costume she deplored. She preferred Grandmother. Either way, she sounded worlds away, and like our dear first mother could only be heard, but never seen. Her words floated in my mind in only the most excruciating times, which obviously meant that impending doom was close. All of us sisters had some sort of disaster-waiting button in us like phones have call waiting.

"Child," Grandmother said, "*I hope all is well for ye. I wish you to travel and travel well to our family land in New York proper where there is something vital waiting.*"

"Got it," I said in low voice, followed by the ask. "Grams, it would be nice if we had time for a proper chat, but just in case I lose you, technically and spiritually speaking, it would be most helpful to have a few clues regarding this thang we're supposed to find."

"Silence!" she commanded. I could hear chains in the background. "For what is to be found cannot be told, but must be discovered."

"One more time for the cheap seats," I replied.

"You will go to the home that burned. Charlatans built a new one that looks exactly like the old. You will absorb the energy of the land and find your destiny," she said in a quivering voice. "More cannot be said in case there are open ears belonging to closed minds."

Really? Destinies were involved. Ears, living and dead, are listening? Could we pass this test? Did we work for her? Or did she work for us? A valid question.

Since 1911, I knew one thing: When you didn't understand parents you just went along with the dance.

"Destiny. Charlatans. On top of it," I said. "All over it."

"If ye are weak of mind and will, I will see you on this side to wish you a happy seventeenth birthday and death day," she said. "I will greet all of you with the sorrow of the centuries."

Not the sorrows-of-the-centuries guilt trip. Not again.

She was going for the big.

AND THEN SHE was gone, along with the flames of about ten candles whose flickers went into the vastness with her. I could feel my sisters staring hard at me, so I gave them the short version of my little trek into the spirit world with way-distant relatives.

"Gran is still excelling at making absolutely no sense combined

THE CLAIRES

with vague threats of our total extinction. Apparently, we're supposed to go back to where she was pickled and where Ma gave birth to us. She hid something she cannot put into words ... in case of prying ears.

"It's one of those find your destiny things wrapped in a riddle and touched by an enigma, yet only found if you are worthy," I said. "So, pass the Pop Tarts."

"I got the address from Ma last week," V filled in the rest. "Said that she didn't hide anything and that her Ma was always slinking around the house doing weird shit like slipping notes that made no sense between bricks . But paper notes will do us no good. The house has burned several times and has been built as an exact replica again and again.

"Ma had no clue regarding what we're supposed to find because she didn't believe in her Ma's crazy old-world magic – but now she does," I said. "Famous last words."

3.
A COGNANT'S STORY: C

"Buckle up, babies," I told my sisters somewhere midflight. I knew where the turbulence was (over Illinois into Ohio – thunderstorms brewing) far before the pilot spotted it on some lame radar. Unfortunately, I also knew that the fruit plate that they were selling was sold out. And old (as in three days molting). Starvation would enter into it.

Somewhere over the bump-shake-and-rattle of being 30,000 feet over Illinois, I mulled over our last day of school before spring break because it was infuriating to say the very least. Sixth period gym class was bad enough, but equally horrifying was the idea that we had to change into ugly maroon shorts and a blinding yellow school tee because the administration clearly worried about sweat leaving the gym area. The truth is they should have been concerned with school colors that made it look like we were prisoners in an upscale mental asylum.

When I returned from a barely carb burning period of volleyball, I opened my locker only to find out that someone had taken all of my clothes and my purse. Pranks were all the rage at school this year including covering all the hallway floors with bubble wrap and removing the top center drawer of every teacher's desk (thanks Rylan and friends). The seniors even swapped their entire class with another senior class at a nearby high school. But it was different with my sisters and I. Instead of not knowing who did it, and chalking it up to end of the school year restlessness, we knew *exactly* who was doing what and why and where.

I found my clothes in the back dumpster and couldn't put them back on thanks to the rancid smell. Wearing my gym clothes for the rest of the day drew snickers in the hallway. I wouldn't allow it to be served as the prank of the week, so I went to my sister V to concoct something for the ages.

V, who was a tech whiz, helped me snap several pictures of the school, inside and out, and then we listed it on the MLS as a building for sale. Don't worry because we also put it up on Zillow and all the other home sale sites. On each, we listed our principal as the real estate agent and also published his private cell phone number. The best part? We listed the school for a whopping price of $25 or best offer. Several foreign countries called the number.

We also listed our principal's house for sale…and said that his wife was also available. Her price, we listed, was negotiable.

THE CLAIRES

Oh, the fun and frolic of high school. There was no time to dwell on these rites of passage.

On the plane, I decided upon on our course of action after we were wheels down at approximately 2:12 p.m. (Our gate wouldn't be ready and we'd sit on the tarmac for exactly 17 minutes and 30 seconds. I knew this now.)

Once sprung, we would go to the Marriott in the city, dump our stuff and then venture out the next morning to find our past. I didn't need Google to figure out how to get there. And the best news was the house was actually there. Luckily, the structure wasn't covered by some ten-story condo unit, but was actually some sort of historically protected piece of architecture with a twist.

Damn thing had burned down five times over the years since our first demise in 1928. Each time it was rebuilt with great precision to erect an exact replica of the original to preserve what the current locals described as "colonial history." No, it wasn't the original structure, but humans were nostalgic, so they took great pains to make it look identical. Gran told us that some of the spirits actually appreciated their efforts. If it felt old and familiar, they would camp there. Stay a while. Haunt the place.

It followed that tourists who spent their days roaming through the past noted that they trembled when they walked in the small front door made out of pine from the trees in the nearby woods Pine that refused to burn. Strangely, each time the house was ablaze, one of the only artifacts that survived was the original front door, which was simply repainted and reattached.

What other surprises were left from the distant past? The

brochure boasted that several pieces of original furniture mysteriously made their way onto the lawn during the blazes along with several glass and hand-crafted tchotchkes that had been found in the front or back lawns and placed once again into the small home.

I was sure that between me and V, once we were there-there, we could figure out where exactly the prize family memento was hidden by Gran over a hundred years ago.

If it was still there. If it survived all of those fires.

If it endured the harsh weather of brutal winters and searing hot summers.

If it eluded the greedy hands of tourists looking to bring home a reminder of days long since gone.

If.

There had to be a clue in there that could lead to heady, untouchable milestones: graduating high school, college, falling in love, marriage, children, and becoming ornery old ladies who were called witches . . . which brought us back to ground zero.

Oh, how delicious it all sounded.

One question remained: What if that bastard Patriarch of the Paranormal had made damn sure that anything left by our first dear mother's mother would be gone, as in forever destroyed by forces in England with their long reach and ocean voyages here to be sure that a *clair* heir wouldn't try to topple their dynasty?

And, what if something old and dangerous was lying in wait, knowing there would be a day when we would come looking. What if they considered that a time for a reckoning?

"Buckle up," the first flight attendant announced. "We're starting our initial descent."

Truer words had never been spoken.

NEW YORK – 1925

C. L. GABER

1.

It was the Roaring Twenties, days of economic prosperity known as the *annees folles* or the crazy years that coined the phrase, "The last of the big-time spenders." Jazz music blasted from our radios and the 14-year-old Claire sisters of that era used the extra money we had from our side hustle of street corner future predictions to buy sparkling white and silver flapper outfits.

S, the book worm who preferred pages to people, practically flew on air that April when she got her hot little hands on F. Scott Fitzgerald's new masterpiece, "The Grapes of Wrath." We could barely rip the thing out of her hands even when Ma bought us our first ever car, a big dream boat called a Chrysler, because travel by horse was just so old-fashioned, plus your car didn't need hay and daily brushings.

She would drive us around at night with all of us dressed to the nines, tens and elevens. One soft summer evening in the big city, we even stopped at a place called The Cotton Club at 142nd St & Lennox Avenue in the heart of Harlem. It was owned and operated by this gangster named Owney Madden who came to our house at least once a week to ask Ma if he would be shot in the next three days. (She saved him so many times because when she said "yes," he simply failed to show up anywhere).

Uncle Owney rushed us through the back door and even gave us a taste of his Number One, a homemade libation known as beer, despite the fact that the government had declared that alcohol was illegal during this time of Prohibition.

The big man liked when Ma stopped by because discreetly she would point out the government agents infiltrating in plain clothes

THE CLAIRES

in order to shut Owney down. One night, Ma took a wrong turn after letting us dance for an hour. We ended up in a back alley where those government types she pointed out were positioned face up and tied up in the middle of the street. I watched as Owney himself revved up his big black car and ran them over, backed up, and then did it again. Ma tucked us in that night and whispered, "Just because you give the information doesn't mean you own the outcome."

We didn't have time to dwell, although A saw a few of those men in her dreams trying to pass on messages to next of kin.

There were too many diversions interrupting what could have been an idyllic childhood if most of the town and all of the children hadn't shunned us. But the bigwigs loved their time spent with tea and Ma in our small kitchen.

One night, John Davison Rockefeller Sr. came knocking on our door, which just about knocked my socks off. He was a Richie-rich, an American oil industry tycoon who was the wealthiest American of the time. In the aftermath of World War 1, the United States became a financial mecca, which meant that businessmen frequented Ma's house late at night to talk wheeling and dealing. (He would ask our Ma about the futures of his five children including his four daughters and his beloved son John Jr.)

"Make sure to enjoy the prosperity now," said C. "Disaster is brewing." Yes, it was a Claire who predicted the Wall Street Crash of 1929, which would end the era of ease and plunge the country into the Great Depression. We would die long before that happened only later to be reborn as infants to a farm family. We were in small cribs by the time men and women started jumping out of tall buildings.

New York was booming, but not without upheaval. It was the police chief who was in turmoil. He knocked on our door just a few years earlier to ask Ma who exactly set off a bomb in Wall

Street. A horse-drawn wagon filled with 100 pounds of dynamite detonated at 12:01 p.m. marking one of the first acts of terrorism on American soil. All attempts to track down the maker of the shoes of the horse went bone dry. "I want names," said the police chief, a man of few words, but with several gold bars. "We have leads that point to that famous tennis player because he …."

"No, he's simply mentally ill, but he's not the bomber," said Ma, who looked deep into her tea leaves for this one. That night, she was a bit perplexed and called upon V and C to sit by her side. Together, they held hands and formed a force of three. "It was an anarchist," C said. "Perhaps a follower of Italian anarchist leader Luigi Galleani who sent those horrible letter bombs to politicos." V stopped her, but agreed that the Galleanists were likely suspects. "Mario," Ma said. V followed with the last name of "Buda."

Later, a man named Mario Buda admitted to being responsible for that bombing and several others to the surprise of many, but none of them named Claire.

Additional gold was sent Ma's way and, as always, she sent a portion of it back to the Patriarch in hopes that her daughter's curse would be reduced if she just out and out bribed him. He thanked her for the funds, but denied her request with the note: "Fertile Claire daughters are another form of a ticking time bomb. But we thank you for your donation."

It would be the last time Ma would ever send money to England, a drafty place always in need of some sort of cash infusion. "Enjoy the bowels of London. I hope you get the plague!" Ma said to the twilight sky. "In America, we take matters into our own calloused hands."

It was tough talk, but scary, too.

We were on our own now – or so we thought.

A VOYANT'S STORY: V

New York, 2013

1.

We keep it rolling all the way to the midtown where we were staying at the New York Marriott Marquis Hotel on Broadway. It would have made our father proud because it was the most economical this side of staying in a pit where we would be murdered. Among the un-swankiness and land of scratchy washcloths, we remained excited as we bounced onto two narrow twin beds that looked like they could fit little children. This was a budget trip, and Dad drove frugality into us, which was a nifty thing. One time, I asked him for a hundred dollars for a pair of shoes and he flipped me a dime. I tossed it right back.

"You had ten cents. Now, you have nothing," he said.

"I should start a GoFundMe account," I said under my breath.

"I've been your GoFundMe account since you were born," Dad replied.

Then I did something that shocked both of us.

"You've been amazing," I replied, running up to him and kissing his warm cheek.

"Why the past tense, honey?"

If he only knew.

I felt deeply despondent for the man who would soon stand at the headstones of his four daughters.

"Don't go nuts or anything," he told us before we left for our fake ocean cleaning trip in Monterrey. For some reason, I felt a little guilty lying to him. Mom was in and out of it to the point she didn't keep track of us anymore. "Don't talk to weird people. Don't accept rides. Don't talk to guys. Don't talk to girls. Don't go down side streets after dark or in the light and avoid all weird alleys.

THE CLAIRES

"Just don't," he said.

"We won't," I promised, "do anything more dangerous than pet a sea otter."

"I have enough worries here," Dad said. "Maybe you girls should have stayed home. Don't go there and get rabies. Did you have your last tetanus shots?" *We didn't need them where we were going.*

"We're here for you, Dad," I said and I meant it. It made me well up when C actually gave him a hard embrace before we left for our faux spring break trip.

We couldn't see this mother's future because it was entwined too closely with our own on a core level . . . and, it can't be said enough -- we can never predict our own destinies. Yet, something deep inside of all of us pointed toward significant pain for the Danko family. As *clairs*, we were strictly against any prolonged suffering.

The clock was ticking with one brilliant touchstone: We had the lingering hours of today to meld into the throngs of tourists, walks down Fifth Avenue and devour fresh pizza and then creamy mint chocolate chip cannoli's in Little Italy. I bought a T-shirt with Tony Soprano's face on it along with the word *Fugetaboutit*. The others opted for the standard I Heart NY hats and tees. We held hands strolling through the Village and smiled at cute boys.

A life slipping away is one that you grasp with both hands. We had eight between us.

2.

EXHUMING ANCIENT CURSES will make you linger over bagels at breakfast or walk slowly in still-chilled spring air to the subway station that takes you back to the past. Our original home in NYC was built in the middle of prime land located in what was once a Dutch-founded town on the East River shore of Long Island. It was now known as the New York borough of Brooklyn, a place that had just experienced a renaissance of sorts, with room for not only ethnic groups, but also for artists and hipsters.

It was S who looked around the minute we emerged from the subway stop and reminded us, "Brooklyn's official motto is *Eendraght Maeckt Maght.*"

"Translation?"

"Unity makes strength," she says and the four of us lock arms.

Nothing like a good motto to keep the demons at bay.

A lesson in history class that stuck: Some old mayor of New York named Philip Hone from 1839 once wrote in some diary that "New York is rebuilt about every ten years." Our history teacher told us that it was true, but New York was also a city that knew how to hold onto its past with an iron glove. We were counting on it during our long subway ride to 36th Street in the Flatlands area and then during a wandering march through the busy neighborhoods of stone walkups and Mom-and-Pop places promising the best of whatever they were selling.

It was already 3:00 p.m., on a cool spring afternoon, and with each step it appeared as if we were walking deeper into something familiar, something that had been covered by the gauze of time.

After a good forty minutes on foot, green grass eventually grew in more than just patches and began to expand as fresh blades poked through the last layers of spring ice covering the tips. It looked more suburban out here, and I knew because there were spaces to breathe marked in lawns between the houses.

I knew A heard lost voices as we got closer to the land where our Ma, the original single mother Lula Pitcher conceived us, and where she once lived as a strange, doomed little girl with her equally expiring mother.

THE CLAIRES

The hairs on my non-superstitious arm began to stand up straight as the history of us began to undo and infiltrate.

This was our family; our story; our land; our beginning. Seeds were planted here that could never be excavated by prying eyes that didn't share our rare and eccentric DNA.

I could tell that my sister S was feeling wave after wave of *what was* because at one point she stopped cold to crouch down onto the side of the road like she was going to be sick.

"I need a minute. I feel their hunger, their pain, their abandonment," she says in a breathless voice. "They cry every single day, all day long."

"They say to keep going," sister A gently tells her.

"They?" I ask.

"They," she repeats.

The ancients were around us and, in typical *clair* form, I gave them a little attitude courtesy of a Beastie Boys classic and sang loudly, "*Foot on the pedal. Never ever false metal. Engine running hotter than a boiling kettle.*"

I finished it with the chorus, "*No sleep 'til, Brooklyn.*"

3.

It was waiting for us like all of the places we leave behind. We say good-bye, but the immovable things remain as physical proof that our murkiest memories were indeed once our realities. Our old homes, for instance, have different owners; different futures, but we still own them in the ways that count. Even childhood houses remain ours because a part of us will forever live within the walls and those walls always exist within us.

"I hear the welcomes. I feel the history. I can almost touch the narratives," A says in a whisper as she jumps up and down. Then she stops on a dime.

"It smells like death," she says. "The souls are all around us. They're measured in decades and they never leave this place."

We have no choice, but to push on. Who knew if we would ever have a chance again in this lifetime, or what was left of it, to travel to New York again... together. C and I stop walking forward and suddenly turn toward the right where there is a small white fence that runs along fresh trimmed green grassland that stretches out like a dainty meadow.

S, who reads places and possessions, feels it down to her bone marrow. "How many summer nights did we run these grounds as little girls trying to catch the twinkling fireflies? Or we'd stand on the fence slats, waving to the horses and buggies who passed by when this was just a dirt path and not a road."

"I remember," she says.

So, do I.

"They shunned us," C recalls of our very first childhood. "Ma put us on the front porch in small, handmade crates with blankets over us on cool fall days. The ravens would fly down and hold watch. But the people would walk by and sneer. Some would spit at us. It was only saliva but it felt like acid. They would yell, "Witches be damned. Witches be gone!"

"Every brick they throw at you is another to stand upon," Lula would calmly tell us.

Would we be able to stand on those bricks now?

Our ancestral land, where the house burned down around us, was indeed now an architectural monument protected by about two acres of thick trees and dense forest land thanks to the government of modern-day New York. It was ironic in a way that would make history buffs snicker. Of course, this was the same

THE CLAIRES

organization that burned down the first house with us in it.

Tourists, who would never know the true history, were supposed to stop at the gate and wait for a guide who showed up on the top of the hour three days a week to show them the property. That little tidbit, clearly etched onto a plaque nailed to that low white fence didn't stop us from climbing over it and then walking up the expansive front lawn where the juniper trees had tiny yellow spring buds just waiting to burst.

My heart began to ache, a combination of pining for the past combined with a lusting hunger for what could never be again.

A few steps closer to the actual house, I heard what could only be described as a low hum buzz in the air, as if something on another frequency was putting out either a welcome or a warning.

I noted that mortals of this city had an insufferable name for the property, an insult of the highest degree. It was carved on a white sign: The Old Witches' House. They were off by a longshot, but it brought the tourists in, men and women who feared spirits and at the same time longed for the scare of their collective lives.

The "official" brochure for the modern-day tour was in one of those weather protected plastic boxes attached to a black stick that was placed in the hard ground. They didn't print the truth. Instead, they made up some moronic lore to make the place even more of a must-see to visitors who were promised a tour that "stepped back in time to the era of colonists and undesirables who crossed the ocean blue and built the American dream."

Strangely the papers describing the house would not stay in my hands although it wasn't a particularly windy day. They fluttered loose, one, two, three times, and I kept picking them up off the ground and dusting them off. It was as if someone or something was toying with me.

"Supposedly, the patriots hid important city documents in our house after the British takeover of Manhattan during the

Revolutionary War, but witches danced on their papers and then burned them," I read to the other girls. Then I played the critic. "What a crock of horse shit. Mom wouldn't even let us light a fire, let alone burn historical documents."

"Horse shit is probably the only thing truly authentic to this place," S sniffed.

There was no driveway because there weren't cars back when we were originally birthed in 1911. Someone had thought to spruce up what was once a hard-packed dirt path and cover it with white, sparkling stones as if they contained magic and weren't just on sale at a local Home Depot. *Our puppy Finley ran in that dirt. After a good rainstorm, we rolled in it until we were so dirty that Ma dunked us in the lake, even allowing A to pull her right in for a high-spirited soaking session with her children.*

I walked to that lake with Mattie Lester's brave son Jesse, who came calling for me on humid nights. I was 15; he was 16. He was six feet four, broad in the shoulders with long blond hair that he slicked back off his face. He almost kissed me on the equinox, but those horrible boys from down the road, Edwin and Lewis, were in the trees and began to taunt Jesse: "Get too close and she will possess you! She's a soul robber. A devil."

I felt him recoil. He couldn't feel my heart or even imagine the breakage.

There was no time to dwell on all the chicken shit boys I loved before. This wasn't an outing about them, but something much bigger. And there it was making my throat catch. The house, which wasn't the original, but it was original enough to make the air in my lungs clog with the memories. I could see our loving Ma tucking each one of us into bed, asking us to make a wish for our tomorrows, however limited they might be.

What's your wish, Ma?

Seventeen years and one day.

THE CLAIRES

And then one after that.
Life.
For my girls.

IT WAS A genteel house comprised of reddish-brown brick with three tall, display windows downstairs and two upstairs that were oddly painted dark across the glass. The color of choice blocking the outside world was ruddy red, the hue of dried blood. There were three sooty chimneys on the roof because there was no central heat in those days and one could freeze to death in those tombs of upstairs bedrooms on bitter nights.

I remembered being five or six and always carrying wood on a return trip from . . . yes, the wooden shack outhouse out back. "Just think of it. An extra glass of milk at dinner and you could lose a toe to frostbite," I joke, but no one laughs. I knew they could feel that freezing north wind on their backs in their slight night dresses from not so long ago.

There was a plaque in the ground by the information box. It *was* old and tarnished and told some of the story, including how an original house was built here in 1702, but it burned down "for some reason" in 1928 when we turned seventeen and then again in the random years of 1936, 1942, 1961, 1975, 1987 and 2001. The brochure noted that the original house before it burned "was the New York sanctuary of a tragic and mysterious widow, a beautiful woman who hailed from London and her four lovely daughters who perished as young ladies in a fire."

"Ladies?" I sniff. *There was a first. For everything.*

There is no time to laugh because we're about to have company.

"Tragedy, right, dear?" she says. And she was not one of my sisters.

Late forties. Female. Maybe Italian.

Her name was Millie and I only knew that because she had one of those little plastic name badges pinned to her clothes, or maybe it was her costume. Oddly, she stood wearing a period gingham dress in faded red and white that went from a high neck all the way down to those twinkling white stones. She was also a chatterbox, which immediately set every nerve in my system on fire.

"People say that they were a family of witches and the town burned them one night when they were in their beds, but that's just lore wrapped up in misfortune and twisted into what some might describe as ridding the world of dark magic," she almost whispers. As if dark magic was a contagion.

"Do tell," C says. My sister. The one who dooms regular people by asking them too many questions.

Millie lowers her voice another notch. If we want gossip, well, by gosh, she will bring the mother ship in. "The mother was supposedly—and don't quote me on this, hun—but some kind of ultra-famous witch or scary fortune teller who was hung by the first government of New York. I'm talking rope around her bony neck and body swinging like a chicken on the chopping block. This happened, historically speaking, in the local jail in 1928 when they made a sport of such things," she says. Finally, she shuts her pie-hole and waits for some kind of reaction.

"Wowie kazowie," I say. Millie is satisfied.

"Rumor is that her daughters were also possessed in some kind of way. And that's not all, huns." Her eyes dance as she winds up verbally for the big finish. "The town burned the entire house down with them in it – and word is their spirits lived on to haunt the place! And they still do!" she concludes.

"Not a very friendly town," I interject. "I mean, keep your

THE CLAIRES

torches to yourself."

"What happened to those bad bitches?" A inquires, sweetly. "Were they teenage toast served extra brown and crispy?"

"Dead. Dead as a doornail," Millie says with a laugh. As if it was nothing more satisfying than great gossip. "The ashes are now six feet under, which is what you get for tampering with what is good and right. You go be unholy in your days and you deserve to barbecue at night, if you ask me."

Which no one did.

"I'm sure," I say.

A loud huff. Obviously, Millie would not stand for anyone contradicting her version of local history.

"You get your flesh burned and your evil bones return to the earth to be cleansed and purified --if you're evil," Millie goes on. "It's what's right, huns. Ever hear of a little thing called karma?"

Wow. How New Age of her.

"Fire and brimstone!" she almost shouts.

Dramatic.

"Are there refreshments on this tour?" C interrupts. I knew she had enough history, and really wanted something refreshing before she took this bitch out.

"Pepsi, not Coke," Millie says in a matter-of-fact voice. "There's a machine out back. I don't make change. So, please don't ask me twice."

"She didn't ask you once," I say in an exasperated voice.

"The next program starts in ten minutes," Millie informs, as a man walks up to the front door. "My husband," Millie whispers although I don't know why it's a secret. A tall, thin middle-aged man in an Edwardian man's suit – a long, plain, loose fitting jacket in dark navy with a wide lapel, and a three-button high closure, tailored pants and a vest – seems to appear out of nowhere.

"Henry Handen," he said, formally putting out a hand to introduce himself. "I'm here to help with the particulars."

I looked at him once, twice. Why did his name sound so familiar? I noted the nose which ran like a spigot. He was six-foot-three, bone thin, late sixties and had deeply hooded eyes.

"Father, it's time to start," says Millie, looking at the sky and then the man she said was her husband. A glance down. Gold wedding bands. They were actually clasping hands as if another tour is filling them with some sort of shimmering thrill. "We're so glad that you're here. Been waiting on you," Henry says, nodding at each of us, but lingering in a way that makes my skin crawl. He can't take his hard, brown eyes off of C.

"You were waiting on us?" I ask.

"For young people to take an interest," Henry says.

"What's with the perv in the suit?" C whispers to me.

"Do we know him?" I say under my breath.

"I certainly hope not," A intervenes. "He's giving my willies the willies."

With a defiant pivot of her black lace-up boots, Millie begins to clomp up to the house, but stops cold to turn around. It's hard for her to move fast dressed up like *Little Haunted Cabin on the Prairie*. "I'm sorry for my rudeness. I never asked you where you were from, dears—and why you are here," she says.

"From?" C inquires. "We're just sinners from New York who park it in Los Angeles now, West Coasters who are fascinated by revisionist history."

"Is there any other kind?" I add, my eyes still attached to her husband.

THE CLAIRES

Millie laughs nervously. Obviously, she had met all kinds.

"Native New Yorkers. That's so interesting, dears," she says. "Incidentally, there is no ice or glasses for your soda, but father can walk you out back and down to the storm cellar where there is a fridge that supposedly makes ice. We never go down there, but there is a first for everything. Henry will take you."

"Um, no thanks," C says, as in *you can keep Henry – who looks like a perp from an upcoming Law & Order SVU -- all to yourself, lady*.

"Suit yourself. Tour begins at five—promptly," Millie says. "Until then you can just . . . amuse yourselves."

I sit on a warm wooden bench for the next hour while the sun dips low behind the clouds and night begins to hint around that another day is closing up shop. Just sitting here made me want to do a final count of our days, but I wouldn't do that here. I couldn't let them see me cry.

And then suddenly, all the time in the world became no time. Five on the dot. Millie unlocked the front door.

4.

IT WAS JUST as we remembered it, down to the little white orbs of light that filtered in through the downstairs window and seemed to separate and float mid-air like thousands of tiny ghosts. A glance upward and my eyes were transfixed onto a small, metal chandelier over the thick pine dining room table. Was I seeing things or was that light fixture perpetually swinging *just the tiniest bit*, although that defied the laws of everything scientific ever invented. The front door was closed and the complete stillness of the air was suffocating and terrifying.

Otherwise, it was like taking a page from our mental photo album and having it rise in front of our faces. Nothing like walking back into a house you haven't stepped foot in for over eighty years, or since those heady days when Mickey Mouse debuted and the yo-yo was invented. We died the year that penicillin was invented. But I digress.

The chandelier continued to sway.

Dark and overly warm, the interior of the tiny cottage felt like a tight hug. The walls were creamy white with dark wood accents and almost black hardwood floors. A light layer of yellow dust covered the sparse amount of furniture that sat in wait, lingering in history and shadows.

Everything was micro-sized in here. There was a small desk in the corner, a wooden rocker in the middle of the room, and homemade white candles burning brightly in murky glass containers on thick oak shelves that lined the walls. There were several small wooden chairs that looked like they belonged only to children.

"Not several chairs," C says. "Four."

Then I remember. *Our original chairs.* They were charred around the edges as if the original arsonist who set a fire to our lives had second thoughts and decided to preserve some of the furniture by tossing it out front after he struck the first match, but before the inferno. *Perhaps the same someone or something did this again and again during the other fires.*

In the old days, they would burn flesh, but not things. The colonists certainly had their priorities.

Things could be reused. People were set to expire.

THE CLAIRES

The wooden dining table was simple and made of dark maple, a replica of the one we owned. There were no chairs around it, but long wooden benches. I spied a tiny bed with white linen in the corner. It was for show because we slept upstairs, which made it far easier to burn us alive because we were little birds in our perch.

We had no choice but to stand next to our chairs because the house was suddenly crammed with a handful of other tourists who also and quite creepily wore period clothing.

What the hell?

One introduced herself as Mrs. Emma Jones and she wore a long dress in thick black fabric that smelled overly natural. She was accompanied by her husband, Declan B. Jones who had that on his nametag. He was in his sixties and wore brown pants, an overly long suit jacket in dull grey, a starch white shirt, and vest with leather brown buttons. It fit him perfect as costumes usually do not. A small black bowler hat topped his head, and two replicas of that headpiece sat smack in the middle of the domes of two gangly-looking teenage sons, around fifteen and sixteen. The boys had big wide faces, thin lips, and eyes that looked like brown marbles. They looked like brothers and were dressed similar to their Pop with collars up and thin silk ties looped around their necks, plus the shirt, vest, long suit jacket, and carefully creased trousers.

"Emmett and Wyatt," Emma says as if introductions are mandatory – and she is the only one to make them.

As if we needed to know the fam tree or would ever see any of them again.

"We didn't get the memo about dress-up day," I say. The four of us were dressed in leggings with long sweaters and various leather jackets. We looked hot, and I was hot. A thin stream of sweat ran down the side of my face.

The infernal Millie waves a second brochure in the air.

"We do dress-up day every Thursday. Read the fine print," Millie informs us. "It's also on the website, hons."

"Isn't it a gas!" Emma whoops to all of us. "Dress-up day at the Old Witches' House! Can you even imagine the Facebook pictures? I made sure the entire family was here this week with bells on! Or should I say, with their britches on! Do you get it?" Then she turned to her sons and took a slew of snaps with her Android phone.

"Unfortunately, we do," I say. "Get it."

"It's bullshit," Emmett says. "I'm sweating like a pig." *I could smell him from across the room.*

"Crapola," Wyatt echoes, telling his brother, "You always smell like a pig." *I believed him. Anyone with a nose would.*

"Why are you here, girls?" Emma asks us.

"History project," I reply. Then I move to avoid C's elbow in my ribs. "Or you could chalk it up to the dark forces of destiny—take your pick."

Our fearless leader Millie looks away because she wasn't really interested in the answer in the first place. She is in monotone as she launches into the same speech she could probably regurgitate in her sleep.

"Gather 'round, people," she commands. "Let me tell you a little story that goes back to when this country was young."

I zone in and out.

"And we know that this house served the patriots during the American Revolution, but I *know* you will find it much more interesting to hear the origin story behind this house and what was trapped here," she says. This catches my attention. "What remained was imprisoned here. But, I better not get too far ahead of myself—and I don't want to scare the chickens out of you."

Heads turned her way, including mine. And it isn't just because she is mutilating the English language.

"It was originally a house that colonists believed was owned by a clever witch named Lola, and I believe it's one hundred percent true. Close your eyes for a moment. Can you feel the presence of spirits stirring?"

Then she makes a mockery of it. "Oh Lola! Lola!" she shouts. "Come out and say hello to your new guests, you mean old ghost woman!"

"Lula, not Lola," I blurt. Now, the eyes are on me.

"I think I know my history, dear," Millie corrects.

One of those gangly boys shoots up a hand. "Is it like *The Conjuring*? This Lola, Lula or whatever gonna come out and get us?" asks the zit king. "Bitchin' movie, if you ask me. I'll post it on YouTube."

The kid had a point. Get Ma mad enough and *who knows what she might do*. I felt a chill wander over the air and then through me, which was technically impossible. It was about 110 degrees in here.

SNAP! In the next moment, the beaded necklace around Millie's neck spontaneously breaks and hard, little nuggets roll down her body, bouncing along for far too long on the wood floor. They stop by the big wooden rocker, Ma's chair, by the fireplace. When a flame suddenly appears, I'm all smiles.

"That was a ne-new necklace," Millie says, her hand on her neck and pinky fingers shaking.

Is this a special effect that came along with the tour price? I didn't think so, although it was a good one. As for Millie, well, she was the Meryl Streep of tour guides, in the middle of an Oscar-worthy performance.

"I mu-must say that has ne-never happened before, but then again, you never know what lurks inside these walls," she says to us with a shaking voice.

"How long have you been here?" I sweetly ask our tour guide.

"Ages."

"What happened to the last tour guide?"

"There was no last guide," Millie says.

"See all those bottles on the kitchen table. Don't ever touch them," Millie continues on with her canned speech. She's back to basics now.

"Just turn and look at them. No touchy. They're Witches' Bottles," she instructs. She looks hard at C. "You – more than any of the others -- must be familiar with them."

"Bitch," C says, under her breath. Then to Millie, she adds, "Why would you say that to me?"

"Familiar with them from your studies, dear," Millie insists. "You just seem so *studious* to me."

I could see C's eyes narrow as she glances at a wobbly wooden shelf filled with about ten cloudy, antique glass bottles that were between eight to ten inches high. C squeezes her baby blues even tighter as she stares at them.

"Back in the eighteen-hundreds, if a witch was threatening you, the defense was to create a witch's bottle, which would then attract her. And then you would capture her by plugging the bottle with a cork stopper, which was a real show stopper!" Millie blurts on autopilot again.

Chills turn into a full body shiver as she explains how a local

THE CLAIRES

folk healer would prepare an average bottle by placing pieces of glass or animal bone, hair or nail clippings, rosemary, needles, and pins in it. "Once the spirit floated inside of the open bottle, then the colonists would rush to pour more pins and needles into the bottle to trap and impale the witch, followed by fresh herbs or other liquids to render them paralyzed—or worse."

I felt sick to my stomach. "Liquids?" I say.

"Do you smell something foul?" she taunts in a lower voice. "Some of the bottles were filled with wine, but many with human urine or menstrual blood, which was thought to kill witches by melting or drowning them in a sea of poison."

Smart colonists, she rattles us, would put a cork stopper on top and burn the bottles in the fireplace believing that once they exploded, then any spells were broken and the witch was thus dead. Others kept the bottles on shelves as their own personal trophies – like the ones before us. Ma would never. This begged the question: Who put these things in our house?

Millie told us that most colonists went to great pains to hide witches' bottles, so they would never be unearthed. These seemed to be on display in the most garish way as if these poor witches were now condemned to eternity as a tourist attraction.

"You must never ever ever open a witch's bottle," Millie warns, as I count another twenty of them on a side table, most filled to the top with the kind of juice that doesn't evaporate for some reason. "If you lift the stopper," she says, with all the drama she could muster for the same speech she made daily, "Well, you'd find a whole pot 'o trouble."

It was only the slightest tremor, but I feel it down to my bones. And then when the bottles on the table begin to tremble softly, I watch in fascination. As the shaking becomes louder, I begin to stare at C, who seems to be in a trance now. The family from Ohio freezes in place. Stupefied. *Petrified.*

I knew this wasn't Hollywood special effects. I knew it because Millie's face drained to a shade beyond pale. The blood continues to rush out of her face and her sudden drop in blood pressure distracts her. It's why she misses it as C actually picks up one of the bottles.

And C, being C, must place it an inch from her face. No one can tell her not to do it although everyone is thinking, *"What the hell are you doing?"* She goes to lick the bottle, but stops short. If I had one percent of her chill, I'd be truly dangerous, too. She brings the bottle to her nose and immediately jets her arm out to go long distance with the thing.

Then she has second thoughts. *Come on. We knew this was coming.*

It took her all of a second to uncork it.

"Freedom-day, bitches!" C cries as the curtains in the room begin to wildly dance.

Every single window is sealed shut.

5.

"What . . . are . . . you . . . doing?" Millie screams. "You'll get us all killed!" *At least now we know. She's a believer.*

Another bottle and C purposely allows it to slip from her hands. Crashing to the hard, oak floor, it bursts into a million pieces that flame indigo blue on their own volition.

"Bet that's not in the brochure—even the fine print," C says with a sinful giggle.

Curtains pulsate and sway as the instant gusts they create snuffs out the candles. In the confusion, I can barely make out an outline of a being, but the feet would haunt me long after today.

The legs were milky white like two spindles of translucent flesh

THE CLAIRES

held together by navy blue veins. Those appendages were wrapped in the tallest, spiked-heel leather boots. The first task at hand was for this "thing" to crush the small phone until it was croaking the greeting, "*This is Millie and I'm not . . .*"

"Alive anymore," C fills in the blank while doing several quick happy twirls in place. My sister stretches her arms to the ceiling while forming peace signs with her index and middle fingers.

The other humans are dazed at first, but this is quickly replaced by banshee-like cursing. And sprinting. The living humans try to find any open hole to get the hell out of this place. That tall husband of Millie screams a curse as he races out of the house, "Kill them all! So, it was written. So, it must be done."

Bodies cram through the small cabin door and I can see that lovely family of four plus our tour host racing at breakneck speed in the pitch dark in the general direction of what must have been their cars, which were probably parked on the now-distant main road. Words of fear—*oh shit, oh shit, oh shit, get me out of here, did you see, don't kill me, don't kill me, don't kill me*—seem to float away on a stray twilight breeze.

I know this won't end well.

A mad dash and the human occupants are outside where we run for a beat or two or three, until I turn around. It's so dark, plus a light fog has rolled in bathing the house in murk and shadows while the mist lingers like lace.

Millie is going on sense memory. She leads the pack, huffing and puffing like many middle agers, until her foot gets caught by what looks like a gnarled oak tree root. She screams like a wounded beast meeting a hunter's spear.

I hear the sharp sound of cracking wood followed by the distinct sound of large planks of timber smashing and bursting. High-pitched screaming starts at our level and becomes hollow as they sink deeply into the earth. The dense evening fog is looser up ahead and I see the outline of bodies running and then being sucked down below. They disappear, one after another, until they're all gone. Like they were never there.

I know how to jam on the brakes—and then I whip both arms open wide to stop my sisters. We stop cold, the front of our torso's hinging forward while our feet stay firmly in place.

In front of us is a large square hole that looks like it jettisons way down into the core of the universe. Upon a closer look, there are stairs, but no one here has walked down them. They've all taken what appears to be a fatal header.

"I think we found the office. It is a storm cellar," I inform my pack. "I guess they forgot that it was located under their feet."

They're all below. . . Millie. Henry. The parents, Declan and Emma. The boys. It was a case of follow the leader until they each tumbled down to their final exit.

Cautiously, the four of us take baby steps until we hover above the hole.

"I don't hear a peep," A says.

"C?"

"With weather and erosion, it's at least thirty feet deep. Maybe forty," she says. "There's just no way . . ."

"That they're alive?" I pose and then try to confirm it. From deep below, I hear a shallow voice utter an unmistakable, "He-help. He-help us."

"We've never murdered anyone before," S whispers.

"Yes . . . we have," I counter. *My sister was a pro at revisionist history.*

"We could call someone . . ." S offers. *The benevolence tour continues.*

"Call 911?" I say. "Yes, let's call 911 and when they say, 'What is your emergency?' we respond by saying, 'Hi, uh, well, we lived on this property a hundred or so years ago in one of our former lives.

THE CLAIRES

And, I'm so sorry officer, but the place is apparently haunted by trapped witches. We popped the cork on the bottles that contained them. And I know it sounds strange, but who knew that real witches were probably still inside of those bottles? But to get to the point, the rest of our tour group subsequently went running out of the house screaming like banshees and some fell through the warped door of an old storm cellar. They're underground now . . . some alive, but who knows. Please send only your hottest paramedics and first responders."

"I see your point," A says.

6.

So what did we do? Answer: A whole lot of nothing.

It's not that we were being utterly cruel. It was just that by the time someone found this house . . . what were the chances that any of them would still be alive? As we weighed the pros and cons, we huddled right there by the large hole freezing and considering the most humane options . . . *for us*. So much for penance. We would be taking the night off from social justice.

We had come this far to find something . . . and our seventeenth birthday was looming. When would we have the chance to explore this house and the grounds, alone and uninterrupted, as our dear granny Penny intended us to do? Maybe she was the one who lured the tourists toward that storm cellar. You never really knew . . . until you knew.

I knelt down and grabbed a bit of dirt. Maybe it was because America has always been about claiming your land, and I wanted to stake my right to our family property. The specks felt solid and wet in my hands and when I brought them up to my face to smell them, I knew this was a sacred place.

Most dirt has a scent that's earthy and fresh with a little whiff of something wet and mossy. Damned, if this didn't have that lavender and vanilla scent that I remembered from our first mother. *I felt her rocking me at night when I was a little girl so sick with consumption. She smelled like flowers and stability.*

I felt her now. But I didn't feel the futures of those in that hole. It was odd. I couldn't find the FLASH! Were they alive? Or dead? And what side would they be on by morning's light?

None of it mattered, which was rude, but necessary.

"We're here for a reason. The rest are trespassers," I say.

I turn on my cell phone flashlight to look into the eyes of my three shivering sisters. "But, the tourists?" S says, with tears in her eyes. "I feel their . . ."

"Causalities," I say. "Of history."

7.
A SENTIENT'S STORY: S

I DON'T WANT to be the askhole here . . . by asking needless and pointless questions, but someone has to speak. "Are we gonna stand out here and let them die or climb in there and help them?" The rest of my sisters look at me like I'm nuts—and they have a point because maybe a thread of insanity – or many threads -- run through our bloodlines.

There is no physical way we can really help them and I can't feel their terror, which might mean their fate has been sealed. A tremor of something else goes through me. *There is something else going on here. I feel it. There is no time to dwell on nagging doubts. Probability of something freaky-odd happening? I feel it stronger now, but push it away. We have to use this time, and the feeling is strong to make the most of it. In fact, it's overwhelming in the same*

THE CLAIRES

way a fever is when you're sick. So, we have our answer. We will not be climbing into the earth tonight for extractions. We'll file it under: None of our business. What will be, will be.

Back on terra firma with that settled, it's time to make a few decisions. We can just stand there in the increasingly frigid elements where we'll probably die of hypothermia or at the very least lose a few toes. Or, we go back into the house to be eaten or worse by witches trapped for who-knew-how-long in piss and blood.

"Do witches eat you or just cast a spell and turn you into something?" I ask. "I just feel the impending doom – and I can't spend my last months as a donkey."

"Are these the only options?" A asks. "Eaten or turned into a mule? I keep trying to tune into Ma to ask, but she's MIA when we need her the most."

For once my hurt feelings are entirely my own. A isn't usually so cutting.

The present world was narrowing by the moment. Millie and the tourists were obviously dead because we didn't hear another word. We didn't have the knowledge or the tools to dig up this house and the grounds to look for some sort of shred from our past. We needed guidance from the source and I wasn't sure if she would be in a giving mood.

"Follow me," says V who began moving into the darkness. I stumbled over hard and soft things in the ground.

"Can you slow down?" I demand.

"No," she snaps. "It's April. I don't have enough weeks left to slow down."

It was full-fledged night now and in the inky distance, I could barely see enough to track her to a far corner of the property. Reaching out with my hands, I felt the sea of waist-high grass that now contained us, punctuated every so often by tall stalks of spring flowers that were daring to burst free.

We crunch over wet mulch for what seems like a century, as we make our way closer to the tall pines and evergreen trees that made up the woods that ran the entire back of the house. I almost bump into V when she stops suddenly. Then I see it, too. It's a small, rusted wooden gate, attached to a low fence that was weathered and peeling. Thick grass grows through it and around it, but it was mostly dead, crispy reeds that were easy to push away. I imagine the fence painted white, but it was peeling gray now.

V jiggles a bar that crosses the front of this makeshift gate. It gives way easily as if no one has ever bothered to lock it. Quietly, we move inside this fenced-in pen and then it dawns on me. Maybe it was a vegetable garden at one point or a chicken pen decades ago. When I look down, I don't see anything that paints such a quaint country-living picture. There is just more of that tall grass interrupted at points by large almost square rocks jutting up through this overgrown jumble.

I'm exhausted, hungry, freezing and needed to take a break. So, I sit—make that plop—down through the weed stalks onto the hard ground. When I lean back to stretch, my spine comes up against smooth stone. It feels good to have some support and I close my eyes, pretending we're back at the hotel and I'm in that soft, cushy bed, leaning on the headboard. Almost immediately, my muscles stop screaming.

I don't know what possesses me to open my arms wide, but I do it to deepen my stretch. It startles me when C clasps one of my hands while A takes the other. It's not long before they are also kneeling on the spongy, cold ground, fingers linked like chains.

Someone has to speak, and I do in the form of a prayer that tumbles from my lips.

"In the name of our mother Lula, and with the permission of the Patriarch, we humbly ask for a window to see what once was

THE CLAIRES

. . . . for the past is in our blood, but not in our eyes," I say.

"In the name of our birthright, we beg for our futures," V says followed by a chorus of "amens" spoken somberly like we are in an open-air church.

A brisk north wind whips up as answers remain hidden. It's not long before a terrifying silence falls over us like a gruesome suffocation. I can hear my sisters breathing. *In, out. In, out.* Four puffs of breath at regular intervals join the night sky as we wait.

And then I see it, a fifth cloud of breath that belonged to no one.

It was across this small pen, close, but far from the four of us, and accompanied by a gentle wheezing. When I smelled the air, it had the unmistakable scent of freshly brewed Earl Grey tea.

"Cl-aaaa---iii—rrrrr---eeee," she moans into the night—and if I hadn't recognized that voice, I might have been running fast now. Our grandmother, Penny, whose voice was low and far away, is so distant that it's like she's speaking to us from another planet.

Long ago, we were informed that one of Penny's many talents was the power of Retrocognition, or the ability to see things that happened in the past—and project them to others.

"Memories are the most potent drug of all, available in doses and overdoses," Penny begins to chatter. "I will show you now, my girls, a small dosage of what was—in the hopes that you will be able to use it to find the gift of longevity."

As always, our home movies were about time and place—and the souls that wandered through both.

NEW YORK

Early 19th Century—Home Movies Courtesy of Lula Fair Pitcher, The Original Bad-Ass Mother

1.

THE PATRIARCH MADE all of the arrangements and had a little house waiting for them at the end of a long street in a borough that would someday be called Brooklyn. He had no choice after Penny refused to abort her daughter. An idea formed in his cleverly deviant mind. Instead of dealing with her, he would "deport" her.

"Road trip?" Penny pondered. And then she packed her things.

In Old New York, the wanderer had her baby and settled in quite nicely, making the necessary home improvements she deemed fit. She painted the windows blood red on the inside and moved a small wooden table into the center of the living room with a chair on one side and another one opposite it. The same lone candle sat in the middle, burning brightly for years for only one reason: She had melted the wax herself, blessed it and only used it for magical moments including the day when she put out the smallest of notices on the front window: Fortunes Told.

Word spread about the odd young woman dressed in that cumbersome woolen black cloak and the little girl called Lula she kept hidden in that house. Some called the two of them witches; some said they were divined. Despite local superstitions about what was called black magic back in the day, the colonist fishermen and washerwomen almost nightly tapped on that dirty window exactly three times, but only well after dark and never on Sundays. They would bring small bowls of sugar, eggs, a baby pig, or a loaf of freshly baked bread as offerings. Some brought a handmade dolly for the "little witch girl" if they wanted to court extra favor.

Everyone had a question; most feared the answers.

Penny reminded each: "You will go blind and hungry if you

THE CLAIRES

speak of me or my girl child in any way or discuss what happens here within these walls. If you try to harm me or my daughter, the consumption will come to your door, slither under it, and down your throat until it chokes off your wind, thus creating a most heinous death."

No one needed to be told twice.

In turn-of-the-century New York, magic was considered a mortal sin of the highest order. There was nowhere for Penny and young Lula to go where it wasn't punishable by death, so they stayed in their little house in New York. In nearby Salem, Mass, where many of the "odder types" had fled the big city, women were being hung as witches at an alarming rate. Not that early NY was a cake walk for mystical types who liked to flex their supernatural muscles. This was risky business at best. The penalty for practicing any kind of magic in New York was either throat slitting or the noose.

Poor Penny didn't have any other trade to put food on the table, so she took the chance that her magic would be so necessary that she would be allowed to live in order to provide a unique and necessary service to such a superstitious community. For her commission and survival, she would sense their pain, hear their unspoken words, and see their futures. She knew the moment their children would be born and the day when the face sitting across from her would draw his or her last breath and exactly why they crossed over. She told them when to sail, when to plant, when to marry and when to run.

As previously noted, she predicted the future of America—three great world wars, a depression, rock music, a machine called the computer, a reality TV star as president, a cure for cancer and an intriguing creature named Miley Cyrus.

Everyone believed her, as the truth isn't just words, but a vibe combined with a knowing that cannot be denied.

She predicted hurricanes, locusts, droughts and floods. She calmed their fears, tickled their fancies, and warned against submitting to the darkness in their souls. And a January in Old New York with little heat and only potatoes as food could make a soul quite angry.

As time passed, Penny finally told young Lula that she also possessed special gifts, but she must always keep this news carefully hidden for her own safety.

"You possess so much more than I," Penny marveled, explaining, "We come from a long line of witches, wizards and clair-types who were banished from England and sailed for America. Our birthright dictates that spiritually we will always fall under the governing of the Patriarch of Paranormal in London, for he is the one responsible for sending us here. Most consider it a banishment.

"I consider it an awakening," she said.

2.

BY THE TIME, she turned sweet and sour sixteen, Lula was already hearing the voices of the dead and couldn't ignore the visitors from beyond who came "calling" late at night. By seventeen, ghosts were visiting her in the wee hours with messages and memories of lives past.

At the same age, she was looking into the futures of others and seeing their lives play out like paintings in her own mind. She also learned how to cross back and forth from the shimmering light to the extreme darkness, telling no one of her travels through both heaven and hell.

Periodically, the Patriarch sent letters to Penny asking if Lula had taken a spirit dulling potion (at the very least) and reminding

THE CLAIRES

all with fully functioning eyes, "It is clear to this board that Lula Fair Pitcher is a rare combination of clairvoyant, clairsentient, clairaudient, and claircognizant, meaning that she possesses four of the most powerful quadrants of knowing. It's a lethal mix, thus the bloodline must end immediately." Of course, there was no return letter, no begging, no cajoling at the time, which sealed the deal. Penny was branded as an "unacceptable," the lowest form of existence, and her file was permanently marked "closed."

"Closed" back in the day wasn't just a filing term.

Lula was grief-stricken on the day she found Penny upside down. She was dead, her body pickled in the barrel of brine outside of the vegetable stand. In her hand was a notice from that newly formed colonial group, The Order: "We found out your true intentions, which are quite sinful. You intend for your daughter to live," it read. "And now you must pay with your life, which will also pave the way for our actions. So, it was written. So, it must be done."

Orphan Lula, at seventeen, was left the black hovel of their house. Oddly, she was not killed as the colonist believed that having tragedy strike twice in one family would then boomerang back onto them. For now, she would simply be shunned. Neighborhood youngsters refused to play on that street. Maybe it was the gargoyle that Lula placed on the front step that terrified them. Or perhaps it was the sight of the strange young woman who occasionally went outside in her long, swirling black wool skirts, dark shawl, and heavy hood. Her eyes burned as bright as the gaslights that lit the streets.

To freak out those vicious neighborhood hooligans called children, Lula perfected the art of having the white parts of her eye disappear until all those flipped out brats could feel was the glow of tempered fires.

Underneath that hood, Lula was actually beautiful with

piercing amber eyes, black hair, and a slightly longer-than-usual nose, which most said predicted shrewdness in those days. Lula was quite the shark, a young woman who secretly managed her rapidly growing powers to the benefit of her growing list of "clients" who defied the idea that her ill fate was catching. They were the ones who eventually demanded that her life span continue on because she was far more useful alive. The same couldn't be said for all of the colonists.

For the longest time, the Order was told that they would be disbanded or worse if anything happened to this precious resource.

For example, politicians from near and far came calling to find out who would be elected the next president. And the president himself visited in the wee hours to talk war plans and economic policy. Mothers of sons lost at sea begged Lula to call out to their boys. Spinsters wanted her potion of attraction. Crews about to go on voyages would arrive in the dark of night to ask if they were safe or would find any treasure. Order leader Henry Handen and his second in command, Declan B. Jones voted for a simple capture followed by blood-letting, but the others out-ruled them for reasons that were also financial. Some felt that her mother knew exactly where treasures were buried in the New World.

"Fools, if I knew where money or gold was buried, I would be a rich woman," she'd laugh, insisting, "No mere mortal knows all or there would only be one mortal."

She was rich in other ways. At the old age of twenty-one, under those dark skirts, she was hiding an amazing secret.

She was pregnant.

With many.

By the time her quadruplets were two, she allowed them to play outside in the front yard, but only in the moonlight. One night, the girl she called V was toying with something strange in the grass. Lula gasped when she saw her baby's bloody hands.

THE CLAIRES

It was a bull's heart pierced with a spike down the middle. Everyone in Old New York knew that animal hearts like this one were placed in vulnerable places to keep the most potent witches away. That wasn't the case here.

The bull was lost and decided to graze.

The girls had other plans for him, which was why Lula cancelled her plans to adopt a puppy. It was too dangerous…for the dog.

3.

As HER DAUGHTERS grew and developed, Lula put them to work in the family business as welcomers. They would receive clients and then serve them the all-important hot elixir, as Lula was now reading tea leaves. Most importantly, the girls would collect the money. If payments were resisted or threats of violence mentioned—many came not knowing why and then resisted—one of the youngsters would race up the back stairs and start pulling a heavy chain across the floor that corresponded with the ceiling in the drawing room.

Yes, they were women of magic. But a few woman-made special effects didn't hurt.

There was one man who went running from the house, his face drained of color, screaming into the night, insisting this home was haunted. Nothing worked to soothe his wildest fears including the small perfume bottle he left on her front step filled with wine, pins, needles, and herbs. It was a classic witch's bottle, but no one could trap Lula or her children because they were *Claires* and not witches. Eventually, that same man threw his money down on the front step. Why tempt fate or irritate the one the town called "The Ivory Witch"?

The name was earned because Lula's skin was almost translucent now and even lighter in the winter.

V was the first to observe how her mother would sit and whirl the tea leaves around and then invert the glass in the saucer. The tea grounds naturally fell into the bottom of the cup and these formations told her the future. It was simple: If the grounds went their separate ways, one was to be unfortunate in love. If the leaves stuck together, one would be happy and wealthy.

A long line of straight leaves meant imminent death.

The beautiful Claires were late into their sixteenth year of life, in 1928, when Lula was finally arrested for witchery (for lack of a better definition) and the practice of illegal magical acts. Hanging was discussed, but just not yet, as the local judge wanted to be sure there was no one who would surrender gold for her life.

It was a brutal winter's day with the sky spitting snow and the corrupt judge drinking his tea at the courthouse. This was where Lula's fate would be decided by a mere man who knew that gold would not be forthcoming. After his last drop, he summoned Lula to his chambers, asked for a quick reading, and then sentenced her to life in The Clink, a common way of referring to prison.

It was days away from The Claires' seventeenth birthday.

4.

THEY WERE ALLOWED to visit Lula the next day, which was brutally cold as a nor'easter brewed. The girls—now lovely, tall, strong, yet brooding—feared their mother would freeze to death, as the jail had no heat. Why they didn't see their mother's fate wasn't clear, as magic was an unpredictable thing.

That's why the girls smuggled in hot tea along with her favorite china cup and saucer for their mother. It was all they could do.

THE CLAIRES

Through the jail bars, Lula asked her daughters for only one thing.

"Hold hands, my darlings," she said. "I want to read your futures."

Gazing down, Lula screamed loudly.

The tea leaves formed into four straight lines.

By morning, Lula was found hanging from the rope in her jail cell. The journal found on the floor contained a last entry that read: "Death is never the end, even if it comes again and again and again."

In her last words, Lula had warned her girls to move far away. "They will come for you. Do not stay in the house."

But, what teenage girl ever listened to her mother – even a dead one?

Two days later, upon the Claires first seventeenth birthday, they woke in four single beds with wrought iron frames once painted white, but now charred black. The beds were unfortunately located in the midst of a raging inferno that was consuming their home. Everything inside was basically made out of wood and it only took minutes for the small ladder that went from the main floor to the loft where they slept to serve as kindling. The upstairs collapsed as if it was being served into the flames. Unfortunately, the girls flailed down until they could fall no more. Bodies and bones were subject to the roasting.

One colonist who dared to look marveled that as each girl fell into the main inferno, they looked so peaceful.

Pristine.

Still.

The Order had decided to end it, once and for all. At midnight, with the mother in her fresh grave in the backyard per her wishes, they quietly removed a few pieces of furniture because it didn't deserve to burn and then set fire to the black hovel, dousing it with all the kerosene they could carry to ensure what wasn't to be saved would prove unsalvageable.

The fire was allowed to rage until dawn while the Order and their children stayed just far enough on the outskirts of the woods to dance and celebrate this victory for humanity and the future of the colonies.

The little witches were gone now.

"So, it was written. So, it must be done," Henry Handen boasted, lifting his glass of ale to toast this American milestone.

5.
1928
DES MOINES, IOWA

NINE MONTHS LATER, a farmer's wife in Des Moines had the longest and most celebrated birth(s) in the small town's history. Much to the dismay of a freaked-out midwife and drunk husband, she had quadruplets.

"I'm sorry. All girls," the midwife apologized to the farmer who needed workers in the form of strong boys and not bony girls.

These unnecessary mouths to feed were all named Claire because the farmer felt…well, compelled to do so, and it was a solid, probably Biblical name. He gave them each different middle names. Claire was his wife's mother's name, after all. He thought.

By age two, the farmer's daughters would wake in the middle of the night, hold hands, and sing old folk songs popular of the day.

THE CLAIRES

The only problem was that neither the farmer nor his wife sang songs about the Queen of England nor played that infernal jazz music popular in sinful big cities like New York. The good citizens of Iowa considered that music to be the devil's boogie.

The farmer and his wife had barely been schooled in English themselves, which was why their daughter's progression educationally speaking was rather upsetting, too. By age five, the girls did numerical equations at a high school level in a town with no high school. Their first mother, Lula, had taught them math to count the money. (Worldly possessions did not travel with them to the next lifetime; smarts did.) By the time they went to the one and only one-room school, the other children dubbed them evil spirits because they knew too much about history, politics and – worst of all – could predict things, which was illegal.

After they blossomed into lovely young ladies, the farmer and his wife decided it was better for their daughters to school them at home and keep them busy by working the land. In the fields, the farmer's face turned purple each time his daughters began to speak to each other in French.

One cold morning just before Christmas, the day before they reached their seventeenth birthday, all four girls were found together in the cornfield. In the dirt. Dead like their hearts just *collectively* gave out. Some said the cows went mad and attacked these strange creatures. Some said that horses trampled them. All of these theories were verging on the impossible. There was no blood; no marks.

They were all face up.

Pristine.

Still.

"It was almost as if they expired," said their father who later that day found his wife quite dead with her head bobbing in the pond, which began a long future of heartbreak for any mortal woman who mothered these young ladies.

You see, on the eve of that seventeenth birthday, before the girls were sent to their deaths, the mothers would be required to perish first, as an eternal punishment for Lula Pitcher's defiance and utter refusal to kill her daughter.

Mere mortals wouldn't know that the Patriarch of Paranormal would put a "suggestion" into the very muddled, pre-birthday minds of the Claire sisters explaining exactly how to sever the mother-daughter relationship. Why? Grieving mothers asked too many questions about their children's deaths, and the Patriarch didn't need any rumblings from those who harbored these girls for their current seventeen years. "Let sleeping dogs and Claires lie," he said.

The mothers had to go.

In a formal way.

It was C—in some sort of dazed frenzy—who lured that farm mother into the water by pretending she was drowning. When the farmer's wife swam out to save her, it was all she (the mother) could do to keep her head above water.

Which…she didn't.

6.
1945
Berlin, Germany

NINE MONTHS LATER in Berlin, a spinster schoolteacher, trying to hide her affair with a married American GI, found out she was pregnant. In the year of our Lord, 1945, she gave birth to quads of all things, who didn't have an easy life. The teacher could not attract another man because none wanted to raise *vier madchens* (four girls) that were not his own. Forced to live in squalor with

THE CLAIRES

her children, this mother was fast with the lash and lethal with her slim, but hurtful hands.

It was only seventeen years later, in the year of 1962, when the teacher was tragically killed at the recently opened Neues Museum, where she took her class of second graders on a field trip to study the early historic collections. Her daughter, who went by the initial A, reported in perfect English and also German: "Our mother was killed when someone pushed the iconic bust of the Egyptian Queen Nefertiti onto her, which smashed her spine."

"*Our* mother?" asked the *Landespolizei,* a member of the German Federal Police.

"I have three sisters," she said. *"Drei Schwestern."*

Outside of the police station after the last of the report was taken, all four girls decided to put their non-existent grief on permanent hold and walk to a local bakery to celebrate their 17th birthday and the upcoming Christmas holiday/December 24 birthday. They were tragically killed when they all—*at the same exact time*— "fell" off the street and plunged into Luisenstadt Canal.

Tragisch.

There was a strong current that day. The bodies – all *vier* of them -- were simply swept away.

14

A COGNIZANT'S STORY: C

1.

I wish I could flip a switch. Turn off the machine. Stop the freaking movie.

It doesn't work that way even when I dig my nails so far into my palm that I draw tiny drops of blood. We're still here at our ancestral home. It's still glacial cold outside…and time is ticking as we're looking for something that's unexplainable. Unlocking my eyes, I fill them again with the peacefulness of a blank night sky after a dense fog lifts. I'm clear knowing, and I expect answers, but instead something seems heavy and strange.

Reaching out to hold one of my sister's hands, my own enters cold pockets of almost frozen air that now permeates this fenced in garden where we've hunkered to regroup. The change in temperature alarms me as I've heard about this phenomenon. In cases of hauntings, the degrees drop in the most dramatic way.

I move my body and realize that I'm also in physical pain. Something is digging into my back as I sit and when I slowly turn to see what's pressing into my flesh, I don't suppress the scream that rises in my already dry throat.

Whipping around, my hands grip what's behind me, which is tall, solid, and icy cold. Upon closer inspection, it's not just a rock, but my backrest is a thick slab of concrete like a large tablet. When a veil of wispy clouds part for just a moment, I can read what's etched onto the front of it for the first time.

My finger traces the name: Pitcher. My eyes follow what I can barely read anymore, thanks to time and elements: Beloved Mother and Spirited Being. *Spirited? It was an odd way to put it.*

THE CLAIRES

Someone had etched something else on the bottom with a knife. The letters are ragged: WITCH.

In the bleak silence, V takes a shaking finger and traces our mother's name—Lula Pitcher—barely readable on the grayish white slab, thanks to decades of abusive weather. I join her and the feeling of chalky dust on my fingers makes me physically ill.

"Ma," I mouth, imagining her warm hands reaching out from below to hold me. But there are no hands, only the soft rustling of ancient trees and the visions of rot.

A low, guttural wail escapes for the second time from my rage-seared lungs. *What they did to her . . . what they did to us . . .*

A, who hadn't been focusing on the particulars finally comes out of what could only be considered a trance. I watch as she kneels and tries to read the engraving of the rock she had been leaning on, which belongs to Lula's short-lived shoemaker husband.

The moon burns bright now and my eyes settle on a row of headstones in what isn't a garden, but our family plot. There are burial sites for us, too. Four in a row, but none of us dares to get too close to that needless decay.

"We are NOT in there. We are NOT," A says before she begins to cry.

It dawns on all of us in that moment. There are graves for us littered across the world filled with bones, but not souls.

This town had burned our house, and they took the ashes of what they assumed were our bones and had indeed placed them deep in the ground. Of course, we were here. Yet, standing in front of what was once our own flesh and blood – at least for that lifetime before we received a new vessel – has now become such a heady trip that I feel myself begin to sway in my shoes. As I wobble backwards, V catches me. She always does and vice versa.

"What matters is never buried," she insists. "We're like

butterflies. We shed the old cocoons and emerge even more beautiful the next time."

"Not more beautiful," V insists, her bravado returning. "More powerful."

I begin to walk away backward, as if expecting to see my own ghost. Eventually, because I cannot see my own life clearly, I trip backward over a lone stone that sits by itself, apart from the family markers.

"Wait, there's one more," I say, as V yanks me to my feet.

"How can there be one more? Because I'm pretty sure we just shook out the entire family tree," V scoffs, which is also her way of coping. "Is there some cat buried in here?"

"Like I know what the hell they did back in those days. They peed in a shack in the woods. Who knows what they did with secret relatives and pets," I razz her. "Let's just see what this is . . . and get the hell out of here."

V shines her phone's flashlight on the words: Here lies the body of Emily Pitcher, beloved sister of Lula Pitcher, loving daughter of Penny Louise Pitcher, father unknown. There was no date announcing her birth or death.

"Trippy," I say. "Ma had a sister." *This was news to us.*

"Let's just go. Leave this place. I feel something awful is coming," V jumps in again.

"What is that . . . over there?" I ask her, swallowing hard as the metallic tang of stone in the air gets stuck in my throat. My eyes connect to a pile of what looks like newly turned earth.

Someone has been here recently.

And there were four new holes in the ground.

Waiting.

Someone had already chiseled our full names into the rock:

Claire Violet. Claire Sophie. Claire Alice. Claire Clover.

"None of this is sparking joy," S suggests. "Let's get out of here."

THE CLAIRES

In the end, we weren't going anywhere. I feel a familiar warm rush flood my upper chest. It serves as my confirmation that we aren't in hot water.

We are in the boiling soup.

2.

My sister A is our road map to the so-called White Pages of the spirit world.

I watched her twirl, which is something she did when she was internally melting into one of her mini-breakdowns. I knew she was trying to connect with *them* . . . instead of *them* trying to connect with her, which was a much harder process. My sib, a slight girl with frozen drops of night dew on her chestnut locks, had her arms wide open as she swirled wildly until her entire body spun in so many small circles that she looked like a flesh and blood tornado.

Northerly wind raged as she rotated hard in that small graveyard until she quit on a dime like a gymnast sticking the landing. "Ma's AWOL, but Grandma Penny said that she came to the New World pregnant with our mother – *only her*," she informed us as we huddled down now, arms around each other for warmth. "She never had sex again. Just once in her entire life. She was never pregnant again or so it follows. There was never an Emily."

"Emily is one hundred percent bull to the shit," she repeats.

"But there is a gravestone," I say and then I run away from them as quickly as my feet will carry me. It's not that I'm afraid. I feel empowered as I approach a small shed just outside the graveyard and touch a small silver lock that looks like it belongs on a high-school locker. This is child's play to me. Closing my eyes, the numbers come to me quickly: 4-44-4.

I return with two sharply pointed gardener's shovels and only one mission on my mind. I hand the other shovel to V, who liked to help me take care of deeds that were more physical in nature. Calmly, we stand over Emily's grave. V states the obvious. "Anything or anyone could be buried in there and this would be considered a spiritual disruption," she says. "If it gets mad . . . then what?"

"Excavate," I reply.

Plan in hand, we dig like our hands are motorized. When we hit what feels like wood, the shovels are tossed aside. We begin to burrow into the earth with our bare hands until we find enough of a grip to hoist out what was approximately a five-foot-long pine wooden casket. It still had the faint smell of butterscotch, which lingers on all of our fingers after we gently place it down on a smooth spot on the frosted lawn.

We stand, hovering above it like it was a recently landed UFO.

V has a plan.

"Rock, paper, scissors?"

She always does paper. Always loses.

"I hate everything in this world and beyond," she says as her bluish fingers pry open, on the fourth try, what something or someone had barely sealed shut. I narrow my eyes just a bit, expecting something dreadful like a pile of rotted bones or a worm-eaten skull minus eyes. Bracing, I knew it would have me screaming into the next county.

There are no bones. No skull. No human matter at all. The casket is completely empty of human matter.

"But it's not empty-empty," I whisper, pulling out something hard and cold. It's a small orange-brownish tin box, the size of a paperback book, caked in thick layers of rust. It has slid to one of the darkened casket corners.

The box has the remnants of faded white paint and I could

make out the outline of a woman in a long flowing gown and matching large hat. In one hand is a needle and the other thread. "A sewing box. Not horrifying – yet," V says, trying to gingerly open it while it remains sealed shut. She tries again and again, finally cracking it apart with great care and muscle.

"Here goes . . . everything," V says as she pulls out a small piece of fabric with words embroidered on it.

It reads: Deny the Past; Revoke the Future.

3.

OUR CLEVER GRANDMOTHER Penney didn't write her message with pen or pencil on parchment or paper. She knew that with weather and age, her words would erode and then disappear. Instead, she had sewn her message into various embroideries or needlepoints onto what feels like thick pieces of linen or maybe even animal skin. I'm afraid to examine all that's in the box because a brisk wind has kicked up.

Imagine coming this far only to have this message from the past snatched up and taken into the yonder.

My sister agrees with me. "Let's just go . . . as in go now," S begs. "We can examine this in the safety of our lovely hotel room over room service pizza." When she grabs her shoulders and starts shaking violently—and not necessarily from the cold—I know she is all things that are right and reasonable.

Whatever causes you to tremble on a cold, dark night should be addressed – immediately. A light freezing rain begins to fall. Without delay, I snap what was ancient shut and slip the box into the deep pocket of my long wool coat.

I punch our location in the app on my cell phone, it says that the nearest vehicle is seventeen minutes away. *Seventeen freaking minutes, damn Uber to hell. Where was your ride share during an otherworldly crisis?*

Vehemently, I vote against going into the house to take advantage of the warmth and the candle light, but A and S are already insisting that they feel some "ill" will pointed directly at us and it's not located within those walls. It's outside. Where we are sitting ducks in a fenced in pen.

I see that all three of my sisters are standing with their eyes pointing towards the trees, which doesn't mean they're opting for a night stroll in the creepy and dank woods. Our house backs up to thick forest land or what might be a mile or two of Mother Nature at her finest. A blink or two later and I see them, too. Shadowy human figures in what appear to be long dark cloaks are staring out from the pines in the uncomfortably near distance.

A few of them are on horseback and all are wearing tall Abraham Lincoln-type hats. The front line is flanked by large hunting hounds whose breath can be seen closer to the ground. What trips me out the most are the small ones. Are they children? Or something worse?

They wear the same long frocks and keep darting out from the woods for a closer look. They use the tall weeds as cover . . . and then bolt back to whisper to the shadowy ones, who lean down off their nags. I know they're forming words, but it's far enough away to sound like hissing.

"Now what?" S seconds in a quivery voice.

"We go home," I say.

Ever so slowly, with our eyes on them and their eyes on ours, we walk backward. It's fifty or so steps back – maybe seventy-five or one hundred. We fall. We stand up. All the time, we are moving, always walking, toward that small house where it all began.

A SENTIENT'S STORY: S

C. L. GABER

1.

First oddity: There is light in the house and I feel with great certainty that there was only absolute darkness inside when we raced outside.

This house doesn't possess electricity in some attempt to maintain the authenticity of the past. My heart sinks to my stomach when I realize that someone lit not one or two of those candles, but all of them. Good news if there is any: It makes the windows of the house instantly glow a warm yellow. Bad news: Who the hell was on the other end of the match?

You can't miss the rest of it.

As we get closer, music is playing.

I recognize a scratchy rendition of Jimmie Rodgers' jazzy, "Waiting for the A Train" that drifts out of some tinny speaker of an old radio. I know this because in one of our former lives, in Germany, our mother schooled us in every musical form available by never turning off the radio.

Still walking backwards with the shadow people advancing forward slowly, I feel the rage and violence from the woods combined with the vengeful emotions of the last hand that touched that old-fashioned radio.

V puts her hand on the front doorknob, half hoping it was locked. Unfortunately, she's curious enough to really find out and the knob twists easily. The heavy wooden door seems to swing open on its own volition and smacks heavily into the creamy white wall. I worry about the witches swarming us, but there are no broomsticks hovering in the air—at least none that are visible. *But*

THE CLAIRES

I still sense it around me. A feeling of malevolence combined with the hunger of a long wait.

Eyes darting to the tiny kitchen, I focus on the slabs of freshly cut wood crackling merrily and burning in the old-fashioned stove. *There was no fire when we raced out of here.* On quaking legs, we take those almost impossible first steps inside only to be greeted by the welcoming smell of meat and vegetables roasting.

If I was a guessing person—and I'm not—I'd bet on beef stew. A glance backward and through the open door, I see the murky figures in the woods moving closer. I am the least cloudy of all my sisters and know there is no choice but to turn and close that door. There is a large lever that I slide to seal it shut.

The emotions inside the house begin to drown me: fury and wrath mixed with the sickly joy of manipulation and a blood thirst that had no limits. These sensations are not my own, and they don't belong to my sisters.

There are other visitors – not the friendly kind. In fact, they are sitting at the little wooden kitchen table, waiting and staring at us. And there are many. No one speaks at first, but one smiles in a way that smells of satisfaction.

The family of tourists who fell to their deaths into that storm cellar are not down below. They are here. Sitting at the table. So is our tour guide Millie and her tall husband with the running nose. When I walk closer, I'm reminded of his name when he stretches out a bony arm.

"Henry," he says as I recoil.

And then I remember.

Ma told us about the day she turned seventeen. The leader of the New World Order...a man named Henry Handen stopped by this house. To put her to death.

Henry might have physically died in the 1900s. But he wasn't gone.

"Welcome home, sinners," Henry says. The sweat above his top lip is licked off by someone who lusts for payback.

I spot the garden ax in his right hand. His black bowler hat is on the table, which anyone knows means bad luck. You don't put hats on tables or beds without expecting a disaster. He doesn't seem to care because no one in this room has ever been described as lucky.

The worst is the teenage sons, Emmett and Wyatt, who are intently staring at us with pure lust as they toy with small handguns.

"But we saw them die," my sister A stammers.

Human matter dies. These people were not human anymore, which was why they were able to survive and crawl their way back from the hole.

The taller, least desirable one, Emmett, is the one who stands up and moves much too close to her before he answers.

"We came back to party with you for a little while before you give us that box you diggedy digged out of the ground," he says.

I want to rip his heart out—and would if I had the skills.

"Guess you girls don't know that there is quite a bounty paid for any magical secrets from Miss Lula Pitcher. She's a legend. A queen," he continues. "We come here all the time just waiting for her kin to start digging. She'd melt the hands of anyone who found that box if it twain't kin. And after 'bout 100 years of waitin' when we saw you, we just knew you'd bring her words to us. You would give it to us, which changes everything. There ain't nothin' she can do if you git the thing out and we taketh away."

"Who the hell are you?" I demand.

THE CLAIRES

"Colonists," Wyatt interrupts. "You could call us greedy settlers. Or you could call us citizens of the good old U S of A with a score to settle."

"A score?"

"Before your mama took her trip to hell," Emmett continues, "She turned in The List."

He was visibly upset when I still looked confused.

"The List," he bit out. "The names. The people whom she thought were witches and warlocks—or ones who crossed her -- so she accused them of magic in order to eliminate them. She gave The List to the governor of New York, a very close friend of hers, who came here to get his fortune read. Everyone in this room and all of those phantoms in the woods were burned at the stake or hung because of your Ma."

"We're souls that cannot rest until we get real justice," he says.

I could see V's eyes flashing horror. "Our mother would never . . ." she began.

"Oh, but she did," the undead Wyatt says. "There was a boy who had night fits. Your mother branded him as a warlock." He stopped only long enough for us to know that he was talking about himself. "Some had seizures like my mother. Your mother called her a witch. Now, they would call it epilepsy," he says. "It was to the point where this settlement began to think that witchcraft was like a virus that would spread through all of New York."

"I was brought to the gallows and hung," the undead Emma says. "My husband was pressed to death with heavy stones after he refused to admit that he was a sorcerer. He was a farmer. Others died in the most heinous ways in colonial prisons or by gashing wounds that bled and bled until the very life just drained away... drip by drip, drop by drop."

"Most were burned," Emma continues in an infuriatingly calm, motherly voice. "Local codes stipulated that malevolent witchcraft need be punished by fire and local leaders oversaw the burning of witches—which we weren't, but your mother gave us that fate because of her own damned life. She passed those curses down to her darling daughters with your *clair* trickery."

"You die each time you turn seventeen," Emmett says. "We know your history. Your curse. And we know that you will kick the can this December, which means the only decent thing is to keep you like pets until you expire. At least, you're all house trained."

"Or we could get rid of them now, which the others might enjoy," Emma interrupts. "Your next death is already on the books. Why not start a little early? I'm sure few will miss you."

Wyatt jumps in. "Some of our friends were beheaded before their bodies burned. It might be fun to do one of those historical reenactments, but with real heads." He laughs viciously before reaching out to grab one of C's curls.

I see her rock backward. Anything to stop him from touching her.

"Don't even think about running, dear," Emma says without moving from her spot at the table. She stabs a beef cube from the stew in front of her like she's killing the cow all over again. "The other colonists have already made a circle around the house. Even though not one of us is a witch, there is always strength in numbers—especially with Earth-bound spirits like those phantoms outside. They're spirits who refuse to leave the general vicinity of their violent deaths."

Emmett saves the best for last.

"I was the one who pissed in those witch bottles a hundred years ago. Pissed on 'em all. And then put the cork on so they could brew in it for all eternity. Maybe we should do the same to the four of you."

He chokes on his own spit while cocking his Smith & Wesson. Oddly, V laughs when he runs the muzzle of the gun down the side of her face. She steps closer to him and asks in a breathless voice: "Really? It was you? You sent the real witches for a swim? How did you do it? Tell me more about those bottles. It's fascinating, really."

"First, I saw the smoke, which is how witches travel. Is that how you travel?" he asks in a low tone.

"Maybe," she says, egging him on with a sweet smile. "Tell me the rest."

"Then I put a bit of pretty ribbon on the bottom of each bottle. I waited until the witch was tempted and the smoke came closer. Then I trapped one of those bitches in one of those bottles," he says. "When the night was almost done, I took my bottles to the woodshed where I pulled down my trousers, pulled out the corks, and then drained the snake right on top of them. I drowned them all." He stops to laugh.

"Human piss is a witch repellant," he informs us. "First you drown 'em. Then you put the stopper back in to keep 'em there for all eternity."

"All of them? You urinated on all?" C joins the laughter.

C then frowns, nudging them toward their mania. "How humiliating—for these poor witches who were just trying to do their own thing only to swim in hot, stinking, germ-filled human waste for the next century of two. All because of you. Vile you."

"Disgusting you," A begins to chant and soon all of us were chanting it while walking in a small circle around him.

Vile you, disgusting you, nasty, offensive, putrid you . . . We take turns finding a new word to describe how loathsome human beings of this variety can be when left . . . alive or undead. You really couldn't win.

Candles flicker wildly as we shout each word. And then I notice that the fireplace bricks have begun to shake until some lose their mortar. I jump when that thick oak mantel crashes to the ground. Antiquated cabinet doors in the kitchen begin to burst off their hinges while pristine white dishes crash to the ground until they are in tiny, chalky pieces.

When the remaining witches' bottles begin to do a slow shimmy-shake dance left and right, I turn toward C who appears to be in some kind of a trance. She stares straight up and speaks to no one in particular.

"We're not fighters," she says, staring into the rafters. "We're women. We're voyants, sentients, audients and cognizants. We're sisters . . . in need of a few more sisters."

2.

ANOTHER VOICE FILLS the room.

"If you can't fight," she advises us. "Then, lovely one, move."

We don't have to be told twice because by now white curls dance, mingling mid-air until they form into see-through indoor clouds. A blink later and these pillows of mist drift higher until they reach loft level. This is where the smoke clears, transforming into young women who form their parts and now sit in sweet repose.

Their legs dangle from the upstairs wooden beams that run the length of the house, and they casually swing them despite the fact they're balancing at the top of a very high perch.

They are blissfully beautiful young ladies, five in all, who appear to be fourteen or fifteen years of age when in human form. One has lux blue-black curls that fell halfway down her regal back and thin frame, which is covered in a dark purple below-the-knee, drop-waist dress and matching modern black boots with pointed tips.

She laughs when V, now hunkering in a corner, finds a shaking

THE CLAIRES

voice to say, "Hello, could we do a quick roll call, please. If not, no problem. Welcome to our home."

"We're nontraditional witches, dear one, who have just found liberation and need a good shower from old pissy pants down there. We were expecting a burning or gallows and instead we received a drowning," she says, adding, "Sorry to be so impudent. I'm the one called Manon."

"Is that a kind of witch?" I query.

"No," she says with a laugh in her tone. "It's a first name. And since you're so curious, you'll probably want to step into the kitchen. The view will be superior."

We scramble as Manon turns her face slowly to the others in her presence—focusing on the two young men, the ones who have gone pale, and then Henry whose ruddy skin flames bright red.

"Excuse me," she says to them. "I do believe you're trespassing."

3.

WHAT FOLLOWED ON that chilly spring evening was prose that was quite inspirational.

"For educational purposes, you, soon-to-be dead, wish-they-had-never-been-reincarnated racist colonists might want to note that most witches are not snaggletoothed old ladies with pointed noses who can be killed by fire or drowned by heinously putrid bodily fluids after trapping their essence in a bottle—although the bottle part works," she states.

"The truth is we're far more dangerous because we're teenage girls with vast upgrades, metaphysically speaking, who roam in packs. We have indestructible bodies and the hearts of raptors when faced with an enemy. Raptors . . . as in the dinosaur. In case you're curious, our bite power exceeds most animals."

"I'm curious," V says from her new spot hiding in a corner by the small chairs. And then she dares to add, "Tell us more about your former existence."

"We live in covens; kill in packs," Manon says. "What else is there to know on a night like tonight when we have guests."

"We're good," I say *and we were. I could feel her intentions toward us and they were pure.*

The other two in her posse nod in an exaggerated way that had their heads launching up and down too quickly. These young witches radiate an innocent glow of eternal youth mingled with some kind of silent, inner knowing – and something freaky to boot. They had overly long teeth filed into points, a sharp contrast from the girl spirit next door look of their strappy party dresses in light blue, steel gray and black. They were stunningly beautiful where it almost hurt to look at their gleaming blonde, red and black hair or nails that were several inches long and painted in bright colors. I watched them change at will…dresses that were black a second ago became deep pink. Hair in high top knots suddenly tumbled down bare backs. They suddenly smell wonderful as if someone mixed fresh lavender with cinnamon bread.

They could be going to Santa Monica High School with us if they allowed broom parking in the student lot and spells that would turn the cheerleaders into trolls.

"We don't sweat your kind."

It spoke. Emmett would not go down easily. Neither would his kin.

"You are an optical illusion," sneers his mother. Like she was trying to convince herself, but wasn't that convincing. "Be gone, devil girls," she begins to chant as if this would actually work. She rubs some sort of crystal around her neck and begins to chant

THE CLAIRES

words in Old English that sound like we're in some sort of remedial Shakespeare class.

Manon shakes her head and launches an eye roll that goes all the way back into her head, literally, because suddenly all I see are her whites. My heart soars as she tells the colonists the truth. "Saying you don't believe in witches is like saying you don't believe in kittens. We're all still here," she admonishes.

One of the young women, with long straight blonde hair and in a green beaded flapper dress with black Mary Jane T-strapped heels, picks up the slack. She introduces herself as Alvina, and I know someday I would never remember such a beautiful name. "But names don't matter. What you need to know is that I'm an elemental witch," she says. "We use the elements of air, earth, wind, and fire. I honor each element—and use it to celebrate life and promote death."

Her friend, in golf knickers, argyle socks, a white blouse and tie, raises her hand. "Chaos Witch. I go by the proper name of Brea," she says. "My main rule is there are no rules. I just ramp up and stir the chaos. You could call me a turn-of-the-century influencer."

"For example?" V asks in a wee voice. I poke her and whisper, "It's not time for the question-answer period of our evening."

Brea smiles warmly and puts up the "just a second" finger, which is when I notice that her digits are about twice the length and girth of anything human.

We watch wide-eyed as she uses that elongated pointer finger to make the planks from the floor boards suddenly begin to pop, creating near misses with the freaked-out colonists whose heads are about to be impaled with wood. When chunks of stew begin to blow out of the cauldron and land in boiling hot plops on their heads, Brea stifles a giggle. "Time to go vegan," she advises. "Dead animals retain their anger in their tissues; dead vegetables ... not so much."

"Hedge witch... My name is Hertha," says the slight girl next to her in a white fur coat that extends from her neck to her ankles. Her own long, raven hair spills out of the back. "I jump between this world and the Other Side. I cross the hedge or the boundary between the two existences to bring messages. And the messages I'm getting from the outside yard are ones of hostility born from generations of hatred."

Inside vibes weren't much better.

Jolted somewhere between fear and desperation, the colonists rise to their feet. They know enough to race for the bolted door, which doesn't move an inch when they try to unlock it. Not that we locked it. But, it's locked now. No amount of body weight versus door works either. It is as if the house has become a tomb.

"All warfare is based on assumption. Sun Tzu," a witch named Maida says, still dangling her legs from the beam. "If your enemy is superior, beat it. If temperamental, irritate. If unprepared, attack. If not, demolish!"

Round balls of red and amber fire burst from the fireplace and land at poor Emmett's feet, charring the remaining floor boards and melting the tennis shoes attached to his toes.

The other witches watch as the fire spreads around him in a small circle that serves as his jail now. Alvina flies downward until she stands in the kitchen.

"I'm also a Hearth Witch, a kitchen witch," she says. "We create magic in the home or specifically in the kitchen. Brews. Herbs. Oils." She waves her hand, motioning for us to gather elsewhere, as she turns and faces the colonists who hover together by the living room hearth. Her hands rotate in small circles and I watch as blue puddles instantly form under their feet. "Paraffin. Lamp oil," she explains. "You might call it Kerosene. It's a highly combustible hydrocarbon."

She nods toward the back of the house and we don't need to be

THE CLAIRES

asked twice. The four of us relocate fast.

Alvina douses the rest of the floor and the furniture with the sticky, sweet fluid. I watch in horror as Manon slowly lifts her fingers into the air until all of the lit candlesticks in the house break free of their holders and begin to rise. When they reach her vicinity, they form a circle. The witch places her hand into the bluest part of the flames until she can draw three small fireballs.

She tosses one sphere of fire at the curtains and another at the wooden cabin wall. The third is lobbed into the middle of that highly flammable oak kitchen table. "Damn, we're going to need more kerosene and we haven't had a general store around here since 1928," she says with a warm smile and arms that reach long enough to close every window.

"You could try Target," I blurt.

"You girls aren't from around here," Maida says.

"Ladies?" Manon says to us, and V nods. It only takes two outstretched arms for all four of us sisters to rise from the actual ground as we are floated up to the beam. A quick scurry through the attic leads us to the only open window and a long wooden ladder leaning against the outside of the house.

As the small abode becomes engulfed in flames, we climb hard, jumping the rest of the way to the soft earth. In the frenzy of the smoke and fresh ash, the posse waiting outside has already retreated into the woods. Fire was the great equalizer and its wrath carried frightening memories across the generations. There was no time to ponder our one lucky break. We sprint hard the other way toward the main road where, of all things, we're saved in the form of a Grey Subaru. License plate BTY128.

Our Uber was parked at the end of the driveway. "Are you V?" asks the bored driver who had been sitting there the entire time listening to his tunes. He was so busy texting that he missed the witch fest, the colonists, and the fact that the house in his GPS was now a blazing inferno.

"No smoking in the car," he tells us because he smells us.

"No problem," I say.

"You having a good night?" he asks.

Standard Uber stuff.

"Nothing for the history books," V says.

4.

BACK AT THE hotel, we call home for the first time during our "trip to save the beaches of California." I'm still so freaked out about the witches that I can barely remember our bullshit. Dad doesn't notice. He's a bit unhinged because he's still in Phoenix at the Mayo Clinic with mom, plus he does the math. "It's one o'clock in the damn morning! I've been trying to call you all day!" he shouts, followed by a lot of other words that are supposed to sound like he's seriously ready to drown us. He goes through his greatest hits: We're always disappearing; where do we go? Why do we never call? Did we almost drown today cleaning up the ocean? Answers: Really. Nowhere, no power on our phone, didn't drown, all A-OK. He ends it with a booming shout into the phone, "I've been calling you all night. Where the hell were you?"

"At a museum," we answer.

It was no lie.

"How's Mom?" I ask because I really do care.

"There was nothing conclusive from the tests today, but the doctor said it's definitely . . . progressing." His voice chokes.

"I'm so sorry, Dad," I say and I feel his pain down to my bone marrow.

Abruptly, he has to go because Mom is sitting in their empty tub, the water is too hot and she's wearing her favorite yellow nightgown and her blue wool winter hat. "Oh Mom," V says, holding back the tears as we settle back into our room. V informs us what will happen next.

"He will call us tomorrow," she says. "And he will tell us, 'We're past the early stages of Alzheimer's. There are drugs that will keep her at h-home as long as poss-possible.'"

"Shit."

"Until December 24," C says and we shoot her daggers. "The mothers always die first. I'm just stating what's on the horizon, girls."

Why, oh why, did we have this kind of bond with these people? They were nothing more than custodians of our current lifetime. I would try to tell myself that over and over again as the next months sped by like they were on fast-forward. I vowed to spend extra time with Mrs. Danko from this lifetime. It was only right.

In our defense, we weren't the only beings who killed what they loved.

We were just experts at it by now.

5.

It is well past three in the morning when we gather on V's bed to open the little metal box.

And so, we have our answers.

And so, we weep.

A VOYANT'S STORY: V

C. L. GABER

1.

"The Seven Karmic Shadows of Life," I say, matter-of-factly, after reading words that were carefully stitched into thick linen used for long colonial stockings that were hidden under cumbersome petticoats. Animal skin would have deteriorated over the decades, but thick fabric like this just yellowed until it was a dirty brown. Our grandmother was a wise one who thought about transmitting this information rather carefully, and painstakingly stitched each word with black yarn that was thicker than thread. She knew that writing might wash out due to the elements, but careful stitch work – double and triple reinforced needlepoint that formed actual words -- had a good chance of enduring.

Tracing each individual word with my finger, I focus on a tactile response instead of allowing what the words meant to sink slowly into my gray matter. The ever-present Patriarch had thought of everything when it came to expelling our kind from the living realm. If he couldn't get us with your standard-issue satchel of poison then he would make sure that we didn't want to live long lives because of this archaic curse he bestowed upon us.

I read our grandmother's words: "All human beings spend their breathing years struggling to come to terms with the Seven Karmic Shadows of Life that are written into our histories and brewed into our DNA."

"Seven Karmic Shadows," I repeated.

Next stocking.

It was stitched: "You need to heal each one and release it in order to achieve the next step in existence. Healing will involve mending energetic and emotional wounds."

THE CLAIRES

Next stocking. But it wasn't really a sock. It was the long hem of a turn of the century shift dress.

I frown and continue to read to my sisters: "These are painful life curses handed down from one's family of origin. In the case of the Claire sisters, they will never come out of the Shadows. Let them be destined to live heighted versions of each one, culminating in their agonizing, painful, and harrowing deaths on the day of their seventeenth birthday, December 24."

"We are so screwed," I mouth. And then I continue to read.

"Let them die en masse unless they can actually stop the Shadows from appearing and hovering. It is the hope of the Patriarch that they will never be able to stop the powerful Shadows, which is the predictable outcome. These Shadows are the equivalent of soul torture and are embed in each lifetime."

Last piece of clothing. It looked like the leg of a man's trousers.

In what was once white thread, she had sewn the specifics: "The Seven Shadows are Abuse, Addiction, Violence, Poverty, Illness, Abandonment and Betrayal."

"In other words, we're shit out of luck," I say.

"And almost shit out of lives because we've already visited most of these curses," interjects S who adds, "My entire being hurts."

Then she poses the big question. "What happens when we run out of curses?"

ON THE PLANE ride home, C says, "Go through the Shadows list again. Let's see how many of them are past tense."

"Okay," I say under my breath. "Here we go. Abuse, Addiction, Violence, Poverty, Illness, Abandonment and Betrayal. Your soul, upon the day of your living birth determines which of the Seven Karmic Shadows you will combat in this lifetime," I remind her.

Grandma Penny had carefully stitched that delightful information, detailing each, into one of the fabric pieces.

"All this time, I thought we were choosing the birth families," C says as her eyes glare out the small airplane window. "But, now I don't think that's true. I think we're pawns for the Patriarch who places us with the families in order to test the Shadows."

"Yeah," I say. "Here's this life's curse. Use it wisely. No do-overs."

Apparently, he even had a sense of humor about it. Why not have a little fun with your torture? I pull out a yellowed piece of paper from the bottom of the box. The envelope was postmarked: London. "Each of their deaths," The Patriarch wrote, "will be predicated by the appearance of a goat since your original grandmother was so fond of that beast and gave it a potion designed for her daughter, which would have easily ended this misery. She chose to turn my demand into a joke, but I will have the last laugh in this way: That first sighting of a goat will cause each Claire girl to become overcome with her most malevolent side. This will also start the death clock running. All four girls will expire before midnight on their 17th birthday. So, it is written. So, it must be done."

"I wonder if Ma counts when it comes to these Shadows," I whisper, and S leans over to shake her head up and down.

"I've been thinking about it, too" she says. "Our Ma was arrested and later hung for being a so-called witch when we were sixteen, causing us to live alone. If that's not a case of abandonment, I don't know what else is."

"The Shadow of Abandonment hovered and was the victor because we died soon after in a massive house fire," I say.

Then I ask, "Don't you remember the day of the fire — how crazy it was."

THE CLAIRES

"Stop it, right now," C says, slapping my hand.

"Ouch."

"I don't ever want to talk about it."

"You drowned those boys that morning," I say. "They were 12 or 13."

"Young men," she counters.

"As if that makes a difference," S says, shivering.

"I still hear them struggling," A interjects. "And I hear them gulping down all of that cold river water."

"We woke up to that little slaughtered goat Belle in the front yard, and she was my favorite. It was a warning sign from the boys in old New York, so I decided there would be no boys left to hurt poor goats."

"And then there was that farm family – another life, another issue," I continue. "We were four healthy girls who just dropped dead at age seventeen in a field. Do you remember how it felt? Our day started with a lovely breakfast. We ate our dear mother's leftover *goat* stew. Then it was off to work in the fields. I can still imagine that sudden, jabbing pain in our left arm. Then the feeling of an elephant on my chest. We didn't just drop dead. We had heart attacks at age 16, which shouldn't have been surprising. That entire lifetime, we walked around with little energy. We could barely run without being winded. We'd wheeze ourselves to sleep at night—and that family was too poor for a doctor."

"The shadow of Illness, and it beat us," I say. "At least, we didn't kill anyone else that day."

"Except that cow," I say.

"And then in Germany, on the last day of a so-called unremarkable lifetime, we woke up in a weird trancelike state. The Patriarch told us to go to the museum. Was it A or C who pushed that statue from behind? It tipped over and fell on her. Crushed her. Maybe I did it. Who remembers? She could see it coming.

The same day, those men we had never seen before followed us on a school trip and violently tossed us off a bridge into the rushing dark brown water. We sunk like four stones.

"The shadow of Violence," I conclude. "But no goat."

"What was on their jackets?" S reminds me. "If you don't remember, I do. It was a badge of valor that included hand-stitched renderings of a sword, a cross and animals on a farm. I'll never forget it because one of those men was a mere boy and so handsome. His animals were a horse, chickens, a pig and a goat."

"So, what's left? And please don't mention our lifetime from 1979 to 1996. I can't take the stress of any past life regressions," says the ghastly pale C who waits until I rattled them off.

"Our futures can be summed up in these shadows," I whisper. "Addiction, betrayal, poverty and abuse. Spin the wheel. Pick your tomorrows."

2.

WE TOUCH DOWN at LAX around 10:00 p.m. (but I knew the exact time from the start) and an hour later, it was home sweet home time again. The p's are home and a frazzled Mom has already been put to bed. Dad hits the backyard to drink a beer and listen to his police scanner, which he finds oddly calming.

And Cass?

Forget the sweet words on how much he missed us. Nix the home-cooked meal. The blond boy-man who could see dead people and seemed taller and wider at the shoulders, if not the mouth, is right there in our faces. His roomy face, strong jaw, and arm muscles that looked even bigger made him appear to be manly. *Flash!* I see my throat in his hand and it's not long before in real life he is overpowering me with exactly that move. He had never been violent with us in the past—and we had already covered the shadow of Abuse long ago.

He was hissing under his breath.

"You," he bites out, "are the reason that Annie and my baby are God only knows where for the last five days." He moves close enough to trap me between him and the milk-colored wall and waits for me to flinch. I just came from a haunted colonial house filled with trapped witches. He would have had to wait several lifetimes.

All I give him is a smile that proves infuriating.

"If I were you—and thank God I'm not—I'd back the hell off," I hiss. "I'd be thinking, 'Work with them for once instead of against them, especially now that there's a poor, innocent child involved." I say it evenly, although I am basically gasping for air now. S, A and C are easily swept aside with his free arm, although they make attempts to launch hard at him. In seconds, he relents thanks to his self-imposed code of honor. He releases my flesh, but I brace because he's still rumbling with fury and wide-eyed at how far he had gone.

"You're an asshole," I choke. *That thin line between love and loathe had moved all the way to the hatred zone. I didn't want to be with him anymore. Not in that way. A smile played on my lower lip. Maybe I could be in the same room with him.... If I were beheading him. Ah, dare to dream.*

"You're a sick bitch," he rants. "I wonder what Dad would have to say about you coming into my room and trying to screw me."

"He would say that you made it up – and we'd back V up until the end of time," C stands up from where she landed on the tile and yells. "Or that you were the cause of it, which could be so much worse. For you."

"Bitchery has been my business since 1911," I wheeze. "You've only been an a-hole for eighteen years, so who is the novice here?"

The sisters look at me harshly. I know I've said too much.

Luckily, there is a diversion. I see it. Plain as day. Cass's eyes fill with tears.

"The right thing to do is to let her come back to you . . . which she will," I offer him, clearing my throat loudly. Yes, I could be the biggest bitch alive for a century, but I could also make him my bitch because he needed information. And our guile did provoke Annie's reaction, so maybe I owed him on some warped level.

"Surely, you can't drag her back here, even if you find her. The only choice is to go back to your life and high school. Try to act normal—if that's possible. And focus on your mother who also needs you now."

The poor idiot couldn't know that she was also living on borrowed time.

Tick.

Tock.

3.

LIFE WENT ON—as it always does for those lucky enough to enjoy that kind of thing called existing. Junior year ended that May for us and I was still a virgin, damn it all to hell. Since I had semi-retired my feelings for Cass, I was wide open to new possibilities although there were none that made any sense. The hot guy who bagged groceries at the local Smith's? Two words: Prison record. Nice six-pack though, and I only knew about it because once he was stocking dairy and I watched. Sue me. It's not my fault that his shirt always hitched because they keep all the good creamers on the highest shelves.

Annoying Declan from school came roaring up in his BMW one day, and we did a little kissing after a movie at the Grove.

THE CLAIRES

The only thing was I felt nada, nothing, zero. The Narcissist-in-Chief of Santa Monica High kept watching himself kiss in his review mirror, which was just plain unappealing. I wasn't donating my virginity to his already long history of girls that he had deflowered, a list that he incidentally once printed out and put on his social media *by mistake*. It was Johnny, who ran into me at the park where he was running, and gave me the link. He was all about the self-improvement that summer and I noted that he tempered that six-foot-four frame by growing some muscles, so he didn't just go up, but also sideways. His skin had cleared; his head was artfully shaved on the sides, but kept longer on top. He left the geek floods at home and opted to wear short blue nylon shorts and a ripped tank. He even looked older. "Keep it up, Johnny," I told the former geek from my English class, "and you might find a girlfriend this summer."

"Yeah, V," he said. "I might… after I work three jobs to help my Mom keep the house."

"You will," I said quietly. *FLASH!* I knew it.

"Find a girlfriend? Nah, I'm gonna spend my summer of leisure reading to impress Miss Ehm when we have her for AP English next year. Gotta pass the AP test in the spring," he said with a smile. We talked during one of his running breaks. I was trying to get my cardio on, too, but it mostly consisted of walking around the park and brooding.

A pang filled my heart because I wouldn't be around for that test. I'd only have her for half of the year before I died.

I never tuned into Johnny before, but when I did in the park I knew that he was a foster child, abandoned at birth and raised in a group home, who was adopted by a nice family and then the Dad split. Now, it was just him and his Mom. I saw that he worked all day at an Amazon plant packing boxes and all night at Santa

Monica Hospital on a janitorial crew. His mother had four jobs to keep the tiny house they had by the airport.

"Yeah, here's hoping for a bright light," he said, waving to me as he left to pound the pavement.

"Always," I said.

After one lap, he turned around to run backwards. "Hey! What's the V stand for? I always meant to ask you," he said.

"Guess."

"Vivid," he said, whipping around and running into the distance.

"Better than vanilla," I shouted.

The sun would rise in ten minutes. I ran home to give our earthly mother a bath and breakfast.

4.

SUMMER MARKED A small tiff with my sister A who could barely leave our room thanks to her doings with fantasy boyfriends. "If you don't investigate someone who is real flesh and blood, you're going to die a sad, sad girl," I reminded her. To which, A just closed the blinds with a huff and stayed in our dark room until three p.m. each day with the fate of Ireland being decided between her multi-hot lovers with dark hair, blue eyes and a penchant for saying romantic things in Gaelic. She boasted that Branigan and Cashel conducted a ghostly sword fight for her honor in our upstairs hallway. All I saw was a vacuum cleaner and a stack of magazines.

Once, when I dared flip on the lights, she sat straight up in bed and said, "Great, just great. I was just about to make out with River Phoenix and you ruined everything."

"But back in the real world, it's dinner time. So why don't you

THE CLAIRES

go downstairs and make out with a slab of meatloaf," I taunted. "To keep up your strength."

C worked with Dad for part of the summer although luckily there weren't any cases as dire as little Ben. The big guy also helped S get a desk job at the station although she could only work half days because of all of the emotional drama involved in police work. She couldn't tell Dad, "I don't want to absorb the feelings of your perps." Luckily, they kept her away from anyone in cuffs. Even better was that several rookie cops flirted with her until Dad gave them the evil eye while fingering his gun.

"Not interested," S would say when we grilled her at night. "Not investing." Deep down, I knew that she had developed some feelings for a young Hispanic rookie named Javier who was eighteen and just accepted into the Santa Monica police academy. He stopped by almost every single day for paperwork, and finally worked up the nerve to ask S if she might want to get a cold drink in the cafeteria. Since it was 97 degrees with 82 percent humidity, our practical sister who always emotionally guarded said, "Um, sure." For purposes of hydration.

"And then what happened," the sisters grilled her that night. Even sister A put a bunch of ghosts including our Ma on a mode she called "spirit waiting" to listen.

"I had a lemonade with Javier," S said. "It was very cold and icy."

"S, before we kill you – and you know we can – spill a few deets," I interrupted. "We don't want to know about the actual drink, you dingdong."

"Oh, well, Javier, is very nice. He wants to save the world. He comes from a lovely family and I know this because I, um, had lunch with them last week. They were really, really nice. They, uh, stopped by the station to take him to lunch and insisted that I go with them. We went swimming, too. Javier is really tall. He's about six foot two with sinewy muscles. Just saying that so you can form a mental picture," she reported. "He holds my hand all the time and then we kissed in his car. And on the sidewalk. And once in front of this salad bar at a restaurant, but only because they were out of cucumbers and there was time. And these were very deep kisses. They were, um, nice. I liked the connection."

"And…." C egged her on.

"And well, he asked me out to hear this band perform on the beach. I went and it was enjoyable," she said. "I just don't know if he or it will be my everything."

"That's okay, honey," I said. "You're a love explorer."

She stayed in bed the following week to recover from the emotional impact of it all.

Then came the crash.

"I think I might like him, but I'm not sure," she said of the kind boy with the glossy black hair and sweet brown eyes. He started coming over for dinner after the big incident, and Dad allowed it since the kid was going to be a cop and all. "But what's the point?" S fretted. "We die in six months. That's only one thing. And I might also ….."

"Like girls. We know. And you're confused," C interjected. Then with a warm smile and a sisterly nod, she added, "Baby, we know. We saw how you used to look at Annie. Just keep figuring it out. That's all any of us are doing here."

"At least one of us was getting lucky. All I kissed today was the neighbor's dog," I interjected and everyone laughed.

5.

BACKING UP A bit, Cass graduated in a rush of long gowns and with Mom trying to walk onto the stage. He refused to cement

THE CLAIRES

any kind of plan for his future, including when Dad said he was allowed to join the marines. Cass rejected signing up until Annie was found, and even took June and July, authorized and funded by Dad, to travel around and look for her.

When he returned one quiet Wednesday night in early August with a lamentable look on his face, I was waiting in the kitchen. I actually made him a plate of food and sympathized. He eyed me warily when I offered to help in a bigger way, but took the bait because he was desperate. Cass handed me an angel necklace Annie had left here. It was one that her mother gave her and Cass was meaning to give it back, but there wasn't time and now it was just a detail. Holding something that belonged to her helped me dial into her future. It didn't have to be ten years from now. The future also meant tomorrow.

"I see her safe with someone she knows, but Gene does not know them," I say. "I see her up in the mountains. In a cabin. Getting bigger. Smiling. She's healthy . . . and happy. She talks to the baby. All the time."

Cass coughs hard to remove the lump in his throat.

"She's six months along and sings to the baby all day long," I offer. "All I got, but I'll try again later."

"Lady G—" Cass begins.

"Yes, she sings Lady Gaga to her," I say.

"Thank you," he says in a quiet voice.

"Is it . . ."

"A girl, yes," I say—and I meant it. "You're having a girl. Congratulations. And I mean it."

If it was possible, Cass finds a millimeter of a smile.

My heart is shattering because I'm not over it. There is a part of me wishing for things that should never be mine including him.

"Good chat," he says.

"Yay," I reply in a soft voice.

As summer progressed, all of the Claires give him a break until he brings that horrible, low-cut-dress-wearing Tara Favre over for dinner. They were doing some kind of volunteer work at the local Boys and Girls Center—Dad's idea to get Cass out of his own head, but I didn't like it. He was in a trance when it came to girls and Ms. Bottle Blonde former cheerleader who couldn't even get into community college with a 1.nothing GPA was ready to pounce.

Of course, I fixed it. Annie was bad enough, but I would not entertain a new girl specimen.

"Tara, dear," I say as we pass the peas, "Who was the one who gave you the Herpes? Chad or was it Declan? I forget." Then I turn to my loving sister C who always has my back and say, "Dear, can you get out the Lysol?"

"Dessert?" I add with a wicked grin.

4.

THE LAST DAYS of summer break are filled with muggy days and trumpet-shaped pink-and-purple petunias. It was about keeping an eye on Mama who was mostly housebound now because she couldn't possibly drive or be allowed to go into public places by herself. She read, slept, and puttered around in her garden. She grieved the death of every Zinnia, and moments later would never remember why she was crying.

"I love you, my girls," Mom would tell us again and again, as if she knew intuitively to say it enough times to make it last.

"Love you, Mama," we would remind her again and again because we did, in our own demented way. Maybe we loved her more than any of the others—and I put the "maybe" on it to not face the truth that we did. Funny that we were calling her Mama again like we did when we were little girls, and she brightened each

THE CLAIRES

time we said it. We never called any of the other mother figures Mama, but it just fit here. It felt right the same way our little heads did when we were young and she would pull us into the soft spot – the pillows that formed in the fold of her sweet neck.

We always would love this Mama. She was kind and selfless, which is what we would remember about her—before we tucked her away in that space we kept for those parents we would never speak of again. It hurt to remember the pain we inflicted and we prayed to never think of them or it again.

So, we didn't. Madmen or madwomen rarely did.

The five of us, including our lonely, depressed brother, took shifts making sure Mama did no physical harm to herself or escape for yonder, which she did. A few times, we found her walking down the street in her short baby blue, cotton sleeping gown and no shoes. Dad brought in reinforcements, like Gene from next door, who didn't exactly forgive our brother, but he didn't want to draw first blood from him anymore either. Sadness can be exhausting, and both families felt as if they could sleep for a year.

Cass was Gene's only link to his missing daughter and possible grandchild and he chose to accept the fact that working with Cass to find them was better than the alternative of losing them forever. He had always considered Cass his almost-son and potential son-in-law. He chose to virtually adopt him now, figuring Cass would marry his daughter, he'd be a grandpop and everything would be alright with the world.

If they could only find her. Them.

It was funny how one could take a hard stand one day and then just give it up on a dime. How easy was it to just let it all go? If you just loosened your grip a little bit, the hate could flow through your fingers and escape for good.

Gene wouldn't allow the other cops to know that he was part of what was now considered a private missing-persons case, meaning the already-skinny case file was kept sealed in his house. He made quiet inquiries to other law enforcement agencies and came up with only dead ends.

We had to hand it to Annie, who proved to be an expert in the art of disappearance although I knew exactly where she was located, which was outside Portland, Oregon at the house of a friend of a friend. I didn't even tell my sisters – and they never asked. I would never tell Cass because if she returned, we wouldn't have our little sessions where I gave him small tips. It was crumbs, but crumbs were often better than starvation.

As for the rest, I knew Annie lived stealthily without a credit card for tracing or crying phone calls throwing herself on the railroad tracks. There was no begging for mercy or money. Her idea of gone was way, way gone without a trace.

Our "brother" was gutted by it.

One night, Cass even wandered into our room to "talk," proving that perhaps hell had frozen over and we should get out our skates. Ever since my late-night love visit, he never came into our room, so this was big.

He made sure all four of us were in there and then settled in. A, our sister whose initial could have stood for "abnormally sappy," couldn't help but bond with him because they shared that "talk to the dead" thing. "Is that a Viking in here?" Cass asked in an astonished voice. To which, A blurted, "Sven, catch you later. Beat it for now. Yeah, I love you. Now go."

Cass parked it for a long, long time on our purple velvet Victorian-era chair where he looked like a giant rhino sitting on a teeny perch. Damn it all to hell, but we even bonded— just a bit. (It was far easier on me to just hate him rather than let him in, which sent my imagination roaring). That night was enough for us to convince him to attend some blowout summer party on the beach the next night. We reminded him that his pitiful youth

THE CLAIRES

(not to mention his good looks and that massive head of fabulous sun-streaked hair) was fleeting and he better grab a handful of life before he was some fat middle-aged guy existing on Netflix, fried cheese puffs and "remember whens."

"Four sisters, no date, and a social event I'd like to avoid," Cass said. "I'm psyched."

"Take your psyched self to your own room," I said. "I see loneliness in your future." *It felt self-protective to return to my most rotten self where he was concerned.*

And it was just like our sap-hearted brother, Mr. Non-Popularity, to spend the entire party sitting on a sand dune talking to what looked like some dweeby eighth grader or freshman who was here with a put-upon cousin who ditched him the minute their shoes hit the sand.

"Girls, meet my friend, Auggie," Cass said, finally snaring us to sit on his own personal lump of sand. He pointed to some tall, wide, pony-tailed dork-a-palooza trying hard not to get his obviously new and possibly hand-ironed Sears blue jeans too dirty. I knew he wasn't from around here – and this had nothing to do with extra abilities. The entire state of California would have dress coded him for wearing a wide, striped shirt with the stripes going in the horizontal direction.

"I'm Auggie. I'm here on vacation. We come here every single year," he stammered. "My mom is really big on me visiting my cousin. She thinks he will make me more social or leap out of my shell. 'Cept, I don't know where he is. He brings me to these things and then dumps me. Did you see him? My cousin, I mean."

"Yes," I said. "There's another big dork in Sears jeans by the bonfire. Don't stand too close. If those pants go up in flames, you might be considered a toxin. This is California."

"That's really funny," he said with a bright smile. *Why did some people – ones you had no intention of getting to know – make it impossible to hate them.* "And no worries about offending me. I'm un-offend-able," the kid said.

He was also unmovable.

This strange kid stayed and stayed while setting our collective ears on fire. "My mom made me go with my cousin to this party, which I really didn't want to do. I thought we were going to see *The Wolverine*," the kid mumbled. He was like one long run-on sentence with a body over it.

No, he didn't. But he did. Auggie raised his fingers, flicked them twice and pretended like he had Wolverine claws. Obviously, we had a winner—someone who was a bigger dolt than Cass *who was …no, please no…. flicking his own faux claws.* If we weren't scheduled to die in a few months, we might have to move.

"Hey, did you girls know that I'm trying out to play tuba next year in the high school band?" Auggie tossed out. "I might go to college on a tuba scholarship. Maybe NYU, you know, because it's in New York. Have you ever been to New York? I hear it's really cool."

"Yes, we did know NYU was in New York. The entire world knows that fact," I said. "And I can see you now in your ice-cream-man white suit with Christmas lights around your tuba. It's beyond definition." *I could actually see some turmoil in this kid's future, but I was off the clock tonight. None of my business, as they say. At the same time, I felt bad for him for shit's sake. What was wrong with me? This wasn't even period related.*

"Do you think I made it on the squad? Do you have a feeling? Are you one of those girls who is intuitive in that way?" Auggie asked with a shit-eating grin.

"I feel something good," S said. *Sweet of her to throw him a bone.*

"Stick to the straight and narrow, kid. It adds to your life expectancy. Don't do drugs. Are you listening to me?" I said.

THE CLAIRES

"I would never," he huffed. "I just say no."

"Good deal, Wolverine," I said.

We ditched them both for the rest of the evening, and didn't return to the party. Instead, we went on a slow prowl and saved two slightly tipsy girls who were being seriously hassled by five rough-looking, tat-covered motorcycle punks in their twenties pretending to own the beach. The girls moved right and the guys kept blocking. Two of the girls were crying now because obstruction turned into unwelcome hands on cold, wind-whipped flesh. Five to two were never good odds, especially for girls who don't have all their wits.

And then the odds evened. Turns out we weren't the only ones on a nightly cleaning mission. Tall types in long black robes with oblong sized heads came out of the shadows or should I say they simply rose from the sand or *underneath* and used what looked like extremely pronged hands, the size of tennis rackets, to make sure those five Romeos pissed their pants.

The hands were everywhere, turning the tormentors into the tormented. One of the guys was sobbing, which was followed by begging because those hands traveled under the collar of his shirt and came out by his socks. Long, gnarled nails drew blood on the lower extremities until there was screaming and negotiating.

"I'll give you my money. My car keys. Just don't touch me, man!" one of the men, and I use that word loosely, cried.

But they did touch them because it was only fair.

There wasn't enough fairness in this mortal world, which was a pity. But the little justice that could be spread in this "natural way" was like sweet frosting on this cake called life.

5.

We had run into their type before, during another near date rape that we were trying to "fix." Those handsy men—in the non-harassing, supernatural sense—looked at us, smiled, and nodded. It seemed as if there was a creed amongst the night creatures including the Claires. If your intentions were pure and you weren't exactly the norm, then you were part of some odd fellowship.

S felt it before I could call it. "We summoned them here. These creatures, these things," she said. "They smell our fear."

One night, a few other odd ones known as Seekers, with their third eye visible, asked us why we were prowling and fixing. "With the time you have left, why not just indulge in every one of life's pleasure and leave such sanitation work for other entities?" one mentioned. *So, they knew about us, which was common. The supernatural world was nothing if not highly intelligent and intuitive.*

"Fixing makes me feel the most alive," C said.

One thing was clear.

"We need to learn how to fight like badass bitches," C said. "All we do is find people doing the worst, but we can't do anything real about it beyond…what? We can't swear them to death. The truth is we're as vulnerable as the victims we're trying to protect."

One of those hands pointed in a direction that was across the street from the beach. What I saw next was large, oh so bright, and landed in the vision patterns of all the sisters. UFO? I wish.

6.

It was a sign, alright, and it said LA Fitness.

We spent the rest of the summer training at this place where

THE CLAIRES

the fees were low, the locker rooms were only half covered in bacteria, and a few of the bored trainers took pity on us and decided to help some micro-leotard-wearing females learn how defend themselves. We went at off-hours and frankly the muscle guys who dwelled there had nothing else to do, but train us.

The younger trainers were hot and on the make, and oh so ordinary that they were morphing into one big, musclebound bore. But there was an older guy named Louis, maybe twenty-two or twenty-three, who was on one leg after a special forces mission in Iraq went south when his truck drove over a hidden bomb. He had a forever reminder of that time of his life in the form of a shiny silver prosthetic that held up his 235 pounds (he told us) and his six-foot-four inches. His arms looked like ripped tree trunks, a fact I mentioned to C a little bit too loudly. His ears were of the supersonic variety and he overheard me.

"Size doesn't give you power," he said in a deep voice. "It begins up here." He tapped his wide forehead three times, which was when I noticed that he had rich green eyes the color of a summer tree at full bloom. There was also a tat of an emerald dragon covering an entire sculpted shoulder and then splaying out magnificently across his defined back.

As a professional who believed in defending her city at all costs, I began to spend copious hours in the gym, and naturally dragged my cardio-loving sisters with me.

For cover. As wing women.

"Louis, I need to know how to defend myself," I said.

"From what?" he asked.

"Everything," I replied. "It's a dangerous world out there."

"Are you hurt?" Louis said, about 45 minutes later, after tossing me halfway across the room. I crashed with a thud onto one of those thick mats, sticking the landing on my now flattened and slightly aching ass.

"Sorry," he said. "But let's do it again. What if someone tries to attack you? Landing is key because if you land submissive then it's all over."

"Yes," I said. "No more submission. Bad for my reputation."

He laughed for some reason—and went along with it. "A few more of these and you can even defend yourself from your standard-variety vampires and werewolves. Please don't tell me you're one of those girls who reads those books. A regular guy can't compete."

Compete. Really? Really.

"Yes," I said. "He can."

"I'm not regular," he said, looking down at the leg.

"Who is anymore….and are you just going to stand there or are you going to throw me again? I mean, I can't get into a guy who just stands there. B-O-R-I-N-G," I retorted.

He threw. I stood. And then I walked back into his face.

"You never know when that will come in handy," I said with a smile because he was helpful . . . and suddenly smoking hot as only a guy who suddenly likes you can look. "What's next, Special Forces?" I asked.

He raised one eyebrow and pointed to the blue mat.

"Gimme fifty," he said meaning sit-ups.

"You're no fun," I moaned

"I used to be," he said.

"How fun?" I taunted because this was fun. And it was much better to try this out on someone who wasn't disgusted by my efforts.

Finally, we got to the good stuff—useable against enemies of this earth and beyond.

"Again," Louis cried. "A round-house kick to the jaw should spin your opponent before it drops him. Don't give me any bullshit that you're female, although you are very much a female."

THE CLAIRES

I felt his look to my toes. In fact, I swore, I was now levitating in my new gym shoes that were black and perfectly matched my hot pink bra top and skimpy little bottoms.

"You have leg bones that, when in perfect working order, are as strong as sledgehammers," Louis said, getting back to business.

Louis seemed distant when he wrapped those tree-trunk arms around me from behind and said, "Tell me how you opt out of someone else deciding your fate."

When I easily twisted around, thanks to some rather oily sunscreen and smiled up at him, he seemed only mildly surprised. When I kissed his cheek sweetly, he nervously muttered, "Yeah, well there's *that*."

"Doesn't work on vampires," I said with a smile.

"Works just fine on the rest of us," he said.

He had excellent planning skills, which is why he stopped talking, and kissed me hard on the lips.

"Fifty more," I joked, before slipping out of his arms. My brain was mush as one thought raced through my entire being: *At least, I could die happy now.* Not happy. Well, you know . . .

"Why V, you're blushing," Louis said. "You gimme fifty more."

He took my hand and wrote something on the palm, which I assumed was his number. Instead, it read: Training/M-W-F/6 a.m. I knew that meant he sort of liked me, too, when he grabbed my other hand. It had to be his number, but wrong again.

He wrote: You're breathtaking.

I felt so high that I went home, took Mom for a walk around the neighborhood, kissed Dad on his cheek and then told Cass that Annie was fine and he should stop worrying because she had a check-up today and the baby was healthy and strong.

"You're welcome," I said.

To further celebrate my newfound, non-faux-relative crush, the girls and I went prowling that night and put a few strokes in our penance journal by stumbling upon a home robbery off Santa Monica Boulevard in one of the nicer sections where well-kept single-family houses exist with exquisite jacaranda trees in the yards marked by papery thin flowers.

In the pale moonlight, we stood a bit down the street and watched two figures in hoodies kick open the side door of a white, two-story house and enter it. C motioned for us to "come on" and we walked up to the house, cut left at the bushes and walked inside just as one of the hooded people was about to stab the man of the house with his own large bread knife. We weren't ninjas by any means, but my crush on Louis meant I didn't miss a training session and regularly practiced in the yard or whenever I could find Cass or Dad. As for my brother, he seemed relieved that I was treating him like a punching bag instead of a crush.

That night, the thick bony part of my bottom leg connected nicely with the head of the young teenage punk girl and she dropped that large jagged knife. Next, I spun her like a top and then projectile-style launched her bony frame, face-first, into a nearby wall.

"Not so tough without your weapon," I spit out, a little shocked myself when her teeth fell out of her head like tiny beads. When she slumped to the floor, I knew I knocked her out cold. *Sorry, I shouldn't have, but I took exactly one photo. Later, I'd make sure that her face, or what was left of it, made its way into Dad's perp files.*

I put my hand out to stop the ten-year-old little man of this house from advancing with his baseball bat. I had to give props to the kid who raced in to save his Daddy O.

"We got this, hon," I said. And for the first time ever, I meant it.

Yeah, baby!

And then there was one.

We circled the other robber and for some reason, I began to hum, a low, steady, *unnerving* buzzing sound I made with my

THE CLAIRES

mouth closed and lips sealed shut. The girls had no idea what the fuck I was doing, but they joined in until we made a sound that was so high and tinny that it probably made the neighbor dogs run for cover. The other robber femme was so perplexed that she spun from side to side until I knew she must be feeling dizzy. That's when I grabbed the kid's bat and with a wink toward him swung for the fences or, rather, her front grill.

After a quick inspection of the damage, we called 911 and slipped out faster than you could say to the kid and his pop (although we did say), "Please keep this on the QT." They did one better when they got into their car to drive to the station to make a police report.

For some reason, we stuck around to make sure these two found their hands in cuffs. During own wait time, I ate a little leftover spaghetti from the fridge and erased the photos on the kid's phone. The ones of us.

When help arrived, we hid in the bushes across the street to watch the coda of the event. When I noticed that the cops were a bit green around the edges, *literally*, and elongated at over seven feet, and missing part of the skin on their lower faces, I checked my phone. There was no record of us ever calling 911 now. Even though we did. But somehow they ... erased it. We almost ran like hell. But I was too curious and had to walk back to the crime scene to ask.

"Who are you?" I inquired, knowing for some reason, at my core, that they wouldn't hurt us. And they didn't even try because the long spear-like weapons on their almost-naked, brown-skinned sides stayed in place.

"Greetings from the Abiku. You summoned; we heed the call of need," one said in what sounded like an Africanese accent. "We come from the Yoruka tribe of West Africa. We're tree spirits who have died several times as you have. We can sense lifetimes—as most spirits can."

"How did you know from so far away?" I asked him.

"You emit what can only be described as a strong beacon when in trouble," he said.

"It turns on when you're in grave danger," said the tallest woman who was completely bald like the rest with large, dark-brown almond eyes. "Spirits sense spirits. Spirits sense lifetimes. Spirits sense when other spirits that don't exactly mesh with the status quo need help. Most spirits do not look for trouble, but if provoked, they will put a cap on a burdensome situation," she said.

"We wish you well," I said, bowing deeply.

"And you," she replied. "But best you be gone now. We like to feed in private. And since you ate all of the pasta . . . "

The police never found body or bone. Neither did the homeowner who did discover a lone silver spear in their family room.

7.

As we sat in our almost empty apartment later that night, C said, "We find the trouble; something else tunes in; it or they arrive to devour the bones," C said. "I actually like it—sometimes too much. We're on the front line. Up until now, they, as in the others, have been the clean-up crew. Most of 'them' don't want to know us beyond initial contact. But a few are friendlier."

I knew she was thinking about that guy Emin and I couldn't blame her. My sweet stolen kisses with Louis were making this a last summer to remember.

"I spoke about this very thing with a spirit who looked it up for me while vacationing at the ancient library at Alexandria,"

THE CLAIRES

said S. "She confirmed that since we're out here doing good deeds, the universe is cooperating by sending in what is known as supernatural reinforcements—and many of those 'helpers' have given us assists in prior lifetimes when they were feeling altruistic.

"For instance, we have seen those water creatures before, in other lifetimes," S continued. "Officially, they practice Hydrokinesis, which is the ability to manipulate and control liquid water and mold it into any desired shape or form."

"They're Nixies," S continued. "Creatures who also enjoy the power of Aquatic Adaptation, or adaption to underwear living."

"They're half human, half fish," she said. "They like to mingle with humans and, when in the water, take on a variety of forms from old women to fair maidens. They're shape-shifting water spirits at the ready for some sort of excitement."

This wasn't street justice; it was spiritual payback.

Mere mortals didn't know that there were supernatural beings who chose to be here for reasons of checks and balance. They were here to tip the scales toward the good and even the odds against what was evil.

Some might even call these visiting entities monsters, but a few knew that these beings were on the side of what was right and were, in fact, running a campaign insisting that others on the side of what was right should join forces with them instead of pushing them away.

"Is that blood on your shirt, honey?" our current Mama had said one night when we got home from a night of prowling. She was far more lucid these days, thanks to new meds prescribed from her Mayo Clinic doc who was "into trying new things," but it was a day-to-day thing. One day was good; the next real bad. We held the good days tight, thanking our lucky stars and then cursing the pills when it all crumbled.

"Now, why would I be bleeding Mama?" I asked her as she

put some antiseptic on a slight gash that opened up after that particularly rough night. Three crazy dudes thought they would rob a little old lady of her purse and steal her food in a dark grocery store parking lot. They didn't get her cash . . . or her half-off coconut cream pie.

"Don't lie to your mother," she replied.

"We don't," I said just as Ma's voice filled A's ears. Our original mother could be a jealous one and she always shunned the new earthly mothers. Sure, they could provide for our basic needs, but anything beyond was her job. *"Enough of this touchy-feely crap. She's not your real mother. She is your host,"* Lula said (translated by A). I had eyes and could see Ma whipping the kitchen curtains into a frenzy. Call it a spiritual temper tantrum.

Mama began to cry, which apparently made Lula feel bad. She wasn't a total bitch and not only cut the crap when it came to the curtains, but curiously did the dinner dishes while (almost) no one was looking. I calmed Mama and set about to make her some tea. When I looked over my shoulder, I saw that Lula was tending to Mama, too, by smoothing her hair down. Mama's eyes were closed. To the naked eye, something was making all the stray hairs suddenly go flat. "Don't stop, honey," she said to no one in particular. "It feels so good. Your hands are so soft."

"I won't," Lula said to A who whispered her words into my ear.

17

CASS

1.

The first message I actually delivered was when I was five. There was a little girl in my kindergarten class whose grandfather had abruptly and swiftly passed. Shannon O'Connor sat without swinging on a hot piece of plastic playground equipment trying hard not to get her pretty yellow funeral dress dirty. She was a skinny little girl with big scabs on her knees from dangerous dares, but death was something that scared her down to her scrappy little soul.

Her mother had dropped her off at school an hour after they dropped her grandfather into the ground. Why not give the kid a break? Something about not missing too much school despite "the sad thing that happened."

I was this stout, tall kid with hair to spare wearing a Batman T-shirt and flood pants because I grew too fast for Dad's wallet. I stopped swinging when I saw him. *Him, as in her grandfather.* He was leaning against one of the wooden poles that held up the little fort next to the swings. Gramps was a tall, skinny man in a red Mr. Rogers sweater, pressed blue trousers and with a sweet-smelling pipe dangling from his lips.

"Hey, Shannon," I said in a low voice because for some reason it felt private, and because the rest of the kids were lined up to try this new jungle gym the school just installed.

"He's right here with you, you know," I finally whispered to her. And for a minute, I thought little Shannon might just get off the swing she wasn't much swinging on and punch me in the face. I knew the only thing between me and her fist were the details—and I saw them clearly. And I caught of whiff of them, too.

THE CLAIRES

"Hey, don't get all mad. I have proof," I said. "Your granddad smells like lemon tea mixed with the black licorice he keeps in his desk, blended with his cherry vanilla pipe smoke and topped with the sweetness of pink roses in Spring, since he likes to dig in the rose garden. And he promises to always stay close if you still eat the little oranges—tangerines, he says—that both of you liked to peel together. From the tree in the yard. He said don't tell grandma about all the peels on the floor of the garage because you're not supposed to be eating in there. But you do."

Shannon stopped looking at her shoes. When her head lifted, her eyes were filled pools of tears. I don't know why, but she reached out to hold my hand.

"Eat in there, I mean," I stammered because I had never held a girl's hand before. "But you do."

"Yes, we do," Shannon said with a tiny smile.

"His name is Albert," I told her. "He said be a big girl and don't . . . *wow* . . . *really?*"

"What did he say?" she begged.

"He said that you should close the pools," I said. I guess he saw that her eyes were filled, too. When she closed her eyes, three or four tears went running.

"Tell him, I drained the pools," she said with a little laugh.

"He said . . . *okay, okay, okay, I'm telling her* . . . that it isn't swim season," I said.

This time she really laughed.

"And he said . . . yes, sir, I'm telling her . . . not to let your grandma drown because she's a real bad swimmer," I said. "And one more thing. He said to always remember that just 'cause you can't 'see' someone doesn't mean they're not right there. Plain as day. He's just a few steps away. You can smell him sometimes. Feel him other times. In your bones."

It was good advice, but maybe too much. Or perhaps Shannon

O'Connor had thought enough about death today.

"You're a total freak, Cass," she finally said, scooting off the swing to run back into the school building.

"She's in room 203, sir," I said to no one.

"*Thanks, son,*" Grandpa Albert replied. "*I'll finish smoking my pipe and then I'll pay her a visit indoors. She might need a little help with that math test.*"

2.

MAYBE I WAS a total freak because my sister wanted to jump me while the only girl I ever loved, Annie, was gone, but hopefully not forever gone, please. She was missing, which was its own torture. A month gone, she had sent a postcard or, as I liked to call it, Proof of Life. POL was a handful of words written in her careless cursive, which she only used when she wanted to get something over and done with fast because it felt uncomfortable: Dear Cass—Doing fine. Left California. Please don't look for me. LOVE YOU. Ann.

She was Ann now.

Evolving.

Things were always changing. I always hated that part of it.

The truth is I would have roamed the earth to find her, but I wasn't sure where to start or if I had the gas money to do an earthly roam. One day, she talked about living the vegan life in Oregon, Idaho, and the next she planned to roam the wilds of Montana where she would rent a cabin in Glacier National Park. Another day and she would proclaim that she was going to get lost in New York City or maybe Boston or Chicago. I could have searched, and planned to during winter break, but where would I start? On what road? Headed for what town? In which direction?

In early December, eight months into her disappearance,

THE CLAIRES

Gene motioned me to come into his house (which was rare now, though we had those driveway chat sessions). He showed me this thing that apparently caused him great shame. They had a joint checking account, so Annie could always buy groceries, clothes, school stuff, and whenever she needed them, other life essentials. She was the little woman of the house because cops were rarely home, and someone had to do all of the mundane tasks. Week of her disappearance, Annie had wiped out the $3500 Gene kept in there. Cleaned them out. I loved her, but what she did seemed heartless on a cop's salary.

She had plotted and executed things brilliantly by figuring out how to finance a brand-new life for her and the baby without her father or me in it.

One night, I asked my sisters, "How hard is it for a teenager to get their own apartment?"

"How did you . . ." S began.

"Know?" I said. "I was worried about you. I followed you there once. Twice. Maybe three times. Nice digs."

"And you never told them," V said. She looked pretty shocked that I wasn't a rat when it came to providing intriguing and totally unexpected news flashes to our parental units. At this point, Mom would have been too confused to understand it; Dad would have imploded and he had enough on his plate. Not telling them was a win-win for all.

"Not too much time left for all of us to be together," S began.

What was she talking about? Where were they going?

"And you wait until now to prove, bro, that you're someone who might be worthwhile knowing?" she concluded.

"Why do we only have a little time left? Are you girls moving to Alaska?" I question her. *What was it about my sisters? They spoke in riddles attached to endless loops of confusion covered in mysteries and enigmas. There were days when I thought we shouldn't be in the same family; others, I wondered if we were the same species.*

"You want a head's up?" she asked, inviting me again into their turn-of-the-century palace that was their not-so-spacious room. As usual, it was Africa hot in this palace of strange rose and cinnamon smells and even odder decor. I was used to my spot in the door, so this was a real treat, if you could call it that in any real way.

They had me curious enough to sink my frame into some overly stuffed purple chair with an odd steel back that looked like it was the velvet version of the much-coveted seat on *Game of Thrones*. A few moves to get comfortable and I felt the bottom breaking, so I stayed still.

"We're leaving before we turn seventeen," V informed me.

As usual, I got it one-hundred percent wrong.

"You're moving out at seventeen? College? Early admission?" I asked her. "How ambitious of you."

"You could call it an eviction," V said in a wistful voice.

I threw my hands up. "You got me curious now."

They went stealth on that one and then changed the subject.

"She's going to come back here, Cass," she added. "The timing won't be the best, but you won't have to look for Annie anymore because she'll be easily found – as in she will be in our kitchen."

"Why does everyone keep talking singularly," I asked, standing up to pace. "There are two of them. She's pregnant."

"Yes, Annie is pregnant," V said with less venom than usual. "She's young, healthy and strong as is the baby. They are living with friends who are taking great care of them. She's eating her veggies. She's not talking to other boys. And it's pretty where she is—giant evergreen trees, water, big mansions. The rest? Who the hell knows?"

"And the baby? When will she be born?"

"I can't really see anything when it comes to the child entering

THE CLAIRES

this world. I seem to be blocked," she said.

"You're . . . what? Did you say blocked? What's blocked? And what other worlds are there? What are you? Or what's in you that can be blocked?" I asked as my head began to throb. There wasn't enough aspirin in the world to deal with my sisters.

"Ladies, first," she taunted. "What are you . . . exactly? In terms of extras – and you know what I mean, so let's not go ten rounds of bullshit."

I never discussed my extracurriculars with them or anyone, but why not trot out your weird in a den of weirdos?

"Ever since I was a little boy, I've been surrounded by dead people at night," I blurted. When there was absolutely no reaction, I went on.

"They're greedy pain-in-the-ass ghosts who want me to pass on messages to their loved ones like I'm some freaking mailman for those who left no forwarding addresses. If you want to think that I'm some freak or weirdo, so be it. I'll be Cass, your resident oddity. At your service for all your freak needs. Prices double on Halloween."

Sister A slid another spoonful of ice cream down her throat. They had their own mini-fridge up here and it was packed with all things Haagan Daz. A flipped me something close to nirvana when she tossed over an unopened Cherry Garcia and a plastic spoon.

"I see dead people, too," she said. *As if it wasn't really a big deal in any real way.* "They are pains in the asses, you're right, but occasionally helpful. Sometimes, the dead can even be amusing or sexy or …well, let's just say they're intriguing in their neediness and persistence."

S jumped in to confess, "I sense the emotions of others . . . I take on their emotions until I can't even begin to feel my own. It's a freakin' nightmare and why I come home from school and lock myself in this room because if I don't find some silence, I will lose my mind. I mean, do you know how many problems of an emotional nature the student body at any high school has in one day. It's in the millions."

"I just thought you were some kind of truancy queen," I said with a slight smile. I was finally beginning to understand what I already read while trying to figure out my sisters through good old-fashioned research. There were times I thought they were witches, so I looked that up. Then the whole "clair" thing become a possibility. That one was true. One was *clair* something . . . what was it . . . *clairsentient*. A was *clairaudient*.

V just shrugged. "I can see the future for everyone, but everyone in this room. It doesn't work for close relatives—even if I don't feel that close to them."

She was the *clairvoyant*.

C looked up from her book. "I can do it all. Anytime. Anywhere. I'm the Yoda of this group – *clair everything*," she said without bragging. She made it sound like a curse when she added, "Yippee for me. Wanna order a pizza? It will arrive in exactly nine minutes and they'll forget the mushrooms."

"Welcome to the circus act that is our family," V said. "Our DNA strands revolve around the *clair* arts, and if you don't know what that means then look it up. I don't have the time to explain it."

What came next shocked me although I brought it on myself.

"But our family doesn't have any *clair* traits," I said. "Mom has a bit of that 'talk to the dead' thing on her 23 and Me. It got handed down to me. Dad has nothing, but some good German blood and lactose issues. So, how do we explain the four of you?"

"Cass, it's complicated," S hedged. "How can I explain this? And frankly, I will explain it because I'm sick of keeping secrets. I always walk around feeling like I'm lying."

The entire room seemed to inhale.

THE CLAIRES

"Your mother is our mother as in she re-birthed us and nourished us when she was pregnant, but we're not from her or your father. You are blood of their blood. You share DNA," she said.

Then she did something even weirder, which was to poke A in the side and say, "Tell Ma that I spilled it. She can send down lightning and fire if she wants," she huffed.

C jumped in. "They had you. And there were complications from the labor. They didn't think your Ma would ever have another baby and then a year into your life, man, did she prove those doctors wrong. She went for a few fertility treatments. And soon she was pregnant with what the docs thought were twins, but were actually quads."

"She did IVF," S said. "But what they implanted wasn't her own eggs and your Dad's sperm. It was something …. else. From someone else."

"They were so desperate for more children that they took it as a miracle," V said. "But sometimes miracles aren't miracles. They're something else. They're spirits . . . looking for someone who can provide . . ."

"A host," S whispered.

"Bottom line," V said. "We're not flesh of her flesh or bone of her bone. Which explains…well, why I've never really thought of you in that typical brotherly slash sisterly way."

Silently, I put down my ice-cream and stared out the window.

"We'll deny this until the end of time if you tell anyone else," C began. "The truth is we're from the past. We die every seventeen years and come back to another host family. We've recently found out that it's part of some sort of ancient curse that has to do with the Seven Shadows of Life, which apparently we must endure as some sort of sick retaliation from some rage-a-holic figurehead in London," C concluded, as she stared at her nails.

Then they explained the Shadows to me, rendering me even further into a non-communicative state. "We've already done abandonment, violence, and illness," V shared. "Our original mother ditched us. We dropped dead of heart attacks the next lifetime around. We were thrown off a bridge the third time we visited this rolling ball."

"So, what's left?" I asked. "Blood-letting? Dragon attack?"

"We'll take addiction, poverty, abuse, or betrayal for five hundred, Alex," C said, mimicking an episode of *Jeopardy*.

I went stealth. Again.

"We should have told him years ago," A smarted. "Turns out this was a great way to finally shut up our big bro, although, again, you're not really our bro in a blood sense. And you can't exactly say we've adopted each other because although we've shared a house, we've virtually had no relationship with each other during the past 16 years. Heartbreaking, isn't it? The truth is—and I will deny it for a few more weeks if pressed—you're an only child!"

The tick of the clock on the wall seemed garishly loud. Finally, a laugh escaped from deep in my stomach and floated up through my throat until my face turned red and I couldn't stop. I could accept the *clair* traits as a possibility because the world was full of unlikely curiosities, but this... They had me at *cursed for life.*

"Oh man, thanks girls," I said, doubling over. "I owe you. I really do. I needed a good laugh. I won't tell Mom and Dad about the apartment until you're much older and someone might actually find it humorous. Like when you're 50 and Dad is 80. I don't know what you do in there. I don't think I want to know, but use condoms."

"Yes," V sniped. "We're drug dealing ho's. You figured it out, idiot."

"Cass, I can suddenly see your future," she added. "You're about to leave this room or we're going to devour you."

THE CLAIRES

I walked away laughing even harder. "You rented mom's womb...I mean....someone better call Stephen King."

In the middle of the night, I looked up every single thing I could find that started with the word *clair*.

AN AUDIENT'S STORY: A

September/October

1.

THERE IS A reason they call it "fall." It's a nicer way of saying dying season. There would be no breaking this curse, although we kept our eyes out for what was left when it came to those Seven Shadows of Life. Addiction seemed unlikely, as did poverty. That left two likely candidates: abuse or betrayal.

Each night, I asked the spirits who visited me and they refused to opine. They felt our pain the same way I felt their need to be heard. It was as if both worlds were living in suspended disbelief as we waited upon a miracle to ease the ache.

Even my Viking lovers tried to console me, but to no avail. "Cross the line, sweet A, and we will be one and the same," said Erik. What I couldn't tell him is that my death would be brief followed by a rebirth that started this hopeless cycle again.

The days seemed to race at max speed because we were living on borrowed time. The worst of the worst in the melancholy department was when the school announced a seniors' winter dance on December 23, the night before Christmas Eve. "Someone owed your fine principal a favor and we're having the holiday prom at the Chateau Marmont," we were told through the morning PA.

I would never admit how much I wanted to go although I would be quite dateless unless I brought one of my boyfriends in the form of an invisible ghost. C was airlifted off a beach by Emin months ago while I knew V had kissed our trainer Louis. All of a sudden, all I wanted before I went again was a sweet kiss at midnight from flesh and blood lips.

While I was wearing a pretty dress. I wanted it badly.

I even heard whispers in the air from students long since

THE CLAIRES

passed who attended a place somewhere called The Academy. They had danced their last dance, but still encouraged me, "Go, go, go. . . . . . these are rites of passages that you will cherish forever, plus a kiss before dying is always a welcome good-bye present."

"Cheesy stuff . . . this dance," I lied to my sisters. S quickly put it all in perspective when she noted that in Los Angeles it was always about location, location, location. Turns out the Chateau Marmont was bat-shit haunted with the spirits of dead celebrities and others who drew their last breath in this castle-like hotel and hot meeting spot. Immediately, I tuned in and saw their stories playing out in a loop in my mind—John Belushi on the last night of his night; Jim Morrison crashing his motorcycle through the dark lobby. Jim actually did something we couldn't do—he lived. F. Scott Fitzgerald wasn't so lucky and had a heart attack right in front of the hotel.

And one of my handsome night suitors, James Dean himself, told me a great story one icy October night about his most infamous night at the Chateau while auditioning with Natalie Wood for *Rebel Without a Cause*. "I jumped right out of a third story window to impress the director and got the role – and a few broken bones," he said with a wink and a smile. "At least I wasn't as stupid as Morrison who climbed onto the roof of the hotel and tried to swing into his room. He fell right on his back, the dumb SOB. Although Jim tells us, it was just an average night where he used up eight of his nine lives."

"I'm in if you're in," I finally told the girls when it came to this social whirl.

It was better to just be observers of the social scene and crush from afar. "We'll be each other's dates," S said, hugging me hard and adding, "At least, there's no mystery. I *will* be going home with my date. Sleeping in the same room with her, too, and listening to her snore and fart."

"Hey, I have acid reflux issues this time around," I sniffed.

It sounded as deliciously normal as V collecting over $1000 from giving out mid-term answers in AP Lit. Thank you, George Orwell and your classic, *1984*. We had enough money now for fancy party dresses and shoes that would make even Carrie Bradshaw jealous.

"Maybe a dance is fitting for our last full night," I began. "You know, live a little."

S shivered. "Yes, that's how I want to spend my last hours. With part of the student body I'm already planning on forgetting."

V hushed her. "Live a little, S?" she said. "Baby, how about *live a lot?*"

"I hope they'll play all my favorite songs," I said, returning to my usual dreamy state where boys danced and dipped you at midnight as the orchestra swelled and played sad music with words that ripped your heart out.

"Someday, when I'm awfully low.
When the world is cold
I will feel a glow just thinking of you . . .

"Yes, dear," V said. "Let's start out with that song, 'Live Like You're Dying' and then conclude with 'Stairway to Heaven.'"

"Cynical again," C said with a wicked grin. "Thank God."

"Practical," V retorted. "You do know what this means? Dance on Dec. 23. Then our death day on December 24, Christmas Eve. What a pedestrian way to go out."

2.
November

"Oh, it will be splendid. My four beauties going to a winter formal," our earthly Mama said during a moment of cherished

THE CLAIRES

clarity that we held dear because they were so fleeting now. She insisted on taking us to a local department store to do mother-daughter things like pile up hundreds of dresses in the dressing room as we looked for those four very special ones. *That dress would be the second to last outfit we would wear on this spin.*

Dad tried to go with us for safety reasons, but she wouldn't hear of it. I knew, as did V, that he couldn't afford what amounted to four expensive winter formal dresses, but Mama's condition was worsening and he wanted to buy her this joy of shopping with her daughters. "We got it covered," I lied. "Babysitting money."

"When do you babysit?" Dad asked, but then he stopped. Asking questions, that is.

There were days when Mama barely remembered our names or why she was in this particular house, which often felt frightening and foreign to her now. She wasn't allowed to be alone anymore, but she seemed lucid enough in this particular moment to enjoy doing something that mothers and daughters had done since tulle was invented.

We went to the local mall.

"These are good people," I whispered to C while V kept track of Mama and pulled the most-expensive frocks off the rack. Why not? A few surprise quizzes provided endless streams of cash. C looked like a queen with mounds of silk on her lap as she sat contently in the dressing room like a princess whose bum was made for clouds of fluff.

"I wonder if we'll get such good ones ever again?" I said.

The parental pool was such a crap shoot. Vegas wouldn't even like the odds.

There was no time to dwell on the great unknown of our next trip around the sun. We pulled up those spaghetti straps, laughed when body parts fell out and cringed when one mermaid dress made V's rear look like it was the size of a Greyhound bus. "Yeah,

I'd like to see you fit those boobs into this . . . contraption!" she yelled, handing me a dress that had so many straps that I felt like I was in a straightjacket.

"Get it off me!" V screamed. "It's cutting off the circulation to my brain!"

"Uh, where's Mama?" I finally said.

Mama had a tendency to wander and after ten heart-stopping minutes, we lost her to the Macy's home goods section, which felt very homey to her. There she was canoodling with some checkered Martha Stewart sheets after she slipped into one of the display beds designed to sell you expensive comforters and 1000-thread-count sheets. She was snoring.

"I'm taking a nap at the hotel," she yawned.

"It's time for shoes, Mama," we said, like this was the most normal thing in the world—uncovering your mother, who suddenly believed that Macys was her actual home.

I tried to push away any thoughts of what would happen to her because the mothers always died slightly before us. Why? I would never know if it was part of the curse or the fact that we went ballistic at the end. She didn't deserve this . . . every single lucid moment with her and all of the mysterious hours in-between were still worth living. Still precious. I prayed that she would be spared.

But it didn't help to dwell on what was out of our collective hands. And it didn't stop the anxious moments in the middle of a dark night when one of us would sit straight up in bed and say, "No. Not yet. Not ready. Not…ready."

Because we weren't. Is anyone ever ready to die?

THE CLAIRES

3.
December 23

THE NIGHT OF the dance, we began the prep work at two in the afternoon because it seemed like a fitting way to live your last full day on earth. We would become beautiful beings that celebrated the best time of the year for most; the worst for us.

All I could do is grab a soft blush brush and paint my sister V's cheeks the perfect petal pink. She returned the favor by applying the thinnest amount of black liner that made my eyes pop. We laughed all the way as we made tiny beige clouds out of the excess powder. I brushed V's red hair until her long tresses shined in the evening light. We put my dark hair up in a bun. The two blondes, C and S, did a glossing treatment. C's short curls were swept back with faux diamond pins while I allowed my long locks to free-fall into a loose, curly tumble.

We were as ready as four girls with a death sentence ever could be for a winter prom.

I wished our Mama could have enjoyed it, but she was in a particularly argumentative mood today, which was happening more frequently. Her words often stung now like millions of little papercuts that you couldn't quite avoid because paper seemed to be everywhere. If you looked at her wrong, she snapped. If you tried to help her, she recoiled. It was bad enough when she spoke, but worse when she remained silent, staring off into some kind of distance to places unknown.

A nurse practitioner named Andrea had stopped by that morning to explain to all of us that we might want to look into care facilities because her confusion could lead to Mama either hurting herself or actual physical violence when she didn't recognize us. Andrea helped by bathing and feeding her on the really tough days and I wished she would never leave.

As a family, we went through the motions. The Christmas tree twinkled, but there wasn't much joy in the house. Cass was stuck in a deep melancholy funk and insisted that he wasn't in the mood to go to "some force-fed, school-sanctioned shindig," although there were several girls at school who would have sacrificed their poor soon-to-be-pulverized toes in order to go out on a date with our supposedly hunky-dory brother.

"Get on it," I prodded him. "Defy the boredom in your soul and take a chance."

V said that she had visions of him someday in the future with a redhead girl with a headstrong personality who would draw him out of his shell in a way that no other could. That made me laugh. What girl with any kind of spirit spark would want our granola-eating marine brother?

"Oh, and she's good at knife tricks," V predicted.

"Does this redheaded ninja stab him?" I asked hopefully, and my three sisters laughed so hard that they began to smear their makeup. Maybe it was an evolved Annie—maybe not. We always teased him about his lack of a dating life because, despite our past struggles, there were some merits to Cass. For starters, he mostly just stood there and took our verbal bashings. We wouldn't think of him fondly, but we would think of him.

"Why would some girl want to go out with me?" Cass asked.

"You have a natural charisma that's infectious," V said.

"Sort of like the Ebola virus," C added with a top spin in her voice before she added, "Close the door on the way out, you handsome big infection."

It hurt to think that by tomorrow night, he would probably come by this door again and again – only to lament. But we would never be "home" because we wouldn't live here anymore. Damn it, they would probably knock down the wall and make him the bachelor bedroom of his computer-geek dreams.

Life was so unfair, especially when you weren't living it.

I would live one last dream in this room. When my sisters were gone, I put a vinyl copy of the classic song "My Girl" on our turntable and called for the spirit of a teenage boy named Billy Furi who died in the 1980s in a fiery car crash. He was a star football player and all around nice guy at Santa Monica High. He started coming to me frequently in the last few weeks and I told him about the dance.

My eyes teared up now when I "saw" Billy appear with his dark hair slicked back and wearing a navy-blue suit. In his wide, QB hand was a dark red rose corsage. He was nervous as most high school boys are, but he still held out a ghostly palm that shook just a bit and asked in a quivering, "Can I have this dance, beautiful?"

I melted into the air, caught by arms that weren't there to the naked eye, twirling around a boy-man who looked as if he was made of fog and film. The flowers he brought from the beyond, ones I couldn't pin, filled my senses and made true my wildest and most romantic dreams.

Until I looked down.

The flowers had turned black.

It was beginning.

The Night of the Big Dance

4.

THE UNIVERSE ISN'T with us anymore. Proof can be found by the fact that our every move is checked by some sort of desperation that seems elevated because the clock is ticking. *Tick-tock, tick-tock.* It is that car that blows the light, swerves, and almost crashes into us on Sunset Boulevard. *Tick-tock.* It is how V trips and almost topples down a staircase the moment we enter the historic Chateau Marmont. *Tick-Tock.* It is only 8:00 p.m. the night before our scheduled deaths, but we know the markers. Hard falls. Impalement. Near misses. Tiny calamities. We were on the brink of transitioning.

"Son of a bitch," says S, with tears in her eyes.

19

A SENTIENT'S STORY: S

1.

I FEEL IMPENDING doom.

"A few beginning pitches, but nothing fatal—yet," C tries to hedge. Then she whispers. "I hadn't really had a chance to wrap my mind around it until we cleaned out the apartment this morning and gave notice to our landlord." When he asked for a following address, we wrote: Unknown.

"You've had seventeen years, dear," I retort. "And just like all the hipsters say . . . you know the drill."

The small warnings of our end being near were always followed by a clarity that swept over each of us. It sharpened our gifts into razor versions of how they were intended to be used by true *clair* wonders. I begin to feel so deeply that it's like an ocean washing over my entire system. I feel so much that I haven't even taken time to process how I felt about Javier, my first kiss, moving to Phoenix to be closer to his family. . . . . and to be a rookie cop there.

"You can lament all you want tonight," V whispers in my ear. "That's what last nights on earth are for.... remembrance and regrets."

THIS MUCH I know: It is best to focus on facts rather than emotions. Facts took you out of your head... and heart. My eldest sister knows it, too, which is why she brings up a topic we will mull over until we draw last breath: Annie. I can picture her with that

THE CLAIRES

flowing red hair standing on our front step. All I ever wanted to do was hug her.

"She's in Oregon," V reminds the sisters, while we wait in line to give our tickets to some annoying, head cheerleading airhead named Tiffany with a much-too-cheerful smile and a dress cut down to her lower intestines. "Annie, the girlfriend who might have been your sister-in-law if you weren't about to drop dead," she snipes under her breath, "was in the land of never ending rain and greenery. Should we even bother to tell Cass her next move or wait for it to play out?"

"Or take it to the grave?" I suggest.

We always had these "take it to the grave" talks at the end. It was morbid, but essential and took our minds off what would actually take us out. Endings were scary enough; finding out how was hideous.

I feel nothing for Annie suddenly.

Another sign.

Detachment from those closest to us. Like turning off a switch.

No feelings = no compassion.

Anyway, it is a weird time to tell us this Annie newsflash. It's also a crucial piece of important family news that we will never have time to certify as true or false, so we will keep it to ourselves. Mean, yes.. . . although I don't give two shits and a flying F. *We were well past the beginning of our end if even I – one of the nicer Claires -- felt this way.*

Our nasty sides emerging in full bloom was another sign of our last breaths: A rage that simmered in all of us seemed to bubble to the top. We were, in a word: Homicidal and hormonal. Okay, those are three words, but I warn you not to spar with any Claire on her death watch. We were in a red zone – running hot – with no brakes.

If we could do someone wrong at this point, it would be the *wrongest* they were ever done.

A sense of evil set into those denied life and it was beyond sinful.

"Oregon, Montana, the seventh ring of hell," I say with a little sniff. "Go hug a tree, Annie. Go raise that kid by yourself under an umbrella so you don't melt from all the rain. Who cares? She's not really our niece, so we don't have to tell the guy who really isn't our brother. Too bad V didn't screw his brains out."

"Screw whose brains out? Your brother's brains!" exclaims a horrified Mrs. Evelyn Ehm, the waterlogged English teacher, who was serving as a chaperone tonight.

V has nothing to lose.

"Yes, his brains," she says. "Imagine my memoir one day. You can read it in the bathroom, Captain Depends."

Mrs. Ehm, luckily, is not the type to kick us out of the dance. She just walks away shaking her head.

"Maybe tone it down a notch," C suggests. "You're starting to sound like me."

Someone did a fast subject change that was somehow still inappropriate, given the lavish setting and the fact that *Rudolph* was playing on a loop in the background.

"You know what would be nice with this death? No surprises. Just something clean like a stabbing or shot to the gut," I suggest. "Something fast—drowning was so painful and that heart attack was a shocker. Fire . . . well, please, never again. We're too tender to burn."

Then I stop cold when I realize the two biggest news queens of the senior class at Santa Monica High have gone stealth silent in line in front of us. No chance that they are not hanging on our every word to feed their social media channels later.

The queens turn oh-so-slowly around. They are horrified.

THE CLAIRES

"We couldn't help but hear your screenplay idea," Amber says. "We'd love to audition."

No one said they were smart. I mean, no one.

"You could play the girl who can't keep her mouth shut and falls down a flight of stairs to her death at a school dance," I announce cheerfully. *Yes, I was getting a mouth on me as it pertained to others I'd never engage with during the living time. No more hiding out under a pillow. Another sign of lights out.*

"I always wanted a death scene," she replies.

I reach in my evening bag to pull out the one thing I have in there: Dad's stun gun, which I stole from his police cruiser. V is quick and grabs the bag with the device in it and takes it away from me.

Those filled with so much life wasted so much of it. That little fact takes me into the rage-a-holic, red zone.

Miss Gossip Queen is so consumed with visions of Disney Plus streaming that she doesn't notice she is standing on the landing of a staircase. My fingers reach out. As Ma says, "Where there's a will …"

"Can I at least dance at this dance before you go batshit?" C begs, stopping me.

My hand return to my side.

I hate this side of me, but it is there.

No one knew this me, but it lurked.

Revealing your truth in your last hours. I could not think of a better death.

2.

HISTORY LESSON: THE Chateau Marmont Hotel, located on Sunset Boulevard in Los Angeles, was built in 1929 by famed architects

Arnold A. Weitzman and William Douglas Lee. Modeled loosely after the Chateau d'Amboise, a royal retreat in France's Loire Valley, it's a sixty-three-room hotel, sometimes called The Castle, which was said to be haunted, and thus was maybe why prices ranged from $575 to $3000 a night. Who wouldn't want a little ghostly action with their 1,000 thread count sheets?

Lore dictated that in 1926, a famous LA attorney named Fred Horowitz decided to construct an apartment building on Marmont Lane and the infamous Sunset Boulevard. He took a boat to Europe for some architectural inspiration and returned to his beloved California with a picture of a Goth Chateau that really existed along the Loire River.

"Build it," he said. And they did build a castle that from ground level looked ominously back at that pair of eyeballs as the building appeared as if it was always ascending upward.

The end result was a Goth castle, seven stories in structure and shaped like a large L plopped on a small hill. It was an apartment house, but eventually the lavish property was converted into a hotel by Albert E. Smith who paid $750,000 in cash for it in 1931.

Oddities ran rampant here. Chateau Marmont survived earthquakes in 1933, 1953, 1971, 1987, and 1994 with nary a bit of damage. By the 1990s, the hotel was modernized by Andre Balazs with the dictate to make it look as if nothing had ever been touched since the day the front door opened and the party started.

Naturally, there were rumors that the place was haunted since the hotel served as a crash pad for the infamous from Marilyn Monroe to John Belushi, who died in one of the guest rooms. Some say that he *checked out,* but never checked out of his favorite bungalow, No. 3.

My sister A told me about the little two-year-old boy who years later was sitting on the floor in one of the guest rooms. His parents found him laughing and laughing and laughing at absolutely

THE CLAIRES

nothing. "What are you laughing at, son?" asked his father. "The funny man," replied the boy. Later, when his mother was looking through a book of celebrity guests of the Chateau, the boy pointed to a picture of Belushi and said, "Mommy, that's the funny man!"

"I'm in no mood for it," A mutters under her breath when the spirits here try to fill her ears now with their sagas and asks. They ring. They buzz her as did our original Ma. We tend to ignore Ma during those last days. I rub A's arm when she begins to talk to herself and says a little too loudly, "Don't even."

Two geeks from the math squad beat a hasty retreat.

The spirits are as invisible as air and when one such ghostly presence floats too closely to A's ear, I hear my sweet sister say in a clipped tone, "Just leave me the hell alone you pain-in-the-ass phantoms."

Then another voice that I heard loud and clearly: "Be gone, you asshole apparitions. It's their night – not yours."

And with those words, he smiles down at us.

My brother Cass, in a forest-green tux, looked like he stepped out of the pages of GQ and was busting ghostly chops like a true baller.

"Why?" I demand.

"Because, unfortunately, you're my sisters" he says with a warm smile.

"You look . . . presentable," I say with a grin.

We had seventeen years to hate each other and less than twenty-four hours and the rest of our existences to lament what could have been. As they say, life's a bitch and then you're just some story. I guess we're all just stories, but in our cases, we were a short story with a looming ending.

3.

Back in La La Land: The pathway along an outdoor bricked trail looks like your standard all-American high school dance, down to the explosion of red-and-white streamers and forest of real evergreen trees that—warning—were not removed from the earth for a mundane teenage social activity. Someone's mom already had them chopped for a fiftieth birthday party three days ago, so why not repurpose them as a path to the actual dance? How green of us.

"Slutever," says V pointing to half of the cheerleading squad.

"Not nice," I reply.

"Nice has left the building," she insists. *This was concerning because when C and V entered their true rage zones, God only knew what could and probably would happen.*

"Level it. Force yourself, honey," I remind her as we wander toward the main party palace.

The ballroom for this ball isn't inside this haunted wonder, but instead is located outside on a large bricked patio hanger that during the day is used for chic celebrity lunches and for entertainment industry wheelers and dealers to sign on the bottom line. Tonight, all of the tables had been moved to make room for a large space under a snowy white plastic tent. The inside is enough to humble even the biggest humbug.

It's filled with thousands of twinkling white lights—simple, potent, and oh-so-magical. Did they really have to pull at the old heart strings with real garland and old-fashioned silver tinsel, suspended in air and dripping down like shimmering vines of holiday splendor? Breathing deeply, I pretend I'm in the deepest trenches of a hidden forest when that unmistakable scent that was so tangy and woodsy fills my system. The Christmas tree, our last one during this California life, is so real, so splendid, that I can

THE CLAIRES

barely hold back my own fury. *It wasn't fair. Why did we have to perish this way? Every single time?* A Shakespeare quote I wrote a paper on pops into my mind: "Fair is foul, and foul is fair." Or perhaps Bill Gates said it best when he opined, "Life is not fair; get used to it."

Heat lamps allow us to shed any sweaters or wraps, because nothing said winter in LA (temp: 52 degrees) like spaghetti-strap gowns with nonexistent backs. Sleeves were for losers or dudes. The DJ pounding tunes provides the rest of the warmth because even the biggest wallflower has been transformed into a dancing fool.

What senior was it who carefully placed mistletoe about every five steps? Even the boys in the chess club are getting their share of lip service while two skinny debaters had their first-ever smudge of lipstick on their overly starched Sears collars.

I watch as one mildly acceptable guy named Chad Johnson, the Timothee Chalamet look-a-like, in a funky green tux with his black nerd glasses asks my sister A to dance.

"Honey, have an experience," I whisper into her ear. "We need something to talk about later on when we're toddlers again. And we can re-live this dance for all eternity."

For once, my sister actually listens to me proving there is a first for everything. And as Chad dips her way, way, way back, she smiles up at those twinkling Christmas lights in a way that dims even their wattage. She has never looked more alive.

I take that back. V is alive down to the fact that her professionally powdered jaw almost hits the floor. She was sitting at one of the tables, lost in her thoughts, when a handsome one in a winter white suit bent down, which wasn't easy on his prosthetic leg. Louis had arrived at the dance looking uneasy, but he was here.

Except for a few stolen kisses in the gym, they had never really gone on an official date let alone done anything else in the name of love, as Bono might sing.

"I don't dance, kid," he told me when I begged him to show up here tonight for her.

"Why is this so important to you, S?" he demanded.

It was the one question I couldn't answer without lying, so I just bent the truth a little bit. "You never know," I told him, "when it's your last chance to dance." He got it and rented a tux.

I couldn't think of a better going-going-gone present.

Until she taps me lightly on the shoulder.

"I was wondering if you want to dance, S?" she says in a flustered voice.

Standing in front of me, shifting her feet, is Karen Miller, a junior who sat behind me in AP History. She has short, brown hair streaked with a hint of pink, big hazel eyes and a hopeful smile. I stand and really look at her because I wanted to memorize these people. There's our school's beautiful Karen in her black velvet, strappy dress, full of nerves and nervous hope. My lips, glistening thanks to slick lip gloss, won't work at first, although my mind is screaming, "You idiot, just say, 'I would love to dance with you, Karen.'" But, I can't form actual sentences.

"Yes," I blurt out, in a breathless rush.

Just. That. Simple.

She takes my hand and lead *us* to the floor where the lights are soft and dreamy and the music features none other than Janis Joplin who in her trademark heartbreaking gritty tone is crooning about having a white Christmas. I shuffle back and forth like some sort of uncoordinated lobster because I don't really dance. *Next lifetime. Arthur Murray, here I come.* Karen places unsteady hands around my back and pulls me closer, so we can just sway.

I almost lose my mind when she leans up and sweetly kisses me on the cheek.

THE CLAIRES

"Can I kiss-kiss you back?" I whisper. Did I mention that she smelled like watermelon body spray and fresh roses?

"Yes," she says, nodding. "But wait."

My heart is sinking as I watch her step back. Will she just walk away? Was I that much of a disaster? If yes, I could just die right now. I mean, maybe I really could *die on the spot. I'm putting it out to the Universe. Take me now.* Bracing for anything, I stare as she fumbles with something stuck in her tiny sparkly purse, eventually, pulling out a wad of green.

"Mistletoe?" I ask in a thunderstruck voice. "Did you…"

"Bring it for you?" she said. "Yes."

I remain stunned.

"Now, S, you can kiss me. Sorry for the delay. I've wanted to do this all year. But I wanted it to be perfect. I'm dorky like that, sorry," she says, leaning in closer and holding the plant over our heads. What follows is shivering flesh on quivering muscle, shaking hands trapped in firm fingers, fiery lips on a burning mouth, a curious tongue tasting raw, rare hunger.

It isn't the right holiday, but it's certainly fireworks.

A COGNIZANT'S STORY: C

C. L. GABER

1.

"Shiver my timbers, ladies," I exclaim under my breath. "It's like the ghost of Christmas past has exploded in this place."

I'm standing in front of a life-sized ice sculpture of Frosty the Freaking Snowman, made of thousands of small crystals and he's flanked by equally large busts of Santa and the Mrs. Claus. One of the senior's fathers owned some swanky jewelry store on Rodeo. "Rudolph's nose?" she kept telling anyone in her vicinity. "Made with real rubies chosen by Dad and the student council."

The dance is a tribute to our talents as seniors—or lack of creativity, as I liked to say. Of course, there are fellow doubters. Who was the joker who drew genitals on the Grinch? "Don't go any closer to him," I had whispered to V. "The Grinch looks like he's in heat."

"We're all in heat. Just look around the room," she joked.

The lighting is courtesy of Mr. Hughes's seventh period honors physics class—nerds to the power of infinity and beyond—who somehow figured out how to make the inside of a tent emit a warm green Christmas glow. Even Mother Nature is cooperating with L.A.'s version of the holiday season. The night is that crispy kind of cold that came with a snap in the air, which isn't normal for California except around the middle of December when you can actually pretend for a moment that you live in Santa friendly places like Vermont or Maine.

A serious breeze is wafting in and out of the festivities, ruffling my curls as I settle into a dark and lonely corner for some advanced placement people watching.

It's downright strange to look around the room, gazing at

THE CLAIRES

the people who have been the very fabric of your life since you were five years old. That's when you put that first little pink toe into the public-school system. Nothing had really changed since that day. Sean and Patrick Coleman were still snorting pretzels, although now in suits, while Taylor Adams and her supposed best friend Paige Perry were making mooning eyes at anyone in pants including a few overly handsome waiters.

It strikes me that I can't stand these people, and at the same time I can't live without them. I hate most of them, but will rabidly miss them because I love them at the same time, if that makes any sense to anyone who ever attended high school. "Hey C," Paige calls out. *What!* She moves closer to whisper into my ear, "I see the way Billy Monroe looks at you. Do you have dibs on him? Hooks in? Hooks out?"

"Go fishing," I say. "Merry Christmas. Happy New Year."

"Really?"

"Merry, merry," I reply.

"Maybe we can do a movie over the holidays?" she suggests.

"Yeah . . . call me." I say it knowing that no one would ever be at the other end of that phone line.

It's strange to look around the room and envy every single person. I was the least contemplative or introspective of my sisters, but this is exactly what I want to do tonight. I want to be alone, wallow in feeling sorry for myself and wonder . . .

How would we die? Would it be painful? Sometimes, it was. *Would it be dismembering? Man, that would hurt. Gunshot? Lightning strike? Car goes into a ditch?* I could never see for myself or my sisters, damn it, but I still made up grand stories in my head. *We would be driving home tonight and that city bus would swerve the wrong way . . . and that train would come barreling into our stuck car . . . or that man with the semiautomatic would start burning clips. Anything could happen after midnight – and it would happen until we didn't draw another breath.*

Another scan of the fine student body and I decide to play with their lives: This one would have two husbands; that one would have five kids. He would live in that big fancy house and die at age eighty-five after years and years and years of time and more time: time savored, time used, time honored, and time pissed away. It was this thing called life, which was enough to make me want to scream and cry at the same time.

"Pastry puff?" asks a handsome waiter in his black tux. In LA, these guys were mostly out-of-work actors who needed to pay the rent this week, although they might be starring on the CW network the next.

"No, thank you."

I can't eat. I can't breathe. I can't dance because my feet don't want to move. I can't even think straight anymore, which was why I'm so easily blindsided.

He shows from nowhere and now stands behind me to speak into my hair while placing warm hands on my bare shoulders. A chill begins on my neck and tracks down my spine until I swear it hits toes. When I whip around, he uses physics or something extra to spin me around one more time, 360 style, until I'm like a dizzy little top in a navy-blue princess dress. Still floating, I settled into his muscular arms that are covered in a silky-smooth fabric that feels cool to the touch. His skin is warm.

I had last seen him in his "work clothes" of black jeans and leather. But I had never witnessed this six-foot-five wonder in a maroon tux, white shirt, and black bow tie. I have to smile. He's wearing white Converses with his formals.

"Wh- are you doing here?" I whisper, afraid that anyone but him might hear me.

Gingerly, he touches, then removes the two small pearl pins I had placed in my hair and watches as my locks tumble free. He

THE CLAIRES

tucks the pins inside his jacket pocket. To keep.

"What I'm doing here is watching you and freezing my bollocks off," he replies. And then with a serious smile, he adds, "Want to dance?"

2.

"Want . . . to . . . dance?" I repeat, like these were the three most ironic words ever said to a dying woman.

"Thought you'd never ask," he smiles, spinning me in another circle without his hands on my waist or hand in my hand. One hand is still in my hair. He seems to be doing the spinning part by some kind of mental telepathy and my body is fully cooperating.

"But it's a lot more fun this way," he smiles, powerful hands slowly wrapping around my middle as he yanks me closer *and then closer again*, until I feel the heat radiating from his skin. Or is it my skin that's on fire? I …cannot … what was the question?

Three or four of the choir girls are singing Christmas standards on a small stage with the band geeks flanking them from behind. Fate cooperated for once when they launch into a sexy version of "Merry Christmas, Baby" with enough thrusting dance moves that our Dean is pretty much ready for a mental institution.

I begin to float. When I open my eyes, he's looking deep.

"Who are you?" I ask with almost no voice.

He replies with a smile.

"Where are you from? Is it of this planet?"

"Chicago. West Side. Cabrini Green housing project," he says.

"This planet."

"Really?"

"Technically, that is of this planet," he says, dipping me back to the music as the front of my dress hitches way too low to be anything but a private show.

"Do you d-do this a lot . . . you know, go to high school dances? Date girls?"

"Not on the everyday menu, but sort of nice to take a break while saving the world from itself," he says. "And you, Claire C? But I prefer your given name of Clover."

"I don't date boys with only one lifetime," I reply, looking around the room. "Limiting."

"By the way, I know about your lifetimes. Happy almost birthday."

I sway—and bring him with me into another low dip.

"Not knowing who I am should scare you," he whispers.

"Knowing who I am should scare you," I retort.

"What I see for our future might make you turn a pleasant shade of crimson," he grins.

And although I can't see my face, I felt the degrees.

3.

How COULD I tell him that after tomorrow, I'd be an embryo again? Then again, it really wasn't necessary to put out an all-points bulletin. It was like he was reading my mind because he was.

"It doesn't matter. I'm right here. You're right here. It's about now," he whispers into my ear. "Let's go."

I felt myself go lax . . .. maybe for the first time in this lifetime.

"Close your blinkers," he says.

That was impossible. I was the Yoda. The watcher.

But they were already shut. He closed them for me.

THE CLAIRES

4.

When I opened my blinkers, we were in our own private cove. It was a small garden in another part of the hotel where the greenery was full and lush while the mood stayed private. "Beat it, you ghosts," I heard Emin say to the "others" who seemed to float away on a winter's gust. That's the thing about most ghosts. Code of honor. They accept it.

What had just happened was hard to explain and even tougher to believe. He had physically moved us, molecule by molecule, without the normal ways of human travel such as moving one leg in front of the other or waiting for some annoying elevator door to open and clink closed. Linked by our hands, he *willed* us here. And here we were. In one piece.

"Astral projection, if you must know. I like to be different than the other blokes," he joked.

"And in layman's terms . . . what did you just do?" I gasped.

"Thanks to my Mum's side, I have the ability to project as an astral body from one place to the other," he explained. He said it like it was no different than inheriting blue eyes.

He did it again, but this time only to move his face closer to mine with record speed. I didn't have this power, but I did have a racing heart and lips that moved closer in normal time. When he leaned down and pressed his soft, but demanding lips to mine, I was projected into some other place where my entire being was wrapped in stars.

He tipped his face for a slow exploration – lips, tongue, breath, again and then again -- and I continued to soar . . . until a sweet joyous ringing of bells broke through the euphoria.

When these chimes stopped sounding, he tried to kiss away the sob that escaped my throat and murmured, "Don't be alarmed, love. It's only midnight."

I wasn't alarmed.

I was frantic.

It was December 24, our birthday.

I was one breath into the day. Two. Three.

I waited for demons to rain down from the sky, lightening to strike from the cloud, or rocks to fall on my head. Even more dreadful than any of those fates—nothing happened. The sky didn't move. The rocks stayed in place. His arms felt firm and mighty, making me imagine that nothing could hurt or hunt us. But, I knew differently. Experience is a brutal teacher.

Time ticked.

12:01

12:02

Our finale was now in progress.

5.

Taking my hand, he kissed the top of it, "Another life?" he requested.

And then he stepped that inch backward that takes someone completely out of your orbit. He knew it was time to go, too.

"I have to go to work," he said. "You have to transition. God bless."

All I could do was close my eyes as he "projected" us back to the dance, of all places. It was all so beautiful there – and claustrophobic now at the same time. Food. That's all anyone cared about now while I'd probably never eat again in this lifetime. Here, however, the ravenous study body was dying to feast on a fresh round of midnight snacks promptly being circulated on shiny silver trays.

I eyed my sisters who were hovering nearby. V was being

kissed deeply by Louis. A was dancing with Johnny from V's English class. His skin had cleared and miraculously his body had filled in. It was A who floated by and smiled sadly at me. She finally found a flesh and blood boy …a first on a night of lasts.

"Mushroom torte?" one of the staff asked Emin and me, but we shook our heads at what was mostly healthy vegan fare because, what else? This was Los Angeles.

Suddenly, I wanted to experience it all and ate ravenously, grabbing twos and threes off those serving trays. When I bit into something chewy—and dare I say gamey tasting—I wondered what faux meat I probably wouldn't have the time to fully digest.

"Ummmmm… What is this?" I asked one of the male models/servers. "This is delicious." My hand snaked up for thirds. "Tofu? Bean burger? Tofurky?"

"Tofurky?" he laughed in that broad, full-body smiling way that beautiful men do. It's like they're always posing for their close-up.

"I'm sorry, miss," he said, still chuckling. "But that wasn't tofu. It's a slider. A goat meat slider. It's the new white meat."

Of course.

The goat.

THE LITTLE GOAT in the 1800s who ate the poison was a marker now of the Patriarch's strange, if not almost perverted, sense of humor. It was as if he was saying to us: "Game over. I got your goat." But this time was different. That four-letter G word wasn't lost on the others – and usually the Patriarch made sure that his private little taunt stayed just that… private.

"Did you say goat?" asked one of the vegetarian dance squad members who had just downed two sliders and now in the pale moonlight looked positively greener than the overhead holiday lights. "Is goat meat vegan?" she pondered. "Is it plant-based?"

The waiter looked at her sadly. "No, miss," he said. "A goat is a critter."

6.

"Ground goat meat comes from an actual slain goat. We blend it with ginger and spices. Baked, of course. Not fried," the waiter said. Just a bit too loudly.

What followed must be described delicately . . . if possible.

The bulimic dancer made a peace sign and stuck those harmony loving fingers down her throat. Chunks came up from 1996. Sally Henderson then opened her professionally plumped lips, slicked by Chanel gloss, and what rose through her taut throat demanded release. What came out were chunks of partially digested goat along with a liquid brown-green sludge that she projectile vomited across a pristine white tablecloth that now sported brown snowflakes.

The sheer violence of the second round, cheesy-smelling to the max, was hurled almost immediately—landing in the face and on the chest of the newly minted Winter Dance Queen.

The queen, a horrid girl named Destiny Nelson, gazed at her brownish yellow silk dress in horror as her nostrils flared like she was some mad farm animal. I couldn't take my eyes off her as she fell to her knees, craning her head upward enough for her own reactionary vomit to splash loudly across the laps of two football players who were sitting in chairs now covered with her innards.

"I'm so sorry," Destiny cried as her date Brian Weber helped

THE CLAIRES

her to her feet. He took one look at her and sprayed goat chunks onto one of the formerly white tent walls. Just watching the pieces ooze in all their warm glory down the thick plastic was enough to create a chain reaction of purging that was so foul and disgusting that the rest of the room could not help but to participate in this one, unifying student activity. Santa Monica HS. Home of the Pukers.

Even an actor playing Santa wasn't immune. I watched as his fat stomach contracted like he was about to give birth, and what was released included some half-chewed pizza and about seven of those goat sliders that he absconded from the trays.

"Who is responsible for this calamity?" Principal Dan Shirley shouted to no one in particular.

My eyes drifted over to my two other sisters knowing that a little bit of goat meat would certainly not be our demise. We never got sick until it was our seventeenth birthday and time for our fatal demise. Normal illness just wasn't part of our *clair* constitution.

All we could do was watch like lookers of some sort of fascinatingly wretched horror movie that you enjoy on one level while wanting your money back on another. It wasn't long before the vomit was everywhere including dangling from that silver tinsel and racing down bare shoulders and pressed jackets.

Our science teacher, Mr. Douglas Melvin, along with our assistant principal Ms. Celine Belden weren't immune. One was folded over in pain while the other had stuffed a floral arrangement into her nostrils to block out a smell that could only be described as blue cheese left out in the sun—for two or perhaps three years.

"This is Security One," one of the guards said into his acid-fluid-covered sleeve. "We have a situation. I repeat. We have a situation. Bring towels from the pool. The throw away kind—and Pepto."

Emin seemed to find it amusing while he kept both of us and

now V out of the saucy fray.

When the student body was down to just small streams, he began to bid me good night and good life. And that's when something even stranger happened. Someone cut all of the lights and the tent was plunged into absolute darkness.

"Now what?" I asked.

7.

I DIDN'T HAVE to wait long for my answer. Someone, or something, had sealed one of the two entrances to the tent, which plunged the dance into pure chaos because by now it stunk so badly in that plastic tomb that everyone needed the fresh air and a quick out.

One of the AV kids worked furiously on the lights, but this time he couldn't bring up your standard Christmas green. "Go to infrared red," I heard him shout. He opted for infrared for a reason. The AV squad actually planned this little joke to happen after midnight. Infrared was often used in night vision goggles to pinpoint human heat patterns. Once Steve Holt flipped the switch to red, I could see the actual "hotness" of the Santa Monica student body. But they weren't burning the hottest. Not even close.

There were others here – six or seven, I counted -- who in this light were as hot as flames. What they "contained" wasn't visible in normal light, but all bets at normal were off now. In this light, some had glistening silvery orbs attached to their heads. Others had eyeballs minus the white because that part burned red. Was it skin or a pelt covering their bones . . . and why were a select few glowing gold? Fingernails or claws? Take your pick.

"But choose wisely," Emin said, reading my mind. "I'd call them talons."

THE CLAIRES

"WTF," I whispered, glancing around at what was trapped in here *with us*.

"The four of you emit some sort of distress signal," Emin said. "I guess now the monsters with ill intent are picking up on it, too. And what's more distressing than a night in the presence of your favorite school mates?"

Those "trolls" from the debate club . . . they were surrounded by real trolls, the kind that were hunched over, backs rounded just a bit and noses just a tad too garishly long. Other "things" had fangs that simply appeared in another light and were lightly wrapped around Rylan and Declan's throats.

If S hadn't pushed both out of the way, they would have been strangled and then devoured.

8.

"Run or fight," Emin said, grabbing my hand while I linked fingers with V, A, and S.

"But we need to say goodbye," said V who wouldn't be given that chance now. Louis was on a trip to the john. Karen stood shaking in a corner. All of us stared at these unfinished stories, but time was up.

Carefully, I stepped out of one high heel and then the other because the fight was in *their* eyes. They crashed this party to feast on things of a non-goat variety, and they didn't want any interference.

I glanced at my sisters. The flight was in *our eyes* now.

A VOYANT'S STORY: V

1.

Sunset Boulevard in Los Angeles stretched from the hustle of downtown to glammed up Malibu. Emin would not allow us to stay in the tent and projected all four Claires, plus his own being, outside of it to reduce the carnage. Those things didn't want the greater student body at SMHS. They wanted to toy with us.

Feet back on the asphalt, we went straight for the actual street, blinded by the touristy neon signs promoting every single movie you never hear of and a few that you did. The rush of oncoming traffic made me dizzy as I ran down the hill from the hotel towards where cars were flying by at upwards of 50 miles an hour. Only once, I looked back and I could see the entities bursting from what once was the white tent, but that was before they ate the plastic.

We had no choice, but to race from the small sidewalk directly into the traffic. The monsters took the same path, the ones who had the ability taking giant leaps until they stood on the hoods of Escalade SUVs and Range Rovers. They were surfing the cement looking for tonight's prey. "FLASH"! I saw the black Beemer and moved slightly right before it could wipe me out. FLASH! I shoved C onto the hood of a black Mustang, which was better than having the LA city bus flatten her.

It was a careful ballet, leaping over cars, sliding over hoods and then fighting whatever was in our way. I connected with a heel-roundhouse kick combo and it hit one of the trolls in his windpipe. When something large covered in scales ripped me off my feet, I bit his hand. Dirty fighting? Was there any other kind? A quick stiletto impaled the flat forehead of something tall with facial skin made up of only raised and connected dark moles. I pierced his

THE CLAIRES

skull and then took the second to bounce two fanged demons to the concrete where a man on a Harley couldn't stop. When he ran over one and then the other, I raised one fist in a victory sign. C was also proving that she was now adept at traffic control. Eight-foot walking stick creatures had no chance when she directed a semi-truck exactly in their direction. S cringed at the sound of bones flattening into the road.

"Fight like a girl," A yelled, nailing something with glowing eyes in the back of its head with a well-aimed front kick shoving it into a sign warning that one must obey the speed limit. "And no jaywalking," A screamed when those eyes burst into millions of tiny shards of light.

Garish red headlights blinded me as I dodged around a Lexus going 60 miles per hour and slid off the front of a stopped Camaro in cherry red.

"S! Run!" I screamed as my sister almost did a face-plant into a moving van whose driver screamed obscenities out of the window. I didn't have time to dwell on her health because something large and sonic fast was racing next to me. When I glanced hard to my side to check for abnormalities, it grabbed me hard from behind and hoisted me ten feet above the street until my feet dangled in the blackened night sky. It had my other sisters hanging onto his side and back, C was practically glued to an expansive chest and had tangled her arms around its neck.

"Ladies, happy birthday," said Emin who flew through the air just over the cars with us as his passengers. "I hope you enjoyed this taste, but this isn't your fight anymore. Peace, out."

"No save," I screamed into the night. "No save! I want to fight. I want to feel something real before I punch out!"

Flailing, I struggled for release. He could save the others, but not me. So what if we didn't all die together? Would it really matter? In the end, he was much too strong.

His last words were for me. "Remind your sister that I was talking about her at the end," he said. "Win a bloke a few points. Tell Clover this: Five by five."

We were disposed of on our front lawn in Santa Monica without a scratch on us. Our only injury was the humiliation of sitting in the middle of a just-watered lawn in a poufy princess dress with makeup now running down our faces.

C, who held his bow tie in her hand, was silent.

I couldn't be sure, but on the ride home, he seemed to have hands everywhere on her.

Every. Freaking. Where.

"Five by five?" I questioned her. "I know you know."

"Used by pilots," she said. "It's about how good or bad a radio signal is when it comes to volume and clarity. On a scale of one to five with five being the best. So, five by five means the best possible."

"Nice – for you," I said, as the adrenalin in my system began to calm.

FLASH! That's when I saw it (in my head, although the ink would follow): Tomorrow's LA Times. The headline read: Prom Gone Wild. High School Gang Rumble Spills Onto Sunset – Students Suspending Pending Investigation.

"There was a large black guy in a blood red tux. He was flying," reported one of the local residents who was immediately given a breathalyzer test by the LAPD. "I think he was a member of the Crips," the neighbor reported. "Or maybe, it was black Superman. I don't know." Funny, but it would take days for the paper to report another story that would be given only an inch of space. Headline: LA Residents Claim to See Supernatural Beings Near the Chateau Marmont.

Hotel officials, however, would release a statement claiming it was simply Hollywood special effects; Steven Spielberg eat your heart out.

THE CLAIRES

2.

We were a bit dazed and confused, dirty and disgusted. At least, the dance was a distraction.

Now, there was just silence, which was fitting for being on your death bed. We couldn't check out on the lawn. A little battered and bruised, somehow, we found the coordination to stand up, brush ourselves off, and then answer the ten million questions courtesy of Cass who had just pulled up in his Jeep. His face flashed furious in his black shirt, which was partly unbuttoned for comfort, and those exquisite forest-green tux pants.

"I went to the dance. People were puking everywhere. I went to get the car when everyone started getting sick. Then I tried to get back into the tent, but the doors were sealed shut and unmovable. Still, I looked for all of you to drive you home. But you were gone. The next thing I saw was my sisters running barefoot down Sunset Boulevard against traffic. In the middle of the road. But I couldn't stop and pick you up because something with eight legs lifted my car and placed it on the freeway."

"Cass," I replied evenly, "get off the drugs."

"Who are you?" Cass barked.

"I'm someone who sees the future. I can see that you're going to get us a nice XL pizza covered in mushrooms and olives." It would serve as our real last meal.

"Get it yourself," he snapped.

He was rude enough that I shouldn't have thrown him a bone, but in that moment, I felt another flicker behind my eyelid. *FLASH!* I saw her in an old car paying the toll and then making her way slowly through the Big Bear Mountain Range. She was about two hours out of town.

"She was in Oregon, but now she's back in the city limits," I blurted as my rage simmered. Yes, this would be a fitting exit if all the players showed up.

It began with a vision I had earlier this night. One that would put all of our fates on a collision course. One thing was certain…our "brother" would never forget us.

I walked right up to Cass and planted a loud smacker of a kiss on his lips. It wasn't romantic. In fact, if you watched mob movies, you knew that it was an assassin's kiss of death indicating that someone in "the family" would soon be executed.

"Get the fuck off me," Cass said, as he recoiled backwards.

"Annie. She just crossed the state line and now she's back in California," I said with a cold smile. "That's a freebie."

"You're such a bitch," he said. *Clearly, he didn't believe me. His loss.*

Cass bolted through the front door, slamming it behind him.

"Have a nice, screwed-up, short life. Hope not to catch you on the flipside," C yelled.

3.

IN THE END, it was Mom who interrupted us. The front door whipped open and I saw her standing there in a long red robe with her hair going every which way like she hadn't brushed it in a year. She was supposed to be drugged and in bed, but her eyes said that she was wide awake and that batty hair said she was frantic. Her dry lips kept opening and shutting. She couldn't find the words.

"Mama?" C said. "We'll take you to bed. You can look at us in our dresses one last time. Don't we look pretty?"

She didn't answer at first. Odd.

Then I heard her. Clearly.

"Well, none of you will ever win a beauty contest. That's for sure," she said, turning and slamming the door behind her.

Forget talons and fangs, knives and guns. Words are the worst weapons of all.

4.

It was such a devastating thing for her to say that my sisters and I rushed through the front door and followed her into the small kitchen where she was now sitting at the big wooden table rocking softly forward and back.

She even lit one of C's hidden cigarettes, which she only did during the most extreme situations, and I watched her bony hand shake as she tried to hold the burning stick. She didn't really smoke it, but let it burn as she waved the cigarette like a small wand making circles of noxious smoke in the air.

"Where's my son?"

"In his bedroom," I said.

She pointed at C. "You," Mama said, "are the devil's daughter."

She pointed at A. "You," she said, "are a freak with your dead visitors."

She pointed at S. "You should be locked in a loony bin, Miss Emotional."

Then she pointed at me.

"You've been in that bedroom with him. You were naked with your brother. You with your deviations. You stay away from my boy," she stood and ranted, throwing the lit cigarette *at me*. "You disgust me!"

She missed by mere inches and I could see that C was furious. When she insisted on taking Mama upstairs solo, I knew it was the bitter end. C would spare the rest of us from the actual doing. Would she strangle her? Knife her? Or simply walk her up the stairs to shove her back down?

The silence upstairs made my skin crawl. C returned with scratch marks down the left side of her face. "It's done," she said.

"She's sleeping?" A said.

"Yes, that is one way to put it," said my sister.

5.

I COULDN'T IMAGINE walking upstairs, so I stayed below as did my sibs. This was our last chance to do things. Normal things. Our hearts weren't in it, but we forced ourselves. Normal is always hopeful.

So, we washed the leftover dinner dishes, raided the fridge, and fed the dog. We took our vitamins for some idiotic reason and S even did a bit of English homework due in January that would never be turned in. She did it for the hell of it. I felt my pulse racing and knew my blood pressure was off the charts. It was the rage. It was like a fever.

I took calming breaths. I sat in yoga poses. I even allowed myself to lament.

We were, in fact, expert lamenters. A few weeks ago, C enrolled in "Algebra 3," a class she would never take, which pained her for some reason while S read the script for our school's upcoming *The King and I* spring play. How she longed to try out for the plum role of Anna, but the auditions were on January 5th. We'd be long-since buried—and the school frowned upon dead girls as their leads.

I took out a calendar and circled all of the upcoming holidays. I would never open my few presents our dear, late Mama had managed to put under the tree, sneak a sip of champagne on New Year's Eve, or feel sorry for myself on Valentine's Day. I'd never feel that first warm rush of spring. I would never see the cherry tree

THE CLAIRES

blooms turn white and rain down like fresh snow on a delightful 70-degree day. I did not lose my virginity although I cared for Louis deeply. He was the one who wanted to wait. How lucky can you get, right? In my case, not very.

I wouldn't dwell on it because it was easier to think about our exit plan. To that end, some of our clothes were already in a Salvation Army drop box for the homeless. Why not? We took the remaining $16,000 we kept in our secret bank account and gave it to a local dog shelter. Bitches supporting bitches. It felt good.

It felt sad.

It felt like moving day, and in a way it was.

We were visitors in this time now.

"It went by so fast . . . as did the others," A said. "In a blink."

"I guess it feels that way if you're blessed enough to hit 80, too," I said.

"It's exhausting thinking about doing it again," S said. "Learning how to walk, talk, run, swing, and not shit in your pants. Solid foods, colors, numbers, reading, boys, girls, hormones, and then the wait until the ripcord is pulled just when we get the hang of it."

"Life," I said. "We remain beginners."

6.

When I wandered into the living room to find the family photo album for just one last, feeling-morbidly-sorry-for-myself look, I smelled that cigarette again and knew it was C having her last puffs. Turns out Mama wasn't dead. C just drugged the crap out of her, hoping for eternal slumber, but suddenly the pills didn't seem to be working. In fact, she fought C the entire way and even scratched her face.

Mama was wandering and now she was in the living room

taking deep drags while sitting stick straight in an overstuffed corner chair. I don't know why it was so startling, but it was. I looked at her as if I was seeing her ghost, but my sister A shook her head. "She's very much alive," she confirmed.

We don't want to do it, I desperately thought. But I also knew the drill. A complete homicidal haze would soon fall over the four of us where we'd operate on some sort of killing autopilot. It was our last-ditch survival mechanism and no one could turn it off until the mother was dead and we were in the morgue. Mothers should never have to bury their children; we took care of that part.

She knew none of the lore. Wouldn't know. Couldn't.

It was just easier that way.

"Oh, you're back," Mama said, looking at me quizzically now. *As if I didn't live here anymore.* "Is my son home yet? I always wait up for him," she said. Her face twisted. I half expected her to growl and show her teeth.

I remembered what the counselor said about how Alzheimer's patients could land both verbal and physical arrows on a whim and then return to perfectly normal. It wasn't her fault, but it still hurt like hell. This was the woman who held us when we slept, who cradled us when we were sick, and who said I love you hundreds of thousands of times. It felt like she had meant it.

But now, maybe stripped bare of restraints, she was being her most honest self.

And that love? It has evaporated like it never existed.

Autopilot began to set into my system, fueled by an unreasonable rage I had for her now. I didn't hate her. I couldn't. But I could be white-hot furious with her.

"Cass came home an hour ago, Mama. I told you. He's sleeping," A said, as she wandered downstairs from our room, where she was reading a book that would never be finished. She sat down on the couch and tried to be normal. Remember: normal = hopeful.

THE CLAIRES

"Can we get you anything? Some juice? Or could we help you into bed?" S asked, fresh from her last bath. She got closer because that was S. She always needed some kind of sentimental closure, but Mama put out an arm to shield herself.

"Don't you dare touch me," Mama said, now slapping S's hand away so hard that my sister actually winced while her flesh reddened. "Don't you *ever* touch me. I couldn't stand it!"

She had never been physically violent before, which is why this felt like a seismic shift. "Why Mama? Why can't I touch you?" S asked her gently.

"Because," Mama spit out. "You're not my real daughter. You're nothing."

"How can you say such hateful things?" C asked her in a quiet voice. "You must be forgetting things again."

Mama rose to her feet in a fury. She took a finger and pointed to each of us.

"You're . . . unnatural," she said in a tone that made it an accusation.

"How could you . . ." I began.

"I know what you are! All of you!" she began to rant. "That fortune teller at the carnival told me all about you devils. I just didn't want to believe her. Stupid, stupid, stupid, me."

She walked in small circles talking to herself. "Stupid, stupid, stupid Mama! But she warned me. 'Do not have more children.' That's what she said. 'Your beautiful boy is enough. He will be your only real child.'"

"But . . . but we're your babies. You birthed us," C cried.

"The fortune teller told me about the man in London who just wanted my womb," she said. "He borrows wombs from around the world. Rents them Poor, poor, poor Mamas. Tricked into being a portal of life."

Her eyes were fixed on the window as she stared outside like she was in a trance. "He said, 'There are womb renters in the universe who force God-fearing women to play host to devils.'"

"Mama!" The anguish flowed through me as she spoke the absolute truth. It was the first lucid thing she had said all night *because on some cellular level she knew. Maybe she always knew.*

"I love my son, Caspian Scott Danko," she said. "And I remember the wish I made the day you were born because I remember everything right now."

"You wished for what?" said S, who was quietly crying now.

"I wished I wasn't your mother," she said. "Your *host*."

7.

Her words produced such an empty, cold feeling in my gut that I almost doubled over. But I wasn't made for collapsing. The monkeys jumping around in my head began to crash against the bars of the cage. The sisters felt just as frantic, especially after C entered the room and went to touch our mother's shoulder. When she dug into Mama's skin with her hand and began to shake the older woman hard, I knew this would end bloody.

Mama fought for it – this thing called life. With her one free hand, she dropped the cigarette on the rug and then stood to crack my sister hard across her hurt cheek with an open palm.

"I hate you now, which makes it easier," C said, tears running as her face burned right. She had her hands around Mama's thin neck now.

I waited for Mama to beg while I rubbed out the smoking stick with my shoe.

"You . . . are unnatural," Mama gasped for air while hissing the words at C. "Abnormal," she choked. "Aberrant." She could barely draw the breath to say, "Mo-monstrous. I gave birth to

THE CLAIRES

monsters ... times four."

It was the ultimate betrayal. Later when we thought back on this lifetime – and we would for closure -- I knew we would check off another of the Seven Shadows.

"Monstrous?" C snapped as she prepared for the kill shot.

One more squeeze. It would be over. C closed her eyes to press hard.

"What's with all the commotion? Is your mother down there with all of you?" called our father who walked down the stairs on his heels like he weighed about five hundred pounds. *Clomp, clomp, clomp.* C immediately released her grip, which caused our mother to recoil back as she fought for air.

"Honey?" Dad said.

"She's trying to kill me," Mama shriek-coughed to Dad. She put her own hands around her neck making it seem as if she inflicted her own red welts that began to rise. Score one for Alzheimer's. The four of us just shook our heads sadly while he put a protective arm around his wife to lead her out of the room.

"It's okay, honey. You're safe. I won't let you hurt yourself," Dad murmured to her. He didn't even look at us when he said, "Tomorrow will be a much better day. It has to be . . . because it's tomorrow."

Our earthly mother severed the final strings by not saying a word. But I would never forget the look on her face when she turned around to stare at us one last time.

It was feral.

Ma confirmed it later as the four of us spent our last night in our soon-to-be former bedroom staring up at the ceiling. "You only have one true mother, my darling daughters," said the original. For a moment, I wondered if it was the Patriarch who insisted we kill the earthly mothers or maybe Ma added that along the way for her own enjoyment. "Happy birthday to my babies and a most joyous transition to the next life. There is nothing left for you here. Good riddance to this life and move forward my dears on your search for lasting peace. It won't be found here."

Autopilot was turned up another notch.

Our death was granted permission.

8.
December 24

Fresh bacon was on the table in a sunny yellow ceramic dish courtesy of Dad who left hours ago to go to work and OJ was already in goofy Mickey Mouse glasses. Dad nudged Cass awake before he went into the shower, but forgot to give him a second wake up call. I could hear our brother snoring from upstairs.

"Do you want cereal with your sausage?" Mama asked sweetly, when she saw us. She wasn't throwing hand grenades the next morning, but instead offering bowls of Cheerios, of all things. She stared straight ahead like the night before and when I went to touch her hand, she pulled it away just so slightly. Did she remember? Was that lucidity – or was it just a knee-jerk reaction born out of instinct? I would never know.

I refused to grab for scraps or cereal and said a curt, "No, thank you."

The cord was cut. I wouldn't bleed for her again.

"We're out of milk," C said sweetly, because she was the most

THE CLAIRES

vicious and the most cunning plotter. "Mama, could you go to the store and get a few things?"

She handed our mother what was akin to a gun: her car keys.

The clock was officially ticking now.

C looked like she was a walking coma when she did it. A glaze had set into all of our eyes. This life was over and out— and we needed to end it, the sooner the better. It was like that last day of vacation. You could only cling so long and then you had to face reality and get out of town.

C was the one who devised the plan of Mama driving for the first time in a year. We knew she would *probably* choose her favorite route, which was the scenic one over a mountain passage. One wrong swerve and goodnight, Santa Monica.

A was the one who looked uber-glazed when she upped the ante. "Can you get the good banana bread? From that place. The bakery we all really like, Mama," she said.

There was only one place—Mission Baked Goods—and it could only be accessed by driving up a twisting road skyward to a plateau on a mountainside. You got the thrill of seeing the ocean on the way up . . . way, way up roads with no guard rails and sheer, deadly drop-offs.

"Maybe I'll get a lemon cake for dinner, too," Mama said. She was already mixing things up as we didn't eat cake for dinner.

I handed her the infamous Mama Coach purse that we kept up high on a cabinet shelf now, so she wouldn't reach for it and potentially try to leave the house.

"You do that, Mama," I said. "You get us that good chocolate cake for dinner."

"And blueberry cupcakes," she said with a sweet smile.

"Sure," I said. "Get an apple pie, too."

"Can you go *now*, Mama?" A asked, looking out the window. It was starting to rain hard, which was an unexpected and welcome element that just played into our hands. Dangerous driving conditions and oil slicked roads would just guarantee a swan dive off the pavement.

"I'll get my purse," she responded.

"It's in your hands," I said, as Mama fumbled with it. With my finger, I jingled the car keys that were in her other hand. As a reminder.

She smiled and took that first step toward her destiny and then stopped cold. That wasn't courtesy of second thoughts. Our back door blew open like someone wanted it to rock off the hinges.

I began to curse the idea of our father returning early and spoiling everything, but it wasn't his large frame in the mood for a second breakfast.

It was Annie who stood in the door jamb like she had so many other times.

She didn't ask for permission.

Headstrong Annie simply just stepped inside our kitchen and back into our lives, allowing a cold wintry blast to help her pull the door shut. She wasn't alone this time. I was so used to seeing her flanked by large-and-in-charge Gene that it took a moment for me to focus on someone smaller.

She was holding a baby carrier and inside of it, I heard the unmistakable sound of gurgling.

If I hadn't been so busy with Mom and dying, I would have seen them coming.

A SENTIENT'S STORY: C

1.

ANNIE WAS IN one of her boho chic outfits that began with a long crimson shirt over black leggings with a cream-colored lace shirt and handmade purple loopy vest that hung low. I have to admit that I would never remember what the baby was wearing. I would recall time and time again during our next lifetime the big hazel eyes on the child and wisps of reddish hair that made her look exactly like her mother. The dimples were pure Cass.

"Is that my baby? Did you bring him home?" Mama asked as Annie looked curiously at the four of us. She could never be sure what was happening, but something told her that she didn't like it. Not one bit.

"Mrs. D. . . ." Annie began and then her gaze settled on Mama's hand and the jangling car keys. Any fool could recognize that our earthly mother was in no mental shape to operate anything that moved.

"I don't think it's a good day for a drive. It's actually raining outside. Pretty slippery, if I do say so myself," Annie chirped. "Maybe you should just stay inside today and curl up with a cup of tea and an old movie."

"Don't be silly," Mama said. "I'm going to buy a puppy."

"Cass!" Annie shouted loudly. She knew from countless homework and bitch sessions in his inner lair that he was within shouting distance just up a short staircase. She also knew he slept until noon on Saturdays. Cass was a such a creature of habit. And, above all, she knew that she needed to even the odds.

Her white-knuckle grip on that baby carrier told the rest of the story. She didn't trust any of us, not with herself and certainly

THE CLAIRES

not with her baby, which was why she was bellowing now for reinforcements.

The back door was still open, which she also used to her advantage. "Dad! Dad!" she shouted as the baby started to cry.

"Cass!" she screamed again and again, but I knew and so did she that he slept with his earphones in and heavy metal music cranked to ten. Anything to drown out the ghosts who visited almost round the clock.

Finally, those ghosts would be our allies.

When the familiar sound of our extra-large brother plodding down the wooden stairs still couldn't be heard, Annie was forced to deal with us, solo. Was that a tiny wince I heard from the back of her throat?

"I know your Dad is out patrolling with our Dad," V said with a smile.

Then she looked at the carrier.

"What's that?" she asked. "Some kind of creature?"

"You bitches are going to let her drive? In her condition?" Annie ignored V and cut to the chase.

"They found my keys and gave them to me," Mama said with a smile.

"It's none of your business, Ann, because this isn't your family," I interrupted her. "If we want her to walk a tightrope over the city that wouldn't be your business either. So, why don't you get your sorry ass out of here – and take that thing with you."

"But if you want to stay, I will go one quick round," I continued. "Such as: Is that really our brother's baby or just another night of whoring yourself around at the beach? Honey, they have DNA tests for this kind of thing, you know."

She began to answer, but was interrupted by a voice that was low and full of gravel.

"What the hell," he spit fire, "is going on in here?"

2.

He lingered in the doorway of the kitchen in navy athletic shorts and nothing else.

His long, light hair was disheveled, so it fell in his face and there were clouds in his eyes. One blink. Then two hard ones. Cass couldn't take his focus off of Annie until he allowed his gaze to drift down toward his newborn daughter who now had him on lock. He was stunned silent; eyes glistening.

"I named her Megan," Annie said in a low voice to make the impossible moment private. "Megan Caspian."

A minute passed. "What a stupid name," V vented.

Another beat. "MC . . . what is she . . . a DJ?" A taunted.

A quick breath. "No, she's just another mistake in Cass's pitiful world," I said.

We didn't necessarily mean any of it, but the rage autopilot shifted those words into our mouths. Plus, our crudeness was for a greater cause. We needed to buy time in order to shift the rest of our fate into gear. Cass remained frozen as he considered the possibilities. Kill us. Hold his baby. Talk to Annie. Kill us. Save Mom. Kill us.

I screwed up his thought pattern when I advanced. Pushing Annie away, I shoved him with all the might left in me. He was shocked when I hurled my entire weight and torpedoed him again. Screaming on the top of my lungs, I advanced like a wild animal, which required him to catch me, grab me and then hold me in place. He had me by at least a hundred pounds.

It was odd, but he'd have plenty of time to mull it all over when most of us in this kitchen were gone.

I was beyond making life choices. All I could cling to were the gaps of time between moments. This is often where the real living occurred.

THE CLAIRES

The garage was attached to the kitchen and I heard a car engine roar to life.

This gap worked in our favor; she was behind the wheel.

3.

EVERYONE HEARD IT—ESPECIALLY Annie and Cass who had that kind of ESP with each other, born out of years of mind melding over topics mundane and significant. Their emotional sauce was as deep as the ocean and they reacted in the same horrified way. But there was a baby now, which required a moment of consideration.

If she wouldn't have handed him the carrier in that instant, I know Cass would have raced out to get Mama, but both knew instinctively that Annie was faster and her feet pumped hard through the back door that led to the garage and then out onto our rain soaked driveway, where Mama was slowly backing out with the '80s radio station cranked to fifty. Def Leopard's *Pour Some Sugar on Me* blasted through the raindrops.

Annie pounded on the driver's window as Mana went about two miles an hour and we watched because by now all four of us Claires were outside in a half trance-like state. Mama took both hands off the wheel and cheerfully waved goodbye to all of us and smiled.

"Stop the car, Mrs. D," Annie shouted, finally realizing the futility of her words. So, she opted for Plan B and jetted around the front of the car toward the passenger's side door. Mama clutched her purse in one hand and it flopped onto the steering wheel as she backed up slowly. She didn't even look, but stared at the four of us standing in a neat line across the top of the asphalt. A fine mist of rain fell, but I could still see Mama looking at us and blowing silent kisses.

Our feet were planted. It was out of our hands now.

But Annie, oh, Annie, wouldn't be daunted by a car moving this slowly. It was lucky that the passenger's side door didn't lock. She opened it in a single move, hurled her body sideways, and jumped right in, slamming the door shut so she didn't fall out.

I gave V a hard look—as in our best laid plans might be screwed—but Mama, in her current state, didn't let us down. She was already at the end of the driveway and during the brief scuffle that followed, somehow managed to throw the car into D.

D for drive.

Just as Cass slammed through the back door and hurled his body toward them, Mama floored it. In her own fog, she was looking out her side window grinning at our house when half a block down, the Thursday garbage truck meandered down the street.

She couldn't possibly see it.

But she felt it as Annie and Mama's little car tried to drive right through that big steel tank. Mama was going sixty miles per hour by now.

It was no real contest. The truck would be deemed the winner.

4.

"Ann-Annnnnnieeeee! Moooommmm!" Cass screamed as he raced toward the wreckage that was now smoldering with plumes of white smoke hanging low to the ground. The four of us ran close to the car just to be sure. Our bare-chested and shoeless brother heard the first tiny flame whoosh violently as it raced around the engine. Tormented between who to help first, I saw that Mama's neck was twisted so far back that she couldn't still be alive. There was only one real choice.

THE CLAIRES

Annie was wedged inside and when he felt for a pulse, he only found a thready one, Cass began to scream one word on the top of his lungs, "No!" he cried. *"No! No! No! No!"*

"Cass," Annie whispered. "The baby. No matter what."

"Forever and always," he said.

"Well, look at you," she whispered. "All grown up."

He threw himself down on the street to be level with her, taking her bloodied head into his hands. "Annie," he began to weep. "Oh, baby."

It was Gene who pulled him back. And back. And back. Both were eventually blown across the street by the fireball as the car exploded into billowing red flames.

There was no saving deadshit Annie now. Turns out it wasn't just a foul name to call her, but my most poignant futuristic vision – and one I didn't even believe until it played out before my eyes.

5.

HE WOULD KILL us. That much was sure. It was a good thing. Cass had so much rage within, he would probably do it quickly. We had planned for that part of it, too, and I was cognizant of it always, despite the deeper haze that had just set into my brain. I knew that we would finish this lifetime as directed by our real Ma who helped us hatch the plan in the first place. She tried to make each of her daughters' deaths as painless as possible. If she didn't orchestrate it, she feared the Patriarch would find the most painful way for our latest demise because he would deem us deserving of anguish.

But we were not to blame for the seemingly multiple casualties on our death day.

Carnage was inevitable.

There was just one new variable.

Our darling little niece.

It was V who calmly went back inside and picked up the baby carrier, which had been left on the red Navaho rug in the living room. She carried it and placed it gingerly in the backseat of Dad's big honking white Cadillac that he kept in the garage. It was his hobby to tinker with that 1970s relic on the weekends. The thing was a real steel tank, too, which was why V stretched out to be comfortable. It was the only way to die. In luxury ... and Zen-like.

Sister A climbed into the car next followed by S and then yours truly. We brought nothing with us and wore absolutely nothing as it was a purer way to die if you were stripped bare of all your possessions and butt naked, ready for a fresh entry into the next phase. We closed the heavy, always malfunctioning garage door behind us first, jamming a key in the inside lock and then breaking it off, so it couldn't be opened from either the inside or the outside without a lot of time and tools.

When we were all safely inside the Caddy, we closed the car doors and locked them. We waited, which was when it happened. A force that was not our own turned on that car's ignition.

We couldn't turn it off. We wouldn't kick out the widows. We would just drift on the fatal fumes.

I turned to my right and blew a kiss to my sister and beloved wing woman, V.

"See you on the flipside, honey," I said to her. "Breathe deeply. End proudly."

THE CLAIRES

"Next life," said S, inhaling because her current fog told her to do so.

"Later, but probably sooner," A said.

"Wish I could see the look on his face," I snarled. "Bye bye, Annie. Bye bye, baby."

6.

Fumes filled the car and we felt a sleepy sort of coma set in. Death was doing her secret work and all we had to do was give ourselves willingly.

Exit. There would be no return visit here.

There was absolutely no sound from the baby carrier.

We knew it would be that way.

7.

As I slipped into a final slumber, I had visions of Dad that I knew were correct. He heard about the accident on his police scanner and roared home. I saw him collapsing on the street and then being taken away by an ambulance as everyone feared that he was having a thunderclap heart attack, but it would only be a mild one. His second. Docs said the world would stop spinning when he recovered from the concussion he also sustained from falling face forward onto the asphalt in shock in front of the burning wreckage.

One of the last sounds I heard in this go-around was the other man in our lives. Cass was screaming in pain in our kitchen. But then he went silent. He smelled the gas and whipped open the inner garage door to find the room hazy with gauzy, white smoke.

Choking, he glimpsed into the car and was confronted by the image of his four naked sisters barely alive. But we were breathing.

"Breathe hard, girls. Just to be sure he knows we're still alive," I instructed.

As he watched our chests rise and fall, Cass just stood there. Bastard didn't try to break a window. Didn't try to open a door.

He made his wishes perfectly clear. Our "brother" wanted us to die for what we did. He didn't cause it, but he wouldn't stop it.

We would oblige him, but still take a little souvenir for the road.

I still had enough life left to push the baby carrier toward the passenger side window. Despite my chest heaving, I grinned when Cass's face went deathly white. I made a motion with my arms as if I was rocking a baby and his eyes widened. When I held her little pink blanket up to the car window, he could hear me laughing.

"It's never over, lover," V wheezed.

And Cass became Cass again.

He was doubled over choking as he tried to break the windshield out first with the Louisville Slugger Dad kept in the garage and then with his own fists. It didn't take long before his fingers were soaked in blood, which he wiped all over those windows as he punched and struck that glass until his skin was ripped and shredded pulp. By the time he smashed a garden shovel against the car's bulletproof and unbreakable back window, we were barely lucid. He did see some of us smiling. My last thought: *Knock yourself out, kid.*

Striking the locked outer garage door was futile, too, but Cass attacked the unforgiving metal with his shoulders and legs until he passed out cold from the fumes.

I wish I knew more, really, but the deceased never get the full story.

Dead girls like us get kicked out of the party early. You go home before it all unfolds and you have nothing to talk about later. You just fade to black. Movie over.

EPILOGUE

CASS

Two Years Later

1.

If you would have told me two years ago that I would rush home for Christmas, I would have told you that you had lost your friggin' mind. Just twenty-four months ago, I couldn't wait to ditch this town and now I was running back to the land of 70 degree Christmases and Santa in flowered swim trunks. I couldn't open that front door fast enough.

"Welcome home, hot shot. First in your class. Elite marine combat unit -- following in the lifesaving footsteps of your not-so-old man," Dad boomed. My arms were weighed down with poorly wrapped holiday presents that came from the heart.

Dad was one of the best presents. Right there in my face. In the laundry room when he heard the garage door open. Wrapping those big arms around me in a giant bear hug.

"Got anything in those packages like a Ferrari?" he stared down at the small boxes and asked before slapping my back again.

"Yeah, Dad. Parked in the driveway," I said. "Cherry red, just how you like it."

He kissed me on my forehead. None of that macho bullshit between us anymore. When we pressed flesh nowadays, we put heart and soul into it.

"Is that your famous spaghetti sauce I smell?" I said. "The kind with the whole bottle of wine in it?"

"What's three more drunks on Christmas Eve in the City of Angels?" Dad said.

"Who you calling drunk?"

There was Gene behind the stove stirring like a madman. He put down his big wooden spoon long enough to walk over and

THE CLAIRES

grab my enormous duffel bag and Dad fought him over who would carry it to my room. "Of course, it's pasta and gravy, Cassy. Is it Wednesday? Are we still on the planet earth?" he said. "You look bigger to me. Guess they're feeding you right in the marines. You must get all the gourmet gruel."

What followed was the same tight hug over and over again. It was just a small family unit now, but it was tight and solid.

"How's life in the Corps? And tell us all the top-secret stuff or we'll beat the shit out of you," Gene said, laughing. "We might be two old, retired cops, but we still got guns. And I'm talking about the arms attached to our shoulders. Plus, I'm taking yoga these days."

"He's does that downward dog and I have to haul him up," Dad said with a laugh.

"I don't want to get my ass kicked, so I'm saying nothing. I'm telling everything," I said to the enormous dude standing there with a kitchen towel draped over one shoulder and a small silver tiara on top of his head. Now that I noticed it, Dad had pink nail polish on his fingers. "You say one word Cass and I'll put you in that spaghetti pot," Dad warned.

He pointed to the living room. "You better get in there," he said.

I swung through the living room portal and the little monkey didn't miss a beat.

"Poppa! Poppa! Poppa!"

"Sugar!"

The little red-headed girl with the bright hazel eyes flew into my arms like a small missile. I got a grip on her and then stood, spinning her around and around until we were both laughing, hugging and kissing.

"Did you grow a tree bigger?"

"Just half a tree, Poppa!" she said. "Can I have a puppy for Christmas?"

"Yes," I said. "Anything you want, MC, princess warrior of this fair land and all the lands in the universe."

2.

We ate like three kings with half of young Megan's spaghetti falling on the pink dress her grandfathers had bought her to celebrate her father's return. Her nanny, Eva, was gone for the day, so it was just us. But we could certainly handle it. We had done just that since the day that my sisters played their last evil trick.

They had taken the baby carrier and pink blanket into the car to scare the shit out of me. They left the baby between pillows on my bed with a note: "Be seeing you. Both of you. Scratch that. All of you. The Claires."

I pushed that out of my mind because all that mattered now was in this room. Dad and Gene had pushed me hard the following year to enter the marines. "We have nothing else to do in life, but raise and protect that little girl," Dad said. "It would be our honor, son. Now, go. We'll be here waiting. You're her father. Build a life for her."

So, I did.

3.

Six months later, I was in Afghanistan on a brutally hot summer day. We lost two men to IED bombs hidden on roads, so I was already in a raw mood when my captain handed me the note to call home. My stomach dropped. "*Shit, Dad had another heart*

THE CLAIRES

attack," I thought. "*Maybe it was Gene's turn. He eats like crap.*"

But, as usual, nothing bad ever happened to the men in our family.

"The pediatric specialist said they've made amazing strides with childhood leukemia. It's the most common type of cancer in children. But we don't know yet if that's what we're facing," Dad told me.

I flew home the next day.

MC had the flu in January after I left, and then what might have been food poisoning a week later. She had been tired and sluggish for weeks, which made the grandfathers go into hyper drive. A visit to the kiddie doc led to the scary road of hospital tests.

A natural red head with pale skin, she looked almost albino when I walked into her hospital room.

"Hi, Poppa," MC said, barely sitting up in her bed now. "I don't feel so good. You can't spin me today."

"It's okay, sugar," I said, holding her tightly in my arms. "It has to be okay. It has to be . . ."

Next came an even more terrifying round of fatigue, weakness, and shortness of breath.

"The abnormal white blood cells form in the bone marrow," said the pediatric cancer specialist. I felt like I was underwater as he spoke. "They quickly travel through the bloodstream and crowd the healthy cells raising the body's risk of infection. Most children are successfully treated," he assured us. "Let's all take a deep breath. Hope for the best."

Hope.

We had no time to breathe. We faced a bone marrow aspiration and biopsy, which came up positive.

"Chemotherapy is the main treatment," said the doctor, who ordered weekly treatments for ten weeks followed by radiation.

I was honorably discharged from the marines and spent the

next year in and out of chemo sessions with my daughter. "Read it again, Poppa. I want to be Cinderella," said the wee voice in the hospital bed after another blood transfusion to fight infections that became wars. "Sugar, I'll have your pumpkin waiting for you when you get out of here and two beautiful glass slippers," I said.

"And a puppy named Bingo?"

"And a puppy named Bingo."

Another night before the antibiotics kicked in and her fever raged, my baby said, "Poppa, tell me about Mama. I see her sometimes. When I'm sleepy. Like now. There she is. Over there behind you."

I couldn't turn to look. I would shatter.

"If you want to Megan, you can run to her," I began with a clogged voice. "You don't have to stay here. You can go if it hurts too much. She will be waiting. You know what to say."

MC cleared her little throat as she shivered under the covers. She knew this by heart.

"I will say, 'Mama, well, look at you.' That's what she used to say to you. Then you Poppa would say . . ."

"Well, look at you, sugar," I said with the kind of grin that always made my baby smile. It took every ounce of strength inside of me to find it.

We buried her later that year in the town cemetery next to my mother and my beloved Annie.

4.

AFTER, ALL I could do was sleep all day and walk the beach until dawn. As the moon graced the evening tide, I tried and tried to imagine the *still* bright future Dad helped set in place. He wasn't just the ultimate optimist bullshit artist. He put plans into action.

THE CLAIRES

"Forward motion, Cass," he told me. "There is no back."

The "for sale" sign was already plunked into the ground. We were moving to Chicago to be near relatives. The plan was I'd use my computer skills to enroll at ITT tech college where I'd live in the dorms for a change in scenery. Dad tried to be happy about it, but I greeted each day bitterly.

There was one shining ray. Dad was going to live with Gene in Chicago. He had enough of California, too. Too many memories. Too many nights when the thinking was too thick and hard, the ghosts were too vibrant and close and the dawn would simply not come, no matter how you tried to will away the dark.

They wanted to be near me, too. By "they," I mean Dad and Gene. I was, after all, their only living relative. The ghosts would come with us as well – as they always do.

We moved that August to a small, red-bricked two-story house they called "a bungalow" in a middle-class neighborhood in Evanston on the outskirts of the city of Chicago.

One moonless night on Labor Day weekend, the California boy in me was jonesing for anything close to an ocean. I found my feet crunching over the gritty, golden sand of Clark Street Beach. It wasn't the Pacific, but Lake Michigan, with its calm waves and fishy smell, would have to do.

I'm not proud to admit it, but I mulled over ending it all. I didn't fit in here and figured that I could wander right into that lake right now, and keep going until the Marines baseball cap I wore on my head was under the murky green water. I could swim in my black tank top and khaki shorts toward the dark horizon using broad strokes until my lungs held no more air. I would keep moving until I couldn't.

And at that point, maybe, just maybe, I wouldn't hear the voices anymore or feel the exquisite pain.

Only two would miss me. And they had each other.

I was lost in diabolical thoughts when I bashed right into her, a freight train striking a feather. Or maybe she knocked into me, because neither of us was paying too much attention on that starless night. She wobbled, but didn't topple. I admired her for it.

A closer glance and I noted that she was slim, but sturdy. Red, loose hair that was wind-whipped tumbled down her back. Her hazel eyes flashed one-hundred percent startled, but ready for action. She reminded me of ….*no, damn it, I wouldn't go there.*

"Hey Palooka, I have pepper spray! So, back off, Jack," she said, reaching into her book bag and then adopting some kickboxing stance that was ridiculous. She looked like Princess Ninja.

"I surrender, sugar," I replied, putting both hands up in the air. "I wave the white flag. Well, I would if I had a flag. Please don't hurt me!"

Shockingly, she walked even closer to see if I was making fun of her. "Annie," I whispered under my breath because she looked enough like her for my mind to fill in the blanks. I knew she wasn't a ghost. Ghosts didn't carry pepper spray, plus I felt the tingle in my arm from where I smashed into her.

She wasn't Annie. But this girl was pretty, actually, beautiful. Taller than my Annie. Skinner, like she needed a good meal. Her emerald-green sundress was covered by a little black sweater that had something white dangling by the back collar. I couldn't help but stare as the price tag blew around in the wind. Nope, ghosts didn't wear price tags. It was official. She was real.

"You wanna borrow some scissors or something?" I asked her. "Not that I have scissors. I'm not dangerous."

At that point, she let the pepper spray fall back into her purse and looked down at her worn flip flops. It was like I gutted her.

"I know," she said following my gaze. "I didn't forget to cut the tag. It's this thing we do. My mom and I have to return it to the store on Monday."

THE CLAIRES

Why she was telling me this, I had no clue. But it disarmed me and charmed me at the same time. In fact, in the sliver of moonlight, I saw the price and wanted to hand her the $19.99 and tell her to keep the thing, on me. But I didn't dare shame her.

The clouds parted like curtains and a bigger moon slice came alive, dancing through the misty shadows of the lake. Blinking hard, I looked again. She was everything I would never be now—young, free, and probably happy. Maybe a junior or senior in high school.

She wore a little white My Name IS sticker on the sweater. I spotted the Northwestern University logo on it, but she certainly didn't look like the type who could afford that kind of tuition.

The good news is she figured out I wasn't some psycho killer. She even felt comfortable enough for some mindless . . . interrogating.

"Do you go to Northwestern? Are you a student there? Or do you go to Loyola?" she quizzed me, rapid-fire style. "Do you like your professors? How tough is it academically? Did you get a scholarship? Will the cafeteria food poison me?"

Deep breath. Hers, not mine

I knew the last one was going to be a good one. "Do you read the school newspaper?"

Maybe this was how they talked in the Midwest.

"Uh . . . no, no, no. I haven't met my professors yet. I don't know. I start school in the fall. No scholarship. I bring my own food. And I never read the newspaper, except for maybe the funny pages," I rambled. I didn't really read the comics, and I had no idea why I was saying that I did. For some odd reason, I felt myself grinning down at her, and damn it . . . it actually felt sorta good.

"You don't read the newspaper!" she exclaimed in disgust, like I had just kicked her dog. "I won this weekend newspaper thing . . . . . well, you don't care."

"You won what kinda weekend thing?" I asked. "And why does it require such a nice sweater?"

"It's just this high school journalism thing at Northwestern," she said. "A prestigious seminar for high school seniors thinking of going there. Not that I can go there. It's crazy expensive, but I can dream, or maybe donate a kidney."

I smiled at her.

"Sorry, you don't care about all this," she concluded. "Have a nice night."

"Resign yourself to thinking that way and you won't go there. You won't go anywhere," I said as she began to walk away. She didn't get far.

"Forward motion," I said. "There is no back."

She turned back around, a strong pivot that took my breath away.

"Thank you, Oprah," she said, peering up at my face that was darkened by my cap. "I'm trying for a scholarship. Either Northwestern or NYU, but who knows what will happen. At this age, they tell us that the possibilities are endless, right?"

"You have your whole life in front of you – and all that good stuff," she rushed. "Who knows what to believe? I'm just enjoying my rental sweater."

For a few seconds, no one said anything.

As the light hit the water, I glanced at her name tag. "See ya, Walker Callaghan," I finally said. "Go slay."

"I think I will," she said, her face glowing before she moved on.

When she was gone, I stood at the water's edge and looked into the blankness of the canvas of my own life. Maybe it was the summer or the water or the pretty girl, but I felt this thing that seemed foreign to me now. It was called hope.

On the way home, I stopped at the pound and begged the guy

THE CLAIRES

behind the desk to let me in. I adopted a homeless lab and named her Hope. It fit.

My cell phone began to buzz in my pocket. "Yeah, Dad," I said, picking it up. "We're on our way home."

AFTERWORD

A VOYANT'S STORY: V

Chicago Illinois, 2017

It all began with a Claire. That's who I am . . . and I would never apologize for it. I was a raven-haired baby now—the owner of several lifetimes and just starting another. I stood up in my crib on wobbly, chunky legs in the middle of a dark night looking into the minds and futures of the city at my feet.

Defiantly, I moved my face away from the light coming in through the nursery door as if too much illumination might highlight the secret spots, thus stealing my reincarnated soul.

Nighttime was our natural state of being. "Daytime is the unfortunate result of a working world. We're part of a wondering world," my golden-haired sister C whispered, which she was required to do, as our new mother wouldn't have known what to do with a twelve-month-old baby speaking in complex sentences.

I was sure that her first daughter, the quite-dead-now Walker didn't speak until . . . well, who knew? We hated her enough to imagine she didn't speak until she was nine.

My sister A stood, her thick thighs wobbling as she grabbed for the crib bars. "Our story reminds me of an Old English quote," she said in her baby tone, but the words were quite grown up when she continued to recite the wisdom of the ages: "The universe is full of magical things patiently waiting for our wits to grow sharper."

The wait would continue.

"Now what are my babies doing up?" said our new mother opening the door wide. "Did I hear something? Must have been the baby monitor."

After the adoption, Madeline Callaghan of Chicago, Illinois, told the world that she was our Mom. Just Mom. Not Ma. Not Mama. Not Madre. It was so difficult to keep track as there had

THE CLAIRES

been so many motherly units in our lives. She was the meat-and-potatoes type.

I imagined her head in one of those cook pots. Turned up to high. I imagined a lot of dark things. After all, we had three shadows left and sixteen years in the bank in order to cast them aside. Addiction, Poverty, or Abuse were up now, spin the wheel.

Pick your poison, Mama. I mean Mom.

We would pick ours.

THE END

ACKNOWLEDGMENTS

My deepest gratitude to the people I'm blessed to have in my life. Thank you to ....

Mary Altbaum, an extraordinary editor, friend and keeper of all things Ascenders. Thank you for your creativity, your 1000 percent perfect editing calls, your razor-sharp attention to the smallest and biggest details and for always keeping the faith. You're a dream editor that only a very lucky writer finds once in a lifetime. Thank you for being as excited each time out to create something big.

Adrijus G from RockingBookCovers.com. You floored me with this cover, but you do that to me with every single one. Getting an email from you with a new cover is like Christmas morning and your birthday rolled into one. Best cover artist ever. Period. Thank you for taking a photo and turning it into beautiful art.

Emily Tippetts and her wonderful team. Thank you for your beyond gorgeous inside design and for allowing me to drive you nuts at the end with all my changes...and for being so darn nice about it. I love your artistry and thank you for making the words look so beautiful and inviting on the page.

Fonda Synder, Fonda Snyder, Fonda Snyder. In the most inspiring way in the world, you pushed me to take a second and third swipe at it and were so, so right on every call. Thank you for bringing your genius talent and keen sense of story to this book. I don't know what I did to deserve both you and Rick Mischel in my life, but it must have been something good. Thank you both for you never-ending belief and for making bigger things come true when it comes to all things Ascenders.

Tiffany S. Bell is one of the all-time great photographers out there. Thank you for joining the team here as the Ascenders official photographer who did such a beautiful shot for the back cover. Can't wait to work more with you in the future.

Erin Shiel, you are a proofreading genius. Again, a new member of the team...and one who is family to boot. Thank you for doing such a great job. Vicki Rose, thank you for doing a killer proofing job, too. You have an amazing eye for words. Also huge thanks to Vicki, Annie Boylan and Louisa Sharamatyan for all of your skills with daily promotions. A huge thank you to the genius Elena Stokes and Brianna Robinson at Wunderkind Public Relations. I'm awed at your creativity, smarts, plus it's so much fun working with you two.

Thank you to dear friends for always listening...Sally Kline, Vickie Chachere, Carrie Healy, Stephen Schaefer and Joyce Persico. Love to my family Gavin and Jill Pearlman Reid, Cade and Wylie Pearlman. Jack "Buzzy" Gaber thank you for being such a wonderful brother-in-law and taking care of the "kids" when we're out of town.

Colton Shepherd and Georgie "The Zim" Doodle...greatest office assistants ever on four legs.

Thank you to my parents, Paul and Renee, who have ascended, but I still feel you always.

To all the Ascenders fans and our fan group Ascenders Nations. We've laughed and cried together while sharing these books and our lives. I love you guys so much...and you know who you are. I look forward to our FaceBook chats and love meeting each and every one of you at events. You're the best! Hearing how these books impacted you means everything and more to me.

Sabrina, my bonus daughter, you're going to college next

year!!! You're a Redbird thanks to your hard work and focus. You are the brightest light and have such an amazing future ahead of you. Love you and I'm so proud of you.

Ron, my love, my heart, my husband, my everything. Thank you for being there in Room 202 when I had a crazy dream that became this book series. And thank you for being wonderful you... so loving, caring and right in the thick of it with me. Love you more.

Made in the USA
San Bernardino, CA
15 January 2020